BY ANY OTHER NAME

KATE KING

Also by Kate King

WILDE FAE

Lords of The Hunt

Lady of the Nightmares

The Last Heir of Elsewhere (March 2024)

Kingdom of the Monsters (Summer 2024)

WILDE THIEVES

The House of Doublecross (Fall 2024)

THE GENTLEMEN SERIES

Red Handed

Thieves' Honor

Damned Souls

THE BLISSFUL OMEGAVERSE

Pack Origin

Pack Bound

Pack Bliss

OMNIBUS EDITIONS

The Gentlemen

The Blissful Omegaverse

BY ANY OTHER NAME

Shakespeare after dark

USA TODAY AND INTERNATIONAL BESTSELLING AUTHOR

KATE KING

ISBN: 979-8-9894640-1-2 (paperback)

ISBN: 979-8-9894640-2-9 (hardback)

First edition April 2023

Cover and typography: Flowers and Forensics

Copy Editing: Noah Sky Editing

Character Art: @Damianintheden

Published by Wicked Good Romance

For Nicole, Renee, and Jennifer

My wicked awesome beta-readers who went so above and beyond to get this book where it needed to be.

BY ANY OTHER NAME

Shakespeare after dark

KATE KING

CHAPTER ONE

ETTA

Junior Year of High School, Five Years Ago

There's blood in my hair, on my face, and splattered across the gold and navy crest on my prep school blazer. Sitting across the hall, Roman Montague looks worse—like the tragic hero of some vampire academy teen drama. Which is kind of funny, because we're not vampires, we're witches, and I've often thought any TV network would fall over themselves for a show about us.

Today alone would make a great episode of a reality show. There's drama, occult magic, pretty, rich assholes misbehaving...the only problem is those assholes are my parents, and the drama is literally splashed across my uniform and half my prep school auditorium.

This isn't how I pictured starting my junior year.

My heart leaps as the doorknob to the headmaster's office shivers, pauses, then stills. I hold my breath, but the doorknob remains motionless, the door unmoving.

Unsure if I'm relieved or disappointed, I flex my fingers, which have unconsciously tightened around the edge of the bench, and lean my head back against the wood-paneled wall. Across the hall, fabric rustles, and I don't have to look to know Roman is also relaxing back into his seat.

Our parents—both sets of them—are inside the office with Headmaster Gregory. It's been over an hour of silence, broken by screaming from inside the office or rattling at the door. Roman and I tense, as if we might get to leave. Then, nothing happens, and we go back to waiting. It's like purgatory; like waiting for Godot, or the toaster to ding, or a guy to text back. It feels like it might never happen. Like we will turn to dust out here waiting for a verdict. For something to *finally happen.*

A loud thump reverberates against the wall directly behind where I'm sitting. I jump, surprised, and nearly tip off my bench.

"What the fuck was that?" Roman barks.

For once, he and I are in total agreement, although I wouldn't have said it quite like *that*. What *was* that? It sounded like someone kicked the wall of Headmaster Gregory's office...but that's crazy. Right?

I open my mouth to voice my theory, then close it again. Today has tested my resolve in so many ways.

I've spent years going out of my way to avoid speaking to Roman Montague. To avoid looking at him. Avoid breathing the same air. We've been in the same grade, had nearly all the same extracurricular activities, and attended fifteen years' worth of holiday and full moon gatherings together, and I've kept our interactions down to the occasional "Blessed Be," or "Please pass the salt."

I've turned avoidance into a fine art.

Yet, looking at him now, I'm compelled to release a lifetime of pent-up feelings. To vocalize every thought, assumption, and errant musing I've had about him and his miserable family all these years.

But I don't.

I say nothing. Because that's what I do. I'm always quiet. I never cause trouble, never fight back or stand up for myself, even though inside I'm screaming.

The telltale tingle of eyes crawling over my skin breaks my musing. I glance up without thinking, only to realize that Roman is staring at me and as his gaze connects with mine, his dark eyes widen for a moment.

The blue light from the phone held loosely in his hand casts a shadow across his pale face and glints off his inky black hair. His phone doesn't even work in the school—too many witches around messing with the technology—yet of course, Roman would have it out, anyway.

Jerk. Attractive, miserable, *jerk.*

"What are you looking at?" I blurt out.

Damn. Years of silent protest ruined in a single moment of weakness. Nice going, Etta.

He sneers. "Just noticing that the blood has turned your hair pink. You look like a fucking troll doll."

The back of my neck heats. Great. That's just wonderful.

Heat climbs my neck, and I avert my eyes, focusing on anything but his steely gaze.

My chest is too tight under my button-down shirt. It's a stupid comment, and I don't care what he thinks, anyway. Still, it feels impossibly unfair that while I look like a troll, *apparently,* he somehow looks better than ever—which is saying something, unfortunately.

He gets to his feet. I keep my head down and all I can see are his shoes, and the bottoms of his blood-spattered, khaki uniform slacks as he stands to his full—considerable—height and crosses the hall to stand in front of the closed door.

"What are you doing?" I hear myself ask.

Roman braces his arms on either side of the door frame, holding himself back like he's doing standing push-ups. "Listening," he says under his breath.

"Well, stop," I hiss.

He looks down his nose at me. "Why? What do you think's going to happen?"

I hate myself for looking up even more than I hate myself for breaking my referendum on speaking to him. "I don't know," I splutter. "We're not supposed to."

"Sure." He turns back to the door. "And I suppose you've never done anything you weren't supposed to do, right? You're a *good girl*."

I flex my jaw, caught between my desire to ignore him and an inability to let his insult go unchallenged. I cross my arms over my chest. "Whatever. I don't care what you think."

He snorts a humorless laugh, and glances sideways, looking me up and down. His gaze is sharp and assessing. Everything about Roman—expressions, insults, jawline—is sharp. "You care what everyone thinks."

For some reason, that stings.

I *do* care what everyone thinks, and I care more that anyone has noticed that. I've never been effortless a day in my life, whereas Roman and his friends don't care about anything and are still winning at *everything*. I suck in a shallow breath. "Even if that's true, I wouldn't care about you. You're no one to me. I don't think about you because you don't matter."

His dark eyes flash dangerously, and I can't read his expression. Anger, maybe? Hurt. But it's gone in a second and he just shrugs. "Do whatever you want, good girl. I'm going to listen."

The seconds tick by, Roman standing at the door, the muffled voices unintelligible through the wall, and me wringing my hands in the fabric of my pleated plaid skirt.

I chance another glance at Roman, and as if feeling my attention, he looks back at me. "Doesn't sound good," he teases. "They're talking about us."

"They're not talking about us. There's absolutely no reason to discuss us in the same sentence."

"Please," he scoffs. "What else would the fight be about?"

I bite my lip, my heart beating too fast considering I'm doing nothing more than sitting. "I don't care."

It's another lie. I care a lot that our parents just caused a huge scene in the middle of my speech-and-debate team competition. I care that four adults were brawling like kindergarteners in front of hundreds of people. And I care that there will be no consequences, because both my mom and Roman's dad are on the Order council—the committee of eight that runs this town.

Another crash reverberates in the office behind me, and the hairs on my arms stand on end.

My father's deep baritone voice rumbles through the door, as clearly as if he was standing beside me. "You won't be so smug when there's a plague on your entire damn house, Montague."

"And we'll throw it right back," Roman's father screams. "Do not think you can fuck with me."

"Oh my gods." I stand up, my heart beating too fast, and march over to the door. "Move over."

For anyone else, that would be a rhetorical statement. Hell, if I threatened a plague, it would be rhetorical, because only adults can pledge themselves to the Order and gain any real power. But when our parents are making threats like that...well, let's just say it's a little concerning.

Roman smirks down at me, like he's won somehow. He's at least a foot taller than I am, and I feel ridiculous looking up as I make my demands. Like a mouse shaking its fist up at a cat right before it gets eaten. He seems to have a similar thought, because his smirk slips as his dark eyes track over me. He looks...hungry.

A shiver of fear travels down my spine, but I refuse to let him win. "Well?" I ask, quietly enough that I hope they can't hear me on the other side of the door. "Are you going to move and give me room?"

He shakes his head, like he's just remembered where he is. "Right."

He doesn't actually move. Instead, he lifts one arm and gestures for me to stand in front of him. I'm debating if I should argue, when there's a crash inside the office, and I hear my mother's voice shrieking for the entire school to hear. "I'll curse you until your ears bleed and you don't know your ass from your eyeballs. Fucking watch me!"

Suddenly, I don't care where I'm standing. I duck under Roman's arm, and press my ear to the door. Though, with the volume of their screaming, it's barely necessary. "What's going on in there?"

He lowers his arm back down, boxing me in. My breathing turns shallow. I haven't been this close to a boy since last summer when Sebastian Cesario felt me up at summer camp, and before that, never.

"I wouldn't worry about it," he drawls.

His statement is undercut by another crash.

"Yeah? Then what would you do?" I ask acidly.

Roman presses both palms flat to the door, and steps back, extending his arms all the way. "Nothing."

There's another unintelligible shout inside the office, and I jump as I feel pressure on the top of my head. It takes me a moment to realize Roman is resting his chin there. I feel him chuckle and I can't breathe. I don't know whether to elbow him in the gut or sink backward into his chest.

"It's not funny," I choke out.

"Come on, good girl, you have to admit it's *kind of* funny. They're not really going to do anything, they never do."

"The blood all over the auditorium begs to differ."

"Touché."

A tiny laugh escapes me, surprising us both. He laughs too, and for the briefest, tiniest second, it seems like we're on the same side. Like we understand each other, on this side of the door, and it's not my family versus his family, but it's them versus us.

Like maybe we've reached some common ground.

Like maybe things might change between us.

Except Roman is wrong; our parents are serious.

And I'm both right and wrong; things do change. They get worse.

So, six years later, when I'm lying beside Roman in a crypt, because all we wanted was to stop the violence, I'll wonder if he still thinks the feud is funny.

CHAPTER TWO

✦ ETTA ✦

PRESENT

I'VE ALWAYS THOUGHT OF ROSES AS FUNERAL FLOWERS.

It's funny how an image can stick in your mind; how you can make an association once, and never be able to banish it. Like, how the scent of tequila can make you sick long after the first—and last—time you drank it, or how a particular song will always make you think of your first kiss. To me, red roses aren't romantic. They're ornaments of the afterlife, with petals like drops of blood on icy February snow. Apparently, whomever chose the flowers for this year's Arcane Auction doesn't agree.

I scowl down at the macabre arrangement on the cocktail table before reaching out to touch the nearest bloom. Bone-deep pain lances through my middle finger and I hiss, pulling my hand back from the stem as petal-red blood wells.

Pretty and vicious. Just like this event. Just like this entire town.

I suck on my finger for a moment before inspecting it. "I guess I've just paid my blood debt for the year."

"Is that what you're trying to do? I thought you were just stealing the decorations."

I look up to find my best friend, Catalina Minola, striding toward me across the crowded castle ballroom, the heels of her Mary Jane pumps clicking against the white marble floor.

Behind her, half the town stands around, chatting and drinking. A string quartet plays in one corner and there's an open bar in the other. Towering, floor-to-ceiling windows look over the twinkling lights of the harbor and over the tops of the Elsinore University buildings. Blood-red flower arrangements cascade from every surface, contrasting with the bright white marble.

"Something like that," I say as Cat reaches me. "What are you doing here?"

"I bowed out early, I thought you might need some back-up." She rolls her eyes and leans back on her heels. "I would have been here sooner, but they stopped me at the door. Like, what do they think I'm trying to do? Who crashes *an auction*?"

I hide a smile. I'm guessing her trouble was less about security, and more about her outfit. She's wearing a brown plaid vest over a ribbed turtleneck with a calf-length pleated skirt. It's a great outfit, but not for a black-tie event. Not that I'm doing much better on the opposite end of the spectrum.

I hadn't planned to attend tonight and had no time to find a dress. My black lace evening gown would have been fine last year, but this year it's several sizes too small in the chest area and I'm attracting more than a few sideways stares from men old enough to be my father.

Champagne problems, but painful, nonetheless.

I nod sympathetically. "Mmm. Who's manning the door?"

She waves her hand as if to say she doesn't care. "I don't even know, but you watch. I'll fucking curse him and his whole damn house."

My smile slips. "Stop, that's not funny."

"I'm not trying to be funny," she says, even as she snorts a laugh. "Anyway, I think you've got the market cornered on family feuds all on your own."

I roll my eyes. Cat has only been here for thirty-seconds, and already we're discussing *them*. I would say it's a record, but it isn't. Like death or getting a suggested follow request for your one-night stand, some things are just inevitable. Whenever we attend an Order event, inevitably the Montague family will come up within five minutes.

"How was the mixer?" I ask, desperate to change the subject.

"Fine."

From Cat, "Fine," means "Excellent," so I appreciate that she left early.

My best friend was attending a student/faculty mixer for our program at Elsinore University, where we are both seniors. I should have attended with her, but my mother asked—no, *demanded*—that I attend this auction instead. Being me, I couldn't work up the courage to tell her "No."

The auction is part of a week's worth of Founder's Day activities. Founder's Day in the town of Stratford, Massachusetts celebrates not only the town's establishment, but the creation of "the Order." A pact between the eight founding families that kept them from being caught up in the hysteria in the nearby city of Salem. Everyone knows about the witch trials; what everyone doesn't know is the real witches survived, and their descendants are living comfortably a few miles down the road, using everyday magic to run hedge funds and mold a new generation of media and tech moguls.

Stratford might seem like any normal, upper-class, New England town from the outside, but it's so much more than that. Stratford is a town built on secrets and magic, where favors flow like currency and debt gives a whole new meaning to the term "blood money."

Cat elbows me in the ribs. "Incoming."

I jump, distracted by my own thoughts, and follow her line of sight. My lips thin into a tight line, but I manage a wave. "Ty! Over here."

My cousin Tyberius strides toward us, immediately noticeable in a maroon suit with a plaid pocket square that reminds me of our old Verona Valley Prep uniforms. "Juliette!" he calls too-loudly. "You should have told me *you* were coming. I would have picked you up."

My nose wrinkles. I hate my name, but Tyberius—a fellow owner of a miserably pretentious and hard to spell name—always forgets. I give him a tight smile. "I didn't know we'd both be here. Mom didn't mention it."

What I want to say is: "What the fuck?" but I hold it together. Fighting with my cousin in public will reflect worse on me than on him. Still, if Tyberius—who has graduated from Elsinore and is a full-fledged member of the Order—is here, why did I have to miss my school event to represent our family?

Ty falls in next to us. He flashes a veneered smile that doesn't quite reach his gray eyes and brushes an ash-blonde curl off his forehead. "Hasn't this started yet?"

I shake my head. "They're running late."

"Of course. And here, I was late on purpose." He looks like this is the disappointment of his entire life. "I'm getting a drink. Do you want something?"

I shake my head, again, even as Cat says: "Yes, *please.*"

Tyberius mutters an unintelligible incantation under his breath and draws a symbol in the air with his middle finger I recognize immediately as a summoning rune.

Nothing happens.

He throws a sideways glance at me, as if I've done something to cause this, and shakes his hand vigorously. He tries drawing the rune again to no avail. "What the hell is going on?"

"Have you tried turning it off and back on again?" Cat asks sweetly.

Tyberius scowls at her as I try not to laugh. "No magic tonight," I inform him, leaning back against the rose adorned cocktail table. "The council thought it would be safer."

"Fuck that," Tyberius grumbles as he wanders away toward the bar. "If I'd known we were playing human I wouldn't have come."

Cat and I share a look of disdain. Champagne problems can be a real pain in the ass.

Tyberius, engaged in a heated discussion with Roman and Bennet Montague.

My stomach does something between a flip and a lurch, like my body isn't sure if I'm excited or horrified.

"What the hell is going on out there?" Cat asks. "I thought he went to get drinks!"

I blow out a breath, pinching the bridge of my nose. "It's just… Tyberius." So much for no magic making everyone safer.

My cousin takes an aggressive step toward Roman Montague, raising both arms, gesticulating wildly. In contrast, Roman shakes dark hair out of his eyes and smiles around the clove cigarette held between his lips. He's wearing his dress shirt partially unbuttoned with his tie slung around his neck like a scarf. He leans back against the railing, seeming completely at ease. Like whatever Tyberius is saying is all some joke to him.

My stomach pangs, as I'm suddenly, painfully, reminded of this same image that's haunted me for years. Except then, his tie was striped maroon and navy, and the sickly licorice scent of Dijaum Black was invading the library of our prep school.

I shake my head to clear it, and turn away before any of them glance inside and see me looking. This is stupid. I am not that idiotic teenager who got flustered by Roman Montague. Not anymore. "Just ignore them. Maybe nothing will happen this time."

"Sure," Cat mutters, disbelieving. "Good gods, when was the last time you saw them?"

I grit my teeth. This is the opposite of "ignoring," but I can tell she's not going to leave it. "The Montagues?"

"Yeah."

"I don't know. High school graduation, I guess."

It's a lie. I vividly remember the last time I saw Roman Montague up close—the last time I spoke to him. It was three years ago at my grandmother's funeral, and I'd made a complete idiot out of myself. Miserable and tipsy, my secret crush had finally come to light, only for him to completely reject me. It was humiliating and made the worst day of my life up until that point all the worse.

Of course, I don't know what I was expecting. He'd warned me over and over that he wasn't a nice guy, and in the end, it turned out to be true.

Since then, I've only seen him in passing, but we don't talk anymore—if we ever really did. Whatever strange common ground we found in the hours between deaths and funerals, was put to rest just like everything and everyone else.

I feel Cat shift beside me, and I know she's watching me watch them, but whatever she's thinking, she doesn't get a chance to voice it.

The set of mahogany French doors explode off their hinges and splintered wood and broken glass pepper the floor. People scream as Tyberius comes tumbling into the room, trying to shake off Roman Montague, who has him trapped in a vicious headlock.

They land in front of the stage, where one of the Cesario sisters is holding up a set of fifteenth century cursed knives for auction. She screams as if she's the one in the fight and trips over her dress as she scrambles to get out of the way. The pleasant, classical music of the string quartet screeches to a halt, replaced by the crowd's panic and angry shouts.

Tyberius and Roman go rolling across the floor after her, like some absurd Hanna-Barbera cartoon. Roman lands on top of Tyberius and wraps his fingers around his neck. Tyberius's face is red, Roman's a morbid shade of pale gray. In their struggle, Roman's shirt has risen up showing the outline of a dark pledge-tattoo curving over his back. Blood has smeared across his hands and over Tyberius's neck, but neither man seems to notice. They're too intent on ripping each other apart.

Blood rushes in my ears and I take a lurching, involuntary step forward. It's stupid, I know, to walk toward the violence instead of running from it, but I can't quite dampen my instinct to play peacekeeper. Even between my cousin and my worst enemies.

Except, someone beats me to it.

There's a horrible screeching sound, like metal-on-metal, and every nerve in my body freezes. I don't know where to turn, unsure where the reverberating sound is coming from. I swing my head toward the stage, where Emrys Lawrence is holding his microphone right next to the speaker, with the volume on full blast. He seems unaffected as he stares stonily at the fight that has paused in the center of his event.

The sound stops everyone except Tyberius, who takes advantage of the moment to move out from under Roman's hold, reversing their positions. He raises an arm and smashes his fist into the side of Roman's face, just as he's turning to look at Councilman Lawrence. I gasp and my gaze travels down to where Roman is lying on the floor, grinning, blood pouring down his face. He barely acknowledges my cousin's fist, as if this madness is what he wanted all along.

"Enough!" Councilman Lawrence says, not quite yelling, but certainly firm enough to be heard over the commotion.

If the men are mollified, they do not show it. If anything, there's an air of defiance to the entire situation. Two houses, alike in every way that matters, yet with only bitterness and pointless violence between us.

Roman shoves Tyberius off him and jumps to his feet, still grinning. He's bleeding from his nose, the blood running down his face and into his mouth. There's a bruise already blooming on his temple, and his eye looks like it may swell shut by tomorrow. Still, his manic glee is evident. Then, as if feeling my gaze on him, his dark eyes snap up to meet mine. A familiar, mocking smirk covers his handsome face, and my breath catches. I feel my cheeks warm, and I wrench my eyes from his.

"I'm so sorry about this." I announce, on behalf of both Tyberius and me. "It won't happen again."

Councilman Lawrence drops his microphone and takes one teetering step toward us, somehow managing to fix the entire room with his piercing gaze.

"You're right, Miss Capulet, it won't." Councilman Lawrence is stern, reminding me uncontrollably of my old prep school headmaster. "We've already lost enough Order members this year. I might be on my way out, but I refuse to have my last months tainted by more violence. I don't know how yet, but you can be sure that this violence will end if it's the last thing I ever do in this town."

CHAPTER FOUR

ETTA

PRESENT

I WAS EIGHT-YEARS-OLD THE FIRST TIME I REALIZED MY family wasn't entirely "normal."

My father was away on business—a code-term, I would later learn meant he was vacationing with his mistress—and my mother had locked herself in her room for the weekend. I didn't mind, because I got to spend the weekend with my Aunt Angelica.

Aunt Angelica didn't know my friends or any of their parents, so when I asked to sleep over at Sarah O'Reilly's house on Saturday night, she had no idea she was sending me to an average human's house, or that Sarah's family was deeply religious. My first clue that something was different was that Sarah's family went to church in the morning. *Church,* during the *day*. The second was that not a single person cast any spells, and there wasn't a pomegranate or an athame in sight.

Aunt Angelica had to explain to me—a few years earlier than anyone really intended—that while religion is common enough in our country, our religion simply isn't accepted. That attributing your success to prayer is okay if you worship one God, but not if you ink a deal with the gods on your skin.

She explained that adult members of the Order are granted the ability to cast magic through runes, bestowed on them by the gods they pledge their life's service to, and that one day I would also have the privilege to pledge my service in exchange for that power.

Even at my young age, I understood all that just fine. What I didn't understand, and still don't if I'm being honest, is how the same gods that accepted my family into their Order of acolytes; that accepted my best friend Cat's family, and four other worthy families, also saw fit to accept a family as dark and corrupt as the Montagues.

Sometimes, I have to remind myself that gods make mistakes too. In that sense, I must be close to godlike, because my mistakes seem like they're racking up lately.

I THROW A VENOMOUS GLANCE OVER MY SHOULDER AT Roman and Bennet Montague and grind my teeth as I drag Tyberius out of the ballroom. I'm not sure who I'm angriest at: Tyberius, for no doubt starting the fight. The Montagues, for whatever they did to provoke it. The gods, for putting us all in the same room again over and over, like lining up little plastic soldiers to fight over a *LEGO* castle. Or myself, for all the stupid, childish thoughts I was having before everything went to hell.

I shove open the front doors of the castle. The castle of the Order, is part temple, part society club, and part office building. The exterior walls are gray stone, worn by the sea air and the wind, and yellow and pink ivy creeps up the sides of the walls, giving it a romantic feel.

The cool autumn night air on my face does nothing to quell my burning indignation as I march Tyberius onto the sweeping, stone front steps. "What the hell was that?"

Ty has the audacity to scoff. "Calm down, Juliette."

"Can you not call me that? Thanks."

Ty shakes off my hand and straightens his jacket. "He was trying to kill me. You aren't going to ask if I'm okay?"

"You look fine."

I really wish I felt bad for Tyberius. I used to, and a better person probably still would. But as much as I despise the Montague's, I have absolutely no doubt that they were minding their own business and Tyberius went and provoked them. They're not innocent, but they're also not my problem.

I take a deep breath through my nose, and try to think calming, happy thoughts. Fluffy kittens. Old books with unbroken spines. Uninterrupted bubble baths. Locking my cousin in a funhouse full of ghost-clowns. Plucking out Roman Montague's eyelashes individually while the noise from the *OPERATION* game buzzes in his head.

Nope, too far.

My cousin cracks his knuckles. "I think I won that. Don't you?"

"That is so far from the point."

"But I did, right?"

I close my eyes and suck in a deep breath. I've seen fights between these two before and Tyberius *never* wins, not even when there's magic involved.

Especially not when there's magic involved, actually.

Tonight, it looked to me like Roman could have killed him but came to his senses before committing actual murder in front of two-hundred witnesses. Then, Tyberius sucker-punched him after the fight was over. But, what do I know?

"It didn't look to me like he was really trying to hit you," I say diplomatically. "What the hell was that even about?"

Tyberius's face falls almost comically. "They were just being pricks. You know how the Montagues are."

"Right." I cross my arms. "I do know how they are, and as much of an ass as Roman Montague is—and oh, he is—he's also not stupid." He wouldn't start shit with Tyberius for no reason, and my cousin and I both know it. "What did you say to him?"

I have a good idea already, but I want to hear him confirm it. I want to hear Ty confirm he's the kind of person who would taunt someone about their dead sister. Feud or not, that's messed up.

"Nothing. That guy's always been unstable," he says. "Come on, I'll take you home."

"No, I have my car and I have to wait for Cat, anyway."

He rolls his eyes. "Fine."

Tyberius storms down the steps into the night, muttering something about overreactions. The irony makes me want to scream, but I don't. I take a deep breath and lean against the banister of the stairs and stare, unseeing, into the dark street. I'm so mad, if I was a cartoon, I would have steam rolling off me in little squiggly lines.

It's not even about Tyberius—not completely—it's about how many events have been ruined by these absurd, childish incidents.

It's about how many incidents weren't just childish fights, and the people who got really hurt.

It's about how I'd love nothing more than to get out of Stratford, but I'm perpetually stuck.

And it's about Roman Montague, and his infuriating, mocking smirk.

The wind picks up and dead leaves pinwheel down the street, as bare branches wave against a backdrop of ivy-covered brick buildings. I wrap my arms around myself as goosebumps rise on my skin. Behind me, the doors open, and I jump.

I whirl, expecting to see Cat, and blanch as Roman Montague steps out onto the stoop. He's not exactly looking at me, more like staring past me onto the dark street, as he lets the door swing closed behind him with a thump that feels like the period at the end of a sentence.

I stand, frozen, somewhere between indignant and confused. Between angry and guilty. It's miserable, and the cocktail of mismatched emotions swirls in my stomach with nowhere to go, making bile rise in my throat.

Not that he can't be out here. It's the steps of a public building after all, but Roman and I have an unspoken agreement to avoid each other—at least, I thought we did. He doesn't seem to care, though, as he reaches into his pocket, extracts his ever-present pack of clove cigarettes and a lighter, and pulls one out with two long fingers.

He's making an absolute mockery of black-tie attire. His tie is still slung around his neck, and he has his shirt sleeves pushed up to the elbows and his jacket slung over one arm. His jet-black hair is sticking up at the back, like he ran his hands through it enough that no gel could compete. His face is, shockingly, more angular with age and I could swear he got even taller after prep school. He's only eight months older than me—twenty-two—but he could pass for thirty in a good way. He hasn't shaved in a few days and there are circles under his eyes that have nothing to do with his black eye. His hair needs a trim and is curling slightly around his ears. It almost makes me angry—shitty people shouldn't get to be effortlessly beautiful.

I'm staring so intently that I don't notice him holding out the cloves to me, offering me one. I jerk, startled, and feel heat flame up my neck and across my cheeks. *Oh my gods.* "Um, no. Thanks."

His lip curls. "Still don't smoke?"

"No."

He cups his hand around his lighter to block the wind, pausing for a second before replying. "I didn't think so. You always were a good girl, Etta."

That needles me. It's like he *knows* me—or, thinks he does.

And he's wrong, anyway. I'm not good. Not really. If I was good, I wouldn't be thinking about how gorgeous he is even with dried blood and bruises all over his face.

I jut my chin up, trying to meet his eyes. "Shouldn't you be inside begging Councilman Lawrence for forgiveness?"

He smirks around his clove. "Shouldn't you be calling *Mommie-Dearest* to do the same?"

He's right and I hate that. I should call my mom, or at least go home to tell her she's going to have to do some social and political damage-control. *Shit.*

"I doubt it will matter since you clearly started it," I lie through my teeth.

"Is that what your cousin said? Come on, you're smarter than that."

I bite my lip, wishing more than ever that Tyberius told me what they fought about. "I still just watched you try to strangle my cousin. I don't care what he said to you, I have no idea why you're talking to me right now."

He raises an eyebrow and winces slightly when the gash on his face pulls open. "Maybe I'm a masochist. Kink shaming isn't nice, Etta."

"Unlikely. If anything, I think you're a sadist."

"Think whatever you want."

I scowl and open my mouth to snap back some kind of insult, but it dies on my tongue. The biting wind kicks up again, picking at my dark-blonde curls, and passing through my dress like tissue paper. I shiver, and I wish for the um-teenth time that I had worn anything else.

Roman clears his throat and holds out his jacket to me.

I freeze, my eyes going wide, and I take a beat to react. "No, it's fine."

"It's just a jacket, good girl."

I stiffen. In theory, sure, but nothing is ever simple with The Montagues, and Roman is no exception. If anything, he's the rule.

Where the hell is Cat? I should just go back inside. Except, I can't decide if going inside to look for her and having people stare at me sounds more painful than freezing to death.

I glance down at the jacket, wavering.

I'm distracted by the black ink tattoos snaking up Roman's forearm. He must have gotten those in the last three years, because I've never seen them before. I can't make out everything, but I recognize the rune for inspiration, and part of a Robert Frost quote. On his other arm, he has scribbled notes in faded sharpie. Upside down, I can read:

> "DENTIST 2:10 WEDNESDAY
> BUY ASPIRIN, MELATONIN.

Then under that, darker, as if written later:

> SARA
> CALL ME! :) 617-555-0149

My hands ball involuntarily into fists, and I take the coat for something to do with them, holding it gingerly, like a bomb. "Did you call her?"

Roman gives me an odd look. "What?"

"Sara." I nod to his arm. "She wrote her name on you."

I can hear the insane bite in my tone and I want to sink into the sidewalk and disappear. I smile, trying to make it better, and feel like the Joker. Oh my gods, there is something seriously wrong with me.

His eyebrows furrow in an expression somewhere between confusion and amusement. "She was my dental hygienist."

I almost want to laugh. *Only* Roman would have someone in his mouth cleaning plaque off his teeth thinking: *Yeah, I want this guy to fuck me.*

My cheeks burn. "Right."

He didn't answer the question, and I don't know why I asked. I don't know why I care. He clearly doesn't care that this random hygienist wrote her name on his arm—teenage Roman would have cared, but he probably grew out of it. I guess we don't really know each other anymore.

I shrug on his jacket, giving into the cold and the desire to hide. Only, now I can't stop thinking about all the sharpie notes on his arm. Why the hell is he going to a *dentist* and taking human sleep-aids? I know for a fact he pledged to the Order, and even if I didn't know, the tattoo was clear enough on his back. He should be able to rune-away any problem as simple as insomnia or gingivitis. *Weird.*

Roman steps back and leans against the railing opposite me. He raises his clove to his lips and takes a drag, watching me intently with his serious, dark eyes. "So, what are you doing here?"

I narrow my eyes. "What do you mean? I have just as much right as—"

He cuts me off. "I thought you were going to England."

It takes me a moment to understand what the hell he's talking about, and then I stiffen. "I was."

Three years ago, I applied to Oxford. Instead, my parents insisted I go to Elsinore. Elsinore is the only college in the country that offers not only regular classes, but also studies of witchcraft, runology and the occult. While I argued that I could study those things in my spare time abroad, my parents were adamant that it wouldn't be enough to pledge to the Order upon my graduation.

I completely forgot I told Roman about this. More importantly, why does he remember?

Roman's eyes bore into me, his face expressionless as he exhales a plume of spicy clove-smoke. "So what are you doing here?"

For some reason I feel the need to explain. "My parents asked me to stay."

His expression is unreadable. "I bet they're thrilled."

"They are." My tone is undeniably defensive. "We all are. It's great."

"I'm sure."

The silence stretches, full of unsaid things. Sparks of energy build in my chest. Like I'm about to explode with everything I ever wished I could say, and then some.

The door opens again, and we both jump.

I look up, and freeze, fear washing over me. "H-hey."

Harrison Dane pokes his blonde head around the door and looks right at me. His eyes are bright blue, even in the low lighting, and at the moment they look as cold as ice as he glances from me to Roman. "Juliette? Are you okay?"

The way he asks is less like he's concerned for me and more like a thinly veiled threat. Like if I'm not okay, he wants Roman to know he's going to do something about it. I sigh. I'd almost prefer to have Tyberius back here than deal with this.

I might be technically betrothed to Harrison—I have been for years—but we hardly know each other. He's not my boyfriend or my family or even a friend. I can count the number of times we've been in the same room since our betrothal on one hand. It's not his job to check on me. Still, good manners win out and I smile. "Yeah, I'm fine."

Roman makes a derisive noise in the back of his throat like a scoff mixed with a laugh. He's evidently unconcerned about Harrison's threat. His mouth twists in a mocking smile. He moves backwards down the steps, one hand shoved in his pocket, the other still holding his clove. "Don't worry, Dane. I haven't corrupted her, yet. Just passing through."

His black eyes dart to me for half a second before turning and walking away into the darkness. My stomach clenches and I have to fight the strangest urge to call after him. But I don't—I can't—that would be unsafe for both of us on so many levels.

"What was that?" Harrison asks.

I swallow, and shake my head to clear it. If Harrison goes and tells Tyberius, or worse, my father that Roman was talking to me... then what? "Uh, he was asking if I had a lighter...which I don't, obviously, so...yeah."

It's the worst excuse I've ever come up with and Harrison looks suspicious as he stares after Roman. "Why didn't he use a rune?"

I furrow my brow, answering honestly this time. "I actually have no idea."

Harrison's frown deepens. "I thought it might be about what Lawrence said. Montague didn't threaten you, did he?"

"No." My brow furrows and I shove my hands in the pockets of Roman's jacket. "Roman Montague doesn't care about the Order enough to bother making threats. Everyone knows he doesn't care about anything."

CHAPTER FIVE

ETTA

Cat finally emerges and I'm tense as we walk to my car.

The street is lined on either side with large brick academic buildings. To our right, the library towers over everything else, the tallest building in the area. On the other side of the road, several dormitories and a science building are still fully lit up, despite the late hour. Everything is quiet, except for the hum of traffic on the adjacent Main Street, wind blowing between the buildings and the murmur of voices in the distance. The odor of cheese wafts all the way down the cobblestone sidewalk from the nearby late night pizza place, blending with the mid-November air and the crisp smell of leaves.

Cat throws a side eye at my borrowed suit-jacket. "Where'd you get that?"

I look sideways at her. I could tell her. She wouldn't say anything...but I'm not ready to talk about whatever the hell just happened on the steps, and telling her the truth would raise too many questions I have no answers to. "It's Harrison's."

Cat stops dead in the middle of the sidewalk and turns to me. "Really? But you hate him."

I cross my arms. "I don't hate him. I hardly know him. There's a difference."

"Ah, yes, all the trappings of a perfect marriage right there."

"We're not getting married. We're betrothed."

She gives me a side-eyed look. "Do you know what 'betrothed' means?"

"Yes, and until that 'betrothed' turns into 'engaged' I'm ignoring it. Practically everyone in the Order is betrothed, especially the founding family kids. It doesn't mean anything."

"O-kay," she draws out the word into two syllables. "Enjoy that fantasy world you live in."

"I will, thank you."

What I don't say, is that I can't help but feel that even a fantasy land wouldn't work for me. Because there's only one person I ever pictured myself marrying, and honestly? Even in a fantasy, I can't see it ever happening.

"You want to drive?" I ask Cat as we reach my car. "I'm exhausted."

I toss her my keys and walk around to the passenger side of my blood-red Mini Cooper, and bend to climb inside. Shutting the door, I lay my head against the window and close my eyes.

"So, what do you think that was about?" Cat asks.

I open one eye. "Which part?"

She takes a long time to answer, and in the interim she bangs an illegal U-turn in the middle of the road, heading toward my parents' house. Cat is staying with us for the rest of the semester while her father, his new girlfriend, and her little sister, Bianca, are in Athens. Given that at twenty-two, her obsessively overprotective father won't let her move out, or even spend a few weeks at her house alone, I don't blame her for wanting to avoid a family vacation.

She glances sideways at me, and puts on a fake, low voice, like Councilman Lawrence. "I'll stop this if it's the last thing I do!" She grins. "Very movie villain of him, don't you think?"

I crack a smile. "Who knows? Maybe he's dying."

"Or retiring," Cat fiddles with her phone, trying to connect her Bluetooth to my car stereo and select a playlist. Finally, she picks something and clears her throat. "I mean, people have been saying he should retire because of those girls. And since he's wicked old and all."

I nod. My mom, who sits on the council representing our family, is one of the contenders for the head position when Lawrence retires. She's not exactly going around with a megaphone demanding his removal, but there have been whispers and I know she's behind half of them.

"To be fair, Lawrence could be doing more. Maybe we should try and do something to help..." I trail off, knowing even as I say it, it's pointless. The Montague's wouldn't accept my help even if I offered.

"For the other families, sure." Cat shoots me a look. "But not the Montagues. They'll think you're making fun of them."

"Yeah." I sigh. "I was just realizing the same thing."

Still, the guilt for not even trying to help eats at me.

I want to voice this, but I don't. Because Cat doesn't know about all the times I met Roman Montague in cemeteries. She doesn't know that I feel guilty because I was too embarrassed about what happened three years ago to go to Marcia's funeral, and that I wonder if Roman even noticed or cared that I wasn't there. I wonder if I'm feeling guilty for nothing—worrying that I hurt someone who takes nothing but pleasure out of hurting me.

IT'S SO DARK WHEN WE ARRIVE HOME IT LOOKS LIKE midnight despite the fact that it's barely 9:00PM. Still, I'm somewhat surprised that my house is fully lit up, and there are at least six cars parked in the enormous, U-shaped driveway.

The gravel of my driveway crunches under the wheels of the car, and dry leaves blow against the windshield as we park behind the last car and traipse into the house. We glance at each other as we ascend the stairs and a crowd of voices rings out from my parents' bedroom.

"I'm going to my room," Cat says. "I have to study."

I nod vaguely. Virtually all she's talked about for weeks is her favorite class: "From Medusa to Fleabag: Feminist Rage Through the Ages." If she studies any more, she'll be able to teach it. Granted, I'm sure this is more about not wanting to be around while I tell my mother about the chaos at the auction.

There are half a dozen people in my mother's bedroom when I walk in. Finally, I spot her, standing on a pedestal on the far side of the room in a robe, with two women kneeling on the floor blow drying her ass. I stop and stare, caught somewhere between confusion and amusement.

It's actually the blow dryer that throws me off more than anything—which is probably saying something. Electronics do work in tandem with magic, but they're inconsistent and most Order members prefer not to use them if they can be avoided, even though the Order is well-entrenched in every level of modern tech and media.

There's sort of an unofficial sliding scale for what tech we'll use, and what is ignored all-together in favor of runes or spell-jars.

Things like cars and planes, where the alternative would be far worse, are always favored over magic and the Order simply avoids too much spell-work while traveling. The internet and all social media is used often, but cell phones and WIFI only work about half the time within town limits. Plug-in appliances, like my mother's blow dryer, are almost obsolete for fully pledged Order members. I still have to use them as I haven't pledged yet, but my mother would be better off casting a heating rune.

I drag my gaze down the cord of the blow dryer and a part of me sags in relief when I realize it's not plugged in. Thank the gods. Things haven't gone completely backwards in the world—what with Roman Montague using a real lighter, and then my mother seeming to plug in an appliance I was nervous. But no…I guess it's just Roman.

"Juliette, come over here," my mom calls over the noise. "I can't hear you from there."

"What…what are you doing?" I ask.

"Semi-permanent firming wrap. It's like Spanx, but it sticks to you." She smacks her own ass and nearly takes the nearest helper's head off. "You want some?"

"No, I'm good," I say firmly, watching a woman spread lotion over my mother's thighs. At least it's not the blood of virgins. That myth came from somewhere, and that somewhere is absolutely Stratford. "Why are you doing this now?"

"It has to sit overnight." She says this like I'm an idiot for not knowing. "It's important to do it right before bed."

"Right." I take a seat on my parent's bed and pick up a book from the bedside table on my father's side—the only part of the room untouched by this madness. He's reading a biography of Pamela Colman Smith and I flip through it for a few minutes, making a mental note to ask him how he's enjoying it. I put the book down and refocus on my mother. "So, can I talk to you?"

"Can it wait?"

"Not really."

Mom opens her mouth in slight surprise. She glances from me, to her attendants, and throws her hands up in exasperations. "Well, you're a bit early. I wasn't expecting you back for another hour, at least."

"Yeah...that's what I need to tell you about."

"Well, go downstairs and I'll find you when I'm done."

"Where's dad?" I ask over the sound of the blow dryer.

"In his office."

My heart leaps. "Really?"

"Yes. Now, go."

For once I don't even care that she's talking to me like I'm twelve. I'm more than happy to go downstairs and find my father while I wait for Mom to finish with...whatever the hell this is.

I drop into my bedroom before heading downstairs. Of everywhere in this house, my room is the only place that I genuinely like—the only place that feels like me, with all its warm tones, spindly antique furniture, and moody florals. Crossing to my canopy bed, I furrow my brow at the black garment bag laid flat against the dark mauve duvet. An electric-yellow post-it note stuck to the front says:

NOTICED YOU MIGHT NEED SOME NEW CLOTHES!

My eye twitches.

It's my mother's handwriting, and I can't decide whether it's meant passive aggressively or not. I gained a tiny bit of weight... and? I'm also not a teenager anymore, gods forbid.

I let out a noise somewhere between a groan and a sigh and cross to the dresser instead, pulling out leggings and a sweatshirt.

Twenty minutes later, I walk into my father's study without knocking. He looks up from his desk and smiles, his eyes only betraying a hint of exhaustion.

"Etta," he says by way of greeting. "I thought you were still at that...what was the thing tonight?"

I smile. I like that my dad, like me, doesn't care much for Order events. He's more interested in the practical magic aspect than Order politics and leaves all council matters to my mother.

"The Arcane Auction," I say, sitting down in the chair across from him. "Although I didn't see much on the list I would consider worthy of that title."

His eyes crease in the corners when he smiles. My father is in his mid-sixties, gray-haired and gray-eyed. To me, he's always seemed calm, mild-mannered, and a little bit lame—like a dad should be.

It's hard to look at this tweed-wearing, tea-drinking man and reconcile what I've learned about him as I've grown up.

"What are you doing here?" I ask, perhaps a little too boldly.

He coughs, uncomfortable—he likes to pretend I don't know he rarely spends a single night at home, or that the book on his side of the bed likely hasn't been touched in six months. I dread the day that I'm older than my dad's girlfriend, and as I've just turned twenty-one I fear we're fast approaching that day.

"Your mother and I wanted to talk to you."

The hair on the back of my neck stands up. "Oh...about what Councilman Lawrence said?"

His eyes narrow. "What?"

Right. I'm flailing. I wish I didn't have the kind of relationship with my parents where every conversation is immediately assumed to be catastrophic, but it's too late to fix that now.

Just then, my mother sweeps into the room. "Alright. What did you want to tell me, Juliette?"

Distantly, I wonder if Mom is supposed to look any different after being air-fried for the last thirty minutes. She looks about the same. Taller and willowier than I am, but with the same ash-blonde hair, which she claims is still natural, and a very pretty face that is mostly still natural even in her late forties. She's a good twenty-five years younger than my father, and it's never been a secret in our house that their marriage is more of a business alliance than a romantic relationship.

Given how miserable she is, one would think she wouldn't want the same for me...but that's "just how things are done."

I lean toward her, my anxiety rising. "I wanted to tell you about the auction..."

Her expression goes as dark as it possibly can as I explain the nights events. She can't furrow her brow, but if she could, I know she'd look furious.

"I'll call Emrys in the morning," she says when I finally finish.

"That's it?" I glance toward my dad for back-up. He's not listening, instead, running one finger over the spine of a leather-bound book on his desk. I roll my eyes. "It's only that Councilman Lawrence seemed mad...he made some comment about how he's on his way out?"

My mom crosses the room, standing behind my father. She taps him on the shoulder to make him pay attention. I frown at them, alarmed by their visual show of unity.

"Actually, Juliette," Mom says. "That's an excellent segue into what we wanted to discuss."

I furrow my brow. "What is? Councilman Lawrence?"

Her expression is odd, like she's trying to look sad, but wants to smile. It comes out as more of a leer. "Emrys has decided to retire. I know council members don't typically retire, but in light of the backlash the community thought it was best."

"Oh," I relax slightly. "So, are you the new head of the council?"

Maybe that's what this is. Maybe we have to move or something, or there's going to be a party...or, I don't know.

The head of the council is an extremely prestigious position, like a combination of president, high priest, and supreme court justice. Not only do they govern the United States witchcraft community, as Stratford acts as the capital city for the magical community, but they oversee the other council positions, and advise human politicians, celebrities, and CEOs on the whims of our gods.

My mother smiles, flashing all her teeth. "Not yet, but hopefully soon. We'd like it if you could help."

"Sure," I say, already uncomfortable.

"Perfect." My mom claps her hands together. "Did you happen to spend any time with Harrison tonight?"

I stiffen. "A bit?"

My stomach sinks as I glance between my parents. Why do I feel like I'm falling off the edge of a cliff? Like I'm teetering, about to spin out of control, and the two people in the world who should want to throw me a lifeline are instead about to push me over the edge.

My father clears his throat, the sound echoing in the otherwise quiet room. "Your mother has been thinking, Juliette, and so have I and we've come to a decision. We think it would be best if you married Harrison Dane."

"Right," I say, even as my heart pounds against my chest. "I know. We had this conversation eight years ago."

My parents exchange a look, and my mother smiles in a way that doesn't quite reach her eyes. "Yes, but we mean immediately."

I can hardly believe my ears and stand rooted to where I am, mouth agape. "But I haven't graduated. I'm not pledged yet."

"You're twenty-one," my father says. "It's possible to pledge now."

"But what about school?"

My mother places her hands on my shoulders and gives them a gentle squeeze as she speaks in a calm voice. Like she's trying to sooth a wild animal. "It's not just about us wanting your happiness Juliette, though we do want that." She looks pointedly at my father before continuing "Our family needs this alliance; your relationship with Harrison could bring great stability for both of our families."

Relationship. As if I even know him.

My breath comes too fast. I feel like I'm in a dream, or maybe even a nightmare. I notice they ignore the question about school, and suddenly the only thing I care about is checking if I'm even registered for next semester.

"Can I go? I'm tired."

My father's brow furrows in concern. He at least seems to care, if only slightly, that I don't seem excited. "Alright. We can talk about all this tomorrow."

"The gala is tomorrow," my mother reminds both of us, "We should announce it then."

I feel like I'm going to be sick. "I'm, uh, going to tell Cat."

"Wonderful," my mother says, as warmly as she's capable of. "Oh, and Juliette?"

I stop in the doorway, nearly shaking. "Yes?"

"Do you happen to know where your birth certificate is? I went to find it in my office, and it wasn't in my cabinet. Didn't you need it for some kind of school paperwork awhile back?"

I stiffen. "Yes, I have it. Why?"

"The seer needs your exact time of birth and for the life of me I can't remember. Would you drop it on the desk in my downstairs office when you get a chance?" She blows a kiss. "Love you."

CHAPTER SIX
⋆ ROMAN ⋆

"You always were a good girl, Etta."

I hear the words over and over in my head, picking them apart with growing disgust as I walk home. What the fuck is wrong with me?

Well, aside from the obvious, that is. What's wrong with me tonight?

That's the kind of thing you think, but don't say out loud. At least, not without prompting. Not to a woman like Etta Capulet. A woman who's impossibly out of reach. A woman who is—for lack of a better phrase, a *good* girl.

The air is sharp, and the cold burns my lungs. It's only a three mile walk back to the apartment I share with Bennet. Any other time, I could run three miles with no difficulty. Tonight, it feels endless. It's too cold to be walking without a jacket, even for me, but I don't begrudge leaving Etta my coat. I know I could technically fix my problem with very little effort.

But I won't.

I'd rather freeze to death than go back to relying on gods who neither listen nor give two shits about me. Who care only for power and those who can channel it, but don't protect their most devout followers.

The gash above my eyebrow throbs in time with my heartbeat, like I'm being punished for my defiance. *Fuck you—I'd rather let it bleed.*

I knew it was stupid to let Tyberius Capulet goad me the moment the pain exploded across my face. Realized it a half second before, actually. Good thing too, or I'd be nursing a broken nose right now rather than a black eye. Capulet might be a worthless prick, but he's got a decent right hook. Not better than mine, but good enough to be fun to spar with if I'm feeling self-loathing enough. Tonight, I was in just a dark enough mood to take his bait.

I reach my apartment building and gratefully duck inside, rubbing my cold hands together. It's a luxury building with six elevators, and I dive into the first open one, punching the button for the top floor several times.

I tap my foot in the elevator, then stride quickly down the long empty hallway with the new paint smell before reaching the only door on the top level.

It takes me two tries to get the door to my apartment open with freezing cold hands, but finally I manage it. The door opens into an open concept apartment. The kitchen is modern, all stainless steel and dark granite kitchen, while the living room is full of leather furniture, most of it worn and showing the signs of heavy use. Huge windows along the back wall overlook the harbor, and the tops of the tall ships are still visible even at night. The walls are decorated with abstract expressionism paintings that I don't have a fucking clue about, and ceiling-high bookshelves are covered with books—lots of books—each of which I've meticulously chosen and read ten times over.

Nothing in the apartment exactly screams "Warlocks afoot." The only things left out in the open are my maps and pendulums, strewn across the coffee table, and the whiteboard in the kitchen, where Bennet tracks our stock investments by the positions of the planets. Jupiter is in the second house. We won't be trading today.

I don't immediately notice Bennet sitting at the kitchen island, but I stop short when he clears his throat. "Where the fuck were you?"

Bennet is usually mild-mannered, especially compared to me. The outburst is unexpected. I raise my eyebrows, and then wince when my black eye throbs. "I walked. That okay with you?"

My cousin runs his hand through his dark hair, fixing angry brown eyes on me that remind me of my dad. Bennet and I look similar, I guess, but not the same. He's shorter and more muscular than I am, with lighter hair. I've always thought it was a shame Bennet was born into an Order family, because he's really built for extreme sports more than political dealings and obsessive academic one-upmanship. We are not a family that values participation in all-American pastimes. We are a family that values the *appearance* of participating in all-American pastimes.

"You couldn't text me back? I thought you passed out or something," he gripes.

"I'm fine, man." I grab a bag of frozen peas from the freezer and then make my way over to the liquor cabinet.

Bennet coughs loudly. "Should you be drinking?"

I reach for the nearest bottle. "It's medicinal."

"Just fix your eye."

"No." I fix him with a dark stare and take a large sip of my drink, and it burns my throat making my throbbing eye water. I scowl at the label. *What the fuck is this?*

Bennet sighs. His expression is somewhere between concern and vague disapproval. "Your funeral."

I blink at Bennet though one eye, as the other is streaming with tears and feels like it's going to permanently swell shut. "Don't look at me like that."

"Like what?" He stands up and crosses to the counter, opening the pantry cabinet and pulling out a loaf of bread. "I have no opinion on your self-destructive phase."

I make a noise somewhere between a cough and a grunt of agreement. He has an opinion—clearly—but I don't care to hear it.

The clinical term for my mood lately is "depression." I'm cognitively aware of it, and yet unable to shake it. When your sister disappears mysteriously without a trace, only to turn up dead a few weeks later, then your mother effectively loses touch with reality, I think some depression is warranted.

"Just tell me one thing," Bennet says, watching me out of the corner of his eye.

I take another sip of my too-strong drink. "What?"

"Could you get over it if it turned out the Capulets did something to Marcia?"

I frown at him, not sure what he's getting at. "Why the fuck would I have to get over it?"

I'm not convinced that Etta's family *did* do something to my sister. If I were, I would have already strangled Tyberius Capulet with my bare hands. Fuck, I might have put aside my issues with the Order and using magic, just to take him on what he considers his own playing field. But ever since Marcia disappeared last summer, that answer hasn't rung true for me.

Tyberius is a fucking asshole. He's a year older than me, which makes—made—him four years older than my sister. I beat the shit out of him back in high school for trying to mess around with her, probably just to upset my family. Still, call me crazy, but I don't think he'd kill her.

It's hard to know how far the Capulets would go—or how far my family would go in retribution, but for some reason I always got the feeling they have at least *some* honor around who is and isn't fair game in a fight. It's a low fucking bar when I'm talking about a family who cursed my grandfather and murdered my uncle in cold blood, but somehow, I don't think they would target someone too young to pledge to the Order. My sister was nineteen. An adult by normal human standards, but not by the Order's standards where the age of pledging is twenty-one. Then, there were the other victims. Two sisters from the same family who had absolutely nothing to do with the Capulets.

I've just never really thought it was them. Even after Etta didn't come to the funeral.

Bennet turns back to me, after taking far too long to put two slices of bread in the toaster. He leans forward against the counter, turning serious again. "I swear I'll drop it after this, but I just want to point out that you're not exactly unbiased."

I take another sip of the too-strong drink. "You're dancing a fine, fucking line, man."

"Unless you're suddenly planning to use magic, I'm not worried." He grins. "Go on, hit me. I'll go a couple rounds with your drunk, half-blind, ass."

I scowl. "How valiant of you. They'll write poems about your courage."

He raises his eyebrows, but when I refuse to continue or feed into his shit he gives up. "Alright, never mind."

I always knew Bennet suspected something had gone on, but he's never come right out and asked me about Etta before. Not even back then. I guess I was asking for questions after the scene tonight. We should have left as soon as I saw her through the window, but the moment I realized she was there, I knew I was done.

I've never been able to walk away from her.

She was staring at the stage, eyes glazed over, as if she was only pretending to listen. It was the same expression she wore during every prep school assembly. Every school council meeting and debate club. Every extracurricular event that she excelled at and clearly hated, where she was pretending to listen for the sake of appearances. Of course, I was pretending to listen too. I was only there because of her.

I knew, the moment I saw her, I had to talk to her. I knew, like I know my own name. And later, when I lied to my cousin about where I was going and followed Etta like a phantom out onto the steps, I knew I was completely fucked.

Because I've been in love with Etta Capulet since I was twelve-years-old, and until this year, it was the worst thing that ever happened to me.

CHAPTER SEVEN

ETTA

JUNIOR YEAR OF HIGH SCHOOL, FIVE YEARS AGO

THE LIBRARY ENVELOPES ME IN A HUSH, ITS STILLNESS only disrupted by the occasional rustle of pages and distant foot-steps. My fingers trace the edges of my textbook, but the words swim before my eyes. Calculus may as well be ancient runes for all the sense it makes.

Actually, no. Ancient runes would be far, *far* easier.

I sigh and lean back in the high-backed wooden chair, feeling its carvings dig into my spine—a reminder that even the furniture at Verona Valley Prep has unreasonably high expectations. I sit up straighter.

"Focus," I mutter under my breath.

As if in defiance of myself, my gaze wanders toward the stained-glass window. The afternoon sun casts bright red patterns across the table where I sit. The splotches remind me of the blood splat-tered across my jacket, and the heated exchange with the

Montagues after last week's speech-and-debate competition. Why can't my parents just act normal for once?

If it weren't for my desperate desire to leave Stratford and go to college literally *anywhere* else in the world, I would leave speech-and-debate on the spot. The club is one of the few I actually like, but the shame is too much to bear. Only, I need the extracurriculars if I have any hope of getting a scholarship. My parents won't pay for any college aside from Elsinore, and without a full ride, the local university looms in my future like a monolithic reminder of my family's expectations.

Maybe there's a way to stay in the club without running into Roman and his self-righteous smirks. I argue with myself, the internal debate as fierce as any club face-off.

Yeah, right—Even I don't believe myself. Not when the image of Roman's taunting grin haunts my every waking thought and even some of my dreams.

As if summoned by my thoughts, someone giggles from the back of the stacks, their voice echoing between the shelves. I frown. "Oh my gods."

Roman fucking Montague. As arrogant as ever, he seems to believe that the world is his for the taking - including secluded corners of the library which he has turned into a love nest with Rosaline Hathaway.

Rosaline, with her super-sleek chestnut hair, perfect body, and condescending smirk, is everything I'm not. In theory, we could have been friends. We're both from founding families, attend the same parties and events, and have known each other our whole lives. But just like Roman, Rosaline wields her popularity like a sword and takes great pleasure in cutting off the heads of lesser mortals.

They're perfect for each other, and I *hate* her.

I close my eyes, taking a deep breath to try and regain focus. I start reading again, but the letters swirl together in an incomprehensible mess.

I bounce my leg against the table, trying to drown out the noise, but it's pointless. Their presence is still the pebble in my shoe, the thorn in my side. A reminder of all the reasons why I need to leave this town.

Rosaline laughs again, and I hear the dull, low murmur of Roman's muffled voice as he says something to her. Hopefully he's telling her they should leave. Probably that they should go out to the parking-lot and hook up in that new car he's been showing-off lately. Whatever, just as long as they're not here.

Footsteps echo through the nearly silent room, and then it's quiet again. I let out a breath. Maybe they've left.

I look up and choke.

They've moved alright. They moved into a different section of the library, and are now pressed up against a shelf right in my direct line of sight. Worse, they're locked in a kiss that seems designed to torment me.

They stand close enough that I can see the way Rosaline's fingers curl into the fabric of his partially unbuttoned dress shirt, how his hand rests possessively on her waist. My heart constricts, and a strange, sick feeling takes root in my stomach.

"Seriously?" I raise my voice to a loud hiss. "If I'd known I was going to be in the splash zone I would have brought an umbrella."

They stiffen, and Roman pulls away from Rosaline to look at me. He runs long fingers through wavy black bangs, and scowls. "Didn't see you there, good girl. Enjoying the view?"

"Hardly," I snap back, my cheeks burning. "Do you mind? I'm sure you can find somewhere else for her to practice her fake orgasm noises."

Roman narrows his eyes. "You working on your stand-up comedy routine or something? It needs work."

"Nope, it's just that unlike some people, I actually care about my future," I retort, feeling the weight of every exam, every club meeting, every application deadline pressing down on me like a physical force. "I don't need to listen to your Discovery Channel impression while I'm trying to study."

Rosaline sniffs at me, rolling her eyes, and grabs Roman's arm. "This is boring. Let's go."

Roman shakes her off. "You can go if you want, I'm fine."

Rosaline doesn't move, even as Roman saunters towards me, each step a deliberate provocation. His eyes never leave mine. My brow furrows in confusion even as my heart speeds up. My entire body hums.

What the hell is going on?

"Get out of my library," I bite out, my words sharp as flint and his presence is a blemish on the sanctity of it all.

"Your library?" he chuckles, leaning back against a shelf as if he owns the very air we breathe. "I don't see your name on it."

I snort a laugh. "What are you, five? Do you write your name on everything you own?"

His dark eyes flash. "What if I do?"

I blink. What are we even talking about? "Uh...then you're pathological, but that feels like a you problem."

"Look out Roman," Rosaline says. "She'll curse you."

I scowl. Apparently, word that my mother curses people for fun has gotten around. Of course, mom is loving it. It's given her an air of infamy her reputation lacked. I am not loving it. It's given me a migraine.

"Good girl wouldn't curse me." Roman's voice is a low drawl, tinged with amusement. "Her mommy's threat hasn't even done anything. I don't think they can do any real magic, it's all talk."

"Shut up," I snap, my cheeks heating. Smart comeback right there. *Shut up. Brilliant.*

He just laughs quietly and snatches a *Sharpie* from the pencil case on the table. Before I can react, my arm is pulled up over my head and he's tracing letters onto my skin with permanent marker.

"What the hell are you doing?" I demand, struggling against his grip. I try to pull away, but he's too strong and moving too quickly.

"Shhh. Just about finished," he responds casually.

I'm seething with rage and look up, searching for Rosaline. Hoping for...help, maybe. Or, at least at witness to this insanity. I find neither. "Your girlfriend left. You should probably go after her."

"She's not my girlfriend," he shrugs off my words.

I scoff, arm still held hostage over my head. "Does she know that?"

"Yeah." I can hear the smirk in his voice. "Not everyone can be a good girl like you, Etta. Some of us like to live a little."

"You're such an asshole," I mutter under my breath.

"Proud of it," he retorts, dropping my arm. "There you go, good girl. Have fun explaining that to Mommy and Daddy at dinner. Hell, maybe call up that boyfriend of yours and see what he's up to."

"Boyfriend?"

I'm so taken aback it takes me a beat to realize he probably means Harrison Dane. Harrison is so, so not my boyfriend—I might be technically supposed to marry him one day, but that "one day" is doing a lot of work. I've barely ever spoken to him.

The mention of Harrison throws me off so much, that I don't look down at my arm until Roman has already taken several long steps away from me. By the time I realize he's leaving—fast—he's already sprinted halfway to the door and there's no way I can catch him. I look down at my arm and my eyes widen in shock.

PROPERTY OF ROMAN MONTAGUE. DO NOT TOUCH.

CHAPTER EIGHT
✦ROMAN✦

PRESENT

I WAKE THE DAY AFTER THE AUCTION TO THE BITTER taste of whisky coating my throat, as if bubbling up from the depths of my alcohol-soaked soul.

My head pounds, feeling about three-times too large for my skull, and the desperate urge to blow my nose wars with the need to sink into the mattress and let it become my tomb.

I open one blurry eye and for a moment, I can't understand why I've woken up at all. My strangely accurate internal clock knows it's well before 9:00AM. I'd say it's before 7:00AM if I were a betting man—which, honestly, I am. I close my eyes again and will myself back to sleep, only to hear my phone chime from somewhere to my left.

That must be it. Someone called and woke me up. Someone has a fucking death wish. Groaning, I throw an arm over my face, then wince. Fuck, I forgot about my eye.

I mumble curses under my breath—some half-magical, some simply profane—and lean over in bed and fumble for my phone, my eyes still closed. It vibrates in my hand, the actual vibration louder than the chime. Forcing myself to open my eyes, I instantly regret it as "Father" flashes across the otherwise black screen.

Fucking hell. If I don't answer it, though, he'll simply keep calling. Worse, he may just show up. "Yeah?"

There's a pause, where my father says nothing. I know he's debating berating me for rudeness, complaining that, "Yeah" is an inappropriate way to answer the phone. Evidently, he decides it's not worth it. "Morning," my father says in his clipped, self-important tone. "Did I wake you?"

"Yeah," I say again.

"Sorry." He's not sorry. "Bennet and I are heading down to the club. I'll pick you both up in an hour."

The club. The club means golf. If there is a more pointless sport than golf, I have yet to find it. "If I go ask Bennet right now, does he know about this plan?"

The pause is answer enough. "You've got an hour."

Pulling my phone away from my head, I look at the time. It's 7:16. Fucking hell.

Sitting up, I suck in a breath as my head spins. "No. I have plans today."

I don't, but I would rather snort crushed glass than play golf, even without a hangover.

"I wasn't asking, Roman," he says flatly. "We need to talk."

"And I wasn't offering to debate it."

We sit in silence for a moment, and I just know he's seething. I can see it perfectly, because I grew up with this man and sometimes, we're a bit too alike for my comfort. "How about 10:00?" he asks with the cautious air of one handing over a briefcase for ransom. "Your mother would appreciate a visit afterwards."

I pinch the bridge of my nose, then wince, as I brush my eye again. I should have known that card would be the next to flip over. "Fine."

I can practically feel his smugness through the phone.

THE POUNDING IN MY HEAD NEARLY DROWNS OUT THE soundtrack of the golf course. If I focus hard enough to make my eyes water, I can pick out the calls of mourning doves in the distance, the swish of clubs against fog-soaked grass, and most audibly, my father's angry mumbling as he tries to line up a shot he will never achieve.

Shifting on the uncomfortable back seat of the cart, I blink and focus on the book in my lap. I've read the same page three times, and still, the words won't penetrate my mind.

"Maybe self-improvement isn't the answer, maybe self-destruction is the answer."

I stretch out my fingers, slightly achy with the November chill, and turn to a random page. Organized chaos.

I focus on a random sentence on the new page. The narrator is talking about his organs in the third person. *"I am Joe's white knuckles...I am Joe's smirking revenge."*

Suddenly aware of a looming presence above me, I slowly look up.

My father stands over me, trying and failing to look menacing in his cable knit sweater and plaid wool hat. He scowls at my book. "It's your turn."

I raise my eyebrows. "I'm getting to the good part."

Realistically there's no "good part" of a Palahniuk novel. It's all good, but that's irrelevant. My father is the kind of man who thinks reading for pleasure isn't a real hobby. I am the kind of man who thinks driving a tiny car on fake grass isn't a real sport. *I am Roman's quiet contempt.*

"We're trying to play a game here," Father says.

I close my book and reach into my pocket for my pack of clove cigarettes. "Yes, but why? You're a warlock and a billionaire. You could do fucking anything, and you're choosing to golf? Do you see how sad that is?"

"Like what, son? Drinking and pissing away my family's money?"

I almost congratulate him on an excellent comeback—albeit an inaccurate one—but my pride won't allow it. "I thought we were here to have a conversation. Isn't that what you said on the phone?"

Father scowls. "Don't light that."

"Why? You have cigars in the glove compartment."

He can't seem to think of a response and gives up as the scent of licorice and tobacco overwhelms us. "Just come take your turn."

I glance up at Bennet, standing behind my father. He shrugs, and I can practically hear his voice, "It's easier just to play along."

It's only because of him that I get up and reach for my clubs.

"I heard about last night," my father says, placated by my participation.

"No shit." I gesture to my face. "What was your first clue?"

"Not that." Apparently, a brawl between enemies isn't newsworthy. "I meant about Lawrence"

I blink, and it's my turn to be confused. "Oh, okay. So?"

Emrys Lawrence is one of the few people in this hell-scape of a town with any real power. Of course, everyone in town would say they have power, especially men like my father who sit on the council, but it was only after my sister's disappearance that I realized just how powerless we all are. How money can buy you a lot of things, but it can't get you answers if you don't know where to look. It can't take pain away. It can't bring back the dead.

My father looks at me as if we're speaking completely different languages, and I could swear we are. "So?" He snaps his fingers. "Roman, keep up."

"You know, I would, but you woke me up at the fucking ass-crack of dawn, I have a headache from hell, you know I hate golf, and I wasn't even in the room for whatever Lawrence was saying because I couldn't care less about the Order."

"Don't fucking swear," he snarls without a hint of irony.

I grind my teeth, reminding myself of my personal vow not to abandon my family...even when I desperately want to.

Before Marcia died, I'd just graduated from Elsinore and thrown myself into work, finding and selling rare manuscripts around the world. While I personally prefer working with classic literature, my affinity for finding and translating runes, ancient magical scrolls and lost works of occult scholars, would have allowed me to stay in the Order, without actually living in Stratford.

It was, in my opinion, a perfect solution.

One that would have put-off my parents for at least a decade before they started demanding I come home and take a seat on the council. One that would've put Etta Capulet out of sight and, hopefully, out of mind. But then my sister disappeared, and now I can't leave. My mother doesn't deserve to lose two kids, no matter how much I hate this town and everything it stands for.

"Emrys emailed the council this morning," my father says, fixing me with a pained stare. "He's concerned about the violence within the Order. Feels he cannot step down while things are so unstable."

I scoff. "What a tragedy."

Father smiles, and this time it touches his eyes. "Quite."

We both know that the violence is only of concern to Lawrence as far as it affects his political career. One of the few things Father and I agree on is that Lawrence has overstayed his welcome.

"Emrys has decided that the next person...or the next house, rather, who draws blood of another Order member will be removed from the council and out of the running for any future seats."

"He can't do that!" Bennet says, speaking for the first time in a quarter of an hour.

"He can with council support," my father gripes. "And, surprisingly, he has it. This is clearly nothing more than a feeble attempt to appear to be cracking down on violence after failing to act on the real problems in this town, however, here we are."

I lean against my golf club and bite my tongue. I'm shocked to find that for once, my father and I might be in agreement. "This is a stunt to look like he's doing something and avoid picking between us or the Capulets."

My father nods, pushing his absurd hat higher on his head and brushes his dark-gray hair from his eyes. "Yes, that was my read on things."

I take a deep breath through my nose, conflicted. While I despise getting involved with the Order, I also despise hypocrisy. Lawrence has shown in the last six months that performative friendship and public words of support often mean nothing behind closed doors. "So, what do you want me to do?"

"Emrys may be inadequate in nearly every way, but for once he might have done something right—if only by accident. It shouldn't be hard for you to provoke Tyberius Capulet into striking first and disqualifying the entire family from the council."

I crack my neck. "Sure, but that's if people even abide by it."

I could easily see them agreeing to kick us out, but not the Capulets. The unblemished, light-magic-wielding Capulets have always managed to worm their way out of everything.

"Make it public," Dad says, a slight gleam in his eyes. "And once they're off the council, not only will Delphine be out of the running to replace Emrys, but he'll step down, feeling like he succeeded in some small way, and the real work can begin to investigate your sister's death."

I run my hand over the back of my head. When he lays it out like that, it all sounds too easy—like by this time next week my father will be happily running the council, Councilman Lawrence will be on an Island somewhere, and the Capulets will be in hell.

Except it's never that easy.

"Are you sure you would win even if Mrs. Capulet wasn't eligible?" Bennet asks, clearly thinking along the same lines I am.

My father looks out over the golf course, as if afraid we'll be overheard acres away from the nearest person. "One of my friends in the dean's office told me that Capulet pulled his daughter out of Elsinore for next semester."

I frown, thrown by the seemingly random change of subject. "That doesn't sound right. E—er, Capulet's daughter is a senior."

"She's twenty-one and promised to Harrison Dane. She doesn't need to graduate to pledge to the Order and get married. That marriage will solidify a strong alliance for Delphine."

"You sound jealous."

He sneers. "Believe me, if I could have found a way to tie us to the Danes, I would have. I'll just have to settle for another alliance, and you're going to help me."

"Right," I say vaguely. "Sure."

I'm not listening anymore. I can't think of anything past the horrifying prospect of Etta married to that prick Harrison Dane. I've known it was inevitable for over a third of my life and yet the actual prospect still makes me homicidal.

I wish my father had picked any other day to have this conversation with me. A day when I was feeling less sick, and up to arguing with him. Except, if I'm being honest, most days have been bad lately.

I'm raising the clove to my mouth when a sense of dread falls over me, and suddenly, I understand what my dad is trying to say. I would have gotten it faster if I'd been having a better morning and my brain didn't feel like it was being steamrolled. Fucking hell.

Sweat beads on my palms and the back of my neck, and this time it has nothing to do with the alcohol literally leaking from my pores. "There are other ways to make alliances...money, or threats. You love threats."

"We're past threats." My father barks. "We need friends at least as strong as whatever the Capulets will get out of using Juliette."

"Like whom?" I practically yell.

I run through the Order members in my head, trying to figure out who he could possibly be planning to align with.

Of the eight families, the Capulets, the Minolas, and the Cesarios tend to vote together. Our house always votes with the MacBeths. The Hathaways, the Danes and what's left of the Lawrences are swing votes. Which must mean…

"Do you remember Rosaline Hathaway?"

Suddenly it's like I'm standing on the tracks watching a train barrel toward me. "…yes."

My father takes out his phone and opens something, like he's reading a list. "She's pretty, well-liked in the community, enjoys tennis and volunteers at the local animal shelter."

She's also calculating, ambitious and borderline sociopathic. We used to have a lot in common.

"Rosaline's reputation is almost on par with Capulet's daughter, and her connections are arguably better. You'll marry her and the Hathaways will vote to support us should Emrys make any rash decisions."

I splutter. "I don't think it's that simple, Father. She might not want—"

He looks me up and down. "Make her want to. For the gods sake, I didn't think you would need dating advice. That always seemed to be one area you excelled at."

I open and close my mouth, unable to form coherent thoughts. "Are we even compatible?"

Every child in the Order has their entire astrological chart mapped out the moment they are born. Often, a reader is brought in within hours of a birth, and sometimes marriage contracts are drawn up that day if there's already another Order child who is a good match.

I had a reading as a child, and as my father has loved to remind me over the years, there wasn't a single good match anywhere in the Order. Like the gods were laughing at me, telling me that I was, in fact, too fucked up for anyone.

I look warily at him, unable to believe he isn't taking this opportunity to bring up this old wound.

My father's gaze darts to the side. Ha, I've got him on something. "She's...close enough," Dad hedges.

Translation: she's not a match and my dad no longer cares. I don't care either, but I still refuse to let this happen.

"No," I blurt out.

"What do you mean, 'No,'" my father drawls.

"Exactly what it sounds like. I don't need to marry Rosaline Hathaway or anyone else so you can be head of the council. That's absurd."

His lip curls. "Oh? And you're so different from every other heir in this community? Better than Juliette Capulet?"

My mind darts to the book in the golf cart. *You are not special. You're not a beautiful and unique snowflake.*

I want to laugh. I'm not special—not in the slightest. I'm nothing, certainly not better than Etta, but not for the reasons my father means. She's infinitely better than me. Still, neither of us deserve to be used this way, and I won't allow it.

I could threaten to leave. To abandon the Order...but I know I can't. Not until we find out what happened to my sister. "Because you just said that it wouldn't be hard to provoke Tyberius," I say. "So, we won't need alliances if the Capulets are gone."

I hold my breath as Father considers. "Fine. Get Tyberius Capulet to attack you in public before Juliette is engaged, or you'll marry Rosaline Hathaway by Yule."

I am Roman's uncontrollable sense of dread.

CHAPTER NINE

ETTA

Junior Year of High School, Five Years Ago

"I think my dad will let me stay at your house, but I know he'll call your mom to check if we're going out anywhere," Cat says as we weave our way down the hall in the direction of our lockers. "Maybe we should get ahead of it and say we're going to the Founders Day carnival."

I glance sideways at her. "No one ever goes to the carnival."

"Yeah, but do they know that?" she muses. "I'm not sure they do."

I'm actually surprised my mom isn't making me get more involved in Founders Day this year. It's usually her favorite event of the season, but something about this year has subdued her slightly. All the better, I guess, since that means Cat and I can actually do something fun for once. Assuming she can escape her over-protective dad.

I sidestep around a group of soccer players, and shrug as I fall back into step with her. "Whatever you want. You know my parents don't care what we do."

Cat continues to spit-ball ideas as we approach our lockers, me nodding along vaguely. Finally, I glance up and stop short. Whomever was walking behind me makes a noise of indignation, like I caused a pile-up on the interstate. I barely notice. "What the hell?"

Roman Montague is leaning against my locker, smirk firmly in place. He's wearing his uniform with a cavalier disregard, shirt untucked and top buttons undone, giving him an air of rebellious aristocracy, and he's flanked by his ever-present shadows, Pierce Avon and his cousin, Bennet.

"What's going on?" Cat mutters under her breath.

Shit. I didn't tell her about the other day in the library, and now I desperately wish I had. "I...nothing. I don't know."

"He's not...waiting for you, right?" She sounds nervous. "Whose lockers are around ours?"

I don't respond, only tugging nervously at the sleeve of my long, white, dress-shirt as I stride forward. "Montague," I say, my tone clipped. "You're blocking the way."

"Am I?" Roman's lips curl into a smirk, eyes glinting with mischief. "Huh. Oops."

"Always the gentleman," Cat mutters under her breath, her annoyance palpable.

Pierce snickers, and takes a sip of a huge, *Dunkin Donuts* iced coffee, holding the straw between his teeth. Bennet doesn't say or do anything, as his gaze darts around nervously, perhaps sensing the brewing storm.

"Move," I insist, feeling the familiar rise of irritation. Roman has the uncanny ability to make my blood boil with nothing more than a glance.

"Make me," he challenges, pushing off the locker with a grace that belies his mocking demeanor.

I consider the situation, weighing the consequences of using just a hint of magic to nudge him aside. But no, that would breach the unspoken truce, as well as breaking all sorts of school rules. Besides, I can't give Roman the satisfaction of seeing me lose control. So instead, I roll my eyes, trying to appear unaffected. "I don't have time for this, Roman. What do you want?"

"Hear that, boys?" Roman says. "She doesn't have time for us."

"Whatever crowd you're playing to, I don't want to be part of it. I just want to get my stuff, so either move, or tell me what you came to tell me so we can all get on with our lives."

I glance at Cat, and she gives me an encouraging nod. I stand a little straighter. That sounded totally rational and mature—not at all like I'm playing into this stupid feud, or whatever absurd mind-games or popularity politics Roman has cooked up. I'm rising above it.

"Why are you wearing long-sleeves, good girl?" Roman drawls. "It's pretty warm out today, don't you think?"

I feel like I can hear a record scratch somewhere in the distance. Heat creeps into my cheeks, not from the temperature but from the way his gaze lingers on my right sleeve, as if he can see through it to the faded pen underneath. No matter how much I scrubbed, it wouldn't come off entirely.

I am not rising above. I am below. Way, way below, in the dark part of the ocean, and even the one-eyed razor-blade fish are like: *what the fuck was that?*

"*Good girl*?" Cat asks, her tone dripping with disdain. "Is that a teacher's pet thing, or a pet-name thing"

To my surprise it's Pierce who answers her, swallowing another gulp of his iced coffee. "Why do you care, Minola?"

"I'm trying to decide how much to hate it."

Pierce grins. "Awe, baby, don't be like that."

"You're disgusting," Cat snaps.

I close my eyes and pinch the skin on the bridge of my nose. "Can we just...not do this? *Please*?"

I refuse to open my eyes as I feel Roman step forward toward me. "You didn't answer the question."

"None of your business," I snap back, eyes still closed. "Maybe I'm just cold."

"Or maybe you're hiding something," he muses, his tone laced with a flirtatious edge that makes my stomach flip-flop.

I open my eyes and glare at him. He's closer than I realized, and I have to tilt my head back to meet his gaze. "Where's Rosaline?"

"How the hell should I know?"

"You should probably at least pretend to care, seeing as you're together."

There's a glint of something else in his gaze—a depth that goes beyond our usual banter and barbs. "You should pretend to listen. I told you, we're not."

"Well, then, you have an image problem," I babble. "Because it seems like you are, and it makes you seem like an asshole not to care."

He laughs and his hand shoots out, snatching at the sleeve of my shirt. I recoil slightly—not from fear, but from an electric shock of unwanted excitement. His touch is infuriatingly light, yet it sends a jolt through me that I loathe to admit even to myself.

His eyes bore into mine—completely focused—so dark they almost look black. "I am an asshole, good girl, and I don't care. I have more important things to focus on, now."

I suck in a small breath, unraveling. Our family feud is the stuff of legends in Stratford, but for a moment, it's just him and me, our own little saga unfolding in the hallowed halls of our prep school.

His phone vibrates loudly in his pocket and the spell breaks.

I jump, and shake my head as if to clear it, and yank my arm from his grip. My cheeks burn. Shit.

I can't even look at Cat. Her expression will tell me all I need to know. Either, I'm blowing this up in my head to be a bigger deal than it was, and from the outside what just happened didn't look like anything. Or, Roman Montague and I just had a major movie-moment in front of three-dozen people in the middle of the hallway at school. Either I'm crazy, or I'm...crazy. *Fuck.*

"What the hell are you thinking?" I stammer, trying to cover my confusion. "You can't talk to me. Everyone is looking."

What I really mean is: Our parents will hear about this within the hour. The entire hall has turned to watch us, and somehow, someone will tell them, and I'll get an earful tonight about how the Montague's are dangerous, black-magic-wielding, liars, who we barely tolerate and would be better off dead. Or, something like that. The feud is preposterous, but this entire town is steeped in secrets and old rivalries, and one wrong move could spell disaster for us all.

Roman glances up, and sees the crowd forming in the hall, as if for the first time. He steps back, but the damage is done. This looks... well, it doesn't look great, and the gods know I have no idea what it even means. Does it look like we like each other? Do I like him? I feel a migraine coming on.

Even Roman's friends seem confused.

I get the feeling Pierce and Bennet were expecting some kind of show-down, especially after the recent drama between our parents. Now that their leader has gone rogue, they don't know what to do.

We have that in common.

Seeming slightly flustered himself, Roman reaches into his pocket where his phone is still buzzing. He looks down at it and scowls, then answers. "Marcia, look, I'm running late. I can't—" he breaks off. "Calm down, what happened?"

Suddenly there's movement around me. Roman turns away, as if completely forgetting what was going on a moment before. Bennet moves to stand next to him, and Roman holds the phone out so his cousin can lean in and listen. It's hardly necessary. From where I'm standing a few feet away, even I can hear that Marcia is sobbing, her words barely coherent between huge, gasping breaths.

"How did it happen?" Roman says, the color draining from his cheeks.

That's not a good phrase—it's the kind of phrase you only hear when something bad happened. An accident...or a death.

"Let's go," I whisper, meeting Cat's gaze.

She nods quickly, already backing up. We turn-tail, and trot in the opposite direction, making it halfway back down the hall before anyone stops us. I can leave my books in my locker overnight, I'll just...

"Juliette!" Roman's voice bounces off the walls, making not only me, but everyone freeze.

My blood runs cold. It's not fear—not exactly. More like dread. I've only ever heard one Montague scream like that—Roman's father—and my mother has nothing nice to say about how confrontations with Mr. Montague tend to go.

Slowly, I turn. The entire hallway has gone silent, and I feel like a tumbleweed should roll past to mark the start of our duel.

Roman stands ten yards away from me, his too-handsome face contorted with rage. It's like I'm coming face-to-face with an entirely different person than was standing here minutes before, and the shift is jarring—a summer sky darkened by sudden storm clouds.

"What happened?" I ask, to break the silence.

"My grandfather's dead."

Sympathy wells up inside me. "Roman, I—"

"Your family!" His accusation is a thunderclap, loud and shocking. "This has your family's dirty fucking fingerprints all over it! Are you happy?"

I recoil, stung by the venom in his voice. "I don't know what you're talking about."

"Of course you don't," he spits, his words laced with bitterness. "And it's just a coincidence that your mother was spitting curses the week before my grandfather dropped dead? Fuck you."

The air in the hallway is thick with whispers and the hallway seems to contract around us. Suddenly, I wonder if Roman bothered to hang-up the phone, or if his little sister is still crying on the line, listening to him yell at me.

"Roman..." I begin again, only to fall flat. I don't know what I can possibly say. Nothing is going to convince him my family didn't do this.

In a swift movement, Roman grabs the iced coffee from Pierce's hand. The condensation kisses his fingers like a cold warning of the chaos about to erupt. I barely have time to register the look of malice in his dark gaze before everything shifts.

A scream of protest dies in my throat as the chilled liquid pours over my head, and streams of coffee trail down my face. It soaks into my hair, a bitter baptism that leaves me gasping for air.

The liquid turns my white shirt completely transparent, and I cross my arms, trying and failing to hide my pink lace bra, as well as the words scrawled across my arm. It's pointless, and I can feel the weight of a hundred eyes baring down on me. A lump rises in my throat and my eyes burn as laughter echoes through the hallway, a cruel chorus to my humiliation.

Roman's voice drips with mock innocence. "Oops."

CHAPTER TEN

ETTA

PRESENT

"DID YOU HEAR ANYTHING I JUST SAID?"

My eyes flick up to meet Cat's reflection in the mirror behind me. "What?"

I'm leaning over the ensuite bathroom vanity in my underwear, a completely mismatched set of too-sexy black-lace panties, and the oldest, ugliest, sports-bra I own.

Cat is lying on my bed in the other room, her reflection still visible through the open door. While I'm barely dressed, she's ready to go, her long, black hair tied back in a sleek bun and her floor-length, emerald gown, lying in a pool all around her. Her face is partially obscured by a book, but her eyes aren't moving, like she's only pretending to read. "Never mind. I was just asking if you'd met with your advisor about next semester today, but I'm guessing the answer is no."

I heave a deep sigh and shake my head. "Not yet."

She looks over the top of her book with her trademark know-it-all stare. "You need to get on that."

I pick up an eyeshadow brush, going over an already too-dark line below my right eye. "Yeah, I know. I will."

"What are you going to say if they tell you you're not enrolled?"

I sigh. "You mean *when* they tell me."

While my parents are avoiding the question, like they do with everything, I know the writing is on the wall. After all, the goal of Elsinore is to churn out good Order citizens. Sure, it's also an elite university, but only in the sense that the Order benefits from members in positions of power, and power often starts with prestigious degrees. If I'm married and inducted early, will they need me to finish school? I doubt it.

I suppose, the real question I should be asking myself is: will I sit back quietly and let them stop me?

"Fine," Cat says. "When you find out you're not enrolled for next semester. What are you going to do?"

"I don't know yet. I guess I need to find out exactly how many credits I need to graduate, and go from there. Maybe Harrison will be nice about it, I don't know."

It's pathetic that I have to hope my husband will be "nice" enough to pay for me to finish school, at a school I never even wanted to go to. I spent my entire prep school career planning for this, aiming for scholarships and ways out of Stratford, but ultimately fell short.

If I'm honest with myself, maybe I just wasn't brave enough to ask for what I wanted.

I look in the mirror again—at this point, I'm ready, and just stalling. There's only so many times one can reapply eyeliner. I look like a raccoon...or a prostitute. Like a really slutty raccoon.

Reaching for the black garment bag hanging on the back of the door, I unzip it to reveal a white ball gown. It's giving "bride." Like, Hilary Duff in *A Cinderella Story*, and not in a good way.

Sighing with exasperation, I tug the gown off the hanger and slip it over my head.

"Slip" is the wrong word. Tug. Suck in my tummy and shimmy. I have to take my bra off, and still my boobs end up near my chin, even before I've done up the back.

Flipping my head up, so my hair—which had been in perfect curls —flies everywhere, I twist in front of the mirror. I wince at the sight of myself trussed up as some sort of sacrificial bride.

"Can you help me with this?" I call to Cat.

The white silk bodice squeezes me until each breath becomes a whispered plea for escape, and it only gets worse when Cat pulls the laces of the back closed.

"You look hot," she says.

"I am hot," I gasp. "I'm suffocating. I can actually feel my temperature rising."

She grins at me in the mirror, and I feel a pang of jealousy for her loose-fitting, airy gown.

Your mom has... unique tastes," she offers diplomatically. "But why so tight? It's not like the Danes don't know what you look like."

"I have no idea. I like to think it's not intentional..." We both know I'm full of shit. "Anyway, she likes when I wear white, I don't know why."

"You hate white."

"Yeah, but this night is more for her than for me."

"That's exactly what a man wants to hear from his fiancé on the night of their engagement," Cat says sarcastically. "You should write Hallmark cards."

"Yeah, well, I don't think I have a choice."

She frowns. "I mean...you do, actually. Like, in a very literal sense, you have a choice about this. You're an adult, your parents can't make you get married."

I stare at her incredulously. I thought she would understand. "You mean like how you're an adult and your dad can't make you live at home and never date until you're forty?"

Her eyes widen. "Okay, fair point."

"I know technically I have a choice, but it's this or basically being disowned and homeless, and since I haven't even finished college and haven't ever had a job or my own money and don't know anyone outside the Order..."

"Right." She sucks on her teeth, seeming to choose her words carefully. "Which part is the problem? Is it Dane, or marriage in general?"

By "marriage," I'm not sure if she means the ceremony—which we both know is infamous in and of itself—or if she means spending the rest of my life married to Harrison. Either way, I don't want to discuss it. "Can we just pretend this isn't happening please? I really don't want to talk about it."

"Fine. We won't talk about it for the next—" she pretends to check a watch "—thirty minutes before you get engaged."

"I hate you."

"I do what I can. We should at least research the ceremony or something. I heard you have to suck his—"

I whirl on her, eyes blazing. "Do you mind?"

Cat laughs. "If you can't even talk about it, how are you going to do it in front of all those witnesses?"

I know the broad strokes of the ritual for marriage in the Order, *The Five-Fold Kiss*. I've sometimes wondered if there was a high priest back in the day who just really wanted to get his cock sucked, because I can't see any other reason for why it's like this.

Technically, it's about each partner worshiping the entire body of their spouse. Blessed be thy feet, then knees—which I think had to have been thrown in there to make the rest seem more reasonable—then genitals, breasts, and lips.

I suppose I can kissing Harrison's knee, maybe even a toe, but the idea of anything higher-up than that coming anywhere near my mouth makes me want to vomit—not a great sign when going into any marriage, but especially not one bound in the Order's black ink.

"You wait, when this happens to you I'm going to be *so* unhelpful."

Cat laughs. "Please. My dad's greatest terror is that his daughters will get married. He wouldn't ask me or Bianca to do anything, even if it made him the president."

We fall into silence, while I consider if I would prefer Cat's father who is overprotective to the point of smothering his fully-grown daughters, or my parents who want to use me as a political chess piece.

THIRTY MINUTES LATER, THE SOUNDS OF LAUGHTER and clinking glasses waft upstairs, and I finally venture out of my room.

The first guests have started to arrive, and I suck in a breath as I descend the stairs into the entry way. It's my own damn house, but somehow, this entrance makes the room feel foreign. The grand staircase looms before me, and I'm not sure if it's nerves, or lack of oxygen, making my head spin. *Please, please, don't let me fall on my face.*

I reach the final step and let out a sigh of relief when my heel connects with the marble floor.

My mother's voice cuts through the hum of conversation. "Juliette, darling!"

Mom stands flanked by my father and Tyberius, their faces carved from the same stoic marble. Across from them, the Danes pose like figures in a wax museum—too perfect, too poised.

"Mrs. Dane," I greet Harrison's mother first. "Thank you for coming."

Gertrude Dane's hawkish gaze sweeps over me, likely cataloging every imperfection. Harrison's stepfather, a man whose smile never seems to reach his eyes, offers me a curt nod. Beside him, Harrison's brother, Hamlin, leans against the wall, disinterest etched into his handsome features.

Truthfully, I suspect my mother would have preferred to set me up with Hamlin, since he's older and he'll eventually inherit both the company and the Dane's council seat, but it's common knowledge that he's been betrothed since infancy. Most Order children have their marriages arranged at birth, however, mine wasn't set up until I was thirteen.

I suppose I should be grateful to have Harrison, who is only six years older than me. Hamlin is ten years older, and rumored to be the wrong kind of crazy.

I should be grateful, but I'm not.

"Juliette," Harrison says, stepping forward and planting a chaste kiss on my cheek. His lips are cool and dry, devoid of any real affection. "You look beautiful."

I plaster on a smile, biting back a scream. "Thank you."

We're both performing for our families like trained dogs. In fact, now that I think about it, the only real thing I've ever seen Harrison do was the other night when he questioned me about Roman—and that hardly told me anything about him. Was he worried for me? Does he hate Roman? Is he an environmentalist, extremely concerned about the proper disposal of cloves? Who knows.

"Isn't she lovely?" my mother gushes, her usually critical eyes now brimming with pride.

"Indeed. Juliette, you'll make a splendid bride," Harrison's mother asserts, her words hanging in the air like an unspoken command.

It feels like a threat, and my palms start to sweat.

"Thank you," I say again. Can anyone hear the panic in my voice, or is that just me?

I can't breathe.

"We should mingle," my mother says. "We'll gather in the grate room for the announcement around nine? Everyone should have arrived by then."

There's a murmur of agreement, and I realize I should be smiling. I think I feel one of my molars crack.

I have to get out of here. Now.

CHAPTER ELEVEN

✦ ROMAN ✦

PRESENT

THE THUMPING BASS FROM PIERCE'S STEREO reverberates through me and the blue light from my phone blurs as I stare down at the screen without really seeing it. My phone vibrates in my hand, and I have to fight the temptation to throw it out the window onto the dark, winding back-road.

"What's she saying?" Bennet asks, looking vaguely nervous.

"I don't care," I say flatly. "You respond."

I try to hand him my phone and he puts his palms up, as if in surrender. "Nah, man. I'm not getting involved."

I feel like we're in fucking prep school again, and I'm playing go between with a friend and his formal date. Only now, I'm the friend, and I need Bennet to tell this woman I've hardly spoken to in years that I don't want to date her, let alone marry her.

The "she" we're referring to is Rosaline Hathaway, but she could be anyone. She has ceased to have a meaning, a face, or a personality in my mind. The list of attributes my father listed off for me earlier have blended into white noise in the face of my life-sentence, where she is both cellmate and jailer.

After golf, my father upheld his promise to facilitate a visit with my mother. Since Marcia's death, Mom has been hovering just on the edge of sanity, but today was a relatively good day. The visit was almost pleasant. That is, until she handed me my grandmother's wedding ring. I don't give a shit about jewelry, or the sentimentality of the ring, but I *do* know that Rosaline Hathaway will wear it over my dead, rotting, maggot-infested corpse.

My phone vibrates again and I growl in frustration. "I'm done with this shit."

"I'll respond." Pierce offers from the driver's seat. "Let me see."

"No," I snap. Partly because he's driving and partly because he'll probably tell her I want ten children or some shit. "Fuck off."

Pierce Avon has been my friend since prep school. He's one of the only few who stuck around after Marcia disappeared and I didn't feel like dealing with anyone or anything. He's a dick, but he's a loyal dick.

I put my phone on silent, shoving it as far into my pocket as it will go. Rosaline is likely to be at the party tonight, anyway. I don't know why she won't leave me the fuck alone beforehand.

"Cheer up, man." Pierce turns up the music, and tries to get me to react. "This doesn't have to be a bad thing. Your family is telling you to go fuck an objectively hot woman, *or else*. That's the stuff of 80s porn."

"Why 80s?" Bennet asks.

"When it had a plot."

I glare at them in the rearview mirror. It honestly sounds less like porn to me and more like the plot of a Bronte novel, but Bennet and Pierce are finance guys, and not really into literature. "They're not forcing me to do anything. Nothing has happened yet."

"Your phone blowing up says otherwise."

"She's just..." *Fucking insane.* "Trying to get clarification on some shit."

"I don't understand what the issue is," Pierce says over the music. "You used to fuck Rose back in the day...why not now?"

And there it is.

He's pointed out the proverbial elephant. The thing everyone is thinking but hasn't dared to bring up to me for fear of having their balls ripped off and shoved down their throats. I growl, low in the back of my throat, a dark cloud settling over my mood. "I know, but that's long over, so what you're essentially saying is: I've already seen all there is to see."

"Took a vacation, but didn't want to move there?" Bennet supplies.

I pinch the bridge of my nose. "Effectively."

It's not that I hate Rose. I don't care about her enough to hate her. We haven't hooked up since we were eighteen. As far as I knew, she's dating someone else, and I really couldn't care less. I thought our indifference to each other was mutual, in the same way that our relationship was mutually understood to be more about appearances than anything else. Except the way she's been blowing up my phone for the last twenty-four hours has me slightly nervous.

"It doesn't matter," I say tonelessly. "I'm not marrying her. We'll fix it."

I'm determined to make this go away. So determined, I put aside everything I've ever said about how much I hate the Order, how I don't like parties I am not personally throwing, and how I refuse to put on suits to please other people, and agreed to go to the fucking Founders Day gala. With the Capulet's hosting, there's every chance that Tyberius will try to punch me for simply being there, and then I'll be free of this entire situation.

At least, that's what I keep telling myself.

THE CAPULET MANSION, LIKE MOST OF THE HOUSES IN the area, is set so far back from the road, it's invisible from the street. The area is wooded, and the driveway twists through the trees, like its own private road. I've sometimes wondered if this is a security measure, or hazing for newcomers who are unfamiliar with how to navigate this sort of driveway in the dark. I don't blink an eye as Pierce speeds around every curve at 50MPH.

The house emerges out of the darkness, a Neo-gothic, brick monstrosity, with ivy crawling up the face. A garden wraps around the right side of the house, and a dozen or more cars are parked around the fountain that sits adjacent to the front door.

Pierce parks his Mercedes S Class between a Tesla and a BMW M6, and we walk up to the front door, its wood inlaid with steel honeycomb.

"I already regret this," I say to no one in particular.

Pierce laughs, like I'm joking, but Bennet's silence tells me he's on the same page.

This is an Order event—technically—so I'm fairly sure the Capulets can't keep us out, but I still don't feel like dealing with the bullshit that will come from being here. Maybe last year, but not now.

The party is well underway, so we let ourselves inside without bothering to knock. The entry hall is massive and opens into the great room. I frown. Nothing about the house reminds me of Etta. The wallpaper is gaudy, and the carpet is deep crimson. The furniture is large and overstuffed, and every light is a dark, black metal. It's all heavy, and overbearing, and nothing like Etta at all.

"Should we split up?" Bennet asks.

"What?"

I turn back to my cousin, and he's watching me, exasperation all over his face. "To get this over with quickly? Should we split up to find Tyberius or stay together?"

"Oh." I glance around, "Um…"

This is one of the reasons that Pierce is here. Aside from being a friend, he's also a member of another family, which provides a social buffer of sorts. Splitting up would negate that advantage.

Some people have spotted us now, and even among the few faces close enough to scrutinize, there are a wide variety of reactions. Older couples seem anxious or disapproving, while a few guys I used to hang out with are waving and their dates are staring, wide-eyed. I suppose I really haven't gone out much lately. Unless you count that auction, but that was far from a party.

"Roman!"

I look up and am incredibly relieved when I recognize the blur in the purple dress hurtling toward me. Of all the people who could be yelling at me right now, I suppose—Violet is one of the least offensive.

"Hey," I say when Violet Cesario reaches me.

"Hey!" She smiles widely. "I can't believe you're here."

"Me neither," I say honestly.

I glance back at Bennet and mutter. "Split up."

He nods, and disappears into the crowd with Pierce, as I refocus on Violet.

I haven't seen her in months. Not since...well, everything. She's Marcia's friend, not mine, and it's not like I've been great about staying up to date with my own friends let alone acquaintances.

"How are you?" I ask, not fully listening as she answers.

Instead, I glance behind her to where the great room is packed to the brim with people. It's November, but still all eight of the double glass doors are wide open onto a large patio where huge, floating blue and purple flames, placed strategically around the space, undoubtedly keeping it warm enough for guests. There's some sort of bespoke bar and a hibachi grill, and a cheer goes up as the chef tosses his knives into the air. Over the noise, the jaunty, festive sounds of a band—half modern, half old-world—waft in from out of sight.

I tune back into Violet for a moment. She's saying something about a theater class. Or maybe attending a show? I don't know, I'm not paying attention because I don't care, and I feel guilty that I don't care, but I can't make myself change it now.

Just as I'm berating myself for not giving a shit about anything around me, I spot something that does hold my interest.

It's actually her hair that catches my attention, which both is and isn't strange. I can't say I've ever been overly observant of hair, or clothing, or anything else aesthetic about women beyond "good" or "bad." Etta's hair was always firmly in the "good" category before. Tonight, I notice it because the blonde is catching the light from the fire and it looks like a halo from this distance, a renaissance idol in the flesh.

She's laughing, talking to someone just out of my sightline. I drag my gaze over her face, down her neck, and over the absurd princess dress she's wearing. The princess dress that looks nothing like anything she would have ever chosen for herself. It's half bride, half Disney character, and the polar opposite of the high-necked, black dress she wore to prom, or the painfully sexy lace thing from last night.

Okay, maybe I do notice things, but only about her. Only ever for her.

"Roman?" Violet asks.

"Sorry? What?"

She turns to follow where I'm looking. "I should have known. What, are you planning to pour a drink on her or something?"

I scowl, because as absurd as that sounds, that isn't...an entirely crazy thing to accuse me of doing. "I did that once."

"Once was memorable," she quips.

"Yeah, well, some of us have changed since we were sixteen," I snap, a bit more aggressively than Violet probably deserves. It's not her fault I feel guilty for the shitty things I used to do. "I'm not going to start anything with Etta, or any of the rest of them."

"Okay, sorry," Violet puts her hands up in surrender, even as she flashes a cat-like grin. "I forgot, you guys have to play nice, now, right?"

"Something like that."

"Good thing, too. It would be shitty to ruin her dress on her engagement night."

Every muscle in my body seizes. "What? How do you know?"

Black spots appear on the edges of my vision. Some part of me knows that I'm focusing on the wrong thing. That Etta's engagement has meaning aside from the stabbing feeling now working its way deeper into my abdomen. Yet, I can't think straight. Can't see straight.

Violet is still speaking. "My mother mentioned—"

I can't hear her, because my entire focus has shifted. Like a search and destroy laser, I've zeroed in on the woman now leaving the patio.

"Well, it was great to see you," I mutter, already melting into the crowd.

Violet's annoyed voice rings after me. "Wait!"

I've spent my whole life reading literature. Memorizing stories about tragic heroes and ill-fated love stories, and distantly, I recognize this moment for what it is. Recognize the simplicity of a metaphor, of the girl in the white dress, definitely not meant for me.

Etta is ethereal. She's Helen of Troy, launching an armada against every defense I've built against her over the last decade.

And I am not the hero of this story. I'm Hades. I'm Heathcliff. I'm Paris of Troy, gone to steal away Helen.

CHAPTER TWELVE

·ROMAN·

THE NOISE OF THE PARTY BELOW DULLS TO A LOW HUM as I jog up the back stairwell of the Capulet mansion. It isn't until I reach the second landing that I realize how reckless this plan is.

I let out a long sigh. Calling it a "plan" might even be too generous. Lapse in sanity? Is it still a lapse if the entirety of the last six months have been one long clusterfuck?

Even if Etta is getting engaged, how will my following her upstairs help? What am I trying to do?

I need to focus.

I need to go find Bennet and Pierce and focus on why we're here; namely, so my engagement isn't the next to be announced.

I freeze in the middle of the empty hallway, about to turn around and go back downstairs, when a figure in a white dress comes around the corner toward me, like an apparition, summoned in a circle of my wildest rambling fantasies.

Etta Capulet stops short some ten feet in front of me. Her huge, round eyes meet mine, and I've never before seen someone embody the phrase "deer in the headlights" so perfectly.

She says nothing, staring at me, her expression wary. Guilty, perhaps. Which makes no sense, as I'm the one creeping around a deserted upstairs hallway of her house, while the party carries on two floors below. She has no reason to be nervous, while I have every reason, yet the longer the silence drags on, my curiosity piques. *What the hell is she doing?*

"What the hell are you doing?" she says finally, as if reading my thoughts.

I smile at the coincidence, and she scowls in response.

"Looking for a bathroom," I lie.

She doesn't look at me, instead reaching behind her back to tug at the laces of her dress. "There's, like, five bathrooms downstairs. Try again."

Right. A year ago, I would have had no problem flirting my way out of this. I can be charming when I want to be, I just usually don't care to bother. Except, Etta never fell for my brand of flirting, even back in prep school. She's probably the only woman on the planet who has never stared at me when they thought I wasn't looking. She's certainly the only one who has told me to my face she doesn't like me, and I suppose she has a good enough reason for that.

"I'll tell you what I'm doing if you tell me what you're doing," I say, trying to insert a note of flirtation into my out of practice tone.

Sure enough, her eyes grow even narrower and she takes a few steps toward me. "Fuck off. I don't need to explain myself to you."

"Fuck off? When did you learn to use grown up words?"

She scowls, like she isn't quite comfortable with it herself, and reaches back to tug at her dress again. "Alright. I'm done with this conversation. I'm sure my parents will love hearing that you were wandering around up here."

I'm 80% sure she's bluffing. Three years ago, Etta would never have sold me out to her family, but now...I'm not sure.

I inhale through my nose, steeling myself, and again, go for man's greatest weapon: delusional confidence. "Sure, but what are you going to do? If you tell anyone, your family will just attack me and then you'll lose your council seats."

She blanches, and the way her eyes dart to the side makes me think I might have just stumbled into a winning argument.

"Fine," she snaps after a moment. "Whatever, just get out...I have to go."

Her eyes dart around the hallway, like she's looking for an escape. This is her own damn house, doesn't she know where she's going?

Interesting.

I should take this win and leave. That's the smart thing to do after dodging a stray fucking missile. I should leave, except she's still here...and now that I've already come this far. "I hear congratulations are in Order."

She looks up sharply. "What did you say?"

"Congratulations?" I'm relieved when my voice sounds normal. Slightly bored. "Or is that not the proper thing to say for an engagement? I can't say I ever paid much attention to those etiquette classes."

The color drains from her face, and her bottom lip trembles slightly as she seems to struggle for a response.

I'm about to continue. Maybe I'll demand to know where Dane is, or ask if she knew this announcement was coming when I spoke to her yesterday on the steps.

Maybe I'll ask her again what she's doing hiding away from the party.

Or maybe I'll ask if she knew I wanted her back then.

If she knows now.

I'll say that I know we'd never have a moments peace from our families, and I know she has no reason to trust me, but if she wanted, I would still leave with her tonight and never look back.

But before I can speak, a voice down the hall makes my blood run cold. *"I've been enjoying the Ardbeg myself, but I'm interested to try one of those new magically aged varieties."*

"Really?" a second voice replies. Male, and not unfamiliar exactly, but not someone I immediately recognize. *"I can't say I'm well-versed enough to know the difference. I'm more of a wine guy."*

"Shit," Etta mutters, the blood draining from her face. "They cannot see me talking to you."

I blink, and in an instant, I can just see the hem of her dress disappearing into the room to her left. I stare after her, my entire body humming. I know I should not want this woman. Not when her very existence seems designed to torture me. Not when her family are my enemies, and when she doesn't want me, anyway.

But I've never done what was good for me, so why start now?

Without stopping to think, I race after her, just managing to slip inside as she tries to close the door. She gasps, surprised as I squeeze in beside her.

She's done something to her hair tonight to make it large and fluffy, falling down her back in golden ringlets, and her eyes are large, dark and defined. I feel slightly guilty as my gaze shifts, falling down the curve over her neck to her chest, where her tits are nearly spilling out of her dress. She never used to dress like this, and I imagine myself pushing her hair off her shoulder and leaning over to sink my teeth into the perfect skin of her breast. How she'd gasp, then wrap her slender fingers in my hair and let me pick her up and press her against the door.

"What the hell are you doing?" Etta hisses, her voice rising at the end.

"Hiding," I say casually. "Same as you, apparently."

I glance around, taking in the room for the first time.

It's a library.

Of course it is. That feels poetic almost. Fitting, given I was in the library of our prep school when I first realized my obsessive hatred of Etta Capulet was really just an obsession.

The Capulet library isn't nearly as vast as the one at Verona Valley Prep, but it's still relatively large with high ceilings and dark, wood-paneled walls. Shelves cover nearly every exposed surface, and stand in rows in the center of the room, like an honest to gods public library. There are two leather chairs by the window, and though it's dark, I would guess that during the day this room looks out on the huge garden along the side of the house. On the table beside one of the armchairs sits an ashtray full of gnome-made cigars, and underfoot, a worn and faded Norn-woven rug gives the space a homey look, and I can picture a young Etta sitting on the carpet, reading one of those old fairytale books she used to read when we were kids.

I wonder if she still has those somewhere. I bet she does. She doesn't seem the type to throw out books.

Reaching into my pocket for my cloves, I stride over to the ashtray.

"No," Etta whispers. "You can't light that in here."

"Can't or shouldn't?"

"Both."

I take a step toward her, clove in hand, and blow the smoke deliberately at her. She doesn't move, but her expression goes from indignant to worried.

"Live a little," I tell her, just to watch her get mad.

I highly fucking doubt there are smoke alarms in here or anywhere on this floor. The Capulets are Order members, and that means lots of candles. Etta seems to know this, because she doesn't even glance up as I approach her. A normal person would be worried about ruining the books with a fire alarm. Etta is worried about...I have to assume, *me.*

"That," she nods at my clove. "Is not living. It's literally dying. You're slowly killing yourself."

I grin. "*Okay*, good girl."

I expect her to get indignant again, but she doesn't. Her brow wrinkles, like something is bothering her. "I'm not," she says.

"Not what?" I ask.

Fucking hell, I'm trembling with curiosity, like if she doesn't answer me fast enough I'll start to shake from withdrawal.

Everything about her is bewitching. Fucking enthralling. And when nothing and no one has been remotely interesting in months, I want to hold on to her and suck every last drop of excitement and color and *life* out of her. To listen to her explain nothing and everything to me, and try to find meaning in it.

"I'm not good," she says.

Ecstasy. Just talking to her, the sheer antithesis of ennui. My little muse—afflatus cocaine.

"What does that mean, anyway?" I cock my head to the side, and take another drag of my clove. She doesn't scold me this time. "What is a *good girl*?"

"Not someone who would be in this library right now talking to you."

Why? Why does she think that? Is it because she thinks I'm inherently bad? Is it because our families hate each other, and she knows she would get in trouble? Or, is it because she's almost engaged...

"So, tell me why you're here, hiding, if you're not supposed to be talking to me. Who are you hiding from?"

"It doesn't matter." Her frustration bleeds through. "I'll have to go back downstairs eventually."

"You're hiding from Dane?" I guess. "Not the best way to start off a marriage."

"What would you know about it?"

I smirk at her. "About marriage? Nothing. About women? Enough to know that if they're hiding from you it's not a good sign."

She scowls. "I shouldn't be talking to you about this."

No, she shouldn't, but it doesn't matter. I've already gleaned enough from what little she has said and more from what she won't say.

She doesn't want anything to do with this wedding any more than I want to marry Rosaline. More than likely her parents want her pledged to the Order and bound to Dane to secure alliances so Delphine will be elected the next head of the Council. My father is right, the Capulets are playing the same game he is, and it doesn't matter what Etta wants any more than it matters what I want.

"Say no," I blurt out.

She looks up at me, and her expression is tumultuous. Again, I wonder if she knew. If she knows now. If I'm not alone in this. But then, her eyes shutter and her face goes as blank as I've trained mine to.

"Even if I wanted to do that, I couldn't."

"Why?"

She takes a step away from me, further into the shadows of the tiny library. I follow, taking careful steps, as if it might all dissolve around me. I'm afraid to make noise. To disturb anything. The room has a silent, untouched magic. Like walking through a cemetery.

Or a church.

And it is, I suppose. A place of worship. The worship of knowledge, and of those who pursue it.

So I look around her library—around her church—and pray for mercy. To be delivered from temptation. Even as I'm ready to sell my soul for a chance to kneel at her feet and declare my undying devotion. To disavow all other gods. To devour her mind and worship at the altar of her cunt.

My gaze falls back to her and she's breathing too hard, her chest rising and falling over the top of her glittering ball gown.

"Because," she gives a tiny miserable laugh, and when she speaks her tone is sarcastic and self-deprecating—like the words aren't really meant for me. "I'm the good girl, remember? I always do what I'm told."

I inhale deeply on my clove, and then, instead of exhaling, lean in toward her. I keep my eyes open to watch her as she watches me, like she's frozen to the spot.

Her lips part, almost like she didn't mean to, and I sear my lips to hers, blowing the smoke into her mouth.

She steps back, coughing slightly, and wipes her mouth with the back of her hand. Her eyes are huge and glassy as she stares up at me, confusion mingling with a hint of intrigue.

I smirk. "Well, there you go, good girl. Now you're tainted."

CHAPTER THIRTEEN
✦ ETTA ✦

PRESENT

"I NEED TO GO."

I stumble backwards, pressing my hand to my mouth, and flee from the room. I can't breathe, and it has nothing to do with the rush of adrenaline swirling in my head. I can't go back downstairs. I just need to get out of here right *now*.

I rush into my bedroom and slam the door, leaning against it as if someone is chasing me. My breath heaves, my chest straining against the bodice of my gown as I slide to the floor, the fussy silk of the skirt pooling around my waist. What the hell is happening?

I feel like I'm under attack. Like at any moment, the door might burst open, and I have no idea why. It's a strange combination of adrenaline and vulnerability that I can't explain. That I don't want to explain, because then I would have to analyze it.

It's been years since I've felt this way. Like my whole world is tipped on its axis and I'm just clinging to the edge by my fingertips, waiting for someone to come step on my hands until I let go and fall into the abyss.

I don't know how I've allowed myself to be alone with Roman twice in the span of forty-eight hours. I know better. Know nothing good can come from it, and worse, there's a whole laundry list of trauma that can come from a single conversation with my dark shadow—my long-time enemy.

Perhaps I can blame it on self-loathing, self-destructive tendencies. I'm upset, so I allow Roman into my life knowing he can only make things worse.

That doesn't sound right, even in my own head, but it's the only explanation I have.

I can't go back downstairs. Not like this.

Maybe I knew when I came up here in the first place I was running away—that I wasn't going back down there. That I wasn't going to go stand beside my parents and Harrison and nearly the entire Order and co-sign a future I don't want.

I take a deep breath through my nose, and will myself to calm down. I need to take this dress off. I can't breathe in this damned thing. My mother, for all her talk of "helping" still managed to buy me something just slightly too small, and it's squeezing hard enough to cut off my air.

That has to be part of my problem. That makes sense.

I stay seated on the floor, but lean forward, tugging frantically at the laces on the back of the dress. When I can't reach those, I give up, and just force it down, over my breasts, to release my ribcage.

"Ahhh." I let out an audible sigh of relief as my chest expands with the first real breath I've been able to take in hours, not even caring that I no doubt look absurd topless, on the floor, in a ballgown skirt.

I stare, unseeing, across the room for what feels like several full minutes, trying to force my pulse to slow down; my breathing to return to normal. Finally, as my panic subsides, goosebumps erupt on my arms and chest, as the air hits my bare skin. My nipples pebble, and I become more aware that I'm sitting topless in front of several windows, none of the curtains drawn.

I yelp, and cross my arms over my chest, unsure what to do. It's dark outside, and brightly lit in here, leaving no way to know if anyone saw me, or can see me now. My bedroom has three large windows, and two glass French doors, which lead out onto a balcony overlooking the garden. It's unlikely for anyone to be in the garden, however if you were standing in just the right spot, you could see right into my room from the driveway.

I try to stretch up to the light switch on the wall, while covering my chest with my arm, and finally succeed in plunging the room into darkness. Relief floods me, and I dash over to my bed, feeling around for the bathrobe I often toss on the bench at the foot of the bed, rather than hanging it up where it goes. I cast a glance at the dark yard through the huge balcony doors as I shrug one arm into my robe, and tiptoe a few steps toward the doors.

All seems quiet down below, thank gods. All I need in addition to humiliating my parents by leaving the party is some blurry iPhone picture of my boobs taken from the driveway.

An image of someone standing down there, watching me, appears unbidden in my mind and a shiver travels down my spine.

I should be revolted by the idea. *Should be.*

It's dark in my room now. So dark that even if there were anyone down there, they wouldn't be able to see me anymore.

I take a tentative step toward the doors and open them. The cool night air whooshes in too fast, tugging at my hair and my robe, blowing the silk of my dress which still hangs around my waist like a skirt. I close my eyes, and breathe in, and I can smell leaves and grass and the coming winter, and whether I'm imagining it or not, I could swear I smell a hint of licorice.

The smell makes me pause and raise my fingers to my mouth. My lips tingle where Roman pressed his mouth to mine—not in a kiss, exactly. More to shock me, I think. To see what I'd do. I suppose, I fulfilled both our expectations when I ran from him.

I lick my lips, nipping at them, shivering now from the cold as well as nervous anticipation. From a wicked thought that good girls most definitely shouldn't have.

Tentatively, I drop the robe, just slightly, letting it gape open at the front. The cold night air is even colder against my exposed nipples, and immediately they become hard little points just begging to be touched. To be sucked and licked.

I part my lips, letting in the scent of the licorice night air, as I reach up and draw a tiny circle around my nipple with my pointer finger. My heart pounds in time to my throbbing clit, and I stifle a moan as I press my thighs together.

What would have happened if I stayed?

"Live a little," Roman says in my head.

I move both hands to run up my sides, squeezing and caressing my breasts. Imagining I have an audience standing below in the yard, watching me. Wanting me.

I open my mouth, gasping slightly as my pulse begins beating in my core. Begging me for more.

I glance behind me at my bed, barely illuminated in the dim light from the windows. No one would see. No one would know.

I cross to the bed and lie down on my back, letting my robe fall open until it hangs off my shoulders. I'm bare from the waist up, with my dress still covering my legs. Somehow that seems dirtier.

More taboo. This whole thing is taboo. I shouldn't be thinking about him. Shouldn't like the idea of anyone watching me, yet I can feel how wet I am already. Can feel my panties soaked just by the idea of him.

"Well, there you go, good girl. Now you're tainted."

How right he was.

I pull the dress up until it pools around my waist again, reach down, running my hands up my bare thighs, over my stomach and hips, and along the waistband of my underwear. I dance my fingers along the simple cotton lace border, not yet dipping inside, prolonging the torture.

My eyes have adjusted to the darkness, and I can just make out the shadowy furniture of my bedroom. The outline of my knees, spread wide on my bed, facing the dark, open doors to the empty balcony. The waving tops of the leafless trees in the yard. The sound of the wind and of distant voices outside, far off, as if they might be on the next street over sends a thrill through me. I'm exposed, yet completely alone.

"What does that mean, anyway?" Roman Montague says in my head. *"What is a good girl?"*

I bite my lip, thinking of that moment. How many ways that conversation could have turned. Now, in my head, in the dark, I don't sass him back.

"Let me show you," I say, and take a step backwards toward the bookshelf. My back presses against the hard ridges of the shelves, but I don't care about the discomfort. My attention is completely focused on the dark, beautiful man in front of me.

Roman smirks at me, and follows, boxing me in. "Show me?" he chuckles, almost mocking. "Is that what you want? To show me how good you can be for me?"

"Yes," I breathe, quaking with anticipation.

He leans in so close, I can taste his breath. Sweet and spicy at the same time. He reaches under my skirt and cups my pussy. I whimper as he slips two fingers inside me and pulls gently upward, as if to lift me off my feet. "I need you to be quiet for me, baby. Can you do that?"

I nod, trembling as he holds me captive, fingers knuckle-deep in my pussy, eyes impossible to turn away from.

A soft whimper escapes my lips as I slide my own fingers down the front of my panties, rubbing gently over my throbbing clit, but already it's not enough. I need more.

I twist my back and reach into my bedside table, pulling out my vibrator, fumbling to close the drawer again without getting up. It's been ages since I used it, yet now, after just one conversation, I'm aching for him.

Roman flips me around, and presses me into the bookcase, his entire body warm and hard against my back. Tingles of pleasure travel all over my body from his mere presence. From his breath in my ear, his masculine scent, his cock, hard and straining against his suit pants to push into my back, his huge hands sliding up the backs of my thighs as his lips graze the shell of my ear.

I slide my ruined panties down my legs and my stomach swirls with arousal as the cold air hits my most sensitive skin.

I run the head of the wand over myself a few times before holding down the button, and the first soft vibration is an electric jolt to my system. It pulses against my slick core as I hold it just on the outside, refusing to move past the barrier of my outer lips.

I bite my tongue, forcing myself to be quiet as he falls to his knees behind me, knocking my legs wider apart with a nudge of his shoulders. I'm trembling with anticipation, knowing there's a party going on in the next room and if anyone walked in here right now I could never explain myself. But I don't care, because I want him so much. I've never wanted anyone else.

My legs fall open even wider and I reach up to lift my hair off my neck as I move the head to press lightly against my clit. All my muscles clench at that first contact. My eyes are already closed, but I squeeze them tighter, as I roll my hips, desperate for more. More friction. More pressure.

My back bows and I whimper as Roman presses his face into me from behind, lapping at my entrance. Running his tongue over my pulsing, needy clit, just like he promised. He licks and sucks at my pussy, tasting me like he's starving, and I writhe against his attention.

I hold the wand against my clit, and roll my hips, my orgasm building in my stomach. The wave is cresting higher and higher, and I could swear I smell that distinctive licorice scent wafting in from the open doors.

I moan, and my legs tremble. My words are unintelligible I think, the moment I speak them I've forgotten what I said.

My feet slide against the duvet of my bed, but in my mind Roman is bending me over further. Undoing his belt, and my heart is beating so fast.

My legs tremble, and just as I'm so close I slide the wand inside, fucking myself with it. Imagining he's fucking me. I'm crying because it's so *so* good. My pussy spasms, clenching, and I shatter with his name on my lips. "Roman."

CHAPTER FOURTEEN
✦ ROMAN ✦

PRESENT

MY HEART STILL POUNDS OUT OF CONTROL AS I descend the last few steps to the first floor. I scan the foyer, but Etta is nowhere in sight. Most people have moved out to the terrace, and I heave a sigh of relief when I manage to find Bennet and Pierce in the crowd. They're standing near the door, and I immediately make connections between their stiff posture and the too-casual group of Capulets hovering nearby

Bennet sees me, and his face splits into a look of combined relief and exasperation. "Where the fuck have you been?"

I reach them in two strides. "Don't worry about it."

Pierce looks ready to argue. "We should get out of here."

I was thinking the same thing, but likely not for the same reason. My brow furrows, my curiosity piqued. "Why?"

Bennet jerks his head to the left, and I turn, just as Tyberius Capulet appears before me, flanked by his idiotic friends.

My heart pounds now for an entirely different reason. This, of course, is why we're here. I should be excited—happy, even. Tyberius is such a dumb prick, he'll likely start a fight not realizing the danger to his aunt and Uncle, or his house.

Except, unlike yesterday, I'm not really in the mood to let myself get hit. I don't need pain to feel alive today, and I'm under no delusion as to why that is.

Tyberius smiles. "Evening, gentlemen."

I grimace. "What do you want?"

He glances over his shoulder at his friends behind him, then back at me. "Just being a good host," he replies, still too smoothly. "How's your eye? I was surprised to see you hadn't healed it."

It's phrased like a statement, but seems more like a question. "Only you would think it was preferable to *need* magic, Capulet. Try and touch me, I'll kill you with my bare hands."

His lip curls, and for a second, I've got him.

But then, Harrison Dane of all people steps up to the Capulets, all authoritative and calm, and claps a hand on Tyberius's shoulder. Playing the older, more reasonable one, he hands Tyberius a cigar and jerks his head toward the patio. "Ty, leave them. It's not worth it."

Tyberius takes a deep breath, keeping his eyes on me. "I know what you're trying to do and it won't work." The smile slips, ever so slightly. "I think you should leave my house now."

I grind my teeth. "We were just leaving, anyway."

I'M STILL ALIGHT WITH MISPLACED ANTICIPATION AS we walk out to the car. I pat my pocket, feeling absently for my phone. As I feel around the pocket of my suit coat, then my pants, my stomach sinks. There's nothing there but cloves.

"I left my phone," I say, more pissed at myself than anything.

Pierce turns around to stare incredulously at me. "Do not tell me that."

I run a hand through my hair. "I know."

"It's theirs now," he laughs. "We're not going back inside."

I glare at him. "I can't just leave it."

It's more the case than anything else. If it was just any phone, I'd leave it—fuck, it might be better to be unreachable. But I can't leave the case.

"If you go back now it'll just start shit," Bennet says.

"That's a good thing, isn't it?" I reply, halfheartedly.

Bennet doesn't look convinced. "Go back tomorrow when everyone is sober."

I'm about to agree with him when I realize where the phone is. I can't go back tomorrow because it's in their library and they'll want to know why I was there. "Shit," I moan. "I can't."

They both turn back to me, now confused. "Why?"

"It's upstairs."

There's a painfully long silence and finally Bennet asks: "Why?" dragging the word out like two syllables.

"It doesn't matter. I'm just going back. Can you wait?"

They're smug as fuck, grinning like henchmen, as I get back out of the car and stride toward the house. The gravel crunches underfoot, and I'm two steps from the door when I change course. Pierce is right, I can't go back inside. Not right now.

Even if Tyberius hits me, there are two dozen people who will swear I hit him first and then we'll lose our seats. Which is frankly something my father should have thought of before sending us out here. If we're going to provoke him we need more witnesses on our side. More of the Avons, the MacBeths and maybe, the Cesarios. It would also be better if there was a police report.

I know nothing about this house, aside from what I've seen tonight, but once you've seen one New-England-style McMansion, you've kind-of seen them all. It seemed like there was a back door off the patio, and I'm willing to bet there's a pool and some kind of in-law-apartment around the other side of the house, which means the right-hand side-yard probably has a terrace. Here's to hoping they've got a trellis.

It's quiet and dark as I walk around the grassy side-yard, the noise from the out back almost entirely muffled by the brick wall of the house. I'm cast in the shadow of the house and the enormous rose bushes all along the side. For a moment, it's almost peaceful.

The yard slopes down in a slight hill, and I step carefully so as to not slip on the dew-covered grass. There's only one room lit up that I can see from this angle, but as I walk the light in that room flicks off. I freeze. Is someone up there?

I'm afraid to move, and I quietly creep forward, positive that the yard is about to flood with light. I don't think I can be arrested for being out here during a private party but I wouldn't put that shit past them. *Fuck.*

I reach down, fumbling in my coat, and pull out my cloves. Lighting one, I shove it quickly in my mouth. Just to look busy.

I look up as the sound of a door opening has the hair rising on the back of my neck. There's a balcony above me I've only just now noticed, the lights off in the room beyond. The doors open a crack and someone must be standing just on the other side. Can they see me standing out here?

Fuck.

I turn to go, holding my cigarette out, to look casual, when a tiny intake of breath makes me stop. I know that voice.

Why the fuck do I know her voice so well that I recognize it from a single gasp? Why am I turning around and peering up at the window, wondering what Etta is doing in the dark?

This is unhealthy on so many levels, yet I can't make myself leave.

I pinch the skin between my eyes and exhale heavily, smoke rising in a cloud in front of me. I try to force my breathing to return to normal. It's painful. Unnatural. When my entire body is buzzing and oh so aware of everything around me. When I'm fighting myself not to say fuck it, and rush up there right now, consequences be damned. When I'm wishing that I'd handled my few moments alone with her differently.

Unbidden, an image of a very different end to our conversation begins to form in my mind. I picture how I would lick into her mouth, stroking her tongue with mine, showing her without words how I would lick her everywhere else. She moans against my lips and I think she must understand as I tangle my fingers in her hair, not caring that I'm destroying her too-perfect curls.

I pull her closer, and I'm almost shocked when she lets me. I'm more shocked at how effortless she feels there, in my arms, like she belongs there and always has. I wonder how she'd feel wrapped around my cock. Riding me, with her tits bouncing in my face, or pressed up against her beloved bookcases while I rub her clit and take her from behind.

I blink several times. Gods. I don't know for certain what defines good, or why she thinks she isn't, but I know that things I want to do with her, to her, right now and every day until the end of time, are very *very* bad.

If I wasn't aware before this moment that I was not the hero of this story, I'm sure as fuck aware of it now.

I've studied every narrative theory, every form of storytelling and character model from *Gilgamesh* to *Superman*. I don't remember a part of the hero's journey where the protagonist stands in the shadows of the heroine's window, achingly hard and barely coherent.

But as I'm standing frozen, hating myself for not having the decency to leave, my entire purpose is shifted in the form of a single word. A single name. "Roman."

What is a name, anyway, when it's spoken like a prayer in the darkness?

Until this moment, I've been stagnant. But now, as the culmination of the last two days, the last three years, the last decade, comes into perspective in that word, I'm transformed.

I'm not alone in this. She wants me too.

And now, I have to have her.

CHAPTER FIFTEEN

ETTA

Junior Year of High School, Five Years Ago

The gates of the Greater Stratford Cemetery loom against the gray, November sky, the intricate iron of the posts like teeth, jagged and threatening. I duck between the jaws, and marvel at the heavy silence, unbroken but for my footsteps trudging down the winding path between rows upon rows of gravestones. The only other sounds are the howling wind and the distant rumble of traffic on the nearby street. The skyline is dotted with monolithic family tombs, grassy knolls dotted with towering oaks, Victorian style obelisks, and the occasional weeping angel, its hands spread as if to welcome me. Fallen leaves pinwheel over the dead city, catching and lingering in my hair.

I don't know exactly where I'm going, but I have a guess: Most of the Order families are buried in the same far corner of the cemetery, in the oldest part, where the plots were purchased hundreds of years ago and the crypts built back when stained glass and lovely gothic carvings were still popular. It will take me a good ten minutes to walk there and would have been far easier to drive, but I was afraid of anyone seeing my car and recognizing me. As it is, this might be one of the stupider things I've done…well, ever.

Knowing that, I don't know why I continue.

After about eight minutes of walking, stopping briefly only to chat with Councilman Lawrence, out for a walk, I can hear distant voices on the breeze, and see the line of black cars, followed by all the normal cars with little funeral home flags stuck to the windshields. It's a large procession, and there must be at least two-hundred people standing on the hill, bundled into wool coats with scarves wrapped around their faces. Like an army of little ebony chess pieces.

I stop. I've gotten close enough. Any closer, and they'll certainly see me, and while I don't think anyone would actively do anything to me, I'm definitely unwelcome.

I scan the crowd, all nearly identical in their winter-wear. Even so, I recognize him immediately.

Roman Montague stands slightly apart from the rest of his friends and family, leaning against a towering beech tree. If I didn't know better, I might think he was bored, or annoyed to be here.

I tear my gaze away. I'm not here for him. I'm here for me, because it's the right thing to do.

I sink onto the grass on a tiny incline across from the hill where the Montagues are gathered as they watch Councilman Lawrence step forward to read a eulogy. I can't hear anything more than the occasional snippet as the wind shifts, but it hardly matters.

I'm only here to pay my own respects, I don't need to hear to do that.

I close my eyes, trying to think of what to say—or to think, I suppose. I've never been good at this sort of thing. Who am I supposed to be talking to? Normally I would feel that funerals are for the living, that paying respect is to the family, but in this case the family doesn't want to talk to me. I heave a sigh...maybe I'm messing this up.

"What are you doing?"

I jolt, my shoulders hitting my ears and my arms flailing as my heart leaps into my throat. My eyes fly open, and I turn to find Roman Montague standing directly in front of me. His shadow looms over me, blocking out everything. His family behind him, the weak November sun, like he's eclipsed all else with his mere presence.

"Uhhh." I flounder for words. "I was just..."

"Gloating?" His tone is unreadable, but his eyes are hard. "Or perhaps choosing another target?"

Even without a drink in sight, I don't like him standing over me like that with his expression so dark, so I struggle to get to my feet, and brush the grass off my legs. Although, when I look back up, I balk. I have the high-ground, so we're nearly eye-to-eye for probably the first time ever, and it's almost more unnerving than before.

I swallow my insecurity, trying to force my voice to remain even. "No, of course not."

He sneers. "Then what the fuck are you doing here?"

Whatever brief respite we had in the hall outside the headmaster's office is evidently over, and Roman is back to being a dick. Back with a vengeance.

"I just wanted to pay my respects. I'm sorry about your grandfather."

He blinks at me, obviously surprised, before his expression goes cold again. "Right. Of course you are."

You didn't even know him, so you're not here for yourself, and I know you're not stupid enough to show-up here for me. So, what are you really doing here."

That comment stings and it shouldn't. He's right—I'm not stupid enough to show-up here for him, especially after the incident in the hall the other day—but some, small, pathetic part of me wishes that he wanted me to show-up anyway.

"It's none of your business," I retort. "This is a public cemetery."

He groans in frustration when my silence makes it clear that I'm not going to elaborate.

The truth is, I'm here just in case my family really did have something to do with this. I'll admit that the timing is a tad suspicious. It was only a few weeks ago that our parents were screaming at each other about curses and plagues, and the next thing anyone knew, Roman's grandfather dropped dead of a sudden and mysterious illness. No doctor, from the Order or from a regular hospital, could figure out what happened to him. It was just...strange. And, okay, so it's not helping that my mother is positively giddy because Mr. Montague was blocking some political thing she was trying to get pushed through on the council. The whole situation looks pretty bad. I'm afraid of being tainted by proxy, and I'm hoping in some strange way that paying my respects will absolve me of any potential crime.

But I'm not going to tell Roman that—I don't want to risk another coffee getting poured on me.

"No one wants you here," Roman growls. "You should leave before anyone else spots you and things get ugly."

And there he goes, proving all my worst impressions of him right. And, at the same time, making me feel like an absolute moron because I still...*like* him.

There. Acceptance is the first step to recovery, I can beat this. It's a stupid crush, not a life-sentence.

"Are you threatening me?" I demand, trying to infuse some fire into my tone.

"If that's what you heard. Just go, Etta.

"Congratulations," I sneer. "You sound just like your dad."

His eyes widen, seeming taken aback. He grumbles something I can't hear over the wind, and I'm not going to ask him to repeat it. He shifts his posture, taking a step toward me, so once again I'm crowded in his shadow, my view of the Montagues down the hill completely obscured. I look up, slightly alarmed, and take a few steps backwards. He follows, like we're playing the strangest game of red-light/green-light ever.

"What, are you trying to herd me away? Are you crazy?"

He laughs harshly, and reaches into the pocket of his long, wool, peacoat and pulls out a shiny, all black pack of cigarettes. "Would that work?"

"No!"

He sighs, and his tone returns to almost normal. "Fine. Then, since you're refusing to be reasonable, I'm smoking alone on this hill."

My eyebrows hit my hair as I watch him pull one out and cup his hand around a lighter to block the wind. I don't think I've ever seen him smoke before.

I wrinkle my nose at the scent of tobacco and nicotine. I lean around him to see if his parents are watching, and he puts an arm out to stop me. "No."

We stand there in semi-charged silence for a few minutes. Finally, my eyes widen, as I catch-on to what he's trying to do. How he's trying to obscure me from view of the rest of his family. I look up at him, assessing. Why do that? Is it for my benefit, or his?

"Is this everything you thought it would be," Roman drawls, his tone matching his condescending expression. "Did you get your good karma for the day, or whatever? Feeling respectful, yet?"

My eyes narrow. "Weren't you taught that if you don't have something nice to say, you should say nothing?"

"No," he replies, deadpan. "I was taught that ridicule would continue until performance improved."

"You don't have to be such an asshole," I say without thinking.

I hear myself, and I nearly clap my hand over my mouth. Ugh, I hardly ever swear. In my head, I have the mouth of a sailor, but I don't say those things out loud. Except Roman Montague makes me want to scream that he can go fuck himself in ways I can't even picture.

He laughs, seemingly in spite of himself. "Actually, good girl, I do."

"Do what?" I ask. "And stop calling me that."

"I *do* need to be an asshole, *good girl*," he says pointedly. "Why do you care? You aiming for Sainthood now?"

The Order doesn't have Saints, which he knows full well, but I know what he means.

Roman thinks aggression and strength are the same thing, and to him, I'm weak. He probably thinks he's weak too, whenever he's nice to me.

If only he knew how hard it is to be nice when I don't want to be. How hard it is to stay quiet and polite. It's actually much easier to be an asshole—I know, because I come from a whole family of assholes.

I take a step back, so I can look at him without having to tilt my head all the way up. "I really am sorry, Roman."

"You shouldn't be," he says, bitterly. "I wouldn't be."

"I know."

He doesn't say anything when I walk away.

Chapter Sixteen

ETTA

Present

"Hey, are you done with that?"

I jump, startled by the clipped, nasal voice, coming from far too close to my ear. "Sorry?"

A woman in a dark-gray suit, oversized but not in an intentionally fashionable way, sighs in exasperation. She pushes a lock of short blonde hair behind her ear, and points at the book in my hand. "Are you all set with that?"

I open and close my mouth a few times, my brain refusing to catch up. I finally realize she's wearing a library name tag, and I'm the idiot who's been standing beside the book-return-cart for the better part of five minutes, doing absolutely nothing, just staring into space. Gods, I am so out of it today.

"Er, yes," I say quickly, color rising in my cheeks. I grab a random book off the top of the cart, just to look like I haven't been spacing out for no reason. "Here, all but this one."

The librarian purses her lips as she pushes the cart away, muttering under her breath. "Undergrads."

I massage my temples and blink a couple of times, turning on the spot to face the main room of the library. What was I doing here again?

Oh, right.

I dragged myself over to the university this morning to set up a meeting with my advisor about my options for next semester, only to realize the office isn't open on Mondays. Unwilling to go straight back home and stare at the walls in my empty house, I dropped by the library. Except now, I can't focus.

I suppose, now that I think about it, a library was not the best place to go to forget about the other night. My sanctuary has been tainted.

Just like me, a tiny voice whispers.

Ah, no! I have to resist the urge to smack myself in the face with my book to dislodge my intrusive thoughts.

I feel like I have this enormous secret. Like I did something hot and forbidden, when in actuality the only hot date in my future is a dinner with Harrison Dane scheduled by my mother.

My mother was less than thrilled that I ran away from the party but softened slightly when I told her I got food poisoning and didn't want to embarrass her by being violently sick in my white dress. Accepting an invitation to dinner was—in her opinion— the least I could do after ruining the perfect public engagement opportunity. If she knew what I was actually doing during the gala—who I'd been talking to, and the temporary insanity that came over me afterward...well, she probably wouldn't think anything because she'd drop dead.

Is it terrible that, right now, that doesn't sound all that bad? I'd be sad of course, but maybe a little relieved?

I'm going to hell.

I sigh, and walk in a zombie-like daze over to the only decent armchairs over by the windows. A beam of sun shines down over the green and blue plaid chairs, and I make a beeline for an open spot. That is, until a dark-haired man seated in the opposite chair looks up at me.

I go stiff.

"We've got to stop meeting like this, Helen," Roman says.

My heart pounds too hard against my chest and I'm frozen, unsure where to go. If I turn around I'm going to look like an idiot. As it is, I'm fairly sure I look like a stalker. How is this possible? In all the years I've been coming here I've never seen him here, and now, today of all days.

"What did you call me?" I say finally, shaking my head as if to clear it. It doesn't work, I still feel like I'm standing in a fog.

"Helen?" he says it like he's asking me.

I furrow my brow. "Why?"

Has my haze of anxiety caused me to actually hallucinate? Not only has Roman Montague never called me anything except "good girl," or the occasional throw away insult, he's smiling at me. Actually smiling. I realize he's getting closer, which must mean I'm still walking toward the chairs. *Oh my gods, what am I doing?*

His smile turns into a smirk. "Read a book once in a while, maybe you'll catch on."

My hackles raise. There's the Roman Montague I know. Dismissive. Taunting. Mean. The guy who proved to be the exception to my theory that anyone can be won over with kindness. He might smile, but he's still a villain. A serpent hiding behind an angelic face.

"I read," I snap, holding up my book.

He puts two fingers between the pages of his own book to make his place and leans forward in his chair to see what I'm holding. "Ah yes, a literary classic. How could I doubt you when you have come to the library to peruse, '*The art of submission: Power dynamics and the psychology of human sexuality.*'"

"What?" My stomach lurches, and I turn to look at the book I'm holding. "No, I—"

Sure enough, he's right. There it is, in blue and white letters, right across the front. *Damned judgmental librarian. Damned random book cart. Why do the gods hate me?*

The back of my neck heats, but I absolutely refuse to admit my mistake with Roman staring at me with clear laughter in his black eyes. I would rather die—which I might if my temperature keeps rising at this rate.

I change course mid-sentence. "Yes," I say indignantly. "Exactly. I am fascinated by all aspects of the human experience."

A smile spreads across his face. "Really? Do tell."

His grin is genuine and even as I want to curl up and die, I can't help but wonder if I've ever seen him this happy before. I don't think I have.

"Yes, now if you don't mind," I turn on my heel intending to walk away.

"Weren't you coming over here to sit?" he says.

"That was before I saw who else was here. I'll find somewhere else."

Much to my horror he stands up and follows me. "I'd hate to think I'm hindering your, er, academic success?" Again, it's posed like a question, but also a joke.

He's fucking with me. Well, fuck him right back.

"Go away," I demand, still marching across the library, no idea where I'm headed.

I need to escape him. There are more chairs upstairs, but he easily keeps pace with me as I dart toward the stairs.

"Are you still in school?" he asks pleasantly.

It's a sore subject, whether or not he realizes it. "Yes. Of course, I am."

"Studying what?"

"Why do you care?"

He's obviously trying not to laugh now. "Honestly, I'm wondering if I should take whatever class that book is for. Is there a practical element?"

"You're finished with school," I grumble.

"Nope," he pops the P. "I'm still here."

I stop walking and turn to face him. "What? You're kidding. You dropped out?"

"Why do you care?" he mimics my words, still smiling, like this is all fun for him.

Why do I care? An interesting question.

The fact that Roman is indisputably intelligent is one of the great injustices of my life. It would be so much easier to dismiss him if he was stupid. If he was a run-of-the-mill village-idiot I could write-off so many of his confusing mixed signals and the way he flip-flops between cruel and flirtatious. I could disregard his enigmatic comments as accidental rather than calculated. But, no. He had the audacity to be born gifted, and then prove it by being the valedictorian of our prep school, and graduating from college an entire year early. Just thinking about it makes me furious.

At least, I thought he graduated early. That was what I was told—what everyone was talking about last spring. But if he really left. If he dropped out and wasted his opportunity, while I would rake myself across hot coals just to come back next semester. I have no words. "I'm just surprised," I say diplomatically. "You always liked school."

He raises an eyebrow. "I didn't drop out. I'm doing my master's now."

He frowns slightly as he speaks, but I'm too distracted to think much of it. I feel my eye twitch and pray it wasn't as obvious as it appeared. "Whatever. I doubt you're getting a master's in sexual expression."

I feel as though I can see him having an actual battle with his inner demons. Like the slight widening of his eyes, the way he almost swallows, and the muscle ticking in his neck. He wants so badly to say: "Why would I, when I already eat pussy at a doctorate level," or something absurd like that.

Damn, now I'm blushing. I back away toward the stairs.

"No," he says. "It's in British and European occult literature through an Elizabethan lens."

"Right." I wave him off as I start climbing the stairs to the second floor, but then I process what he said. "Wait, really?"

He jogs after me. "Yes? Is that a problem."

I lick my lips. Gods, why is that hot?

"No." My tone is short. "It's just, that's almost what I'm studying. Or will be, I guess. After I finish my undergrad. I want to do Arthurian, though, not Elizabethan."

He barely reacts. "Small world."

I need to get out of here. This conversation is only reminding me that I probably won't be able to do any of that. The way things are going, I won't even be allowed to finish my degree.

I climb faster, annoyed when he has no trouble keeping up. I can't believe he won't go away and leave me to melt into the floor in peace.

"So, what are you studying, then, with such interesting books?"

I let out a sound that is half sigh, half growl. "Are you having some kind of break with reality? I don't know what gave you the impression we could just—" I glance around, finding that we are completely alone, the second floor being entirely deserted. "—Interact in public, but you're begging to turn that black-eye into a set."

He raises an eyebrow, following my gaze around the room. "What public?"

I huff in exasperation. "You know what I mean."

"I don't. Tell me, in explicit detail."

I roll my eyes. That's like the pretentious way of saying "talk dirty to me," and I can't tell whether he meant it like that or not. From approaching me after the auction, to sneaking around upstairs at my house, to whatever the hell this is, Roman seems to have completely forgotten that we don't talk. We can't talk, and anyone seeing us together would go very badly for both of us. Is this flirtation, torment, or genuine lunacy?

"I feel like you're forgetting what happened the last time you tried to talk to me in public."

He scoffs. "That was years ago, people change. Anyway, this is a library, good girl. We do well with accidental meetings in libraries."

Oh my gods.

The armchairs on the second floor are tucked all the way in the back of the room behind several rows of shelves. I cross to the nearest one and sit. It doesn't occur to me that perhaps it's not my best idea ever to lure Roman Montague to a deserted, quiet corner of the library, armed with my sex book, until I'm already there, but by then I've committed.

Face burning, I sit down firmly in the armchair and open the book at random. Of course it's an extremely accurate diagram. I'm going to burst into flames. This is so insanely stupid, and yet, I can't breathe. I'm a live wire, and I'm afraid to move the book and actually make eye-contact because either I will spontaneously combust from mortification or I'm going to jump him, there is no in between.

So, it's lunacy then. And it's contagious.

"What am I supposed to tell people about why we were here together?" I bite out.

"I won't tell if you won't." He shrugs. "Actually, Helen, I did want to ask you something."

"What?" I mutter under my breath.

"I think I left my phone in your library on Saturday."

I hear him, and the words don't penetrate. What a normal thing to say. I don't know what I was expecting, I guess my entire perception has been a little unfairly warped by my own embarrassment over the last time we saw each other three years ago. Still, Roman is, and always has been, a self-proclaimed asshole. I was expecting a taunt at the very least. A reminder of my mistakes.

Something.

"I didn't see it."

"That's okay, but can you look and let me know?"

I nod. It's been two days since the party. I'd be going out of my mind if I lost my phone for that long, especially with no great way to get it back. Roman can't exactly swing by my house uninvited.

Actually though, that reminds me of a good question. I take a deep breath and compose myself before lowering my book. Immediately, my body goes into hyperdrive. "If you tell me what the hell you were doing up there I'll get it for you."

He smirks. "Would you believe I just wanted to talk to you?"

I wish. "No."

He shrugs. "Then I guess I'll just have to trust in your better nature to return it. It really is important that I get it back."

I narrow my eyes. If the situation were reversed, he'd probably throw my phone off a bridge and make me dive for it. Yet, I hate to say he's right. I will probably do the right thing and return it, because I'm *nice*; It's my biggest flaw.

I press my lips together, but nod. "Okay."

"Okay?" He sounds unsure, like I'm messing with him.

"Yeah," I say. "I have a date tonight, but I could drop it off somewhere tomorrow?"

His eyes darken, clear anger flashing on his face for a moment before he can bury it. Who the hell is he to dictate how fast I need to do him a favor? It's not like we're friends. The opposite, in fact.

"How about here, tomorrow," he says, his tone measured. "Same time."

Maybe I should tell him to leap off that bridge after all, but I don't. I'm never as mean out loud as I want to be in my head. Not even to Roman Montague. "Fine."

Neither of us seem sure what to do after that. It's like the scene has ended, and the lights have come up, ruining the theatrical magic of whatever the hell was just going on. The prop of my sex book now feels all the more comical and Roman looks around, realizing seemingly for the first time that we're alone in the back of the library.

This time, it's him who walks away first, and I wait five minutes before following so we won't bump into each other.

CHAPTER SEVETEEN
ETTA

PRESENT

I PEER OUT AT THE SHADOWY DARKNESS WHIPPING PAST the car, the occasional distant porch light or headlights passing in the opposite direction. The ride reminds me oddly of wintertime drives with my parents when I was little, going to and from relatives' houses or late-night holiday parties. It's certainly the wrong vibe for a date—perhaps it's the silence.

I glance over at Harrison in the driver's seat. I've learned two things about him in the last twenty minutes that I never needed to know about anyone. He finds the light from cell phones—even other people's—intensely distracting, and drives in complete silence. No music. No podcasts. No chatting.

Like a serial killer.

I don't think he's an actual serial killer, and this isn't exactly the worst thing that anyone has ever done, but it's certainly not something I would list as an attribute on a dating profile. I envision a lot of very silent dinners in our future. Silent car rides. Weirdly silent sex.

I shiver.

Harrison spares me a look. "Are you cold?"

"No," I say too fast. "I'm fine."

He smiles benignly. "Okay."

I feel guilty. He's not even bad, just very quiet. I suck in a breath. Okay—he's not going to take the conversational lead, so I guess I'm going to have to.

"So," I begin, and then realize I have no idea what to ask him. Where do you see yourself in five years? What are your biggest strengths and weaknesses? Do you have any questions for me? "Tell me about yourself."

He laughs ruefully. "I know it's hard to believe, but I'm actually pretty boring."

I want to bang my head against the dashboard. "No, I'm sure that's not true."

I cast around for anything I know about him. Anything I can ask about.

The Dane family is one of the original eight founding families in the Order, along with my family, the Lawrences, the Avons, the Hathaways, the Minolas, the MacBeths, the Cesarios, and the Montagues.

They own a multi-media empire, with arms in news, print, and Hollywood. They're responsible for both the laws against subliminal messaging, and for creating ways to creatively skirt those laws. The company was taken over a few years ago by Harrison's uncle after his father died. Harrison's brother, Hamlin, is the vice president, but I don't know what Harrison does. "Which division of your family's business do you work in?"

To my surprise, he bristles. "The news," he says shortly. "Do you follow the papers?"

I raise my eyebrows, shrinking back slightly. "Sometimes. I'm more of a fiction reader."

"Ah. So, you don't understand current events, then?"

I recoil. "No, I wouldn't say that."

"You'll have to start following the news. The entire family works in the business in some way. You can consider that when you pledge. What are you bringing to the table, Juliette?"

We fall silent again, as unease settles over me. He doesn't ask me anything about myself, or seem inclined to elaborate.

The silence seems to stretch on forever. I grew up silenced, in an empty house, and now I'm driving in a silent car, toward my silent future.

WE PULL UP IN FRONT OF A RESTAURANT I'VE NEVER seen before, nestled in a silent little nook off the main road. The building is elegant and quietly imposing, with walls of dark-red brick and white trim that glows in the moonlight. The windows are warmly lit from within, giving a cozy air to the otherwise intimidating exterior.

I step out of the car, my heeled boots clicking against the cobblestones as I walk towards the entrance. Harrison holds open the door for me, and we enter a grand foyer with soft music playing in the background.

The hostess leads us to a small, white-linen covered table in the corner of the restaurant. A whole row of forks beside my place setting shines under the low light of the flickering candles. I frown and glance around at the other diners, all of whom are probably older than my parents by twenty years.

Harrison gives a broad, self-satisfied smile. "You don't have to be nervous," he says. "It's just dinner."

"I know. I'm not nervous."

"You're quiet."

I quirk a brow. Is he serious? "Sorry."

"I guess this is a little strange," he continues. "Trying to have a first date when we're already engaged."

I shrug, my eyes darting away from his intense stare. I resist the urge to point out that we're not engaged—we're betrothed. The difference is minor, but it feels important right now. I avoided the engagement last night, and until someone ties me down and shoves a ring on my finger I'm still just *betrothed*. I will die on this hill.

"I suppose I would have spent more time trying to get to know you over the years," he drawls. "But I couldn't imagine it would be enjoyable to spend time with a child."

He keeps smiling, like this is a completely understandable thing to say, and I grimace, struck momentarily dumb. Should I be glad he wasn't trying to pounce the moment I turned eighteen, or offended that he never wanted to get to know me? There are no good options here, and I'm starting to miss the silence.

I look down at the menu to hide my discomfort, and my heart falls. It's extensive, and I realize that I don't recognize most of the dishes. Not for nothing, but I've traveled quite a bit, and been to my fair share of fancy restaurants over the years. Still, this is extreme.

Harrison seems to know what he wants, and I watch as the waiter arrives and he orders confidently, his voice smooth and practiced. I, on the other hand, can barely ask for a glass of wine. I speak Latin, Italian, and a smattering of Spanish, but no French.

The waiter nods patiently, and I can feel my cheeks heating. I motion to Harrison. "I'll just have what he's having."

The waiter nods again and disappears as quickly as he arrived. Harrison watches him go, then turns back to me. "You didn't want to try anything else?"

I shake my head. "No, thank you. I'm sure…" I don't even bother to try and pronounce whatever we're eating "…what you picked is the best."

He beams at this, while I just pray it's something edible.

OUR FOOD ARRIVES, AND I PICK NERVOUSLY AT IT, trying to work up the courage to mention school to Harrison. Nothing about the evening so far has implied it will go well, but if I don't at least ask, I won't know what my options are. Maybe I'm blowing this up in my mind to be worse than it is. Maybe he's not expecting me to leave school at all?

I suck in a breath and take a sip of Pinot Noir for courage. "You went to Elsinore, correct?"

"Yes." He nods. "I enjoyed my fraternity and not much else."

Perfect. Off to a wonderful start.

"Right, well, I'm really looking forward to next semester. I'm working on my thesis already. I'd love to show you my research if you're interested, I—"

He pauses with his fork halfway to his mouth and I break off, catching on to his clear confusion. My stomach sinks. Here's the confirmation I knew was coming.

"Won't you have a lot to do?" he asks. "What with the wedding and pledging?"

"Yes, but I'm very organized." I laugh, and it comes out more hysterical than amiable. "Really, if you'd just take a look at my research, you'd see I can definitely handle taking on a lot at once."

He nods slowly, a small smile playing at the corners of his lips. "Juliette."

"Etta," I correct, my throat already feeling tight.

He ignores me. "I don't think—"

His phone rings, and we both jump. I'm startled mostly by the sound of the ringer—I hardly know anyone who leaves their ringers on anymore. I'm even more shocked when he pulls it out of his pocket and answers without a second thought. "Harrison Dane."

It's work. I can tell immediately by the sharp tone in his voice, the way he straightens in his chair and stares off into the distance. "Right...excuse me? Are you fucking kidding me?"

I jump, surprised, when his voice raises abruptly.

"That's unacceptable," Harrison snaps. He's abrupt and curt, barking orders with a tone of authority that I've never heard before. It's clear that whoever he speaks to on the other end is not happy, but Harrison is relentless.

"Tell Claudius that I have no time for incompetence." He pauses. "I don't care if it was already fixed, I want the message received that stupidity is no excuse for laziness. Gods, why am I surrounded by fucking imbeciles?"

I sip at my wine, and sink low in my chair, half-mortified, half-transfixed. It goes on and on, and my glass is nearly empty when finally, Harrison hangs up, lowering his phone back to the table.

"Sorry about that," he says, his tone is calm. His smile is light, as if nothing just happened. "You know how work can be."

I blink at him, still shell-shocked by the extreme tonal shift. "Is something wrong?"

He frowns, looking confused. "No, why do you ask?"

A feeling of dread settles over me like a cloak. "I—you—you sounded mad."

He just shrugs. "This isn't kindergarten, Juliette."

My dread takes shape, a sickening creature crawling around in my stomach. Either he really doesn't know what I mean and that's just how he speaks when he's inconvenienced, or worse, he does know what I mean, and he's openly dismissing me. He's assuming I'll get disoriented and drop the subject, which to be honest, isn't a bad assumption.

What am I supposed to do? Demand he admit I'm right? He drove. I'm stuck in the middle of nowhere with him.

Part of me says I'm overreacting. Another part knows I'm not.

I always worry I might be being paranoid, or that my intuition is lying to me, but I'm also rarely wrong, and my gut is telling me to get the hell out of here.

My heart starts to beat a little too fast, and I stand abruptly, my chair screeching against the floor. "I'm going to the ladies room. Excuse me."

CHAPTER EIGHTTEEN
·ROMAN·

PRESENT

HARRISON DANE IS THE KIND OF ASSHOLE WHO TAGS his location everywhere he goes. Normally, I would scoff at that, but today I'm almost embarrassingly grateful.

Fog presses in on the windows, and my windshield wipers seem to strain with the effort of trying to shove it out of the way as I drive down the winding back road on the edge of town. The scent of rain lingers in the air, and the woods are eerily silent, the road dark and empty.

I keep telling myself that I don't know where I'm going. That I'm just out for a drive, or going to see one of my friends, but it's bullshit. I know it's bullshit. I keep trying to pretend that I'm not driving in the direction of Dane's stupid fucking pin, yet I've never been more on edge than I am right now. My pulse hums as if it's trying to escape my body. The sound is so loud I can almost hear it. Like a warning trying to force me to move. To go do something—anything.

Ever since Saturday night, I've thought of virtually nothing but *her*.

Heard nothing but her breathy moans in my head.

Seen nothing but her huge, too-innocent eyes when I close my own. The relentless thoughts of all the things I could have and should have said to her, or done *to* her, have crawled inside my brain and taken root.

The moment I heard her whisper my name, I planned out all sorts of ways to have her. Then, like some kind of cosmic intervention, there she was in the library. Only, before I could say anything real. Before I could tell her what I heard and admit I want her too, or ask her to leave with me, or any of the other ideas swirling in my overstimulated mind, she poured icy water over the entire thing.

"I have a date tonight."

I saw red for all the wrong reasons. I should care that the closer to marriage Etta gets, the more the walls close in on me. That her engagement will prompt my own. Yet, I wasn't thinking of any of that—not earlier, and not now.

Wanting her isn't enough. What felt possible in the dark, is more complicated in the light of day, and now I'll need to take a more delicate, measured approach.

Delicate, like spending hours obsessing over the date she mentioned.

Measured, like breaking my referendum on using magic so I could scry for Etta's location.

Etta Capulet has been tormenting me for as long as I can remember. Longer, probably. She has the kind of personality that's as infuriating as it is fascinating. That gets in your head and lingers, making you stew for hours about what she meant by some glance or throw-away comment.

It took me years to realize that my problem was that I liked her. Longer than it should have by any stretch of the imagination.

She made me borderline homicidal between the ages of twelve and fourteen. Every single rant and complaint, every hormone-fueled shit-fit was about her holier-than-thou attitude, how she was a teacher's pet and didn't deserve her achievements, how she wasn't even that pretty, anyway.

When we were fifteen, she attended our freshman formal with Sebastian Cesario. Up until then, I'd been friendly with Sebastian, but after I heard him talking about getting into her panties after the dance, I nearly lost my mind.

All of my current friends were there for all of it. They helped beat the shit out of Sebastian and then watched while I fumbled through the next few years, teasing her, following her around, threatening her dates while parading my girlfriends in front of her, and generally leaning hard on every toxic stereotype I hadn't yet learned I was fulfilling.

Only Bennet—and my sister, Marcia, come to think of it—ever suggested that I might be tormenting Etta for any reason other than our long-standing feud. Marcia, because she was perceptive like that, and maybe girls just know things, I don't know. And Bennet, because he would have had to be blind not to see it with how much time we spend together.

In retrospect, I should have realized then that I liked her, but no.

It took years for me to put it together. Even when she started showing up in the cemetery, I didn't realize that my obsession with Etta had shifted beyond hatred. That it had shifted a long time ago. But by then, it was too late.

I've never heard of the restaurant Dane tagged himself and Etta at. From the description, I can't imagine Etta there either, but it doesn't matter. Every restaurant has a bar, and I'm going to go sit at that bar and...I'm not sure yet.

As I drive, the music emanating from my satellite radio suddenly cuts out. *Damn, no signal.*

I look down at the screen, flipping through channels trying to get something to work. Nothing does, and I sigh, glancing back at the empty road.

My heart leaps into my throat. What the fuck?

A bluish light is coming toward me, giving the impression of a lantern appearing out of the mist, or a will-o-wisp luring a traveler off their path.

I blink furiously and squint into the fog, and I make out the faint outline of a cell phone. Someone is walking along the shoulder of the road, illuminating their path through the darkness with their phone.

Primal instinct kicks in and I slow down to look—partly out of concern for their safety, considering the lack of visibility; but largely from curiosity. It's not unusual to spot people biking or jogging at night, but they usually wear some sort of reflective material. What is someone doing walking on a main road—in all black clothing—at night?

As I approach the figure, my annoyance and confusion shifts into a gut-wrenching shock. I slam my foot down on the break without thinking, and my car lurches forward too fast as the engine tries to compensate for my sudden movement. My tires screech, then skid on wet pavement, and my seatbelt cuts into my neck, nearly knocking the wind out of me.

"Fuck!" I gasp, knuckles white on the wheel.

I sit there for half a second, processing the fact that I just almost flipped my car, before rolling down my window. I lean my head out all the way and yell: "What the fuck are you doing?"

Etta looks up at me. Her face is illuminated by both my headlights and her phone. I watch as fear crosses her face, only to be replaced by recognition, and finally, annoyance. Her wide eyes go narrow, and she scowls at me.

"Enjoying the nice weather," she yells back.

Mixed emotions war in my chest: I'm livid—she shouldn't be out here alone at night like this. It's far too dangerous. Where the hell is Dane? And yet, beneath the rising tide of anger, a hint of satisfaction coils itself within me—another chance meeting. If that's not fate, I don't know what is.

Pulling my car onto the shoulder of the road behind her, I throw my door open and step out. Etta is already walking again, faster this time, evidently intent on escaping me. I almost laugh. She's kidding herself if she thinks she can outrun me, but I like that she's stubborn enough to try.

"Etta!" I yell again, louder this time. "You need a ride?"

Without warning, a memory flashes in the back of my mind. A memory of years ago, trying to persuade Etta to let me drive her home from the cemetery. At the time, I had no idea why I cared. No idea where my irrational fear of something happening to her was coming from. Nothing has changed in the last five years. Etta is still stubborn to a fault, and I'm still desperate to protect her.

She stares at me for a moment before shaking her head no. "No, thanks," she responds curtly, stepping off to the side of the road into taller grasses.

Yeah, fuck that. I'm not going to let her say no.

I race after her. "What are you doing out here?"

"None of your business," she shouts back without looking at me. Then, quieter, she mutters. "I actually thought this night couldn't get worse, but shame on me, I should have knocked on wood."

A growl of frustration bubbles up in my chest. I scan over her outfit. I didn't notice immediately, too shocked to see her here at all, but she's wearing a tight white dress and heeled boots. Her coat is long and black, but it doesn't completely hide how tight and sheer that dress is. The anger rises in my throat again. "Didn't you say you had a date tonight?"

I try to make it sound as if I've only just remembered. As if this hasn't been my constant thought for the better part of the day. I'm not sure if I'm successful, but she seems too preoccupied to notice.

She stops, and I catch up to her in two strides. My breathing is labored, as every possible worst-case scenario runs through my head. "Tell me what happened."

"No," she snaps. "The last thing I want is you here witnessing this."

"And what exactly am I witnessing?"

Etta lets out an exasperated sigh. "Nothing."

I run a hand through my hair, frustrated with her and angry with myself for being frustrated. It's not even only about Etta. My sister's belongings were found on the side of a road in the middle of nowhere, miles from where we later found her body. I refuse to let Etta become another statistic. I refuse to fail twice.

I lower my voice, taking a step toward her. "Get in the car Etta, because the only thing stopping me from going to find Dane right now is taking care of you."

Her eyes widen. "Why the hell would you do that?"

I let out a humorless bark of laughter. "You're walking alone, at night, clearly coming from your date. You won't tell me what happened, so I'm forced to jump to the worst possible conclusion."

She worries her bottom lip. "Nothing happened, and even if it did, why would you care?"

Irrational rage surges in my chest, exasperated by every other over-saturated emotion of the last few days. Does it fucking matter why I care? She's testing my patience in the worst way, and soon she's about to hit my limit. I'm not going to let her keep walking alone, I'm not going to stand here and listen to her mouth-off, and frankly, I'm done with this conversation. "Get in the car, or I'll put you in. Your choice."

"So, you're kidnapping me? How do you think that will work out for you?"

Her tone is strong, but her eyes betray a hint of anxiety. Honestly, if I were trying to kidnap her, I think she'd drive me up the fucking wall. I love everything about this woman, never get tired of hearing her talk, but I do think I might get tired of listening to her whine—eventually.

I take another step toward her, so we're practically nose to nose. "Look. I might have said some fucked up shit to you when we were kids, and I'm genuinely sorry for that. I'm sorry that my parents hate your parents and things have gotten so out of hand, but don't imply that I wouldn't care if someone was hurting women. I've never done anything to make you think I'd hurt you or that I wouldn't care if someone was hurting women. My fucking sister is dead for god's sake, don't you think I might care if something happened to you too?"

It's probably more than I've said to her in one conversation ever, and I'm panting, my breath leaving me and allowing no more words.

Etta blinks at me, surprised, and then her angry brow softens slightly. "I didn't know you were capable of an apology."

I blink, rolling back what I said in my mind, and wince. I don't enjoy apologizing—although, if anyone deserves one, Etta does. She deserves everything. But from the way she's already blushing, I don't think she's ready to hear more. Not yet, anyway. "Don't get used to it."

"Okay, fine," she says. "I'll get in the car, but only until I can get a phone signal. My phone isn't working."

I glance down at the phone in her hands. There's almost nowhere in densely settled areas where you can't get a phone signal anymore. Nowhere, except for Stratford. Phones, and most technology in general—like my radio—don't work that well around magic. Landlines and desktops with ethernet cords tend to work better than anything running on wireless alone, but it's a mixed bag. "We must have been near an Order member's house. My radio cut out a little ways back."

"Okay, so just take me to where the signal works."

"Fine," I lie.

I lead her to the car, open the passenger door and wait until she's settled in before I round to the driver's side. Neither of us is happy. Her, because she clearly feels as though she's lost something by accepting help. Me, because I don't want to see her unsafe.

At first, neither of us speak. Finally, the satellite radio kicks back in and I breathe a sigh of relief. I don't even care that the song is awful, I just need noise to break the tension.

Alone with her in the library earlier, I could barely think of anything else but pulling her into one of those overstuffed armchairs, or perhaps fucking her against the bookshelves. In my car, with only inches between us, there's little to keep me from thinking of it again.

I can feel her eyes on me, and I try not to think about the way her dress clings to her curves or how her hair falls in loose waves around her shoulders. I know it's wrong to be attracted to her given the circumstances, but I can't help it. The fact that she's had a bad night should make her less appealing, but it doesn't. What does that say about my moral compass?

She's beautiful and infuriating and I want her. It's as simple as that.

"My phone is working again," Etta says. She glances back out the rear window, then from her phone to the screen in the dashboard. "You can let me out."

There's not a chance in hell I'm letting her out of this car. "It's starting to rain. I'm taking you home, and that's the end of it."

"Is there any point in arguing with you about this?"

"No."

As we speed through the quietly deserted downtown. The streetlights blur together, one after another until they form a single glowing line. The rain intensifies, pelting my windows, and I bite the inside of my cheek to keep from pointing it out to her—as if she hadn't noticed the increased downpour. *This* is what she would've been walking in. She'd have been lucky not to get hypothermia.

Finally, we reach Etta's house. She directs me to pull into the driveway, then, before I can turn the car off, she is already pushing her door open with one hand and gathering her things with the other. She looks at me sideways. "Oh, don't do anything stupid when you leave here."

I raise an eyebrow. "Like?"

"Like go look for Harrison. I'm not lying, nothing happened on my date."

So she thinks she knows me now? She's right, I was thinking of doing that, but still. "Then why are you walking?"

"Because—" She rolls her eyes, but this time it seems like it's more to herself than me. "—this isn't kindergarten, Roman."

"I don't know what the fuck that's supposed to mean."

She smiles, and reaches for her door handle. "I know. You should go before someone sees you."

"I don't give a fuck."

"I do."

Of course she does. She cares about everything, while I couldn't care less who sees me. I don't care what happens if it means a few more minutes of her time, especially after what I heard the other night. I don't care whether her family burns me at the stake, or my life goes up in smoke, I'll happily stand in the flames and burn myself alive.

I lean over the center console, reaching across her to hold the handle of her door closed. "Wait."

CHAPTER NINETEEN
ETTA

PRESENT

"WAIT."

My heart is pounding too fast, my pulse thrumming like butterfly wings against my throat, as he leans over me to hold my door closed. I'm suddenly aware of how close we are. Of his eyes darting down to my lips, and the heat I feel radiating from his body. It's making my head spin, reminding me of all the crazy ideas and fantasies I had as a teenager.

If I did something stupid—disastrous—right now, could I convince myself it meant nothing? That the wild evening had rendered me temporarily insane?

No. I've been down this road before. It's a bad idea. Convincing myself that Roman is a good person, like some sort of misunderstood hero, will only lead to disaster. He's proven time and time again that he's no hero, and every shred of kindness from him comes with a bitter aftertaste of malice.

Except for tonight, a tiny traitorous part of me argues. He didn't have to stop and help. I gave him every opportunity to change his mind. No matter which way I look at it, what he did tonight was beyond nice. I don't even know where he was going, or what plans were interrupted by him helping me.

"You're a nice guy when you want to be," I say, without thinking.

To my surprise, he recoils slightly, like I've physically hit him. His face twists, a storm of turbulent emotions flying across his eyes before he manages to revert to his usual flat facade. "You've got it wrong, good girl. This had nothing to do with being nice. It was entirely selfish."

I furrow my brow. "I don't believe that."

He clenches his jaw. "Believe whatever you want."

My heart pounds too hard and fast. What are we doing? What am *I* doing? I shouldn't still be sitting here. Shouldn't want him. Shouldn't be thinking or doing so many damn things lately.

Yet, I'm not moving to get out of the car, and he's not leaning back to give me room. Our faces are so close, and the darkness presses in around us. The sound of the rain pounds on the car, and our breathing grows heavier, falling in sync.

He stops moving. There's only a fraction of an inch of space left between us, and it's like he's waiting to see if I'll close it.

I'm an idiot to risk humiliating rejection all over again, but I can't bring myself to make that stop me. Our eyes meet, and I shift forward on a breath. His lips brush against mine, whisper soft, so lightly it's hard to know if I imagined them being there in the first place.

Light floods the driveway, blinding us. I jump, and shrink away from Roman's proximity. Whipping my head around, my heartbeat quickens for an entirely different reason. Raindrops slide down my window, and it's dark outside, but even so I can make out my cousin Tyberius's car pulling down the driveway. "You need to leave right now."

Roman turns as well to look, then smirks at me. "Why? If he attacks me he'll get kicked out of the Order."

Pinching the skin between my eyes, I take a deep breath. This is the last thing I need. "I obviously spoke too soon."

"About what?"

"You're right. You're not nice."

His lip curls up in a smile. "So soon? What happened, good girl?"

"If Tyberius gets kicked out then so will I. Did you ever think of that? And that's if the bare minimum happens. What if you guys kill each other."

He scoffs. "He can't kill me."

My stomach lurches. Deep down, I know that. Deep down, I'm not scared for Roman. I'm scared that Roman really isn't the nice guy I like to pretend he is. That, if Tyberius keeps provoking him, one of these days, Roman will kill my cousin.

I bit my lip. "If we get thrown out because of you, don't think I won't make sure you get kicked out with us."

He cocks his head curiously. "You act like I give a shit about the Order. Getting kicked out is fine with me."

I purse my lips. I'm sure it is fine for him. He's already pledged. He can do magic if he wants to, and getting kicked out would only give him more freedom. Me, on the other hand? I haven't pledged yet, and if my family is forced out I'll never be able to do more than kitchen witchery and basic runology.

"Is it really though?" I snap. "If you didn't care you could have left already. You could leave at any time."

"But you're here," he says. "If you get kicked out too, why would I stay?"

My heart stutters and I look up too quickly. I can't read his expression. Can't tell if he's joking, or worse, trying to goad me into leaving.

But what if he's not joking.

My eyes dart to my cousin now getting out of his car, holding an umbrella high as he strides toward us. "Look, I'll meet you in the library tomorrow with your phone. Please just leave, I don't want there to be a fight."

I gather my purse and my phone and fling my door open before Roman can say anything else. The rain pelts down on me as I dash toward the door, my hands shaking.

"Juliette," Tyberius calls across the driveway.

Reaching the porch, I turn back and see my cousin looking from me to Roman's car as he zips back up the driveway. I heave a sigh of relief that for once someone listened to me.

"Was that Dane?" Tyberius asks as he steps up onto the porch and shakes out his umbrella. "I thought his car was white?"

I shake my head, "I guess not."

We step into the foyer and I close the door. Tyberius rounds on me, his eyes narrow with suspicion. "Why wouldn't he come in to say hi?"

"I don't know. The rain I guess." I shrug. "What are you doing here?"

"Your dad and I have some business," he says vaguely.

I would bet all the money I have that the "business," has something to do with either the Montague family or Lawrence's recent declaration. I shudder at what would have happened if Tyberius and Roman crossed paths.

And that's just it, isn't it? It doesn't really matter who Roman is —if he's a nice person under all his dark armor, or if he's really the villain he seems to want to portray himself as. It doesn't matter, because first, he'll always be a Montague.

I stare at my cousin—my infuriating, brash, pompous cousin— who is still the closest thing to a sibling I have, and I can picture all too clearly how he'll be the next victim of the feud. Probably by his own stupidity. "Right, well, I need to go change."

Pushing the melancholy from my mind, I march toward my room. My gaze darts toward the closed door to the library as I pass, and I nearly stop.

No, not right now. I can look for the phone later. It's not that important.

I make it two more steps before turning back. I don't know who I think I'm kidding, trying to lie to myself. That phone is the single interesting thing in this house at the moment. The only thing distracting me from the doom-spiral in my mind.

"It's just the phone," I promise myself, as I swing open the door to the library. "That's it."

I'll just grab the phone, give it back, and pretend this week never happened. Because nothing really did happen. My imagination running away with me doesn't mean anything, and I have bigger problems right now than Roman Montague. Problems like what will happen when my parents find out I ran out on Harrison, or how to avoid having to marry him when everyone else around me seems intent on it.

I wish Cat was here, but she has her study group tonight and wasn't expecting me back this early, anyway. I suppose I should be grateful for that, though, since it makes it far easier to slip into the library with no awkward questions.

The smell of cloves immediately hits me, and the scent alone is enough to make my conviction waiver. Gritting my teeth, I dash across the room and yank open a window. Cold air comes rushing in, tugging at my clothes and hair and raising the exposed skin on my arms.

I bend down and flick on a table lamp as a creeping feeling crawls up my spine. I'm being stupid, getting creeped out by wind like a child in the dark. Then again, it's not like I don't know there are real things that go bump in the night—human and otherwise.

My eyes dart around the room, wondering where Roman might have left his phone. We weren't in here all that long and we barely moved away from the door. Although, I did leave first...

But then, I spot it on the rug near the door. Like it must have fallen out of his pocket at some point. I can't even imagine how we were both too distracted not to notice that.

Brow furrowed, I cross the room and pick up the phone. It's simple and relatively unassuming. Like the heroine of some mid-00s detective witch show, I make a list in my head of things I'd deduce from this phone.

It's an iPhone, maybe one generation back. So, he can afford new tech, but doesn't care enough to run out and buy every new iteration right away. The case is bright purple, filthy on the edges, and scratched to all hell—in far worse shape than it should be considering how new the phone is. I frown. I'm a shitty detective because that makes no sense.

Curious now, I walk back over to the table lamp, and hold the phone face down under the stream of light to get a better look. The mess on the edges of the case that I first took as dirt is actually more of a light tan color. My stomach sinking, I pull out my own phone and compare them. Sure enough, I have similar smudges on my case. It's make-up. Foundation to be specific.

My throat goes tight, as I examine what I'm now almost sure is Roman's phone and his little sister's case.

I shove my own phone back in my pocket and bend to turn the light back off. I leave the window open to air out the library and close the door again before heading back to my room, phone held tight in my fist like it's some forbidden contraband. Flopping on my bed, I stare at it.

I feel weird looking at anyone's texts. But then again, he would absolutely do it to me...right? Isn't he the one who's always making fun of me for being "too moral"—as if that's possible.

It probably doesn't matter, I assume the phone is password protected, anyway.

I hesitate for half a second, then light it up again just to check if there is, in fact, a password. Sure enough, a numbers screen pops up. I let out a sigh of relief.

So, that decision is made for me then. But then, after a minute, the code screen disappears, and up pops the previews of every message and notification from the last few days. *Shit.*

Roman's stupid voice rings in my head. *"You always were a good girl, Etta."*

I scowl. Alright, I'm not a saint. I can't be expected not to look at this.

I leap off my bed and race across the room to lock my bedroom door, then dart around the room closing all the shades. I am so aware this is absurd, but I feel like I'm doing something wrong here, and no one can know the clear depth of my obsession while I venture into this gold mine of information.

Once I'm sure I'm completely hidden, I return to my bed and dive in.

There's days' worth of shit here, and the first thing I notice is that Roman doesn't clear his notifications. *At all*.

The very top things are from *Amazon*, social media, *Kindle*, podcasts and news—none of which are recent. He has no sports or stock market apps, both of which my father checks religiously. He needs to update his IOS and hasn't backed up to the cloud in 96 weeks. I cringe. Who does that?

For half a second, I'm shocked by the *Kindle* notifications, and then I realize that not everyone reads exclusively smut. Kindle can be used for other things...I just haven't found a reason to indulge in those things. I bet the most recent thing in Roman's library is a Shirley Jackson book, or maybe Toni Morrison.

Going back to the phone, there's nearly a dozen missed phone calls. It looks like both Bennet and Pierce called him a few times, probably trying to find the phone. I am guessing it's Bennet based on context, because the contact actually says "Eggs Benedict" but Pierce's says "Pierce N. Avon," which I find funny for some reason.

His parents are listed as "Father" and "Mom." They both called twice.

Then, the texts.

My eyes grow wide as I scan down all the messages from "Maybe: Rosaline Hathaway." I raise my eyebrows. That's a name I haven't heard in a while.

Rosaline *freaking* Hathaway. Roman's prep school girlfriend and the object of much of my teenage angst. I can't help feeling a little smug that he didn't save her number, the phone did. They must not have ended on good terms.

That smugness dies, my stomach plummeting as I scan through their messages.

While I can't see more than the first few words of each message, it's enough to understand the gist.

It starts out relatively normal:

> MAYBE: ROSALINE HATHAWAY:
>
> Are you coming?
>
> I just heard from V…
>
> Are you here yet?

She's probably talking about the party on Saturday where he lost his phone. She follows that up with some questions about music, which seems to be what they were discussing. Or, perhaps something he mentioned to her? It's hard to tell without the whole message showing. Then, the next morning, it starts to go off the rails.

> MAYBE: ROSALINE HATHAWAY:
>
> Did you get the pic I se…
>
> I think we should anno…
>
> What do you think?
>
> Call me back when yo…

I furrow my brow. Gods, I wish I could see the rest of what she's asking about. If only for, er, academic curiosity. I scroll to the following day, moving my face closer to the screen with the manic glee of a prospector sifting for gold. *We wants it. We needs it. Must have the precious.*

> MAYBE: ROSALINE HATHAWAY:
>
> Roman what the fu…
>
> My mom wants to k…

> If we're getting engag...

"Oh my god," I say out loud, staring blankly at nothing in particular.

My heart is suddenly beating so hard against my chest I can't breathe. "Engag," can only be "Engaged," right? He's engaged? Or, engaged to be engaged? And to Rosaline Hathaway of all people?

I flop back on my bed as my mind races, conjuring long buried memories of every time I would walk down a hallway in prep school behind Roman and Rosaline. Every time they made out in the library, or in front of my locker or in the parking lot next to my car. If I didn't know better, I would have thought it was on purpose.

Could they have been betrothed that whole time? It never even occurred to me that Roman might be promised to someone, which now in retrospect, seems insane.

Of course, that had to be what this was. Half of Order kids got betrothed at birth, and almost all have been set up by their fifth birthday. It almost never takes more than five years for another Order baby to be born with a compatible star chart, and then, if the families agree, the match will be set up right then and there.

About two-thirds of betrothed couples who grow up knowing they are promised to each other start dating by prep school. Why didn't I realize that Roman and Rosaline were one of those couples? Why do I even care?

I stare down at Roman's phone in his sister's purple case, and frown. I suck in deep breaths, trying to think about this rationally. Like a puzzle. Because this engagement, like every other thing I've ever known about him, doesn't add up.

Another long-forgotten comment bubbles up from the depths of my memory, jumbled together by the intervening years.

"She's not my girlfriend...I don't care. I have more important things to focus on.."

That doesn't seem like something someone would say about their betrothed. Anyway, if Roman is engaged to Rosaline then what would he be doing sitting in a dark car in my driveway late at night? If he's engaged to Rosaline, why would he look at me with that dark, raw, hunger that sends shivers all over my body.

Maybe I'm delusional, or feeding into years of half-crazed fantasies, or maybe, Roman and I could help each other.

CHAPTER TWENTY
⋆·ROMAN·⋆

THE TASTE OF ROSALINE'S WINTERGREEN GUM FILLS MY mouth as she swipes her tongue over mine. I grab the back of her head, trying to tilt her head up to a more convenient angle, and she whimpers. I don't know whether I'm hurting her, pulling on her curly, chestnut ponytail, or she thinks I'm into it when she makes noises like that.

I don't know what it says about me that I don't care either way.

The minutes tick by in my head—my strangely accurate internal clock knowing we have about five minutes until the end of H block, when this stairwell will flood with our classmates moving to their next period.

I push Rose harder against the faded brick wall and run my hand up the inside of her thigh under her pleated plaid skirt. I'm almost shocked when she makes no move to stop me—not even a false protest. *"We can't do this here."* Or, *"Let's go out to your car."*

The first few times we hooked-up were like that, but maybe now she's realized I don't want her in the back seat of my SUV in the back of the student parking lot, or anywhere else where no one will see us. That's never been the point.

I think if she's honest with herself Rose feels the same way about me. We accessorize each other well, but we're not dating.

The door at the top of the stairs bangs open and footsteps clatter against the marble, coming around the corner at the top of the landing above us. Instead of stopping, I press closer to Rosaline, sucking her bottom lip into my mouth as my fingers snake their way under the cotton lace of her panties.

"Fuck! Are there no safe stairs in this place?" a familiar voice barks.

I freeze, surprised, and turn my head too quickly, nearly knocking Rose's head back against the wall.

Bennet raises an eyebrow at me as he descends the stairs toward us, Pierce close on his heels. They're both wearing their maroon and navy uniforms, but while Bennet's tie is straight, his hair combed, Pierce looks like he got dressed in a wind-tunnel.

Rose looks from my friends to me and rolls her eyes. "Shit."

I don't reply. I don't trust myself to say anything.

Rosaline ducks out from under my arm, picks up her abandoned messenger bag off the landing, and smooths her ponytail. "See you this afternoon?"

I shake my head. "Tomorrow, maybe."

She shrugs, as if she cares about as much as I do. "Okay."

Pierce and Bennet watch her go with very different expressions. Pierce is grinning, amused, while my cousin seems vaguely annoyed.

"You don't appreciate how good you have it with her, man," Pierce says, watching Rose walk away. "It's like a relationship without any of the work."

I give him a flat look. "What are you assholes doing here?"

"Why? Were you expecting someone else?" Bennet asks mildly.

My cousin's expression is a little too perceptive and I don't like it. I narrow my eyes. "What? No! You couldn't have waited five minutes?"

"Only five?" Pierce smirks.

"The bells are about to ring," I say, defensively. "Wait, don't you have Brit Lit right now?"

"There was a test, we finished early," Pierce says, still grinning. "See, Roman? You're not the only genius. I think I just did myself proud with a very respectable C-."

I ignore him, instead watching the door at the top of the stairs. There's only another minute until the end of the block. This stairwell is located perfectly between the library and the history hallway, and I happen to know that on Mondays and Wednesdays I'm not the only one with a free block, or the only one who might leave the library a few minutes before the bell to beat the crowd...

"She's not coming."

I glance at Bennet. "Who?"

Again, he raises his eyebrows. "She's not here. She wasn't in A block this morning."

My stomach lurches, my breath catching in the worst way, yet I force my face to remain impassive. I practically crawling out of my skin wanting to ask why Etta wasn't in class, but that would be the same as admitting that I was waiting for her. Yeah, no thanks. "I don't know who you're talking about."

"Sure, whatever." He glances at the door that Rosaline walked out, then back to me. "This is fucked up, you know. If you don't want her, you should let her go."

I furrow my brow, truly confused now. "Who, Rose?"

Bennet huffs in frustration. "No. Not Rose."

I blink at him, incredulous, as he moves past me. I open my mouth to reply just as the bell announces the end of class and a cacophony of voices fills the stairwell

"I don't know who you're talking about!" I yell over the din.

No one answers.

I PULL INTO MY DRIVEWAY TOO FAST, AND SKID TO A stop in front of the open garage door. There are no other cars here, though we could comfortably fit thirty in our driveway before we even needed to use the garage. My parents are rarely home, so I expected nothing less.

The side door groans on its hinges as I swing it open, stepping into the lemon-scented kitchen. Before I can take two steps, I freeze.

Marcia—my kid sister—is sitting alone, slumped over the kitchen Island. All I can see of her is a mop of black hair and a pile of crumpled tissues.

At the sound of my footsteps, she sits up and looks at me with red-rimmed eyes. "Hey," she says, with forced cheerfulness. "What's up?"

"Hey," I start, my voice softening despite myself. "You okay?"

Marcia sniffles punctuating the silence that stretches between us.

She's been crying a lot lately, ever since our grandfather died. It makes me fucking uncomfortable. I don't deal with emotions well, and crying freaks me out, but I won't ignore her.

"Are you okay?" I ask, awkwardly.

"Yeah," she lies, sniffing loudly.

"If it's about Grandfather I can call mom or something..."

She shakes her head, causing her long hair to fly around her tear-stained face. "No, it's not that. It's not a big deal."

I look up, my interest piqued. "Assholes at school?"

"No." She lets out another wail and I flinch, waiting for her to blow her nose. "It's just...I wanted to go to the Senior Prom, and I told everyone I was going to get to go so now all the girls at school will think I lied. I really thought he was going to take me, we'd talked about it."

My eyes narrow. "Marcia...what the fuck are you talking about? Who was going to take you to the Senior Prom? You're in the eighth grade."

"It doesn't matter," she says quickly. "I don't want to talk about it anymore."

"I'm just trying to figure out who I need to kill."

Her face goes white. "No, don't. I was being stupid."

She starts to get up to leave, and I realize I'm probably scaring her. I need to reel it in. "You're not stupid, but whoever did this to you is," I say through gritted teeth. "What happened?"

"Nothing!" Marcia says, side-stepping me to escape the kitchen. "I don't want you to do anything. Just leave it alone."

I let her go, grinding my teeth.

She probably just needs to calm down. She'll tell me later.

And if not, I'll still find out eventually. And then I'm going to commit actual fucking murder.

CHAPTER TWENTY-ONE

✦ ETTA ✦

"OKAY, I LOVE THAT," CAT'S VOICE RINGS enthusiastically through the dressing room. "You look like...sexy Morticia Adams."

"Morticia Adams already is sexy," I reply.

"Precisely." She nods sagely, eyes scanning over my dress.

I smile slightly at my reflection in the three-way mirror. I have to admit, I like the dress too. Plus, it's black, which means my mother will hate it—always a plus.

It's Saturday afternoon, and Cat and I are cloistered in the dressing room of our local boutique. It's fall-formal season, and the air is heavy with the scent of fresh silk and lilac perfume, and the overhead lighting is trying to be something other than what it is—fluorescent. The sounds of laughter and other girls and their mothers discussing gowns travels over the top of every dressing-room door. My mom wouldn't be caught dead in a place like this.

But then, she doesn't have to, because technically I haven't been asked to formal yet...I'm just, hoping.

"I think I'll get it," I say, fingering the neckline of the long, black-lace gown. "Worst-case scenario, I'm sure I can wear it to some Order function at some point. It's not too prom-y."

Cat nods. "True."

Shockingly, Cat actually has a date to prom already—one her father approves of. She's not exactly into the guy, but her little sister, Bianca, is a sophomore this year and got asked to the dance as well. Bianca was only allowed to go if Cat went, so she's taking one for the team and doing some kind of double-date scenario.

Now, if I only had a date, everything would be perfect.

I step into the dressing room to take off my dress and close the door. Biting my lip, I call through the door: "Does Bianca's boyfriend have any more friends?"

My face heats, and I'm glad Cat can't see my face through the door. How the hell did I end up being the desperate girl without a date three weeks before the dance? Why is this my life?

There's silence on the other side. My embarrassment thickens. Oh my gods, did I suddenly grow three heads overnight?

"I'll ask," Cat says finally. She doesn't sound hopeful. "But I think everyone's a little nervous."

I freeze, the dress halfway over my head. My heart speeds up, and a hot, sick feeling starts in my stomach and creeps up my chest. Anxiety, mixed with an intense, shameful dread. Does she know something I don't? Is there actually something wrong with me? "Nervous about what?" I say, my voice nearly quavering.

Thank the gods, this time she doesn't pause before answering. "Well, after what happened to Sebastian—not that he didn't deserve it—and then, with all the rumors after that coffee incident..."

"Wait, what?" I squawk. I pull the dress the rest of the way over my head so fast, it's a miracle it doesn't tear in half. Tossing it in a ball on the floor, I yank my jeans on, and don't even bother to finish tugging my shirt over my head before I'm swinging the door open again. "What are you talking about?"

Cat stares at me, eyes wide, as my head pops out of the top of my t-shirt. "If there was ever a time for the phrase 'keep your shirt on,'" she quips.

"Ha. Ha," I say sardonically, "tell me now. What are you talking about?"

She shakes her head, her long, dark hair swishing all around her shoulders. "You know, the whole fight after sophomore-semi." Her hands wave wildly in the air. "You do know...right?"

I gape at her. "What fight?"

"Oh my gods," she almost yells. "I totally thought you were doing like, the world's best job of rising above the drama. Do you not know?"

"Catalina!" I scream. There's silence in the dressing room, as clearly I have disturbed all the other shoppers. Abashed, I lower my voice. "Catalina. What happened after semi? What fight?"

"Roman Montague beat up Sebastian Cesario in the parking lot. They were both out of school for days, remember?"

I wrack my brain, trying to remember either of them being out of school, or when I might have heard about this. "Roman fights all the time. That's just what he does," I say dismissively. "Pardon me if I can't keep up with every time he's suspended and his dad has to donate a new science lab or something. Anyway, Roman and Sebastian are friends."

"Not anymore," Cat says. "I don't give a shit about that kind of gossip and even I know that."

I wave her off. "Whatever. What does that have to do with me?"

She looks uncomfortable again, and there's another long pause that feels like an eternity. "I mean, maybe nothing?" She says, and it sounds like a question. "But there's kind of an understanding going around that anyone who goes out with you should expect to get their ass handed to them."

I gape at her. "That can't be true. When has Roman Montague ever said—" I break off, realizing what happened.

He didn't say it.

He wrote it, in black, permeant marker all down my arm. And then, he revealed his psychotic cattle-brand in the most demeaning possible way, by turning my shirt completely transparent in front of an entire hallway of people. Anyone who saw me that day would have been able to read my arm just as clearly as they could see the rest of me.

Anger flares within me, hot and fierce, igniting every nerve. "He has no right," I seethe, the words a venomous whisper. "Roman Montague is the absolute scum of the earth."

"Maybe there's more to it?"

"More?" I let out a hysterical laugh. "Like what? What could he possibly do to me next?"

Honestly, it's starting to feel like some mean joke. Some twist of fate gone wrong. I can't possibly be meant to spend my life constantly crossing paths with Roman Montague, always at war. It's too cruel. I thought I could somehow ignore the feud, but he's making it impossible.

"I don't know," Cat shrugs. "It seems like maybe he likes you."

I scoff. "No. This isn't like getting my ponytail tugged on the playground. Roman Montague is actually trying to ruin my life. He's deranged."

"Fine," Cat says. "What are you going to do?"

I guess I got my secret, terrible wish. I have Roman's full attention, and it's nothing like I pictured it would be. I'm not pulling him into the light with me, he's tainting me, making me bitter and resentful and mean, just like him.

I grit my teeth, still seething. "Nothing. I'm going to do absolutely nothing."

She quirks a brow. "That's anti-climactic."

Yup, is it ever. I'm already regretting it and I haven't even started.

"The only way to stop this stupid game is not to play anymore, so I'm doing nothing. Roman Montague can keep trying to torture me, and I'm still going to be nice to him." I grimace. "Even if it kills me."

Chapter Twenty-Two
•✦• ROMAN •✦•

Present

I sprint into the library five minutes late and dash up the stairs two at a time. A surly blonde librarian scowls at me as I run, making a loud "shhh!" sound that is far louder than my pounding feet. I give her a nod and a smile, as if to say sorry, and she looks away.

Skidding into the alcove in the back of the second floor, I'm shocked and a little disappointed when Etta is nowhere in sight. She's usually painfully on time. Or at least, she used to be. I don't necessarily know how she is now, but I remember how she would complain when I was late to Model UN or SAT prep or whatever other activity I was only taking because of her.

Her comment yesterday proved to me that I was a better actor than I had always feared. *"You always liked school."*

She's wrong. I didn't like school, I was just good at it. What I liked was seeing her, so I took every damn extracurricular activity I could and spent countless hours in the library. Etta is the reason I was the Valedictorian, though she would hate to realize that.

It's amazing what a seventeen-year-old guy will pretend to like to spend time with a girl.

I sit down in one of the armchairs to wait, and toss my bag on the one across from me. The little group of four chairs is clustered in a corner, with a blank white wall on one side and a bookshelf on the other. There's a fire exit behind the chair furthest from me, and a large sign stating that the door is alarmed. I have no idea why this seating area is here, or frankly, why more people aren't using it—if only that maybe no one realizes it's back here.

Footsteps sound behind me and I crane my neck, looking back, as excitement leaps in my stomach. "Hi."

Fucking hell. There are so many words in the English language, and beyond that, I can hold my own in both Latin and French, and yet all I can come up with is "Hi."

Etta is standing in the three feet of space between the edge of the bookcase and the wall that separates this strange little alcove from the rest of the library. She's backlit, as the shadows of the tall bookcase cast me in darkness, and slightly out of breath as she drops her bag on the floor at her feet. "Hi. Sorry, my class ran long."

I stand up, so I'm not sitting while she stands, and look her up and down, before settling on her face. She's flushed pink, like she ran all the way up here, and she's gnawing nervously on her bottom lip.

"Oh, here." She steps over her bag and slightly further into the alcove. "I brought your phone."

She's wearing a white turtleneck sweater with a black skirt and some kind of see-through tights today. I stare at her legs for half a second too long, while she fishes around in the pocket of her skirt.

Pulling out my phone, she hands it to me, and I inspect it. It's not really the phone I care about, it's the case, but everything looks okay. I tap the screen and notice that the battery is almost fully charged.

"Thanks," I say, slipping the phone into my own pocket.

"No problem."

There's a pause that feels painfully long. I'm not sure why, but this feels ten times more awkward than any other interaction we've ever had—which doesn't bode well for the plan that I've been ruminating on. Is she uncomfortable? Am I completely off base here?

"Did you go through it?" I tease.

I assume she didn't. Etta is too nice for that. She would assume it was an invasion of privacy or something. I don't even know why I want her to have looked. Maybe because I would have looked without a second thought if given the same opportunity and I want her to be just a little morally gray, like me. Maybe because I want her to care. Maybe for the same reason I would take my prep school girlfriends to make out in the library where Etta was studying. Because as much as I don't care about Rosaline, I want Etta to know that she might not want me, but other women do.

That's fucked, I know.

"Yeah," she says quietly.

I swear, I can hear a record scratch. "You did?"

"Yes. Sorry." She looks uncomfortable. "So, looks like congratulations are in Order?"

The words sound familiar. Practiced. Like she's quoting something I don't recognize. My delight turns to confusion, and I look down at the phone. The first text blinks up at me, words like engagement and ring popping out. *Fuck.* "Oh. No, that's not—"

But surprisingly she waves a hand, cutting me off. "I get it, *believe me.*"

Right. I'll bet she does.

She steps back and reaches for her bag again, and panic jolts through me. She's going to leave. She's going to leave, and there's no reason we would have to talk to each other again. We've gone years without speaking, and it's only through coincidence and, well, me chasing her down that we've spoken at all in the last week.

I can picture it, too. Etta will leave and I'll end up marrying Rosaline fucking Hathaway because there's no good reason not to and my mother will guilt me into it. She'll say something about how Marcia died and she wants a full family again, and my father will threaten to cut off my inheritance and I'll cave because there's nothing objectively wrong with Rosaline. And Etta will marry Harrison Dane, and whoever ends up being the head of the council won't ultimately matter because we'll all end up there in a few years, anyway, when our parents retire. And I'll fight with Etta on the council about shit I don't care about, just like I fought with her in debate club and model UN and every other fucking after school activity, and go home and fuck my boring wife about it, just like I fucked my boring prep school girlfriends pretending they were her. And maybe we won't literally kill anyone or get in fist fights at fundraisers, but people will still gossip about our feud and how the Montagues hate the Capulets—or the Danes, I guess, if that's what she's called. They'll still talk about the curse, for generations on generations, until no one really knows what happened or why we all hate each other.

Or, I could stop her from leaving.

"Etta," I say, having no idea what I'm going to say to keep her here.

But at the same moment, she spins back to me, her expression hard and determined. It's the same look she used to get right before a debate final, or when I would tease her and she was trying not to cry: Heavy concentration.

"Roman," she says, in a flat emotionless tone unlike anything I've heard from her in years. "I actually wanted to talk to you about what I saw on your phone. See...I was wondering. If you wanted... maybe if you didn't want to go through with...you know. I was thinking that..."

I blink at her, trying to follow what the hell she's trying to say.

Etta takes a deep breath. "I was thinking we should get married."

I can't breathe.

I stare at her, sure I must have imagined her words. It's finally happened, my diet of clove cigarettes and protein shakes combined with booze and lack of sleep has caused me to halluci-nate. This should be a wake-up call, probably. Inspiration alone can't save me, I can't literally sustain myself on Etta's life-force. I'm going the way of Poe or Wilde, but without the ambiance to make it anything other than depressing.

The object of my obsession takes a deep breath and shakes her head, like she's trying to clear it. "Roman?" she asks. "Did you hear me?"

The color is rising in her cheeks, in a way that's as confusing as it is endearing.

"No," I blurt out. "I'm not sure I did."

She wrings her hands in her skirt. "Right. Never mind then. Have a nice afternoon."

Fuck. She's closer to the exit than I am, and the urge to physically grab her and make her stay is almost overwhelming. "No, wait," I say instead. "You want to get married." It's not really a question, more of a statement.

She hovers on the balls of her feet, still looking like she's about to bolt. "Yes?"

I lean backwards, sitting on the back of the armchair behind me. It's not exactly comfortable, but I'm starting to feel like my legs can't hold my own weight. "Why?"

Stop it, you fucking idiot! I scream at myself. *Don't ask why. Go with it, take her and run.*

She takes a breath through her nose, and I get the feeling she's decided to go all in as she walks around to the opposite side of the little circle of chairs so she's facing me, her back to the fire exit, both hands planted on the back of the armchair across from mine, and I'm forced to swivel to keep her in view.

"Don't you see?" she asks. "It's perfect."

I blink at her. I do see. Yes, it's fucking perfect. She's perfect. But I don't think that's what she means. "I don't understand."

"I saw your phone, and I know I only saw one half of the conversation, but it looked to me like we're in very similar situations."

"...what situation is that?"

She waves her hands in the air, agitated. "A sudden unwanted engagement mandated by the powers that be."

I'm not sure if she means the Order, our respective parents, the council, or all of the above, but I can't help but see the irony no matter what she means. I bark a laugh. "So, you're suggesting the same thing in a different font?"

"No, I'm suggesting a better option. An option where we can exert some control over the whole thing."

I lick over my lips and try to force myself to focus. Married. Married to Etta. To Juliette Capulet, and I didn't even have to be the one to suggest it.

Earlier I was coming up with my own plan to this effect, but I can't honestly say now whether I would have gone through with asking her or not. If she hadn't said it first, it would have sounded absurd. It still sounds absurd, but in a wonderful sort of way.

Still, I feel like I need to tell her she has at least one thing wrong. "I'm not engaged."

She reels back, all the color draining from her face. "You're not? Oh my gods. I thought...never mind. I'm so sorry."

I look down at the phone and only have to take a quick glance to understand what she thought. "It's complicated. I'm not engaged *yet*, but it's not dissimilar to your situation I suppose."

"Okay..." her expression turns slightly hopeful again. "And you don't *want* to marry Rosaline?"

I shake my head. If she only knew how much I don't. How this exact conversation is something out of my perfect fantasy and nightmare at the same time. This is my Faustian bargain, and she is my vice.

"Do you really hate Dane that much?" I ask, incredulous.

She bites her lip, and glances to the side, uncomfortable. "No, it's not that."

From her expression, it's not *not* that, though. A hint of smug satisfaction rises in my chest. "Then what is it?"

She furrows her brow, and there's a spark of frustration behind her eyes. "They won't let me go back to school."

My mouth turns into a thin line. I'm not sure if by "they" she means her parents, or Dane, or both, but either way I'm humming with anger. I recall my father mentioning this—mentioning his friend in the Dean's office saying Etta wasn't registered for classes, but I didn't fully understand the magnitude of it until now. I simply...couldn't understand it. Not only has Etta always loved school, she's known for it, she fucking excels at it, but our community prizes education. Not allowing her to finish is not only unusual, it's...

"That's—" I can't think of a word bad enough and just stare at her.

She purses her lips, her tone, clipped and almost bored. "Fucked, I know." From Etta, who swears so sparingly, the word has more impact. "I'm glad you agree."

I examine her, trying to read her intentions in her wide, gray eyes. I shake my head. *Focus.* "That can't be all," I scoff, trying to seem unbothered. Amused. "Letting you finish school isn't unusual. There are half a dozen guys in this library alone who would probably pay your tuition if you went on one date with them."

She cocks her head to the side, looking vaguely confused. "Is that a compliment?"

I wave her off. "A fact."

Pink spots appear on her cheeks and I don't understand. She has to know people want her, right? She can't not know.

"You told me the other day we're studying the same thing. I assume you'll have to travel at some point for your research?"

I nod slowly. "So, you're trying to tell me you want to get *married*. Legally married, because I would pay for you to go to school and take you with me to England?"

"I didn't ask you to pay," she says quickly, her hair bouncing with every word. "I'd figure that out on my own. I just want to finish school and do my research."

"You realize that makes this less believable, right?" I ask, running my fingers through my hair so hard I think I might have no hair left when this conversation is over. "I might have believed you if you asked for money."

"Oh," she says, looking furious with herself. Like she can't believe she didn't think to ask for money.

I stare, in awe of how someone can exist in this fucked up town and still have the kind of integrity where they wouldn't even think to ask for money. In awe of both how insanely beautiful she is and how absurd this afternoon has become in only a few short minutes. "If it's not money and it's not school then what's this about?"

"It is about school," she says fiercely. "Partly."

Fine. It's partly about school. I don't dare to hope that the other part is because she wants me the way I've always wanted her. Even with what I heard the other night, even with the way she looked at me in the car last night, I'm not delusional. That was lust.

If I've gleaned anything from literature—learned anything from the countless tales of heroes and villains, comedy and tragedy, it's that kings do not launch armies over lust. Money, power, and love —those are the things that send men into war.

What Etta is talking about is a marriage, and not just any marriage, but one that won't be accepted by anyone in either of our families—that could cause catastrophic fallout. Lust is not a good enough reason for that fallout, and neither is school, or going to England.

Money could be, in the right context.

Or love.

Etta has *never* given any indication that she felt anything real toward me. Not even back when we spent days hidden on the top floor of the library, she was always untouchable.

Honestly, as fucked up as it is, that's part of why I liked her to begin with. I'm not unaware of being attractive, or of how that makes people project personalities onto you before they've ever even spoken to you. Etta is the only woman I've ever met who wasn't a little too impressed at first, and then disappointed later when I wasn't the same person she imagined. She just hated me from the word "go." It was refreshing. Exhilarating.

Etta's spine goes rigid and she draws herself up to her full height. "I'm running out of family members."

It's my turn to frown. "What do you mean?"

"Councilman Lawrence might think he's made things better with this threat against anyone hurting each other, but it's a bottle-neck. The next fight will just be worse. I frankly don't know how Lawrence didn't realize that," she says bitterly. "All that will happen here is more violence, and more than likely one of our families will be expelled from the council entirely."

I rub a hand over the back of my neck, feeling slightly guilty about the conversation I had with my father only the other day. Granted, I don't doubt Tyberius is planning something similar.

"All my parents care about is politics. My marriage is a means to an end," Etta says. "They want allies on the council and they want to be able to investigate the missing girls."

"Via your mother as head of the council," I point out.

"Sure," she concedes. "But your parents want the exact same thing, right? Aside from who is technically in charge. In another world they'd be working together."

I shrug. It's an interesting point. "But I don't care about your parents. Or mine for that matter. Their happiness is immaterial to me."

"But you'd rather they were alive, right?" she snaps.

Sometimes I think she gives me too much credit. "I suppose."

She looks down, and I know she's thinking of her cousin Tyberius. Hell, at the same moment I'm thinking of Bennet. Of my sister. Of all my own dead family members.

It's hard to exactly prove any direct responsibility for the deaths. For all the public fighting, we're not the godsdamn mafia. Everyone has high enough profile jobs that literal murder would be out of the question. But still, I know what Etta means. With the exception of Marcia, just because none of the deaths could be pinned on the feud, didn't mean it wasn't abundantly clear what was happening.

"I want the fighting to stop. I want no more pointless deaths or violence or secrets. If we were to be married they would have to stop, if not for the sake of our happiness then because they needed our cooperation on the damn council. We're both only children —" She winces, apologetically. "So, our house seats won't go to anyone else. Plus, the core alliances on the council stem from us. In theory, if we started voting together, there would be total bipartisan agreement. It's too good of an opportunity; our parents will *have* to get over it."

I stare at her, and my heart pounds too loud in my ears. She's right of course. It makes perfect sense. So much sense that I can't believe no one suggested it before. Well, maybe I can believe it, because that would require everyone to get their heads out of their asses and put their issues aside long enough to think.

But can I do that? Can I put my own issues with her family aside? Can I make small talk with Tyberius, and have Christmas with her sadistic parents, and bury everything from the last ten years if it means I get Etta as a reward?

"Roman?" she asks. "Are you still with me?"

Yes. Yes, I'm with you. Yes, I want this.

She's dancing back and forth between her feet, nervous and painfully uncomfortable. Like she wants to bolt and pretend this conversation never happened. Suddenly, I'm getting to my feet and taking a step toward her.

"Have you thought about this," I ask, my words coming out low and a little rough.

"Yes," she says firmly. "Of course I have. Were you listening just now? I—"

"No," I interrupt her and she jumps at the harsh command of my tone. I almost laugh at that. If she is shocked by that, then she really isn't prepared for what it would mean to be bound to each other. "Have you really thought about it? Being perfect on paper doesn't mean shit if we don't work as a couple."

"What about the ceremony?" I croak, my mouth going completely dry.

"Oh." A flush rises to her cheeks and she looks down and away. "I mean. I figured we could just..."

"Just what?" I ask her.

"Figure it out?" she breathes. "That part doesn't seem all that hard to me."

I let out a strangled laugh. Bad choice of words.

I run my tongue over my lips, suddenly harder than I've ever been in my entire life, because I get the feeling she has thought about how we might "figure it out." A lot. Was that possibly what she was thinking about the other night when I heard her whisper my name? Does she want this?

She looks up at me with wide eyes, her pupils dilated, her breathing uneven, and seems unable to find the words. But I need her to. I need to hear it, though I already know what she's thinking, because there's really only one option; It might be possible to have a fake, sexless marriage in a secular community, but not in the Order.

This wouldn't be a sham relationship or a marriage of convenience, like in some Austen novel. What she's asking for would be real. Till Death Do Us Part.

CHAPTER TWENTY-THREE
ETTA

PRESENT

ROMAN TAKES A SLOW, CAREFUL, STEP FORWARD. His eyes dart over me and I can't think. I can hardly breathe when he's watching me like this, when he's standing so close that it would be only too easy to close the distance between us.

My breathing is ragged, my eyes wide, and I truly feel like I must look like prey to him, with the way he's stalking me. Yet, I'm not scared. Not exactly. A little embarrassed, certainly. Overwhelmed. But mostly, excited.

"I thought we would just..."

"Figure it out?" he finishes for me, his lip tipping up at the corner.

"Yes," I say almost defensively, taking a step back until I nearly hit the wall. "Why? Do you have a better idea?"

He chuckles, and I would give any amount of money in the world to know what he's thinking.

My inner teenager, the part of me that was relentlessly teased and tormented by this man from the age of twelve onward, wonders if he's just making fun of me. That part of me wars with my adult brain. The part of me that knows what his expression means, and who can tell the difference between a laugh of contempt and a sexy laugh, meant to make my thighs clench and send shivers up my spine. He may not like me, but I'm almost positive that Roman Montague wants me—at least a little. That's certainly an improvement from three years ago, but it's not enough to make him agree to marry me.

"So, are you in?" I ask, rolling my shoulders back. "Or am I wasting my time here?"

He takes another step closer. "Oh, I'm in, good girl."

I relax slightly, even as a tiny part of me wonders *why*. I'm not sure I've made my case strongly enough, and the debater in me wants to hammer home my win. "Good," I say instead. "Fantastic. That's just great." I'm babbling and I want to die.

"On two conditions," he says.

My stomach lurches. There it is: the catch.

I knew this was too easy. Knew I hadn't made my point strong enough.

I've laid out all my reasons for wanting this marriage, and they're all valid. I'll protect my family. I can go to school. I'll get away from miserable Harrison, and Roman would probably take me to England with him like I always wanted.

I didn't even mention all my other reasons for wanting this marriage. All the smaller, pettier things, that I was almost too ashamed to add to my own pro/con list in the privacy of my bedroom.

Like, that there's part of me that would really like to see the shock on my mother's face. Like, every fantasy I've ever had late at night about Roman, and finally getting some closure on my humiliation three years ago. Like, I would love nothing more than for no one to ever be able to call me a good girl or the perfect daughter, again. The perfect daughter would marry Harrison Dane and live in perpetual silent car rides and eat dinner at restaurants for eighty-year-olds. I don't know what kind of woman marries Roman Montague, but I think she's probably a lot more interesting.

But none of those things matter to Roman.

He doesn't care about his family the way I do—not now that his sister is gone. I'm getting far more out of this than he is, and what the hell is he getting in return? Me? Why would he want me? Maybe we used to talk on occasion, but we haven't spent any real time together in years. Between those talks he was nothing but cruel and indifferent toward me. Why would he want me, when he could have anyone—when he could have Rosaline Hathaway instead?

Oh my gods, maybe I'm making an idiot out of myself, and there's no logic that would make this work for him because he hates me that much. Fuck, I need to go fling myself into traffic.

"What do you want?" I ask, and try to keep the accusatory note out of my voice.

"First," he says. "I don't want to tell anyone this is an arrangement."

That's not what I expected. "So, what are we supposed to say? We've been secretly in love for years?"

He puts one hand on the wall, leaning forward so he's looming over me. "Sounds good to me."

"And you really think people will believe that? Forget the general public, what about your friends?"

His expression is unreadable. "I think you would be surprised what people will believe."

My anxiety bubbles just on the edge of boiling at the idea of lying to everyone I know. My thoughts dart immediately to Cat, and I try to imagine telling her I've been secretly dating Roman and can't. The image crumbles—it's impossible. "Cat won't believe it."

"Catalina Minola?"

I nod, feeling incredibly short as we stand in this position. "There's absolutely no chance."

He ponders this, licking over his bottom lip. "Just her, then."

I blink, distracted by his mouth. "Okay, fine. And the other condition?"

He leans even further in, and I could swear my personal space has completely evaporated. I'm caught somewhere between the urge to duck out from under his arm and get some air, and say fuck all and push up on my toes to close the two inches of space left between us.

"Let's call this less of a condition and more of a suggestion," he says, his voice low and rough. "I don't believe you've really thought this through."

"I did, I made a list—"

He cuts me off. "It's a public ceremony. Can you handle that?"

Whether I can handle the ritual has never really been the question. I would have to participate in the same bonding ceremony no matter who I married. When I picture the scene with Harrison or some other faceless groom it feels like a mandate. Something clinical to be endured.

When I imagine it with Roman...I shiver bodily. "Of course I can. It's one night."

He misinterprets the reason for my trembling. "I don't know, good girl. You look like you're already thinking about running screaming for your ivory tower."

"You say that like it's some kind of orgy."

I'm joking. Kind of.

The Order marriage ceremony isn't an orgy. It's not even sex in a traditional sense, although it definitely takes the phrase "you may kiss the bride" to an extreme that would scandalize most other religious groups beyond repair. Except that now, the way Roman is talking about it, the way he's watching me, I'm starting to wonder if I misunderstood something. I need to double check the rules...

He sets his jaw. "No orgies. I don't share."

I raise an eyebrow, even my forearm prickles. "Fine. Whatever you say."

He still looks unconvinced. "I might suggest a few practice runs first. To make sure everything looks...authentic."

My breath catches and he raises an eyebrow as if to say "see?"

But it's not fear that has me holding my breath. It's anticipation. I close my eyes for half a second, forcing myself to think. To breathe again, before I force false confidence into my voice. "Is that all?"

He fully laughs now, like he can see right through my bluff. "That's all."

The part of me that's, well, good, knows I should tell him to go to hell. That, "practicing" is a flimsy as fuck excuse, and if we wanted to fuck we could just do that. But there's also a part of me that wonders if he has half a point. It wouldn't make much sense for secret lovers to look like they've never even kissed. And I suppose, if I can work up the nerve to ask for a marriage, I should be able to admit what else I want.

My eyes dart to the opening between shelves that leads to the rest of the library. I've never seen anyone else up here, but that doesn't change the fact that it is a public building. There are undoubtedly other people nearby. On this floor, certainly, and someone *could* walk in on us at any moment.

And something about that makes fucking my enemy turned secret fiancé so much hotter.

I step into him, tilting my face up. "Here?" I ask breathlessly. "Starting now?"

He exhales sharply and his eyes flare, somehow showing equal heat and surprise. A jolt of excitement travels through my system as he shifts closer, like that was all the confirmation he was waiting for. "Well, it is a public ceremony."

He presses into me and I can feel him hard against my side as he uses his free hand to push my hair away from my ear and whispers low so I can feel his voice everywhere. "I need you to be quiet, for me."

I nod as he reaches down, sliding a hand up my nearly bare thigh and tracing fingers along the edge of my panties. My tights provide the thinnest barrier—enough to drive me crazy with wanting him closer, but not enough that he can't feel exactly how wet I already am just from this alone.

I whimper, just the smallest noise.

He smiles at that. "Good girl, Etta."

I gasp.

In magic, intent matters more than the actual words. "Good girl," has always seemed like an insult to me. Like he's calling me a teacher's pet or a goodie-two-shoes. Except now, it doesn't sound like that at all. Maybe it was never intended to. It sounds beyond a pet-name. As much a declaration as a term of endearment.

Praise and a prayer.

I lean forward, moaning a little as he moves his hand up to cup my core, stroking fingers back and forth enough to drive me insane. This is so incredibly unlike me. Or rather, unlike the persona I have portrayed publicly for so long that it has become my default.

"More," I say, desperate for him to actually touch me for real.

But instead of giving me what I crave, he slows his fingers, moving back a fraction of an inch. "Before my self-control goes to shit, are you on birth control?"

My brain comes to a screeching halt, half because of how he phrased that question. I love the idea of him losing control. I want to see that, more than I'd care to admit. Maybe not in this library, but where? When?

But then, I process the rest of his question. "Uh...what?"

Part of me is wondering what the hell is wrong with me right now that I'm the one not thinking about that. Me. The one who thinks about everything. Me, who makes pro con lists and actually uses the cross-compare feature on amazon and is in a long-term relationship with my label maker. This is catastrophic on so many levels.

The other part of me is wondering why he's even asking.

Birth control of any kind is a human necessity. I would need it to have sex with someone not pledged...but Roman shouldn't have that problem. Every guy in our prep school knows the rune for contraception, it's like a rite of passage.

He keeps staring at me, so I just shake my head. "No, but you can just—"

Suddenly my feet are leaving the floor. "Ah!"

Roman picks me up with seemingly no difficulty, and spins us around. I barely have a second to panic about him thinking I'm too heavy, or about how I've gained weight this year, feel self-conscious before he's depositing me on one of the huge arm chairs.

"That wasn't very quiet, Juliette."

I stare at him, a little disheveled, and feeling shocked by our sudden switch in positions. "But—"

Standing in front of me, while I'm seated, I'm painfully aware that I'm face level with his cock which is still clearly visible through his pants. It's a herculean task to look up as he speaks. "What if that sullen librarian heard you scream and comes running up here?"

"Well, at this point there's not much for her to see." I sound more than a little petulant and I don't care.

"Isn't there?"

He smirks, an almost feline smile, and sinks to his knees before me. We're nearly eye to eye as he wraps his hands around my upper calves just below my knees and tugs me forward until I'm sitting just at the edge of the chair, my skirt bunching around my waist. "I want to hear you when you come for me, but I don't want the whole library to hear you. Can you do that?"

Oh my gods. I nod again, my entire body already tense and somehow responsive and malleable at the same time.

"Tell me."

"Yes," I whisper. "I can do that."

His smile is oddly triumphant. "Good. I have a theory, and I never thought I'd get such a perfect opportunity to test it."

I don't know what that means and I don't care. All I care about is that he stops stalling and gets on with it, because the anticipation is going to kill me.

"Next time," he says, running both hands up my thighs, to my stomach, where he finds the top of my tights. "Don't wear these."

I lift my hips, to help as he rolls them down, stopping when they're banded around my ankles. "No promises."

"Next time, I'll tear them in half."

I feel a little jolt of excitement every time he says "next time," but I'm afraid to point it out. Afraid to ask what it means.

I want to keep arguing back, but then, all other thoughts flee because Roman's hands are on me again, and this time there's barely anything left separating us. He loops his fingers in the elastic of my panties and begins to ease them down and over my ass. The air hits me and I shudder in a breath. Then, finally, he tugs me as far as I can be to the edge of the chair, until I'm about to fall off the edge, and supported only by his shoulders holding my knees apart, my bound feet in his lap.

"Fuck," he says under his breath.

I think he's going to elaborate. Maybe give me some other sexy command, or say something quippy. One thing I've never been able to ever find fault with about Roman is his eloquence. He has a comment for everything, and I would expect him to have an entire dictionary's worth of auto-reply phrases ready to go for every sexual scenario under the sun.

But he says nothing else, and I'm oddly satisfied by that.

Instead, he leans forward at last and presses a kiss to my clit. It's a kiss that quickly turns to licking and sucking, and then he shifts, dragging his tongue over me in long strokes.

He slides his hands under my ass, lifting me up, as if to taste me more thoroughly and I dig my fingers into the arms of the chair, my breathing ragged.

My heart is pounding too hard and the rational part of me wants to overthink this already even as it's happening, but the sensation is too much and I can't make my brain function long enough to form a coherent thought.

Waves of pleasure wrack my body, building higher and higher. My hips rise of their own accord, chasing my pleasure. I move my hands from the arms of the chair to his hair and he practically growls at that, seeming spurred on by my reaction.

My knees clamp around his head and sounds I barely recognize come from my mouth and I know I'm not being good. Not following the rules. But Roman isn't bothering to correct me, seeming too distracted himself to care.

He pulls his hand out from under me and I already know what's coming before he teases my entrance with his fingers. I gasp, pressing my hand over my mouth to keep from crying out.

Roman seems to hear that, because he stops licking me and looks up. I want to cry when he stops because I'm so, *so*, close.

He smiles, and I swear he's never looked hotter than when he's between my legs, chin wet, his hair a mess from where I've grabbed it. He keeps teasing me with his fingers, slowly petting over my pussy, occasionally dipping inside just enough to make me squirm.

"Don't do that," he says.

I gasp for breath, and try to focus. "What?"

"Don't cover your mouth. I want to hear you, Etta. It's up to you to make sure no one comes running."

I blink. Holy shit. "And what if I do cover my mouth?"

He stops moving his fingers. "Then I'll stop."

I completely believe him, and I hate that I'm not stubborn enough to tell him to fuck off and stop touching me right now if he's going to play games like that. I lower my hands back to the arms of the chair. "Better?"

His smile grows wider. "Good girl."

Gods, I'm fucked.

Without warning, he pushes his fingers all the way inside me and my back bows, my intake of breath so loud that I might as well have screamed. And then his tongue is back on my clit, his lips are kissing and sucking over me, and my hips are moving without my permission.

I feel like I could speak in tongues and it would make absolute sense, like I'm nothing but sensation and color. My breathing is too sharp and too much, and then I'm rising and falling back down, shattering with his name on my lips.

I lie there for a good minute, knowing I should move and unable to, my legs shaking, until I hear his voice.

"I knew it."

Chapter Twenty-Four

✦ ROMAN ✦

Senior Year of High School, Four Years Ago

The hushed whispers of the library are a goddamn lullaby for the weary, but not for me.

My fingers drum a staccato rhythm on the mahogany table, each beat echoing my pent-up frustration. I'm trying to study, but the words blur before my eyes, as if taunting me with their simplicity.

I don't do well with "simple."

Everything in this whole school is too damn easy; every historical date, every scientific formula, they all line up in my head like obedient soldiers. I should've skipped a grade—hell, maybe two. Then, perhaps, the boredom wouldn't gnaw at my insides like a ravenous beast.

I'm sitting at a table at the back of the school library, half-a-dozen books spread out before me. I don't often study here—hell, I don't often study at all, as there's hardly any subject I can't ace without even trying, but my final in Modern World History is the exception to the long-standing rule. History is all about memorizing names and dates, rather than basic intellect. No IQ score can read this shit for me—unfortunately.

And then she walks in.

Etta walks gracefully, her long, wavy blond hair flying out behind her without wind, like there's some kind of soundtrack playing only for her. It's like a goddamn Disney movie—next thing I know, she'll be singing to mice.

I scowl, and look away, only to glance up again a moment later; a man possessed.

Etta stops to talk to the librarian, then makes her way over to the American history section. She selects a book from the shelf, her slender fingers brushing the spine with an almost reverent touch. I watch, venom rising in my throat, as several guys turn to look at her. My hand clenches around my pen so tightly I'm half afraid it'll snap.

"Get your shit together," I breathe, the words barely a whisper.

Ten minutes later, a stack of books lands on the table in front of me with a loud thwack. I jump, and look up, dropping my pen against the mahogany wood. "What the hell?"

"Hello, Satan," Etta says cheerfully. "Happy Monday."

I freeze, my heart hammering against my ribs like it's desperate to escape. I gaze up at her, then drag a hand down my face, blinking several times to clear the cobwebs from my eyes. "I don't *feel* asleep..." I mutter. "This must be one of those hyper-realistic dreams. Take your shirt off."

She scowls at me, for half a second, before she masks her annoyance. "I'm going to choose not to have heard that."

My eyes narrow. What the fuck is going on? "Are you lost? The children's section is on the other side of the library."

She ignores me. "Mind if I sit here?"

"Actually, I do," I say without looking up, hoping the ice in my tone will send her scuttling away.

But Etta has never been one to be frightened off that easily.

She takes a seat across from me and pulls out her textbooks with deliberate slowness. I drive my pen through the paper in front of me, accidentally creating a blue ink-stained hole in the center of my notes. Fucking perfect.

"What are you working on?" she asks cheerfully.

I gape at her, uncomprehending of what she's trying to accomplish with this. "Are you fucking with me?"

She looks almost amused, but her voice is tinged with exasperation. "When I'm fucking with you, you'll know it."

I blink, and heat floods me, blood rushing straight to my cock. I close my eyes, willing it away. I'm not sure I've ever heard her swear before—damn, now I want to know what else I could make her say...

No. No, I can't think like that.

"Are you a masochist, good girl?" I bite out. "I can't think of any other reason why you'd willingly come over here."

She opens her notebook and reaches into her bag for a pen. "I'm going to be nice to you whether you like it or not."

"Why?" I demand, practically shaking with indignation.

"I'm just choosing civility over animosity. It makes life easier, don't you think?"

"Life isn't meant to be easy," I counter, my voice a low growl. "It's a battlefield. You of all people should know that."

The air between us crackles with something unspoken, something that should not exist between two sworn enemies.

"Maybe," she concedes, the warmth in her gaze disarming. "But we could all use a ceasefire now and then."

CHAPTER TWENTY-FIVE
✦ ROMAN ✦

PRESENT

FOR THE FIRST TIME IN LONGER THAN I CARE TO remember, I wake up early.

It's not the kind of "early" I've started to convince myself is good enough—9:00AM instead of 12:00PM, like it's some grand achievement to defeat the afternoon. It's not like when I wake up at 5:00AM, anxious and confused, before falling back asleep until 1:00PM, wondering if I was ever awake to begin with. No, today I'm up by 7:00AM, and the ever-present fog in my mind is lessened.

That is, until I realize I have no idea what to do with myself at this hour.

I don't know what kind of person is awake at 7:00AM, but it's not me. The time brings to mind old ladies gardening, good church-going citizens, early morning joggers, and parents with small children. While I am none of those things, renouncing them completely is also a bit much. I am one step away from claiming to be raised and molded by the darkness, and even to myself that sounds both over dramatic and absurd.

Yesterday afternoon, once Etta had come apart screaming against my tongue and we'd agreed on the broad strokes of the plan, she pulled her clothes back on and went back to business, explaining to me the details of how she wanted to move forward. In a way, I was wrong. She had thought a lot of it through—starting with how, if at all possible, we should avoid having Councilman Lawrence perform the ceremony.

I'm just completing my third lap back and forth between my room and the kitchen when the front door opens. I look up, unsurprised to see Bennet walking in, pulling earbuds from his ears. He is an early morning runner—it's astounding we get along.

He sees me, and jumps, eyes going wide. "What the fuck." It's neither a question nor a true exclamation—just a kind of loud statement. Like he's not quite able to process what he's seeing. "What are you doing?"

I laugh. "Nothing?"

He seems more alarmed by my laugh even than my presence and I wonder if that's indicative of my mood lately, or my mood this morning. Am I usually miserable, or especially happy today? Both?

"No, really." He kicks off his muddy sneakers by the door and crosses the kitchen, pulling out a chair. "What are you doing?"

"Just thinking." I cross to the fridge and pull it open. Inside there's a stark contrast between my cousin's food and mine. I'm subsisting on takeout and protein shakes, while Bennet actually cooks. There are heaps of ingredients in here I haven't bothered to notice in months. I pull my head back out of the fridge. "Can I use your eggs?"

He blinks, surprised. "Sure. Take whatever you want."

I take him literally and start pulling eggs, cheese, and half the crisper drawer worth of vegetables out and pile them on the granite countertop beside the stove. I'm not incapable of cooking, I just don't—at least, not lately, but this morning I'm having the worst craving for something aside from flavorless, vanilla protein powder.

Bennet watches as I dig around in the cabinet over the stove for a cutting board and begin chopping an onion to make an omelet. "What's different this morning?"

I don't know how to explain to him what's different without sounding like a fifteen-year-old girl in a teen movie. And moreover, I don't know what to say, period. I know Etta and I agreed to pretend this had been going on for a long time, and that it was my idea to do so. It's a good idea, and I stand by it...but at least in Bennet's case, I'm not sure.

I glance over my shoulder, debating my answer. Bennet's watching me expectantly.

"Do you want the complex truth or the simpler lie?" I ask.

He cocks his head to the side and actually thinks about it. We are very different people. I wouldn't have thought about it for a second. I would always want the truth, no matter what it cost me. Bennet would genuinely not want to know something if it's going to be inconvenient or illegal. He should become a lawyer.

"What's it about?" he asks.

I reach for a package of mushrooms and savagely rip into the plastic, dumping them out on my cutting board. A few roll across the counter and I don't bother to collect them. "Etta Capulet."

"Truth."

I smile, and tell him the story while I finish making an omelet.

LATER THAT AFTERNOON, MY KNEE BANGS AGAINST THE edge of my desk, over and over, the noise creating a dull pounding rhythm in the back of my mind. I'm more aware of the sound than the feeling. The relentless, throbbing, sensation of metal on denim covered flesh. Not quite painful, but not comfortable either.

That in and of itself is enough to make me vaguely aware that I'm dissociating. That I don't really know how long I've been doing this, or how much time has passed. That I've missed whatever the professor said for the last few minutes or perhaps the last hour.

I need a cigarette.

There's a clock on the wall that lets me know it's only been about ten minutes, and that's a relief. Every moment of time I've spent in this lecture hall over the last semester has made me question my conviction to avoid practical magic. To return to school rather than following the path laid out for me since birth. Sometimes, in moments of clarity, I know it was a decision made out of panic and grief and not enough sleep. A decision I made when the only sources of inspiration I had were death and dying.

The decision to return to school seemed to make sense, even if a master's in occult literature isn't an ideal choice in the eyes of my family. The only son of house Montague can't become a High Priest, or devote his life to research—especially not now that I'm suddenly an only child, and without an heir our house will die with me.

Yet, Professor Abram, another Order member, was more than supportive of my desire to question our existence. Why are we here and who is pulling our puppet strings? I only wish I wasn't so bored. After an entire semester of this, I've never been more uncertain. Uncertain of the Order and of why we pledge our lives to its service when no one seems particularly happy. Uncertain of what I want to do and what even matters. And uncertain of the path laid out for me, of those I've been taught to hate and ordered to love, and if those mandates can possibly be correct when they feel like life sentences.

Chairs scrape around me and I startle, realizing that everyone is standing up to leave. The class must be over, and I can't remember a single thing that was discussed. I grind my teeth, hoping I'll be able to piece it together from the reading.

Professor Abram is standing by the podium gathering worn out parchment into his faded leather bag. I throw my own bag over my shoulder and make my way up to the front of the room.

"Hey!" someone calls behind me. "Roman!"

I stop, and turn automatically at the sound of my name, and freeze as a familiar face smiles at me.

Rosaline Hathaway darts toward me between the crowd flooding out of the lecture hall. Though we're inside, she's wearing a wool coat and a thick knitted scarf wrapped halfway around her face. Her short, blunt bangs combined with the scarf, give the illusion that she's wearing some sort of ski mask. She's carrying a leather book bag over one shoulder, and I recall vaguely that last I heard she was getting a degree in...something. Education, maybe. I raise a hand in an unenthusiastic greeting. "Hey, Rose. I didn't know you were in this class."

She reaches me and stops short, about three feet away. "I'm not. I had a meeting in the same building."

"Right." I wrack my brain to remember the name of the guy I thought she'd been dating for the last few years. "How's Samuel?"

"Sampson," she corrects.

Whatever.

She wrinkles her nose. "Engaged. I guess he was betrothed at birth and never felt the need to mention it."

I raise an eyebrow. I almost have the energy to tell her that guy is a dick—I probably would, but her timing is bad. She's preventing me from catching Professor Abram. "Oh."

She laughs sardonically. "You always could be counted on to say the least comforting thing, Roman. At least you're consistent."

I stare flatly at her. I don't know what she wants me to say. Sorry? Behind me, Abram is almost done putting his papers in his bag. "Listen, I need to go."

"Wait," Rosaline says urgently as I'm already backing away. "I've been trying to reach you. We have to figure out what we're going to do. I know it's not official yet, but you have to know that your dad talked to my dad...right?" She widens her eyes, seeming almost worried for a moment that maybe I *don't* know. "We're going to be engaged soon."

Yeah, absolutely fucking not.

"Do you want that?" I blurt out.

She gives me an odd look, like she's trying to solve a difficult math equation. "What do you mean?"

Fuck, I wasn't trying to turn this into a longer conversation. I glance back to where Abram was standing. Fuck—he's gone. I press my lips together, and shrug my bag higher on my shoulder, impatient to leave.

"Do you want to get married?"

She laughs. "Please, Roman. *Wanting* things is for infants and advertising executives."

Alright, this conversation needs to end. "Right. Well, text me."

Her eyes narrow. "I have texted you. You don't answer."

"I lost my phone. I've got it back now." I'm already backing away. "I really need to go."

I know I should feel bad for leaving Rosaline standing there alone, but I can't. Even if the stars hadn't somehow just aligned for me, and Etta hadn't miraculously thrown herself into my path without my having to lift a finger, I wouldn't have wanted to marry Rosaline. But now especially, I'll never be able to look at another woman and not compare her to Etta. Not now that I've tasted her. Not now that I know the little noises she makes when she comes, know how soft her skin is, or what my name sounds like on her lips. I've imagined her for years, but nothing could compare to the real thing, and I won't give her up. I can't.

Professor Abram's office is on the ground floor at the end of a maze of twisting halls, nowhere near the classroom I'm used to seeing him in. His door is open, but I knock on the frame, anyway, more out of habit than manners.

He looks up from where he's sitting at his huge, dark oak desk, and jumps. "Roman. I don't think I was expecting you. Did you have a question about the lecture?"

"Hi." I take a step into the room. "No, you weren't. Do you have a sec?"

Professor Abram is an average man in pretty much every way. Average build, average height, neither attractive nor particularly unattractive. He dresses like I'd expect a professor to dress, usually in tweed and carrying some sort of scuffed leather briefcase. He smiles as I walk in, and pushes his glasses up the bridge of his nose. "Sure, what can I do for you?"

I glance at the open door. "Can I shut this?"

"Allow me." Abram draws a half-circle in the air, causing the door to swing shut, and frowns as I sit down. "Is this about your paper, because it was fine."

"I need your advice," I say slowly. "Or, opinion, I guess."

He raises his eyebrows. "About school?"

"No."

"What's going on?"

I pause for a moment, wishing I'd planned better how to ask for what I want—what Etta and I agreed I would ask him.

I know that Professor Abram is in the Order. He's not part of one of the founding families, but you don't have to be to practice. In this case, his lack of ties to any of the founding families is exactly why I want to talk to him. Abram knows who we are. He knows who Etta is. He's a theology professor and a member of the Order, so he'll know how all the rituals work, and best of all I actually like him, which is more than I can say for 80% of the rest of this miserable damn town.

"Is Councilman Lawrence the only person who can perform a handfasting?"

His eyebrows raise. "Why?"

"Just, in theory."

"No. Not if both parties were already members of the Order."

My eye twitches slightly. This, right here, is the entire purpose of this conversation. A marriage ceremony—bonding, handfasting, whatever you want to call it—and an induction into the Order are not synonymous, yet they often get lumped together because, as far as I know, you do need to be pledged to marry another Order member.

It would be possible to have a bonding in secret and then announce to our families that it was simply too late to stop it, but not to have a secret pledging. The council would need to be involved in that.

"What if one or both of the...er...couple wasn't pledged?"

His eyebrows disappear into his hairline. "Roman, what is this about?"

"Just, theoretically. What then?"

"Theoretically..." Abram considers, and I know he doesn't believe this is hypothetical. "The handfasting would amount to nothing more than a spiritual marriage. Like a human ceremony. Which might be fine if that's what you were intending."

I deflate. I was afraid of that. I don't personally care, but Etta will argue that it will matter because our families will try to say it's breakable. Order marriages can't be ended through divorce.

I rise from my seat and turn toward the door. "Thanks for your help."

"Roman?" Professor Abram says. "Should I assume that you've decided to return to the service of the Order?"

I turn back to him, and am slightly taken aback to find that he's watching me with an intensity I haven't seen before. Like this answer matters to him—I can't fathom why. He's a decent professor, sure. Was helpful after my sister's death, but he has no stake in the council or anything else that might be affected by this.

I shrug. "Considering it."

CHAPTER TWENTY-SIX
⋆ROMAN⋆

SENIOR YEAR OF HIGH SCHOOL, FOUR YEARS AGO

SOMETIMES I WONDER IF I BELIEVE IN GOD, OR THE gods, or whatever.

It's a stupid thing to contemplate, really, because obviously there are gods — here's an Order, there's fucking magic — they have to be real.

But what if they're not, gods exactly? What if we're following the wrong thing? What if nothing fucking matters and nothing exists?

"Do you ever just, wonder what the point is?"

I peel my cheek off the glass of the passenger side window, and turn to face my cousin fully. He's driving, for once, because I wasn't in the mood.

Bennet looks at me sideways. "Of...what?"

"Existence?"

"Are you high?" Pierce asks from the back seat.

I sigh. No, but fuck, I wish I was. I'm having a godsdamned existential crisis. "Never mind."

I glance at the clock on the dashboard. It's 9:12 on a Friday night. We should already be at a party or something by now, but nothing is going on.

I wonder what Etta does on Friday nights. Probably knits, or reorganizes her closet or some shit. "I'm fucking board," I say, trying to change the subject.

"No one is throwing tonight," Pierce whines. "Well...except Capulet."

I perk up at that. "Etta is having a party?"

Again, Bennet gives me a sideways look, but this time it's more smug than alarmed. "No, Tyberius."

"Oh."

There it is—the cause of my crisis: I can't get her out of my head.

Etta keeps showing up everywhere. Never in public, like I would do, but in the library, or near my locker, or in the parking lot after school. She's just...being nice. She just sits there and studies, or says "Good Morning," or smiles across a room.

The conniving bitch is trying to drive me insane, and it's working. I need to exercise her from my life in the worst way, but at the same time, I constantly look forward to seeing her.

"Let's go," I blurt out.

"To Capulets party?" Pierce asks.

"Yeah."

"No seriously, are you high?" Bennet asks. "That's a stupid fucking idea."

I grin, trying to get them on board with...whatever this is. "Look, I want to do something. He's throwing. It'll be big, I'm sure no one will even notice we're there."

"I'm down," Pierce says.

"You're trying to get us killed," Bennet complains, even as he bangs a U-turn in the middle of the road.

"It's good to test your mortality now and then. Makes you glad to be alive."

To my disappointment, the party isn't at Etta's house.

Bennet pulls up to what looks like just a deserted stretch of woods alongside a dark empty road. The only thing going on is a bunch of SUVs parked along the shoulder, and the sound of distant screams and laughter as soon as we open the doors and get out.

"Why didn't you say this was a woods-hang," Pierce complains, walking around the back of the SUV to open the trunk.

"Cause no one fucking asked," Bennet snaps.

Pierce shrugs, and hoists a thirty-rack out of the trunk. I watch, considering. "Leave it. Capulet can play host tonight."

"Whatever, man."

Trudging through the forest takes about five minutes. I can smell a bonfire now, mingling with the fresh scent of pine. Twigs and dried leaves crunch under foot, and all the while the distant sounds of the party grow ever louder.

The trees part, revealing a clearing in the middle of the forest. It's pitch dark out, but the whole area is illuminated by an enormous bonfire, and the light of four-dozen cell phones. Guys in *North Face* jackets and *Tims* stand around chatting to girls wearing skin-tight skirts and heels. Typical woods-hang.

I scan the crowd, looking for anyone we know.

Sebastian Cesario and the Macbeth twins are over by the keg. I grind my teeth, turning away. I spot Rosaline but pretend not to see her waving. Half these people are from the college, but still, they're familiar. Many faces turn to us—well, to me—and nod in recognition. It's partly that Bennet and I are from a founding family. People always seem to give a shit about that for some reason.

My mood sinks lower and lower. I know who I'm looking for and don't want to admit it, even to myself. Yet, the longer I don't see her the more I wish we hadn't come at all.

"Are we just going to stand here?" Pierce asks.

"Yeah, I—" I break off, my stomach leaping into my throat.

Etta is here.

She's standing in the shadows, with her cousin and some of his friends, half obscured by the smoke from the bonfire. She's not wearing one of those skin-tight dresses, but instead has on jeans, and what looks like a guy's jacket. Who the fuck gave her their jacket?

"Come on," I say, already striding off in the direction of the keg. "I want a fucking beer."

AN HOUR LATER, I'M FOUR BEERS IN, AND ETTA HASN'T moved from her spot across the clearing. I watch her over the rim of my red solo cup, the alcohol making me forget to be discreet in my staring.

"Hey," a cheerful female voice says somewhere to my left.

I glance over, uninterested. "Hey."

I wish I could go anywhere where I didn't know every single person at the party, at least by sight, but that's impossible in Stratford. Tonight is no different. The brunette standing next to me is Maria...something. No, Mariah...no...

"Miranda," she introduces herself, grinning.

There it is. I remember now, Miranda Prospero, she graduated a couple years back.

"Roman," I reply without inflection.

"I know. How have you been?"

I raise an eyebrow. We've never spoken, but she probably doesn't want to just walk up to me and say "Wanna fuck?" so she's going to try and make small talk for a few minutes until I suggest it. I look her over again, assessing this time.

Nice body. Cute face. Not interested.

Craning my neck, I yell over my shoulder: "Bennet!"

My cousin appears next to me, and also looks Mariah up and down. He grins. "Yeah?"

I clap him on the shoulder. "This is Mariah. She wants a beer, give her a hand."

"Miranda," she corrects me.

Whatever. I go back to watching Etta, while Bennet takes care of Maria.

Three more beers later, things are getting a little fuzzy around the edges. Bennet and Pierce have long since disappeared with Maria and one of her friends, and I'm sitting alone near the keg.

I should have brought a book.

"You know this is my cousins party, right?"

My head snaps up so fast I hear it crack. "He doesn't own the woods."

Etta looks down at me, framed by the dying bonfire behind her she looks almost angelic. Or maybe I'm just drunk. "He bought the keg, though."

"I'll toss him a couple bucks if he's really hurting for it."

She rolls her eyes and starts to walk away. I jump to my feet and wobble slightly. "Since when do you come out to these things? I thought you'd be home knitting or some shit."

She scowls. "I have a life, you know, despite your best efforts."

"What's that supposed to mean?"

"Nothing." She raises her cup, as if saluting me, and drinks. I watch the column of her throat work, and for a fleeting moment, I wonder what it would be like to trace the line of her jaw with my fingertips, to feel the heat of her skin beneath my hands.

"Enjoy the party, Roman," Etta says, breaking the spell as she takes another step away from me.

"Wait!"

She pauses, and I riffle through my foggy mind, having no idea what I'd planned to say. But then, before I can think of anything, a shadow falls over Etta.

"Juliette," Tyberius says. "What's going on here?"

"Nothing." Etta lets out an exasperated sigh. "We just bumped into each other."

She marches back toward the fire, clearly hoping that Tyberius will follow her. He doesn't.

"What are you doing here, Montague?"

"Drinking all your shitty beer." I shrug. "What are you doing here with a bunch of high school kids? Aren't you supposed to be in college?"

He flushes slightly, then his eyes narrow. "How's your sister, Montague?"

"My...what?" It takes me a minute to comprehend what he said. "What the fuck do you want with my fifteen-year-old sister?"

"Nice girl," he drawls. "A little naive. You should really tell her not to talk to strangers."

My gut clenches, a reflex of both anger and protectiveness. I can almost taste the bitterness of this conversation on my tongue, mixed with the stale aftertaste of cheap beer. "Stay the fuck away from her, Capulet."

"Or what?"

I don't wait for any further invitation. My fist connects with his jaw, the impact vibrating up my arm as he staggers back and I follow, taking us both to the ground.

His fists find my ribs, mine slams into his stomach. The fight has its own momentum now, something primal and ugly.

In the background, I can hear Etta screaming, and someone— Bennet maybe—trying to calm everyone down, but their voices are just part of the background noise.

I feel more than see the next punch coming. I sidestep, grab his arm, and twist. There's a satisfying yelp of pain as Tyberius crumbles, but it's short-lived. He's back on his feet in seconds, eyes blazing with hatred.

"If you come near my family again, I will fucking kill you," I hiss.

Capulet reaches up and wipes blood from his lip. "Likewise."

CHAPTER TWENTY-SEVEN

✦ ETTA ✦

PRESENT

LAVENDER, ROSEMARY, EGGSHELLS...I LOOK AROUND for my crystals and salt, then gather the rest of my haphazard ingredients, before stuffing them all into a jar without much concern for the order. Herbs and salt spill over the vanity counter alongside my curling iron and several make-up pallets that are probably expired. My reflection in the mirror over the sink looks anxious, which is exactly how I feel. I hardly ever make spell-jars anymore, but if there was ever a time...

I reach for the matches on the shelf above the toilet and light one against the top of my jar before dropping it in. The smoke from the lavender and other herbs rises for a second, before I screw on the lid, trapping it inside. The label on the lid of my recycled jar smiles up at me, proclaiming to calm dry and flaky skin. I snort a laugh. There are Pinterest witches everywhere cringing at my lack of aesthetic. Whatever. Pagan gods do not care if you perfectly layer ingredients or use brand new jars or even if all the ingredients are exact. I could have thrown dirt into the air with intention, and it would have probably been close enough, but I'll feel better knowing I at least made the effort to throw a spell together.

I huff out a sigh and my shoulders slump as I place the jar on the counter with slightly too much force. The crystals inside rattle. This is something like a protection spell plus a 'calm the fuck down bitch' potion. At least, that was the intention. I'll bury it in the garden later, and let it simmer.

Rolling my neck, I exit the ensuite and walk back over to my bed, flopping on top of the haphazardly made covers. Usually, the simple act of making a spell calms me down, even if it's barely more than a prayer as I have no real magic yet to put into it. Still, maybe a marriage of convenience to my enemy and hooking up in the library is beyond the capacity of my jar.

It's been just over twenty-four hours since I left the library, and in that time, I've gone from satisfied to horrified to a basket-case. What seemed like a completely reasonable idea in the secluded corner of the second floor now seems insane. I don't know what I was thinking.

Actually, I do know. I wasn't thinking. People don't do shit like this in real life.

Most people don't make spell-jars or pledge their souls to demons either.

Playing devil's advocate with myself has been exhausting.

It also doesn't help that I haven't heard from Roman at all. Granted, I don't know what I'm expecting him to say. Until he speaks with Professor Abram there's no reason for him to contact me. It's not like we text just to chat, but still. I'm losing it. Especially as I'm fairly sure he must have had class already.

What if he's planning to back out? What if he's regretting the entire scene in the library, or worse, just didn't care about it at all?

If this was literally anyone else, I would assume that the scene in the library yesterday meant that Roman at least sort-of liked me. Yesterday I was fairly sure he wanted me, but what if I was wrong? For better or worse, I've known Roman for most of my life. I've heard the gossip from quite literally hundreds of his dates. It doesn't seem like affection is a prerequisite for sex for him the way it is for me.

Oh my gods, why is it that it only takes a single interaction with Roman Montague to ruin years of work I've done on myself, and turn me back into an insecure teenager?

A distant crash sounds outside and I tense, glancing toward the open balcony doors.

It's not too cold out, and I like the fresh air, so the doors are cracked open. A slight breeze rustles the curtains on occasion, but otherwise, everything seems quiet. It's probably nothing—an animal in the yard, or something from the nearby street.

Without warning, a shadowed figure throws his leg over the edge of my balcony. I jolt, and my mind darts to the women disappearing from the Order, and my blood runs cold.

Holy shit, I'm about to be a statistic!

I turn and sprint toward my bedroom door just as a soft "Oomph," tells me that the prowler has made it over the railing. Terror shoots through me, and I stretch my hand out for the doorknob.

"Etta?"

I register the sound of my name, but not the tone or the voice over my own labored breathing. Panicked, I reach for the nearest item—an oil diffuser on the dresser to my right—and swipe my arm out. The force of my momentum makes the diffuser go flying across the room behind me. Glass shatters, and a man yells. "Ow! What the fuck?"

My mind processes the yell, the breaking glass, and the feeling of huge arms wrapping around my waist, as all happening at once. Later, I realize that makes no sense—that all those things cannot have happened in exactly the same second, and that my panic has warped my memory. But for now, I feel as if I'm drowning in sound and sensation.

"Hey," Roman says. "Breathe."

"What are you doing?" I whisper-scream.

"Sorry, I didn't know how to let you know I was here."

My heartbeat is slowing down now that I've realized it's him, but my panic is slowly being replaced with rage. "It's called a phone."

"I don't have your number." He shrugs, giving me a smile I'm sure he thinks is disarming. "Imagine not having my fiancé's number? Crazy."

"Don't try to be cute," I practically growl. "You terrified me. I thought you were the witch-killer."

His face turns solemn. "I'm sorry. You're right, this was stupid."

I should probably calm down now, but my adrenaline is so high and I'm so surprised by the apology I don't know where to go from here. Since when does Roman Montague apologize? "Why not just use the damn door? Or magic? Or message me on social media?"

He cocks his head to the side. "I assume you blocked me on social media because I can't find you."

I open my mouth to tell him that's insane, and then close it again.

He's right.

I did block him, but it was quite literally ten years ago, and I completely forgot. I don't even remember why I did it. He prob- ably said something to upset me in the eighth grade to get himself blocked, and because I rarely use social media and have had the same accounts since I was twelve...well, here we are.

I put my hands on my hips. "And the door? Or a spell?"

The number of times he's avoided using spells or runes in favor of ridiculous alternatives is starting to seriously concern me. Is it possible he didn't pledge? But why not just say that?

He runs a hand through his hair, and then digs in his pocket for his cloves. I'm stressing him out, obviously. I don't feel the slightest bit guilty about it.

Roman pulls out one of the cloves, but doesn't light it, just flips it between his fingers. "I figured you wouldn't want me to use the door. I wasn't going to stand down in your yard and scream up at your window, that would be apocalyptically stupid and would definitely get us caught. I thought you would recognize me right away...your doors were open."

I grind my teeth. While I can see the logic there—kind of—there's still just so many issues. I look past Roman to the oil diffuser now smashed on the floor and sigh. I really liked using that.

He somehow manages to look up through his eyelashes even though he's a foot taller than me. I'm sure it's an expression he's perfected over many, *many* screw-ups. "I really am sorry I scared you."

I grab a sweater off my desk chair and follow him outside. Roman steps up behind me, crowding me against the railing, his arms on either side of my body. I shiver at the feel of his breath on my neck but make no move to shrug out of his hold, or ask him to step away.

Roman pulls a lighter out of his pocket and flicks it but doesn't raise it to light his clove. "I came to tell you I spoke to Abram today."

"You don't sound happy."

"It's not a death sentence." He sighs and I feel it against my back. "But there's a setback."

I hold my breath. Here it comes...new conditions. Or maybe he's come to tell me face-to-face he can't do this. "Right. Well, anyway. What's the verdict?"

"You need to pledge, and Abram pointed out that it doesn't matter whether we have Lawrence officiate or not, he'll have to be there as a witness to your pledging. A wedding could have any witnesses, but a pledging needs a witness from every house."

I blanch. Nothing is ever simple, is it? "Fine. Shall we go see Lawrence, then?"

He chuckles, low and sexy, and the sound goes straight to my core. "That fast?"

"Yeah," I say briskly. "Unless there's something you're leaving out?"

"There isn't."

"Fine. So, there's no point in whining about what we can't change. Let's go see Lawrence."

"It's getting kind of late." He leans over my shoulder to look at his watch. "He'll probably be eating dinner or something, and shouldn't we come up with a plan first?"

I bite my lip. He's probably right, but I'm more than a little nervous that if there are too many hold-ups, he'll realize how crazy this is and back out. I have way more reasons to need this than he does and if it gets too hard...well, I just can't let that happen.

My eyes catch on the still unlit cigarette he's now just holding between his lips. "Are you going to smoke that?" I ask, distracted.

"Why?" I can hear the grin in his voice. "You want it?"

I roll my eyes. "No...just wondering why we're out here otherwise. It's cold."

"I'm thinking about quitting," he says, contemplation in his tone. "It's really more of an oral fixation than an addiction, anyway, and I'm sure I could find other ways to occupy my mouth...unless you still wanted to go see Lawrence right this second."

My eyes widen, my entire body going tense as a flush blooms on my cheeks. The seconds tick by, and I know he's waiting for me to set the tone. We're still in a strange gray area—are we hooking up now, or was yesterday a one-off? What exactly does "practicing," mean?

I lick my lips, my pulse pounding in my ears. There's no one here, and nothing but gardens and woods stretched out in front of us. Unless someone happened to be standing in the yard directly under my window...we're completely alone.

"I guess we don't have to go right now," I say breathlessly.

Wordlessly, Roman puts the unlit clove back in the box and there's a rustle of fabric as he stows it in his pocket. I suck in a breath, my skin growing hot, my every nerve tingling.

Roman grasps my waist, his breath hot in my ear, and I arch my back, pushing my ass against his hips. His cock grows hard pressing into me. A shiver travels down my spine and my pulse pounds in my core, my clit throbbing in anticipation of what we both know is about to happen—regardless of who might hear us.

He spins me around, so we're standing chest to chest. I feel a pang of dizziness, with my back braced by nothing but the open air, and the railing at waist level, but then Roman places his right hand over mine on the railing, linking our fingers together. My heart speeds to a rapid thrum.

"No tights today, good girl?" he says in my ear.

"It's not for you," I whisper. "It was warm out."

It's bullshit and we both know it. Roman reaches under the hem of my skirt, trailing his fingers over the wetness soaking my panties. "Is this not for me either?"

I palm his cock through his jeans. "I could ask you the same thing."

He laughs low in my ear. "I don't care who knows that I only ever get hard for you. I've never wanted anyone else but you."

My heart leaps, stutters, and my breath catches in my throat.

If it's a line he's used a thousand times before, it's a damned good one, because I could swear it sounds like he means it only for me.

I forget to wonder about the label of our relationship, or what he's thinking, and finally give in.

Roman bends slightly and yanks my panties down in a single swift motion until they're banded around my knees. "Step out," he says firmly.

I immediately respond, lifting one foot, then the other so he can remove my underwear. My breathing is ragged, and my head spins, as I look down at him eye-level with my waist.

He smirks, rising to his full height again. He shoves my panties in his pocket. "These are mine now."

I make an indignant squeak in the back of my throat. "Why—"

He holds my gaze as he reaches under my skirt and without preamble, shoves two fingers inside me. His thumb rubs over my clit, in firm, rhythmic strokes. "This is mine too, good girl. No one else touches this pussy except me."

"What, are you going to write your name on it?"

His eyes flash, darting toward my arm as if he can still see the scribbled Sharpie-brand that set off so many other events. "Don't tempt me. You know I'll do it."

My pulse throbs low in my core, pleasure coursing through me as he continues to stroke. I let out an involuntary whimper, my legs spreading wider, almost of their own accord.

"Fine," I hear myself agree. "Whatever."

"You don't come unless I say so. Not even on your own."

Huh? Wait, no.

I meet his gaze, blinking through my lust-soaked haze, and scowl. "I'm not so sure about that."

His smirk turns into a full grin, and his fingers move faster, driving me closer and closer to the edge. "If you want to come, you find me, and I'll always make time for you...assuming you've earned it."

I moan as he pulls his fingers out of me and shoves them in his mouth, sucking them clean. My eyes widen. Holy shit. What did I get myself into?

"Now," he says. "Let's go."

I gasp for all the wrong reasons. "Go? Where?"

"You wanted to go see Lawrence, right? Let's go, good girl."

"But—" I stutter, somewhere between confused and indignant. "I knew you were a sadist."

"No, this is still masochism, good girl. Trust me."

My scowl intensifies. I doubt that. "At least give me my underwear."

He shakes his head. "No, these are mine now. Try to avoid wind, or any grates."

My face heats. Am I going along with this...yes, yes I am.

"We can take the stairs," I say, a little breathless. "Unless you feel some need to bring it full circle and fling yourself off my balcony."

He scowls, but there's no real malice behind it. "Let's not discuss that again."

I shake my head, grinning. "As if I won't be bringing this up for the next twenty years."

We both freeze in the doorway to my room, and I know we're thinking the same thing: Will we actually be together in twenty years? Is that a possibility? Do I hate that idea?

CHAPTER TWENTY-EIGHT
ETTA

PRESENT

THE AIR SMELLS LIKE RAIN AND THE SKY IS DARK IN THE distance as Roman and I drive off in the direction of Councilman Lawrence's house. I fidget in my seat and try not to watch him, but it's impossible. It was a mistake to let him drive. At least if I'd driven, I'd have something to focus on aside from our painfully forced proximity, and the fact that I'm entirely bare under my skirt.

I should've known better—I was just as much of a basket-case the last time I was in a car with him. I'd chalked that up to adrenaline after the incident with Harrison, but no. Now I realize it's just Roman. I can't be within six feet of him without feeling like I've been dosed.

I take a deep breath, trying to collect myself, and glance at the GPS. We're twenty-five minutes away, but that doesn't tell me anything. "Where does Lawrence live?"

Roman flips on the wipers as the first drops fall on the windshield. "Pretty far out, he's barely in town limits."

"Assuming Lawrence says yes, any ideas for other witnesses?"

Out of the corner of my eye I see him nod, his absurdly sharp jaw slightly tense. "Yeah, actually. Grab my phone, I have a list."

I glance around. "Where is it?"

"In my left pocket."

In other words, the pocket on the side furthest from me. I narrow my eyes, even as the back of my neck heats. "You've got to be kidding me. I am not reaching into your pocket, get it yourself."

He frowns very seriously, but there's still laughter behind his eyes. He's messing with me. "Both hands on the wheel, good girl. Safety is important."

"Uh huh. You're not even watching the road."

"And that is precisely why I cannot be trusted to take my hands off the wheel." His lips tip up, betraying his amusement. "If you're worried, I'm going to crash, I've managed to drive while much more distracting things were going on in my lap. I promise, I've got this."

"You're absurd."

"And you're uptight. I'd be happy to help with that, if you would just show me how much you want it."

I cough on air, my breath getting stuck in my throat. He's unknowingly come quite close to the same words as my fantasy version of him. Or maybe, I unknowingly came close to imagining what the real Roman would be like.

Help.

I know my cheeks are flaming as I lean over the center console to reach into the pocket of his jeans. I try to imagine explaining this to the police if we were pulled over for reckless driving and can't. "Well, you see, Officer, it was all in the name of safety. He called me uptight, I couldn't let that stand!"

I pull out the phone and quickly retreat into my seat, my heart beating a little too fast, for little more than a graze of his thigh.

"The code is 3882," he says, without prompting. "Go to the notes app."

I'm skeptical as I type in the code. I don't know why—it's just a phone, but I feel a bit like I'm accepting the poison apple from Snow White.

"You already thought about this." My tone is half surprise, half accusation. I laugh lightly. "It took you long enough to get around to the point."

He runs a hand over the back of his neck. "I should also mention that I told my cousin the truth."

I raise my eyebrows. "I thought you wanted to keep this a secret."

"I do, but he wouldn't have believed it. Like your friend Catalina."

"Cat," I correct absently, as I scan down the list he made. "Did Bennet help you with this, then?"

He's listed out all eight founding families and potential witnesses from each house, as well as which one of us knows them. It's actually fairly thorough. I'm...impressed that he cares.

"Yeah, but don't sound so skeptical. I could have made that list on my own."

I glance up and see that he's grinning. I suck in a sharp breath. Holy shit, I'm like a lobster in boiling water. I'm getting used to being around him, forgetting how absolutely, insanely gorgeous he is, and then I'll look up and realize I'm burning alive.

"I didn't mean it like that," I stammer. "If there's one thing you're not, it's stupid, I just wondered why you brought up your cousin."

"Right." He glances down at his shoes. "Well, what do you think?"

Under Montague he'd listed himself and Bennet and under Capulet he'd put a question mark, which really summed up the entire thing for me. Aside from that, almost every house had someone represented, even house Hathaway which I thought might be a problem. I nod at most of them, giving my silent assent.

"Why Violet Cesario? Aren't you friends with Sebastian?"

His gaze turns unexpectedly dark. "I don't want him there."

I raise my eyebrows. "Why?"

"I just don't. Violet was friends with Marcia, she'll do it."

We fall silent. The drizzle turns into rain so heavy, I have virtually no idea where we are. Hell, without the GPS I'm pretty sure Roman wouldn't either. Yet, somehow, we manage to pull into a winding little driveway off the main road without much trouble. I grimace, and steel myself to get out of the car. I wish I brought an umbrella.

As if reading my mind, Roman leans over my lap to open the glove compartment. He pulls out a little fold up umbrella with his father's company logo on it and hands it to me. "Here."

I stare down at it, an odd mix of feelings washing over me. It's like warmth, passing over the back of my neck and down my arms and leaving too-cold goosebumps in their wake. Like, the physical manifestation of one emotion bleeding into another. It's a bit overwhelming for a single umbrella.

I'm not sure I like this. Not sure I can handle this.

It's just a stupid umbrella, but I don't want him to start trying to take care of me even unconsciously. That's not what this is. That's not what this was ever supposed to be.

I've only ever been alone, and I'll be alone again one day. Just the thought earlier, of if Roman and I would be keeping up this ruse for decades should have been enough to give me this wake-up call. That's crazy. There's no chance we'll do that. This arrangement may not have an expiration date stamped in black and white, but common sense says there is one. Maybe when our parents retire, which could be as early as a few years. The minimum age to sit on the council is twenty-five. Roman is only three years off, and I'm eight months behind him.

I can't let myself start to rely on someone who isn't a real fixture in my life—who isn't capable of that. I can't let myself start to believe this is more than the business arrangement that it is.

I shake my head, no. "Thanks. I'm all set."

"Suit yourself." Roman cocks an eyebrow at me and grasps my upper thigh for a moment before getting out of the car. "Careful of the wind, good girl."

The damp air is cool against my face as I step onto the pavement, water pelting my hair and dead leaves whipping at my ankles. A cacophony of crickets and marsh toads chirp, and a nearby river rushes in the distance.

Councilman Lawrence's house is the exact opposite from what I'd expect. Rather than one of the stunning estates on several acres, we pull up in front of a tiny bungalow with two-tone wooden shingles and a well-kept front porch. Two Adirondack chairs sit on the porch, and a pile of firewood lays in disarray in the side yard beside an overgrown rose bush.

"Is this the right place?"

Roman shakes out his wet hair, not looking at me as he replies. "Definitely. Why?"

"Just not what I was picturing. It's very...normal."

"I'm positive this is it." Roman says with a shrug. "Are you ready?"

I shake myself and draw in a nervous breath. "Yes, of course."

I still wish there had been a way to avoid Councilman Lawrence.

He isn't evil, I remind myself. He doesn't hate you...he's just old and not all that helpful. Still, incompetence at one thing doesn't necessarily mean incompetence in all areas. Maybe this will be fine.

Even in my head, it's the lowest-energy pep talk I've ever heard.

This is going to suck.

The damp pavement and wet leaves slip under my boots as we dash from the car to the front porch. The freezing rain soaks through my hair in less than thirty-seconds, and I hate myself for not accepting the umbrella.

"Here," Roman tugs off his scarf and tries to hand it to me.

I turn on the front step to look up at him, bewildered. His wet hair is plastered to his forehead and his dark, intense eyes seem to penetrate through me. "What's that for?"

In answer, he uses the end of the scarf to dab at the water streaming down the side of my face. I suck in a breath at his nearness, and our gazes connect. Suddenly, I'm not so cold anymore.

The door opens with a creak so loud I jump. We spring apart, and I feel like a teenager caught breaking the rules. Heat rises up the back of my neck, and without thinking I snatch the scarf and toss it over my shoulder like some kind of sash. Distantly, I wonder if the scarf will join Roman's suit jacket in a ball at the bottom of my closet—like a dead body I'm ashamed of and trying to hide.

Turning, I meet the gaze of Councilman Lawrence standing in the doorway. His white hair is a little less perfectly combed today than I'm used to seeing at events, but I immediately notice that he's dressed as if to go out in a dark brown wool blazer and collared shirt.

Lawrence looks down at us. Well, he looks down at me. Even standing a step up, he's nearly eye-level with Roman. His pale eyes are shrewd as he considers us. "Hello?" It's almost a question. "This is unusual."

"Afternoon, Emrys," Roman says calmly, as if he sees Councilman Lawrence every day. "Do you have a second?"

I turn and gape at him. It's not only that he's calling the councilman "Emrys" like they're peers, it's that he doesn't seem nervous at all. I'm practically shaking.

"Of course," Councilman Lawrence says pleasantly. "Come on in. Terrible weather, isn't it?"

"Yeah," I say, awkwardly.

As we step inside, I immediately realize I was wrong to think this house was out of character. It's small, but immaculately decorated and practically dripping in prestige. The dimly lit entryway has a large, old-fashioned coat rack in one corner and a floor-length silver mirror on the opposite wall. I blush when the councilman takes our coats, wondering if it's obvious I'm not wearing my own scarf...or my underwear.

"Can I get either of you anything?" The Councilman asks as he leads us into the living room. "I'll admit I was about to go out so I don't have much, but I can make coffee?"

"I'm sorry," I say. "We should have called. Do you have to go?"

He waves us off. "No, I'm just going to dinner alone. I'm all yours."

That makes me a little sad for him, and I don't know what to say. "Coffee would be great, thanks."

We sit while Lawrence retreats into the kitchen. His living room is full of antique furniture, crystal vases, and old paintings. The fireplace is lit and crackling, casting a warm glow over the room. The air smells of freshly brewed coffee and a hint of something else, something herbal and fragrant.

"Nervous?" Roman asks.

"No," I lie.

He looks down his nose at me. "You're shaking."

I press my hands to my knees, which are held so tight together that honestly might be half the cause of my alleged shaking. "I'm fine."

Roman smirks, like he is all too aware of what I'm thinking. "You're such a bad liar, good girl. Maybe let me do the talking."

"You're a good liar then?" I scowl. "Is that supposed to make me feel safe and secure?"

"I'm decent, it depends. And you can feel whatever you want, it's just a fact."

I lick my lips, hating myself for my curiosity. "Depends on what?"

"If I care enough to bother."

Councilman Lawrence returns with a tray and places it on the table in front of us before taking a seat on the green velvet sofa across from us. He draws a rune, and a silver pot begins to pour coffee of its own accord. "So, what can I do for you?"

I bite my lip, realizing that I should have planned out the answer to this question. It's the obvious thing to say and sitting and staring at Councilman Lawrence in silence is not only awkward it's painfully rude. Yet, I have no idea how to voice what I want. It was embarrassing enough to voice it to Roman the other day, and I will probably remember that moment for the rest of my life. I can't do it again.

Fortunately, I don't have to.

I nearly melt with relief when Roman leans forward and takes charge of the conversation. "We're here to discuss a solution to the...problem...that you identified the other night."

The Councilman's gaze falls on the bruise still healing on Roman's face, and his gaze darkens for a moment. It's funny, I've almost stopped registering his black eye. It looks much better now than it did the night of the auction—and as much as I hate to admit it, he looks sexy like that.

If Councilman Lawrence's expression is anything to go on, he seems to think the bruise is a representation of all that is wrong with the world. "Enlighten me."

Roman reaches for my hand and pulls it into his lap, like we're really in love. "We'd like you to stand witness to our marriage."

Roman says it so matter-of-factly, like he has absolutely no reservations. His expression is firm, but then he looks over at me and smiles. It lights up his entire face, and I have to stifle a gasp. If I was standing, I would need to sit.

Damn, he is good at this.

I gape at him for a moment, before I remember to smile, like I'm in love and this is exactly what I want.

"Well." Councilman Lawrence clears his throat. "I can't say I'm surprised."

I turn my head so quickly I'm fairly sure I whip Roman across the face with my hair. "Really?"

He tips his head in something like a shrug, and I'm about to push him further about why he's not surprised when Roman cuts in. "So, will you do it?"

He assesses us, and I have this feeling like he's seeing more than just us sitting in front of him. I know there are some witches who are clairvoyant, but I've never heard of Councilman Lawrence being one of them. Maybe I'm just paranoid.

"I assume you are trying to avoid standing in front of the entire council, or you wouldn't have come to me personally."

I nod, sheepishly. "Right."

"How do you intend to have witnesses from your own houses?"

I wince. Just like that, he's managed to pick up on our problem. "Well, we were hoping to act as our own representatives..." I trail off as the Councilman starts shaking his head.

"No. No, that's not how it's done."

"My house isn't a problem," Roman says. "My cousin will do it."

"Right," I grumble. "It's just me."

A wave of bitterness washes over me, that not only am I an only child, but most of my relatives are either dead or so angry at the Montagues they can't see straight. I sigh, I guess that's the end of that.

"What about Angelica?" Councilman Lawrence says.

I raise an eyebrow, surprised that Lawrence even knows my aunt's name. "Would she count?"

He ponders it. "Normally no, but under the circumstances... maybe we could make an exception."

I smile. "Really?"

He tips his head, as if still unsure if it's the best idea. "...Yes. Assuming she agrees, of course."

I feel a rush of affection for the old man. I always liked Councilman Lawrence prior to this year. Maybe he's really just getting old, and his inaction is more about struggling to fulfill all his responsibilities than neglect or political maneuvering. Maybe retirement is the best thing for him.

"Who's Angelica?" Roman asks, blankly.

"My father's youngest sister." I explain, taking a sip of my coffee. "She was my nanny when I was a baby actually."

Roman furrows his brow. "I didn't know you had another aunt."

Aside from the dead one, he means. Tyberius's mother, who died "mysteriously," along with her husband, while I was in prep school. I bite the inside of my cheek. Nope, not going there today.

"Angelica was expelled from the Order some fifteen years ago," Councilman Lawrence says with the same tone I might say, "Nice weather we're having."

I look down, uncomfortable. I know this story, but it's better that Roman knows I guess, if we're going to see her. "Aunt Angelica was betrothed at birth just like most Order kids, but it was kind of an unusual situation. My dad said the man was more than twice her age and already pledged when she was born."

"That doesn't happen." Roman says flatly, shifting beside me.

I narrow my eyes. What, so he thinks that because it doesn't usually happen, I'm what? Lying?

"It did," Councilman Lawrence says, leaning back in his chair. "I remember the whole thing. While the match would have been advantageous for both families, Angelica grew up to be quite headstrong and didn't want to go through with it. She embarrassed your grandparents dreadfully by leaving her groom at the altar and running away with a man they didn't approve of. I believe they disowned her, although I doubt it mattered as she'd already left."

I blink at him, surprised at how much he knows. "Were you already the head of the council back then?"

He nods. "It wasn't that long ago in the grand scheme of things."

"Do you know where she is now?" Roman asks.

Councilman Lawrence reaches for his coffee cup again and takes a sip. "I believe she now works in Salem at one of those Tarot reading shops. Interesting, don't you think? I wonder if her upbringing makes any difference there, or if it's just a personal inside joke."

"Er, okay." I lean forward. "So, if we find her and she agrees, you'll perform the ceremony?"

He smiles a little knowing smile. "Yes, assuming you can get all the other witnesses of course."

Well, that won't be an issue.

Feeling somewhat bolstered, I stand and Roman follows my lead.

"Thank you," I say earnestly.

"Of course," the councilman says. "And if I might give you some advice, I would learn from your aunt's mistakes."

"What are those?" I ask.

"You two are only children. If this ends in tragedy, it could mean the end of two founding lines. Just make sure you keep that in mind, and don't tempt fate."

"Right," Roman says, already heading for the door, "Thanks."

CHAPTER TWENTY-NINE
✦ ROMAN ✦

SENIOR YEAR OF HIGH SCHOOL, FOUR YEARS AGO

THIS IS A BAD FUCKING IDEA.

It's early spring, but unseasonably warm for New England and sweat pools on the back of my neck, sticking to the collar of my shirt. By all accounts, it's a nice day, but I've hardly taken the time to notice.

The cemetery is empty and quiet as I drive through the gates. I instinctively roll-up my windows and turn down my music, as if my presence might disturb the slumber of the dead, then scowl down at the two bouquets of flowers in my passenger seat.

I'm furious. First, at the mere existence of the flowers, and second, because I didn't buy the bigger bouquets that I really wanted. I'd usually go-big-or-go-home, but I tried to thread the needle— choosing something in the middle—and now I'm dissatisfied on all fronts.

I don't know why I'm doing this, except that Etta did, and I'll be damned if I let her always be the better person. The more thoughtful person. The winner of this strange, morality competition that exists only in my head. It's a lost cause, anyway, because I've already lost by the simple fact that she's not playing. She showed up to this shit out of actual kindness, rather than to even the score.

Well, to even the score and because Etta has stopped turning up everywhere. She hasn't sat next to me in the library, or said good morning in the parking lot in days.

I didn't think anything could make me crazier than her kindness, but I was wrong; her indifference is infinitely worse.

I tense as I drive past where my grandfather's grave sits. We were close, he and I, and the memory of his death is still painful to think about. The memory of Etta turning up at his funeral is still as confused and tangled as it was the day it happened. As confusing as Etta herself, who is, and always has been, a contradiction.

A girl I was raised to hate. Told constantly was just the latest in a long line of liars and thieves. Yet, has never shown that side of herself to me once, no matter how often I tried to provoke it out of her. No matter how often I've tried to prove the duplicity of the Capulet bloodline, Etta has always been too good, and I'm starting to wonder if in this generation, *I'm* the problem.

I scowl at the flowers again.

I refuse to lie down and accept being the villain in my own narrative. If Etta can do nice shit like go to her enemy's funerals, the least I can do is turn up with flowers three days late.

I drive in circles for a few minutes, wave to Councilman Lawrence walking by with his dog, and eventually park and get out of my car. It will be easier to find on foot. I doubt her aunt and uncle will have a headstone yet, but there should be some sort of grave markers or...something. Unless they were buried in the crypt? I square my shoulders. This just can't be that hard.

It's nearly eighty degrees out and sweat beads on my forehead as I wander down row after row.

But then I stop short.

As if summoned by my thoughts of her, Etta is crouching by a gravestone twenty feet in front of me. Her back is turned, and the sun glints off her dark blonde hair, making it much lighter in the sun. She's wearing a sundress, unlike anything I've ever seen her wear—which makes sense, as I rarely see her outside of a school, or at the occasional formal function. Still, it's unmistakably her.

My stomach turns over. What is she doing here? It's not even the actual funeral. What are the odds that she would be here at the exact moment I am?

I back up a few steps. I could leave. Turn back before she ever sees me here. Or just wait until she leaves? *Fuck.*

My decision is made for me when she turns around. Her eyes widen as we stare at each other across the headstones. Her gaze travels down from my face to the flowers in my hands. I wait, expecting her to say something. Instead, she turns away, ignoring me, and it's even worse than if she had looked up and yelled at me for daring to come here.

My eye twitches. *Look at me.*

"Hey," I hear myself say, like my voice is coming from a different person, completely disassociated.

She doesn't greet me back. "What are you doing here?"

I'm tempted to taunt her, just out of habit. "Paying respects," I say, mimicking her phrase from my grandfather's funeral.

"The funeral was three days ago. If that were true, you would have shown up then."

"Maybe I didn't want to get beaten up by your insane family."

She shrugs, her eyes narrowing. "Then I guess it wasn't that important."

I'm annoyed by how I sort of agree with her, and more annoyed that she's clearly pissed. I don't owe her anything. She is not my Jimmy fucking cockroach, or whatever that puppet's conscience was called.

"Look, I just heard today, okay?" I lie. "I wanted to leave these."

She looks like she thinks giant scorpions are going to jump out of the flowers. If so, it's the fault of *Whole Foods*, not me. I move to place the flowers on the plots of displaced earth she was kneeling beside, but she won't move. She stands, blocking me.

I raise my eyebrows, bemused. She's like a kitten trying to pick a fight with a tiger, but the effort is appreciated. "What's your problem? Weren't you the one who was all into paying respects and shit?"

"And shit," she mocks, then her lips tighten, as if she's not used to the curse coming out of her mouth. "Yeah, something like that."

"Okay." My eyes narrow, and I raise my flowers higher, like I'm brandishing a torch. "So, what's your problem? Can I leave these and go, please?"

She sniffs dismissively, and I see red. Where the fuck does she get off ignoring me? I don't even know what I did to piss her off.

Okay, that's not true. I can think of a ton of things I've done that could have potentially pissed-off Etta, but not lately...

She's the most frustrating, person I've ever met. I want to shake her. Suck every last drop of ridiculous optimism and excitement out of her. I hate how crazy I sound—how obsessive this is. How I can't stop thinking about what she might be thinking about.

"You know these are Tyberius's parents, right?" she demands, pointing at her aunt and uncle's graves. "Did you ever think maybe they wouldn't want your respect?"

"Why?" I drawl. "Cause their son is a prick? I don't see the connection?"

She stands and practically vibrates with anger. Cute. "Because you beat up their son for no reason."

I take a step back, slightly surprised at how upset she is. Of all the things I thought she would be mad about; her cousin hadn't even crossed my mind. "For no reason?"

"Yeah. I saw what happened, you attacked him."

I bark a laugh. She's serious, and It's almost funny how wrong she is. Could she not hear us from where she was standing? I was pretty drunk—I don't remember where Etta was when the fight started. It's interesting, though, that she never reacts when I poke at her, but the one time she thinks her family has been slighted, she's furious. "Sure, good girl. Believe whatever you want."

The day after the party in the woods, I finally got the entire story out of Marcia.

Tyberius Capulet had spent months talking to my sister, going so far as to convince her she could go to the Senior prom, all so that —as far as I could tell—he could get her computer password and try to get into our dad's files. I could only assume his aunt had put him up to it.

I was fairly sure Capulet wasn't actually trying to do anything with my sister and didn't really want to take her to the prom, because once he realized the only things on Marcia's laptop are homework and fan fiction, he got bored and gave up. It wasn't quite as fucked up a situation as I'd been afraid it was, but I still felt pretty justified in kicking his ass—if only to deter any future ideas.

I snort a bitter laugh. If Etta doesn't know any of that, and wants to think I start fights for no fucking reason, that's her prerogative. She should know who her family is by now. If she's still putting her head in the sand it's not my job to educate her.

Her expression shifts, slightly, turning conflicted, but she doesn't say anything as I back away. There are about ten yards between us. I almost wince. It's about the same distance as when I screamed at her in the hallway after grandfather died. Not my proudest moment, even if it was Etta I was yelling at.

My parents would probably consider that little outburst a net-positive, proof that I might have some hope that I'd turn out something like my dad after-all.

I'd never been more concerned about that very thing.

My father is the kind of man who screams to express mild inconvenience and takes out his problems on random bystanders. I don't know who I want to be, but not that. I don't need to be a fucking Saint—I'll never be the good-guy. Never the hero, like Etta Capulet seems to expect of herself and everyone around her, but I don't want that.

"Use them or throw them out, I don't care." I put the flowers on the grass, then. I turn and start to walk away, reaching into my pocket for my clove cigarettes.

Just talking to her stresses me out in a way little else does, when I notice that there's no car parked along the road in between the various plots. I stop, looking around. Did she walk?

I glance back. Etta has turned away from me again and is facing the headstone. From here, it would be all-too easy for anyone to grab her or hit her in the back of the head...it would sound paranoid, if there weren't three fresh graves surrounding us.

A strange, foreign feeling rises in my throat, nearly choking me—like anger, but bitter. I lower my cigarette, unlit, and spin back around. "Are you out here alone?"

Etta looks up from where she's crouched by her aunt's grave, seeming surprised I'm still here. "Amazing deduction, Sherlock."

My gaze hardens. So much for her speech about kindness or whatever—I must be a special case, because I've never heard Etta be quite so caustic as she is with me, especially today. "Where's your car?"

"Why?"

"It's a long walk back to your house."

"Yes, thank you for that observation."

"You shouldn't walk alone, it's dangerous."

I hear myself, and I don't recognize the person using my mouth. What the fuck am I talking about? Dangerous, how? This is fucking Stratford Massachusetts, a suburban college town with a population of 11,000 and a median income of 1.3 million per household. The crime rate is 1%, exclusively due to fights caused by our respective relatives. If anyone is in danger, it would be me if any member of Etta's family saw her in my car.

Etta seems to be thinking the same thing. "Pardon? Stratford is... dangerous? Since when?"

I ignore her. "Come on, I'll take you home."

She stares at me with so much contempt I can practically feel the flames licking over my skin. "So, to sum up, you're saying I should let you drive me home in case I run into some weird guy in the cemetery who wants me to get into his car?"

"Exactly." I nod, glad she's agreeing, and then realize what she's getting at. "Wait, no."

She shakes her head. "I'm all set, thanks."

"Etta—"

She raises her eyebrows, probably because I've said her name. It sounds weird to me too, and we both pause for a moment. Suddenly I'm trying to remember if I've *ever* used her real name, and why that's even relevant.

"Etta," I try again. "Don't be stupid."

The noise she makes is somewhere between a scoff and a choke. "Oh, I'm definitely going to listen to you now," she says sarcastically. "Just leave me alone, Roman. I wouldn't get in your car without a blue light and some Lysol, anyway."

Fine. Never mind. The good girl is way too good for me. She cares about everyone but me, so I don't care about her either. If she wants to get murdered in a graveyard that's her godsdamn prerogative. "I would ask who shoved the stick up your ass, but it's very clear you've never been fucked—in the ass or otherwise."

Something in my stomach revolts, seizing in a way I don't like. Maybe that was kind of too far...should I apologize?

She turns away, and I catch a glimpse of the side of her face. She looks...actually hurt? "You make it impossible to be nice to you."

CHAPTER THIRTY
·✦· ROMAN ·✦·

PRESENT

ETTA PRESSES HER NOSE TO THE FOGGY CAR WINDOW. I shoot furtive glances at her, but trying to both watch her, and keep my eyes on the road is impossible. Especially as it's raining, and visibility is low.

"You good?" I ask.

She tenses, and I cringe as I hear myself. That sounded stupid. I don't know why every time I speak to her, I sound like I'm making fun of her or like my vocabulary has deteriorated to that of a nineteen-year-old frat bro. I could *write* sonnets about her beauty if given the chance, but I couldn't say them out loud. If forced to recite anything, apparently all I'd come out with is "Fuck baby, nice tits."

"Yeah," she says, "I'm fine."

I shoot another quick look at Etta, because something about her statement sounds off. I can't pretend to be an expert of women's tones—she could be sulking or angry or hungry, or something else, but she's not fine. Maybe she's nervous?

I crane my neck and try to get a look at Etta's face in the mirror. She's worrying her lip, her eyes wide, yet unfocused. Yes, *nervous*. That's got to be it. It's not an expression I'm used to seeing on her.

I'm used to seeing her defiant, frustrated and defensive when talking to me. Sometimes embarrassed when I tease her or smug when she thinks she's beaten me. She's concentrated and curious while reading, bored and indifferent in classes or at events she doesn't like and euphoric in ones she does. She laughs with her friends, is resentful of her mother, and very occasionally, lately, I've gotten to see what lust looks like in her huge gray eyes.

Nervous, however, isn't really part of her repertoire.

"Are you worried about talking to your aunt?" I ask, feeling somewhat pleased with myself for decoding her mood.

"What?" She says quickly, turning to look at me. "No. Why?"

Fuck, okay, I suck at this. "You seem uncomfortable."

She laughs, and it's more of a nervous giggle. I can only describe it as, well, uncomfortable, but still, she's cute. I've never found anyone cute. Never cared about expressions or feelings or laughs. But then again, I've been completely focused on those things for her for years, so I guess there would be no time to care about anyone else's mannerisms. Fuck, maybe I should send apology cards to my past girlfriends. Fruit Baskets. Condolences for dating me, sorry I'm an asshole. It really wasn't you; it was me.

"I just realized that my parents might disown me, and I don't know why that didn't occur to me before? Maybe because it happened to Aunt Angelica when I was really young, or because I kind of didn't think we'd get this far, but this might all turn out really *really* badly and I don't really have a back-up plan, you know? I don't think they would disown me, but then again, I wouldn't have thought they would pick Harrison for me either, and here we are. I just don't think I could handle being cut off like that."

She says all of this in one breath, and then sucks in a huge sigh—like she stayed underwater too long and has just popped up for air. I try and fail not to look at her chest as she heaves another breath, then shakes her head. I'm caught between wanting to laugh—not at her exactly, but with her, because she's funny for forgetting how to talk and breathe at the same time—and the fact that I'm suddenly hard, my dick pressing against my jeans, and I feel sixteen again nearly unable to control myself.

"I don't think your parents will disown you," I bite out, willing myself to focus on the road and not think about her panties in my pocket or her perfect tits bouncing as she breathes too hard, or how her nipples show in little points through her sweater. About how easy it would be too easy to reach over and slide my hand under her skirt. To pull over and suck her nipples into my mouth while I bounce her—

"How do you know?" she asks.

Focus.

"Because your mom is a social vampire, and your dad is an asshole but he's not stupid."

"Hey," she glares at me. "My dad is not an asshole...he's flawed."

I notice she doesn't even bother to defend her mother. "You're an only child, they don't have any other options to inherit their council seat or their businesses."

"They have Tyberius."

I grimace. I doubt they will give a cent to Tyberius ...not with his gambling problem, but Etta doesn't need to know that. It would just upset her. "Maybe? But I still don't think they would just throw away their only kid."

"You're underestimating how much they hate you," she quips.

"Look, if I'm not worried about being disowned, you shouldn't be."

It's a bald-faced lie. She's actually bringing up a good point—maybe I should be worried about it. I actually do think she's safe, but me? Not so much. My parents actually have a pretty good alternative heir in Bennet. He's more responsible than I am, and I'm fairly sure my dad likes him better than me. I'm actually at a pretty severe risk of disownment...except I don't care. Because all I've ever cared about is sitting in the passenger seat next to me, and I'm so close to getting to keep her forever I can taste it.

It's pitch dark as I pull into Etta's driveway. It's only five, but daylight savings makes it feel like midnight. I suggest we meet up tomorrow—same time—to go see her aunt in Salem. She bites her lip, seeming unsure and my stomach plummets...if she's going to back out.

"I can't tomorrow," she says.

"Why?"

"I have class. I'm still enrolled for the moment, and then I have to have dinner with my parents and Harrison. It's probably best to keep up the pretense, don't you think?"

I raise an eyebrow. She doesn't know it, but I didn't just drive home and go to bed after finding her on the side of the road the other night. Of fucking course not. But even after driving around, checking social media, and scrying again, Harrison Dane was nowhere. He'd vanished, like a fucking ghost. I sort of assumed that he bolted after whatever went down with Etta, maybe afraid of her family's retaliation if he offended her or something.

"You're still saying he didn't hurt you the other night," I ask, my anger from the other evening rising again full force.

"He didn't," she insists. "And if he did I could have handled it. If I don't go to this dinner, he'll definitely say something to my parents about how bad Monday went."

I press my lips together. It's not that I think she's weak or unable to handle herself, it's that Harrison Dane is a full-fledged member of the Order and Etta isn't. Size and strength aside, she's at a power disadvantage. I pinch the bridge of my nose, willing myself not to lose my shit. "Fine. So, is this dinner at least with other people?" I bite out. *If it's not there's no way she's going.*

"Yeah, it's here, with my parents. I'm shocked he even wants to, but..." she shrugs, her mouth disappearing into a flat, upset line.

A vein throbs in my temple. *It's temporary,* I remind myself. Soon I'll have her all to myself and exploding now in a fit of jealousy over a man she clearly despises will only scare her. "That's at night, though. Not in the afternoon, right? When will your last class get out?"

"4:30."

Damn, that's probably too late to make it over there. "Okay, the next day, then. I'll pick you up."

She bites her lip, obviously unsure. In any normal circumstance I wouldn't be pushing so hard for this. I hate seers, especially card readers, and I'm tempted to admit that to her—admit that the revelation that the only potential witness from her family is a reader isn't a welcome one.

I didn't think to ask Etta if she cares about star charts and predestined matches when we were making our plans because, to me, all that matters is her. Now, a horrible idea has taken root.

What if we're not compatible?

What if she cares about that shit and calls the whole thing off?

She can't possibly care, right? Someone who followed birth charts wouldn't be looking for a political marriage.

I imagine the reader telling us we're wildly incompatible and that she has some other, faceless, nameless perfect match out there. The man is fictional, and still, I'm furious. Already, my hands clench into fists, as I imagine wrapping my hands around his throat. She's mine. She's only ever been mine, and I don't care what her aunt or her parents or the fucking stars say. I defy you, stars!

"Alright." Etta nods. "Just be careful. We should figure out a meeting spot or something."

"Or you could give me your number."

She pauses, one hand on the car door. She looks uncertain for a second, then I can practically see her deciding it's ludicrous to argue about this. "Yeah, okay."

She takes out her phone and rattles off her number, before taking mine as well. I notice her glancing at me as she does this, her gaze seeming to linger on my hands. I furrow my brows. "What?"

"Nothing," she says, her tone clipped. "I'm just surprised you didn't write it below the hygienist."

It takes me a moment to understand what she means. I laugh, glancing at the faded sharpie on my hand. "Jealous?"

"Gods, no," she says too fast.

I grin. *At least it's not just me.* "Don't be, I didn't call her."

"Good, I guess. It might look bad when you have to tell her you're married."

I don't care what it looks like, I'm fully intending to tell everyone I meet for the rest of my fucking life that I'm married.

. . .

"WOULD YOU LIKE PAPER OR PLASTIC?"

"Paper, and have I mentioned I'm married?"

"ARE YOU READY TO ORDER?"

"My wife and I will need another minute."

ONLY, I CAN'T TELL HER THAT, SHE'S NOT READY TO hear the extent of my obsession with her. Etta has grown up since high school, but she's still her. She's still performing for a fake audience, and cares too much what everyone thinks about her. I can't shake her world view too much, she'll run away screaming.

"Actually, on that note, though," she says "Maybe we should get our story straight. And set some ground rules."

I raise an eyebrow at her. "Like what?"

"Like how long we've been together, how it started, when we got engaged, that kind of thing. Oh, why don't I have a ring?"

A ring. I knew I was forgetting something. My mind immediately flies to the velvet box containing my grandmother's ring that my mother thrust on me after golf with my father. I stuffed it in a drawer in the kitchen at my apartment and promptly forgot about it until now. "We'll get you a ring."

She looks down, blushing. "No, that's stupid."

It's not. "It's not. Don't worry about it."

Even if I didn't give her my grandmother's ring, it's not like I don't have the money to get her a new one. I don't want to give her excuses to act like this isn't real.

"So, any ideas?" she asks, clearly uncomfortable.

I don't even have to think before a story comes to me fully formed. It's half-fantasy, half-logic. "We dated on and off since prep school in secret, no need to say how we met, everyone knows we've always known each other, and we decided to get married this week when our families were going to make us marry other people. That's it."

She licks her lips, eyes going wide. "Okay. I guess that's sort of believable."

That, "sort of" is doing a lot of work and we both know it, but there's not a great alternative. "Anything else?"

"Yes." Her tone turns unexpectedly clipped. "I don't think we should date other people. It's a small community and it will look bad. At least not right away, maybe after we're established, or— "

"Done," I say immediately. Did she really think I was going to date other women? Or for that matter, tolerate her bringing home other guys? Not fucking likely. I don't share. "Next?"

She blinks. "Are you sure you understood me? I know how you are."

My lip curls into something between a sneer and a smirk, and I can't help the slight annoyance that shines through at her comment. "Oh? How am I?"

"You...*you know*."

I let mockery lace my tone. "I'm shocked, Juliette. Are you not the same person who organized an anti slut-shaming campaign for your senior project? How the mighty have fallen."

"Don't call me that," she snaps. "And I'm not shaming, I'm observing. I *clearly* have no qualms about sex. I *do* care if your sexual escapades make me look bad."

Just like that, I'm thinking about the library again. Thinking about everything I could do to her—with her. About pulling her onto my lap and pushing her skirt up around her waist. "It's not a problem. I'm assuming our practice sessions are still on the table considering you're currently wearing no underwear."

She sucks in a startled breath, and she shivers. Her teeth sink into her full lower lip, and I have the feeling she's considering telling me to fuck off, perhaps just on principal. But then, shocking us both, I think, she nods. "Of course."

Fuck, just like that I'm hard. I haven't been this out of control in years, but just her nodding, just the idea of sex with her is enough to turn me on. "Is anyone home right now?" I hear myself ask.

She shakes her head. "No."

"Fuck. Why did you tell me that, pretty girl??

Why tell me that I can make you scream as loud as I want? That I can do whatever I want to you, in your asshole father's house and they'll never be the wiser. Why tell me that you want this, but not why, leaving me to speculate wildly. Leaving me to consider all the ways I could torture answers out of you.

I reach across the center console and slide my hand up the inside of her thigh. She doesn't move, and her breath catches. Her breathing is uneven, her pupils dilated. I prompt her again. "Were you hoping I'd pet your pretty pussy while we drove?"

"Mmm." Is her noncommittal agreement.

"Did you get wet knowing I might touch you at any moment?"

"Maybe."

I doubt I'm going to get a better answer out of her, so I let it go. Someday, I'll get her to talk dirty to me.

Moving my hand from her thigh to between her legs, running my fingers over her bare folds until she lets out a breathy moan, squirming in her seat. Etta is stubborn and bratty, and I'm dominant, but I'm not exactly into the 'call me sir and do as I say, or I'll deny you orgasms indefinitely' thing. I'm not going to cut off my nose to spite my face—I want her to come, often and as hard as possible.

"You should invite me inside."

She hesitates for only a second, probably weighing the likelihood of someone coming home with wanting more room to get properly fucked. My dick swells painfully at the thought, straining against my jeans.

"Okay," she says, breathless. "But move your car around to behind the garage."

Chapter Thirty-One
✦ ROMAN ✦

ETTA LEADS THE WAY THROUGH A GARAGE LARGE enough to hold ten cars, and into the house. We pass only two cars —her's, and one I assume must be an extra, or she wouldn't let me come inside. I follow close behind her and wrap my arms around her waist as we step through a back door and into a dark kitchen. I take a step toward her and reach out, my palm finding the side of her face. Her lips part for a moment as I lean in, intending to finally, really kiss her for the first time.

Etta turns her head. "Wait. Just...don't kiss me."

I raise an eyebrow. "Why?"

"I just don't think we should forget what this is?" she says in a rush.

I step back. "What is it?"

"Not a relationship. This is a partnership, like a business."

I scoff. "Not any business I've ever heard of."

"I thought you liked to read?" She snaps back. "Until the last hundred years most marriages were about business. That's all I want."

My lip curls. She's trying too hard to maintain the distance between us—protesting too much. "And kissing will ruin that for you?"

"Yes," she says haughtily. "I understand you can't be with anyone else and that we both have...needs, I guess." Her blush is intoxicating. "But that's all this is, and I don't want to forget it."

Satisfaction settles over me. She might think this request is pushing me further away, but she's wrong. She's only proving to me what I realized on Saturday—what's been becoming more and more apparent every moment I spend with her since: My feelings for her aren't one sided.

She might not be fully aware of it yet—might not be ready to hear the words out loud—but this is more than her extremely delayed teenage rebellion, or a convenient way to end a feud. There's something here, beyond lust, beyond the forbidden, and beyond the fulfillment of a childhood crush. She might think that's all this is, and I'm happy to let her think that for as long as she needs to. Eventually she'll realize it too. I'm sure of it. "Whatever you say, good girl, but that just means I'm going to have to kiss you everywhere else to make up for it."

She shivers, her eyes flaring with lust. The corner of her mouth tips up, but yet her tone is indifferent when she replies. "I guess I can agree to that."

Brat. We'll see how indifferent she is in a few minutes.

Etta bites her lip and places her hands on my shoulders before trailing them down my chest until she reaches the top button of my shirt. She looks up at me through her lashes as she fiddles with the button, running the tip of her finger over the edge of the lapel. It's not a sexual gesture in any sense, but for some reason I'm harder than ever. There's just something about her being casual that makes me want to disregard the promise I literally just made her and press my lips to hers. Yet, I can't ignore a direct request. Even if I'm fairly sure she wants it too. I'll wait for her to initiate a kiss when she can't wait anymore.

I pick her up and sit her on the granite countertop, then step between her bare thighs, her skirt pooling around her hips.

"Wait," she laughs, as I bury my face in her neck. "We need to go upstairs."

I nip at her ear. "There's no one here."

"But someone could come home."

I lean back, giving her a look that tells her exactly how little I care. "So?"

"So, I'm not so sure I'm into that."

I roll my eyes. It doesn't take a genius to realize that Etta's into the danger of getting caught. She both cares too much what everyone thinks about her and likes the idea of being bad. Otherwise, I wouldn't be here at all. Not that I'm complaining. "You have exactly thirty-seconds to decide where you want to go, good girl, cause I'm done talking about all your new conditions."

Rather than answering, she says: "Yeah?" she asks, jutting her lip out. "What are you going to do about it?"

My mouth falls open slightly. Fuck, just when I think I know what she's going to do, Etta does the exact opposite. She has to know what she's doing to me. Has to know how infuriating and sexy she is when she talks back.

What am I going to do about it? Well, rather than wasting more time with taunts or teasing, I yank her back down off the counter, and she yelps in surprise when the heels of her boots hit the floor with a sharp clatter. Even in heels, she barely reaches my chin, so it's not hard to put my hands on her shoulders and push her to her knees in front of me.

Etta looks up at me from her kitchen floor.

"You're taking your life in your hands, Montague. Or rather, your future children's lives. I could get very vindictive down here, you know."

I smirk down at her. "Don't you mean *our* children?"

She blanches, looking like she swallowed a hot pepper whole. "Uh—"

I probably would have let her avoid this particular type of "practice," despite the fact that I'd have every right to argue it's necessary, but if she's going to be a brat...

I run one hand over the top of her head and down her cheek, tipping her chin up. Her expression is defiant, but she doesn't try to stand up and leave, and makes no effort to shove me away as I use my other hand to unzip my fly. I pull my jeans down just enough for my cock to spring free. Gripping myself with one hand, I drag the head of my cock over her lips. "Suck."

As if waking from a trance, Etta's gray eyes go wide and her mouth parts on a gasp.

My back straightens when her breath feathers over my pulsing dick, the anticipation of what she's going to do close to driving me out of my mind.

And then, her tongue darts out to taste me. She wraps her lips around my cock, her hand coming up to cover what she can't fit into her mouth, and as the head hits the back of her throat and I bite back a groan, I realize my error. If I thought for a moment, I was controlling Etta by asking her to do this, I was entirely wrong —she holds all the power here.

My hand finds her hair and I'm mesmerized, watching her head bob up and down. "Fuck, Etta, you need to stop."

She needs to stop because I want to come inside her, not down her throat,

She keeps going, and panic mingles with pleasure as my balls begin to go tight.

I yank hard on her hair, pulling her up. She's smirking, knowing she's won this round. "What's wrong? I thought we were practicing?"

Yeah, she knows what's wrong. She can't pull that shit during the ceremony.

Spinning her around, I crowd myself against her back, pressing her against the edge of the marble. "Are you trying to drive me insane?"

"Maybe," she says.

I take that as a yes. She's doing an excellent job of it. I've been halfway insane for years and being this close to her is making it so, so much worse.

I press my cock harder into the curve of her ass, grinding against her and leaving no doubt for either of us what I'm intending to do to her. "Bend over and put your hands flat on the counter," I tell her, as I step back and flip up her maroon, pleated skirt.

I'm shocked when this time she doesn't protest, immediately pressing her hands flat, spreading her legs wider, and curving her back to press her ass higher into the air. My eyes widen, and I press my fist into my mouth to stifle a groan, because *fuck*. I can't believe I finally have her like this, laid out before me, ready, and waiting, and *mine*.

I reach down and run a hand over the curve of her ass, as I've wanted to do so many times before. I can see the evidence of how wet she is for me and my cock twitches against my jeans in response.

I bend and press kisses to her hair, her neck and the shell of her ear. "Have you been this wet all afternoon?"

She gasps, arching into me. "Touch me."

I smack her ass, hard, and she yelps. "That's not the answer to my question. Try again."

"Yes," she says quickly. "I can't take this. I need more."

I'm tempted to keep torturing her, given how difficult she's been, but honestly, I can't take it anymore either.

I cup Etta between her thighs with the other, running my fingers over her until she's squirming against me. My thumb finds her clit as my fingers stroke over her entrance. I wince as she moans and grip myself tighter. Just knowing that soon I'll be inside her is enough to nearly send me over the edge.

Except, even as part of me is dying to slide inside her, another part is saying it shouldn't be like this.

Fuck, I sound like a fifteen-year-old virgin, wanting to lay out rose petals and make our first time special. That's not exactly it—as much as I care about Etta, I'll also never be that kind of person. I'll never be able to be not an asshole the majority of the time or turn into the kind of guy who likes roses. But I also know I don't want the first time I fuck Etta to be over her parents' kitchen counter. Maybe—definitely—a different time, once I've claimed her as mine for real and she's accepted that there's more than an agreement and inconvenient lust between us. But not the first time.

I want to take my time with it, have her all night, every way and as much as I want, and this isn't going to work.

Etta looks back at me, confused as to why I've stopped. "What's wrong?"

Shit. I search around for any reason that would even remotely make sense and wouldn't offend her. I want to tell her the truth, but I'm almost positive she isn't ready to hear it. That any confession of feelings would send her running for the hills, or at best, she wouldn't believe me.

"I—"

A light flares overhead, so bright and surprising it's almost blinding. I blink, startled, and instinctively flip Etta's skirt down, fumbling to shove my dick back in my pants.

It takes me a moment to realize no one is screaming or cursing. No one is trying to punch me in the face.

I turn slowly and find Catalina Minola standing in the doorway of the kitchen wearing some kind of plastic bag over her hair and a giant t-shirt as a dress. She raises a pink paint brush at me like a sword and scowls. "Um, what the fuck am I seeing right now?"

CHAPTER THIRTY-TWO
ETTA

PRESENT

EVERY MUSCLE IN MY BODY TENSES AS I MAKE EYE-contact with Cat over Roman's shoulder. She has black dye dripping down the side of her face out of her shower cap and is brandishing a dye brush at us like a weapon. Her expression reads violence, and I suddenly regret more than anything not making more of an effort to talk to her about this.

"Hey..." I say, knowing it's not nearly enough.

"Oh hey," she sing-songs, voice dripping with sarcasm. "Again, what the fuck am I looking at? I'm honestly hoping my gummies were laced with something, because that's the thing that would make the most sense right now."

"It's not what you're looking at, it's what you're doing, which is cock-blocking..." Roman mutters.

I roll my eyes. I'm 90% sure he's joking. Actually, as we've spoken to each other more in the last few days than we did in the

307

combined fifteen years prior, I've started to wonder if he actually just has a very deadpan sense of humor that teenage-me was a little too sensitive to understand. Not that it excuses the worst of his behavior, but in retrospect, maybe he wasn't so much "bullying" me as "teasing," me.

Potato/Po-tah-to, I guess.

Cat does not seem to understand he's joking, and her expression turns feral. I need to head this off before things get ugly and I have another feud on my hands. "Alright, maybe we should just calm down." I look at Roman a bit helplessly. "Let's just call it a night. I'll see you tomorrow."

"Sure. See you tomorrow, good girl." He backs away, but I stiffen, alert to the mischief in his dark gaze. He glances at Cat, before smacking me on the ass as he walks out. "Remember, no tights."

Cat's eyes bug out of her head, and she looks from me to the doorway, like I just personally set feminism back one hundred years and took a shit on Gloria Steinem's lawn.

I sigh. Just...why me?

"Do you have any more of those gummies? You might want to prepare for this conversation."

THE FOLLOWING DAY, I SIT IN CLASS, STARING INTO space as my professor rattles off something about the most recent reading: Percy Shelley's *Queen Mab*.

My mind is elsewhere. Specifically, on Roman and on what Cat must think of me after the catastrophe last night. I fidget with the strap of my bag. Then, abruptly, I realize the room has gone silent.

Confused, I look up and my stomach drops out. Everyone is staring at me.

My eyes fly to the professor, and he gives me an expectant nod. Shit. Apparently, it's my turn to contribute to the roundtable and I don't have a clue what's going on or what's already been said.

"Uh..." Heat rises to my face as I scramble for literally anything to say. "Uh, I think that while Mab is most often a representation of dreams in a literal sense, for instance in chapter thirty-one of Melville's Moby Dick, I think here Shelley is using her to mean dreams in a figurative way. Like utopia. A dream of revolution."

I relax as the professor grunts his lukewarm approval. "I think we'll end there today."

My face is still flaming with embarrassment when I step into the hallway five minutes later and find Roman Montague leaning against the wall waiting for me. "Well, look who it is, the queen of dreams." He raises a fist in the air. "Viva la revolution."

I scowl. "What, are you stalking me now?"

His eyes flash with amusement. "Would you be mad if I said yes?"

I stop in my tracks, genuine alarm in my voice. "Yes!"

Roman moves away from the wall and falls into step beside me. "Don't worry, good girl. As much as I enjoy looking at you, I only just happened to hear the end of that." He grins with mischief. "It wasn't the *worst* answer I've ever heard, but then again, I have taken classes with Pierce, so..."

"Well, we can't all have read every book under the sun." I look sideways together. "What are you doing here? We can't walk together; someone will see us."

He grins. "Are you getting Deja vu, or is it just me?"

"No seriously. I thought I was going to see you tomorrow."

"I decided I don't care."

My heart speeds up, suddenly anxious. What doesn't he care about? Is he done doing this? Already? What could I have possibly done? We haven't even seen each other and—

"I don't care if people see us," he adds. "Gods, good girl. You're not only a bad liar, even your expressions are obvious. Good thing too, since you never actually say what you're thinking."

Is he insane? He can't just decide not to care if people see us together. "But...you can't do that."

"I can. I did. Here I am."

I grind my teeth. In a way, I probably should have expected something like this. Roman was always...is "possessive" the right word? Maybe just "Obvious."

It's thoughts like this that make me wonder if I should have viewed some of the things that went on back in high school differently. Was he tormenting me, or just...I don't even know.

"What did Catalina say when I left?" Roman asks, clearly unwilling to continue talking about this.

"Cat," I correct reflexively.

He frowns. "I don't think I'm going to get used to that."

"Why?"

We turn the corner into a crowded stone hallway. "Do you have any people that you grew up with that are first name/last name people?"

"What?"

"You always call them by both their first name and their last name, like…" he thinks for a minute. "You always say 'Sebastian Cesariao.' We went to all the same schools for almost twenty years. There was only one Sebastian, I know who you mean without the last name."

I shrug. "Oh, yeah I guess."

Roman nudges some guy out of the way so I can keep walking beside him undeterred. "Well, it would take an act of the gods for Catalina Minola to become 'Cat' to me."

"Like marrying her best friend?" I say, then immediately glance over my shoulder to see if anyone heard me.

He scoffs. "That's not an act of the gods, good girl. God is nowhere near this union. This is entirely sinful."

The back of my neck heats and I bite my lip. I tangle my fingers in my skirt, knowing full-well why I didn't wear tights today, even though I didn't even think I would see him, and he's right—there were no gods involved.

"You're a first name/last name person for me."

Mostly. I don't want to think about how easily it's starting to shift.

His brow furrows. "Really? Strange. You're not for me."

"Well, of course not, you always called me, 'good girl.'"

He flashes a grin at me. "And looks like I was right, you turned out to be just as good as I thought you'd be."

I cough and pat myself on the chest with an open palm, as if to dislodge the air choking me.

"You okay?" he asks.

"F-fine."

"Well, what did *Cat* say?"

"Nothing," I lie. "She didn't care."

He raises his eyebrows. "Bullshit."

He's right. In reality, my friend spent over an hour complaining that I didn't tell her about this. Then, just when I thought it couldn't get worse, she started in on very specific sex questions. Hell. On. Earth.

"No really," I say airily. She wasn't fazed. That was, um, hardly the first time Cat's seen something like that."

Roman's expression alone is enough to tell me I haven't quite hit the "no big deal," vibe I was going for. His mouth has become a tight line. "Is that so?"

"We were roommates freshman year, so..." I trail off, realizing that by inventing this story out of thin-air, I'm making myself sound *so* much worse than I ever needed to. *Why, why do I open my mouth?*

He exhales sharply through his nose. "It's a good thing you're a bad liar, good girl, or I'd be calling Catalina right now to get a list of every man who's ever touched you."

A shiver travels down my spine. I might be a bad liar myself, but I'm good at spotting lies, and Roman has never been more serious.

He grabs my hand and pulls me around a corner into a less crowded hallway. "Less," being the key word. It's not empty, just not packed, and I can still see the outlines of people walking past his shoulder behind him as he backs me up against the wall. "So where are we going, good girl?"

"Stop." My voice is nearly pleading. "We can't be seen here."

His exasperation is evident, but still, he grabs my hand and drags me behind him down the hall toward the nearest door. I doubt he even knows where we're going. We could be about to barge into a full classroom.

Thank the gods, Roman opens a door onto an empty dimly lit classroom full of four-seater worktables and yanks me inside.

"Happy?" he asks, low and dangerous.

"Never better," I snap.

We hold each other's gaze and electricity seems to charge between us. I bite my lip and his gaze tracks the movement. I feel my pulse shift lower.

Roman's tongue darts out to run over his bottom lip, his black eyes following my every tiny shift and intake of breath. "Come back to my place."

A shiver of excitement travels over my entire body, hardening my nipples and making my pulse pound in my core. Gods, I hate him for how much he affects me. I hate that I want to go with him more than anything, even though I know it's a terrible idea. My attempts to put distance between us are failing miserably, and I'm flailing.

I suck in a quick breath, my gaze darting between his black eyes. "I can't."

"Can't or won't?"

"I really can't. I told you I have to go to dinner with Harrison and my parents."

"Fuck that," he says emphatically. "It doesn't matter what Dane thinks about you, anyway."

"This isn't about that. It's about following the plan."

He leans in closer, his face only inches from mine, and his tone is mocking as he runs his fingers up the inside of my thigh. "Do I need to remind you who owns this?"

"Excuse me if I don't want to screw up the plan and have it be my fault if my cousin kills you."

He stares at me with so much intensity I almost can't hold his gaze. It's all-consuming, yet I have no idea what he's thinking; if he's angry, or about to start shouting.

I shiver.

Everything about Roman's personality is too intense—too saturated—like he was born with the contrast settings up too high. Yet knowing that, seeing it from afar, and having all that feverish, near-fanatical energy solely focused on me, are three entirely different experiences.

When he speaks, it's so low, I strain my ears to hear him. "Fine, good girl. We'll stick to your plan for now."

"Good," I mutter, confused at how easy that was. Why do I feel like I'm not out of the woods yet?

Roman glances over at one of the long, workbench style desks in the empty classroom and his lip curls in a half-smile. "Come here."

I shouldn't. I *should* argue, except I don't have a single leg to stand on, that isn't shaking or bare of tights.

I take two, wobbling steps toward the nearest table as he asks: "What time is it, good girl?"

I quirk an eyebrow at him, confused, before fumbling in my pocket for my phone. "Um, it's 4:50." I glance back up at him, as I speak and realize belatedly, he's wearing a watch. I scoff. "But you already knew that, right?"

He smiles. "I'm guessing this classroom will get used at 5:00, which means you have exactly ten minutes."

"To what?"

"To persuade me to let you go to your insipid dinner."

I blanch. "That's not how this works. You said we'd stick to my plan."

"And if you can provide me with an adequate incentive, we will." He smirks. "What did you say the other night? This isn't kindergarten, Etta."

My stomach drops out. "Don't say that."

Roman's eyes flash back and forth between mine and he must realize I'm serious, because for once, he drops it without question. He takes a step toward me instead, backing me in against the table. "Come on, good girl. I know you're a good debater."

I laugh lightly. I am, in fact. Structured debates were one of the few times I was ever able to argue to my heart's content without the fear of coming off rude, or the judgement of being beholden to my own anger. In a way, it's a bit like this. Hiding behind practice, to act out the fantasy of what I want.

I glance at the clock on the wall. Roman doesn't want a debate. He wants me to convince him.

With a boldness I didn't know I was capable of—at least, not without more prompting—I reach forward and trail my fingers along the edge of his belt until I reach the buckle. Leaning forward to brush my mouth against his collar bone, I undo the belt and unbutton his pants.

"I thought you said no kissing," Roman rasps.

"This doesn't count."

I slip my hand into his pants and I'm momentarily shocked as my fingers brush smooth skin. Roman is neither a boxers nor a briefs guy, apparently, and I hate how that both fits perfectly, and somehow changes every interaction I've ever had with him.

My fingers stroke up and down his length, teasing, my thumb rolling over the head. I gently explore while I graze my mouth over the exposed skin of his neck just above the collar of his shirt. I'm almost glad it's the highest point I could reach. He'd have to bend down for our lips to connect, saving me from myself.

"You have eight minutes," he says roughly. "Unless you want to practice with a real audience."

My stomach lurches. I'm pretty sure he's joking. I don't *think* he wants that—but then again, it's hard to tell sometimes. Better just to get a move on.

I sink to my knees in front of him. It's just like last night, in my kitchen, but this time I'm in control. I'm choosing to do this, rather than Roman leading me through the motions.

"No, that's not what I meant," he says sharply, trying to tug me back up.

"You just said I had to convince you."

It's a twisted little game we've started, battling for control, and I'm not sure how it happened or when it started. If it was in the library when we decided to do this, or that day on the steps outside the auction, or upstairs at my parents' party. Or maybe it was years ago, in cemeteries, or outside our headmaster's office.

I know I'm already at a disadvantage in our game. Know that Roman wants to own me and thinks he already does, and that in a way he's a little bit right. Yet, as I look up at him through my lashes and lean forward to run my tongue up his cock. As I wrap my hand around the base and suck the head into my mouth, swirling my tongue with each long, teasing strokes, I feel like I might be closing the distance on his lead.

I smile around his tip, enjoying this power I have over him, and speed up my pace taking more and more into my mouth with each motion.

"Fuck." Roman makes a strangled sound and digs his fingers into my hair. "You don't know me as well as you seem to think you do, good girl."

My eyes narrow. I don't know what that means because he's clearly enjoying this. His nails scrape my scalp, half holding me there, half petting me. Like a caress against the top of my head as he moves me back and forth over his length.

My clit throbs as he speeds his pace, fucking my mouth, deeper and deeper until he hits the back of my throat, I blink against the burn in my eyes and mascara tears pour down my face.

Finally, his hips jerk and then he's erupting down my throat in long, hot bursts and I swallow instinctively.

"Good girl," Roman breathes, face almost pained as he gently wipes the tears from my cheeks with his thumbs.

I tense, my brain warring with the way my body hums when he calls me that: "good" uttered in this entirely new context. Not like I'm "good" but I'm good for him. I've pleased him.

I smile and move to stand, licking my lips, but Roman's hand shoots out to stop me. "Where do you think you're going?"

"I thought there was a class coming in," I gasp.

"There is. You've still got about fifteen-seconds and I remain unconvinced. Better make it quick."

I gape at him. What the hell? "What else did you want me to do?"

He shakes his head at me, mischief in his eyes. "You should have used that time to make yourself come, good girl. I'm not the one who needs reminding who they belong to."

My mouth falls open. I—he—what? Does he mean what that sounds like, or did he misspeak?

"Well, I guess I lose then," I mutter, reaching for my abandoned bag.

Roman reaches out and catches me around the waist and yanks me back before I can take a single step toward the door. Pressing his lips to the curve of my neck, he kisses along my pulse point, nipping and sucking over my skin. I gasp, going half-limp in his arms. I guess this isn't technically kissing...and it feels so good, sending tingles of pleasure all over my body.

But then I realize what he's doing. He won't let go, sucking so hard against the same spot on my skin it's bound to leave a mark. I bring my hands up, shoving his chest, but he's already letting me go.

"What the hell?" I hiss, even as I glance around. There's no way someone didn't see that.

"Just in case you or anyone else needs a reminder that you're mine." Roman looks down at my neck with smug satisfaction and runs a thumb over the bruise. "Have a nice dinner, good girl."

CHAPTER THIRTY-THREE

ETTA

PRESENT

I SWAY ANXIOUSLY BETWEEN MY FEET AND JUMP AT every sign of movement from outside. The sausage-casing dress my mother laid out on my bed sticks uncomfortably to my skin and sweat beads on my hairline.

"You look like you're about to bolt," Cat says from behind me.

I snort. If I didn't know my mother would move mansions to find me, I'd be halfway across town by now. "What was your first clue?"

"If you do, let me know this time. I'll help."

Cat still hasn't forgiven me for yesterday. Not that I can blame her exactly—I'd be traumatized for life. Hell, I *am* traumatized for life.

Maybe it's that trauma that has me on edge as I stand at the window, staring out into the dark driveway. Maybe it's that Harrison Dane is coming to dinner. *One guess which one.*

I drop the curtain on the window to the dining room and turn to face her. Her tone is light, but her eyes tell me she's halfway serious. "Have I said I'm sorry enough?"

"Maybe a few more times." She examines her nails, not meeting my eyes. "We're close, I think."

I shake my head. At least she's direct, I guess. "I really would have told you—"

"—If you'd processed it yourself, I know," she finishes.

"Right."

Personally, I think that's a good excuse. For someone like me, who takes time to think things through and doesn't blurt everything out as it occurs to me, it makes total sense. Cat isn't like that. Her thoughts seem to erupt from her mouth, fully formed and functional.

"I would never have told anyone, you know."

"I know, but you would have reminded me—"

"—How dumb this is?"

Yeah, that.

I shake my head. Trust Cat to be the world's bluntest voice of reason, just when you don't want it.

She sucks on her teeth, like she's thinking hard. "Look. You know I think all privileged men are the scum of the earth."

"You exclusively date privileged men."

"Yes, and I hate them. I was just going to say, I get it why you'd do it, I mean, he doesn't even look real...but there are plenty of hot guys out there who don't come with emotional damage and red flags the size of circus tents."

I nod. "Mmm."

Honestly, Roman isn't the only walking red flag in this…whatever we are. I'm not putting my best foot forward lately either.

I hear the doorbell and my heart seizes. Cat turns toward me. "Don't worry. I doubt Dane will bring up the restaurant if he hasn't already."

It seems that Harrison's pride prevented him from telling my parents or anyone else I walked out on him the other night—at least so far. I wish that was my only fear about this evening.

With a few days' distance and Cat's reassurance, I'm surer than ever that I didn't overreact the other night—I was right to get out of there. I just wish I could trust my parents to take my side.

Right now, I wouldn't trust either of them as far as I can throw them. They could tell me it was raining while I was looking outside at a thunderstorm and I would still go outside and soak myself, just to check.

As if summoned by my thoughts, my mother appears in the doorway like a dark specter. She wordlessly beckons Cat and I toward the living room, her expression pinched. I feel my feet move without my permission, as if I'm a puppet on someone else's strings. Sometimes I wonder if my mom is using spells, or if she's just *that* manipulative.

"Tilt your head," Cat mutters.

I glance at her, hissing under my breath. "What?"

"That thing on your neck is not subtle. Like, at all. My gods, get some better concealer."

The three of us step into the room and find Harrison, Tyberius, and my father already gathered around the drink cart. Now I realize why Cat was invited to stay—she might be staying with us while her family is away, but my mom would have absolutely no problem telling her to go out for dinner if her presence would mess up the symmetry of the place settings. With Ty here, and his on-again-off-again girlfriend nowhere in sight, it looks like Cat is about to be thrown to the wolves.

"Sorry," I mouth at her.

She shrugs, plastering a grin on her face. "Whatever."

Taking my friend's lead, I also force myself to smile, slipping into the easygoing beauty queen façade my mother has cultivated for me over the last twenty-one years. At the last second, I remember to tilt my head down to hide my neck. "Hello."

Harrison turns, and his gaze frosts over as he takes me in. He's wearing a brown tweed blazer over a black turtleneck sweater with no tie. His pale lips are turned up in an unamused smile, his arms folded in front of his chest. His back is to my father, who can't see his expression, and therefore smiles genuinely, unaware anything is amiss.

"There you are, Etta." My dad beams. "I was starting to think you got lost."

I focus on my dad, ignoring Harrison. Of my entire family, he's the only one who never calls me Juliette, for which I am grateful.

I grin, nodding at the drink he just poured. "Is that for me?"

Dad pretends to frown, before handing it over with a jovial wink. My heart squeezes. I rarely see him, now that he spends so much time with his barely legal mistress. "How was work, dad?"

I immediately cringe. What a basic question—I'd been meaning to ask him about that book I spotted in his room, or my pledging, or talk about school, or *anything* that might result in a conversation longer than a few sentences.

Sure enough, my father waves me off. "Uneventful. Harrison was just telling us about the business."

I deflate. I don't care about Harrison—worse than that, I actively despise Harrison, which I'm fairly sure my mother realizes, and my father would realize if he'd been present for a single, solitary day since I've been home.

But I don't say that. I don't say anything. Like Pavlov's dog, the dismissal from my father has me smiling sweetly as I fall back into old patterns. "Fascinating. Please continue."

We all fall into seats around the dimly lit living room. The ice in Harrison's glass clinks against the crystal as he takes a sip of the scotch. He glances at me with his pale eyes and smiles tightly. "As I was saying, we've been having success with our venture capital investments. It's a good time to be in the media."

I couldn't care less about what he's saying, and it must show because as he speaks, my mother glares daggers at me across the room. I stifle a groan. Usually, silence is my best option, but apparently not tonight. Dinner hasn't even started yet, and already I'm in trouble.

I don't know what my mother is expecting me to say. I know little about Harrison's role in his family business and have nothing to add to this conversation. Cat looks across the room and at me and smiles encouragingly.

I take a deep breath. "So, do you have any fun stories?"

Harrison blinks at me, as the room falls silent. "Fun?"

"Yeah, you know...what's the point of working in news if you don't get all the gossip first, right? Have you ever had to bury a scandal?"

My mother looks like I've asked Harrison about his porn watching habits and followed it up by uttering a vile slur. I blink, confused as to what I've possibly said that's so offensive. To my credit, even Tyberius —difficult and fussy as he is—seems perplexed.

"No, Juliette," Harrison snaps. "We report the news fairly and accurately, exactly as it is. *Every. Single. Day.* We don't *bury scandals.*"

I bite my tongue. I have never been surer that he absolutely has bodies in his yard—probably literally, but that's none of my business, I guess. "Right. Okay, sorry. So, what's the headline for tomorrow then?"

Harrison's expression darkens and he presses his lips together as he leans back against the chez lounge. "If you must know, there's been another disappearance in the community.

"Oh my gods. I'm sorry." I immediately regret my question. I'm not sorry for him—or for asking, but for the family and for whomever has gone missing. "Who was it?"

He ignores my question. Harrison nods sagely, as if I should be sorry. "Yes, well, it is a trying time for the community."

My mother glares at me, as if there was any way I could have known what the answer would be when I asked about the headline. My eye twitches. I shouldn't be annoyed when someone is missing and likely dead. There are clearly larger problems in the world. But *come on! This* is why I stay quiet.

Tyberius gets to his feet. He casts me a sympathetic glance, before placing his glass on a side table and turning toward the door. "If you'll excuse me. I need to go check on something."

I would bet money he's going to call Adriana—his sometimes girl-friend. He might be a douchebag, but he's not completely heartless.

My father waves Ty away, his gaze shifting between Harrison and I, an unspoken question in his eyes. He looks as though he's struggling to understand the tension between us. *Yes, dad, stop this.* I silently beg. *I hate this guy.*

But before anyone else can speak, Harrison jumps in again. "Sorry to sour the mood," he says, not sounding sorry at all.

"Not at all," my mother rushes to say. "How many is that? Four this year?"

"Five, I think," my father says. "Who was the most recent victim?"

"Another girl from the school. Her name hasn't been released yet."

The air around us thickens while my parents exchange wary glances—clearly unsettled.

"This is exactly why we need a shift on the council," my mother says. "I like Emrys, but this cannot continue."

"Quite right," Harrison agrees.

My back straightens and I glance at Cat, meeting her eyes. *See?* I want to say. *It's political.*

Maybe if I had the kind of relationship with my parents where I could simply ask them their plans and trust that they would be honest with me I would have known about this days ago, rather than having to guess and plot, while they were no doubt doing the same behind my back.

If only they'd included me in the conversation. I would, of course, agree that not investigating the disappearance of multiple women from the Order could never continue. We could have come up with another solution to get more votes—a solution like the one I found with Roman.

Except, that's the problem, isn't it? My parents would never have accepted that option, even if it was the simplest and the most obvious. Because their hatred stems so deep it overshadows everything, even their love for me and their better judgment.

"Maybe we should consider moving up the wedding," my father muses.

I choke on the drink I'd only just raised to my lips and bang the glass painfully against my teeth. No one seems to notice. "What? Why?" I nearly choke on my own shock.

My mother looks over at me and frowns, practically daring me to argue. "You'll pledge at the same time as your wedding ceremony, Juliette. Surely, I don't have to explain the advantages of that to you."

I swallow. She doesn't have to. It's only that I refuse to marry Harrison. Even the thought of performing the bonding ritual with him makes me want to climb out of my own skin.

"If we're going to do that, we should really get around to officially announcing the engagement," my mother says, shooting me a dirty look.

"Can't we just post on social media like normal people?" I ask.

Everyone laughs, like I'm joking.

"How about we have a party on..." my mother thinks for a moment "...the day after tomorrow? I think I can pull something together in 48 hours."

"Perfect," Harrison agrees.

I swallow thickly, holding onto my sanity with every shred of my control. I take a deep breath. All I need is to make it through dinner and call Roman. I'll talk to him, we'll figure this out, and everything will be okay.

I don't want to think about how easily Roman has worked his way into my life. How after only a few days, I'm thinking of him as the person I need to run to for help. I can't think about that. Because if I do, I'll have to confront every other way Roman Montague is invading every part of me.

And if I do that, I'm afraid I won't be able to turn back.

I MANAGE TO GET THROUGH THE REST OF DINNER without incident—without running screaming from the room or stabbing Harrison with my dessert fork. Yet, as my mother goes over plans for moving up the wedding, my anxiety rises in my chest, my mood growing darker by the minute.

Cat meets my gaze across the table, and we share a silent understanding. The moment Harrison says Goodnight and has closed the front door behind him, she and I dash upstairs to my room before my mother can call us back.

"What the hell am I going to do?" I hiss as I close my bedroom door behind me, turning the lock with a snap. "This is insane."

Before Cat can reply, we both stiffen as my mother's shrill voice sounds through the door. "Juliette!"

"Damn!" I whisper. "Tell her I'm in the shower."

"Why?"

"I just don't want to talk to her."

I dive into the ensuite bathroom and turn on the shower before lying my entire body flat against the closed door to hear what my mother is saying to Cat. There's a pause outside, before the hinges of my bedroom door creak and my mother's muffled voice sounds again.

"Oh, Catalina. Where's my daughter?"

"In the shower, Mrs. Capulet."

"Well, would you tell her to come to me when she gets out? I don't care how late it is."

"Sure."

There's a pause, and my stomach roils with anxiety—I wish I could see their faces. "It would help if you could remind Juliette that Harrison, is a good match. He's wealthy and powerful and despite her sulking actually wants to marry her. She's doing herself no favors by trying to ruin this."

I struggle not to bang my head against the wall, knowing the sound will give away that I can hear them.

The door clicks shut, and I burst out of the bathroom. "See? See how insane this is?"

Cat nods. "I never said it wasn't."

I sink onto my bed, massaging my temples where a stress headache began to form over an hour ago. It's not the arranged marriage that's getting to me—it's the speed, and the fact that my parents don't seem to care at all that I barely know Harrison, and from what I've seen, I don't want to know him.

"You have a plan, though, right?"

I look up, finding her leaning against my bedroom door, arms crossed over her chest. "What do you mean?"

"Well, we knew this was coming...right? I thought you were already planning to marry Montague instead."

Her nose wrinkles when she speaks, her expression telling me she still can't quite believe I'm speaking to Roman Montague, let alone want to marry him. I can't quite believe it either.

I pinch the bridge of my nose. She acts like it's so simple. "Sure, but I wasn't expecting the wedding to be moved up."

Cat walks over to sit next to me on the bed. "So?"

I bark a humorless laugh. "Very helpful, thank you."

"No, I'm serious," she says, her eyes wide. "So what? You were already hanging off the deep end, let's just jump all the way in."

I blink at her. "I don't know what you're talking about. You need to spell it out."

She sighs, exasperated, and flicks her long black hair over her shoulder. "Gimme your phone."

I hand it over without question. Cat has been my partner in crime since we were kids, always there to help me in times of crisis. The gods know I wasn't exactly killing it without her input all week, so time to make a change. *Catalina, take the wheel.*

My heart thumps heavily in my chest as I hear the muffled sound of the line ringing, as Cat holds my phone to her ear.

"Who are you calling?" I ask anxiously.

She holds the phone out to me. "Your boyfriend."

I snatch the phone from her, pressing it to my ear. "He's not my boyfriend. And, anyway, I could have done that."

"Yeah, but you wouldn't have. At least not before going back and forth about it for the next hour."

True. Voicemail picks up, the standard phone-company message that means Roman never recorded a personal greeting, and I scowl. "Well, he's not answering. So, now what?"

I glance at the time. It is almost midnight. With anyone else I would say they were sleeping, but people with normal sleep schedules don't write "BUY MELATONIN" on their hands or have vampire-esque circles under their eyes.

My eyes dart to the balcony doors, and the image of Roman launching himself over my railing pops into my mind.

A small smile curves my lips.

Chapter Thirty-Four

✦ ROMAN ✦

PRESENT

"Your bet," Bennet says from seemingly very far away.

I look up and am almost surprised to see my kitchen table full, my friends staring at me expectantly. I shake my head to clear it, blinking down at the cards laid out in the center of the table. I can barely remember what's in my own hand, so it makes no difference what's been turned over since I stopped paying attention to the game.

I toss a few bills into the center without enthusiasm. "Check."

Pierce rolls his eyes. "You just raised the last bet by $20. At least pretend to pay attention."

My expression is stony. "I don't know what gave you the impression I wanted to play at all."

There's a Hunter S. Thompson book in my room calling my name, and a woman I love having dinner with some other man right now. I have better things to do than play poker with my dickhead friends.

Luca, another one of our friends, leans over and fishes my $20 out of the pot in the center of the table, handing it back to me. "No one thinks you want to play, Roman."

I growl in the back of my throat. "Then why—"

"—Because we're better people than you." Bennet interrupts me. "Accept it and move on."

He's not wrong. They are better people than me—it's part of why I can't understand why they won't go away. I've been moody and mean and borderline unstable for a decade, and that was before Marcia died and things got infinitely worse.

I watch my friends talking and laughing, tossing money on the table, winning and losing, and in a way I'm grateful that they haven't abandoned me. Even if I deserve it. Even if I've done my best to drive them away time and time again in a thousand different ways—tonight being no exception.

I can't think. Can't focus, knowing that Etta is at dinner with that fucking prick, Dane, right now. I keep imagining wild scenarios where she leaves and gets married tonight or comes over tomorrow to tell me that she met someone else and is moving to England with him.

It won't matter. I try to tell myself as I toss a few more dollars onto the table. All the reasons she wants this will still count, even if her parents are pressuring her, or Dane turns out to be not such a prick after all. I can take her traveling. We'll fix the feud. She'll get to go to school. She'll still be mine.

A sharp knock sounds on the door and I jump, nearly sloshing the beer in my hand over the front of my sweater. Bennet and I make eye-contact across the table.

"Did you invite anyone else?" I ask, leaning forward, the front legs of my chair hitting the floor with a clatter.

Bennet shakes his head, then glances over at Luca "I didn't, but..."

I know what he's implying—we all do. Luca is fucking some girl and is so pussy-whipped he will invite her anywhere he is without a second thought. Not that I have a single leg to stand on, but no one but Bennet knows that yet, and he's not going to point it out. He likes his teeth where they are.

"Not me," Luca says, putting his hands up. "Bianca is on vacation. I'm texting her now."

I grumble in the back of my throat, as whoever is outside knocks again. Realizing I will have to get up and answer the door, I put my drink down and push my chair back from the table. "If it's the neighbors complaining about noise again..."

"Curse 'em," Bennet says, slurring his words slightly.

To be honest, if I hadn't sworn off magic, I would. Our neighbor could do with a good curse. I suppose I could always hit him...

I make my way to the door and pull it open with more force than necessary, sure I'm about to come face-to-face with one of the needier tenants in the building. I need an assistant.

"Listen," I say as I open the door. "We didn't—" I stop short, my words dying in my throat.

"Hi," Etta says breathlessly.

Her eyes are wide, her hands bunched in the wool coat she's wearing over casual leggings. I blink at her, nonplussed, while behind me, I'm distantly aware that the kitchen has fallen silent, my friends clearly knowing that something is going on.

"What are you doing here?" I ask, finally.

She dances between her feet. "Can we come in?"

I glance behind her and realize that she's not alone. Catalina Minola is standing maybe ten feet back down the hall.

My brain stutters. I'm still frustrated about earlier, but not enough to not be glad to see her. But I can't help focusing on that dinner she was at. Fuck, why is it that every time she sees that asshole something happens? "What's wrong?"

Etta shuffles between her feet. "Nothing...exactly. You just didn't answer your phone and," she takes a deep breath. "I didn't know where else to go."

She didn't know where else to go?

My mind spins as I step aside to let her in. Etta and Catalina follow me into the house with an apprehension that contradicts the confidence Etta showed in the door only moments before.

My friends all look up, as if only just noticing we're here. I roll my eyes. It's bullshit. We were playing Texas hold 'em, and Pierce is holding at least ten cards in front of his face, while Bennet is counting crumpled dollar bills with an enthusiasm that implies, he's never seen money before.

Only Luca frowns, seeming disturbed by their presence. He texts furiously, his thumbs flying across the screen of his phone.

I open my mouth, and come up short, realizing I have no idea how to introduce Etta or her friend. Not that we don't all know each other. We do. Yet, it's impossible to ignore that this is an unusual situation. I glance at Etta, and my stomach seizes. She's uncomfortable. She came here to see me—for my help, and she's uncomfortable. Un-fucking-acceptable.

Digging deep into the recesses of my personality—whoever I used to be before Marcia died, before things stopped mattering, I reach for her hand and drag her forward and into my lap. No gods-damned introduction necessary.

"Lu!" I bark, and he looks up from his phone, startled. "Get a chair for Catalina."

"Cat," Etta mutters.

Whatever.

"I didn't know you had company," Etta murmurs as the guys shift around, moving chairs and offering drinks.

"We're not company," Bennet says before I can say anything.

"Not at all," Pierce adds. "I promise, Montague would prefer we'd all leave."

He's not wrong. Especially now, when I want to pull Etta into my room and wipe that frown off her face. That I want to show her exactly what she's getting herself into by coming here—I want to lock her in my room and never let her out. I would too—I will, but if I know a single thing about her, it's that she'll be nervous to leave her friend, and embarrassed if I drag her away with an audience within seconds of her arrival.

Etta looks up at me with mild confusion at Bennet's statement, but it's Catalina who replies. "Then why don't you leave?"

"I live here," Bennet says, taking another sip of his drink.

"I like poker," Luca answers, almost nervously, as Catalina turns her gaze to him.

When Pierce says nothing, she fixes him with a dark stare and crosses her arms. He blinks up at her, seeming almost bemused. "I don't answer to you."

Catalina pauses for what seems like a very long moment, then smiles, seeming to accept his response.

As if she's not even listening to their exchange, Etta shifts in my lap, and I can feel the tension in her body.

I lean in, whispering in her ear so only she can hear. "You shouldn't be here, good girl. You're not safe in this house."

She shivers, her eyes flashing with doubt as she cranes her neck around to meet my gaze. "I know. I'm sorry about earlier. I just... I thought—"

I cut her off before she can finish whatever thought is in her head, and plant whatever seed of doubt is there. "To be clear, you're not safe here because if you stay too long, I might never let you go."

Etta blinks, seeming taken aback before her gray eyes darken with lust. "That's fine. I'm not all that interested in, 'safe.' I would have thought that was already clear, but if not I'm happy to give you another demonstration."

I choke on a laugh, and wrap my arms around her waist, pulling her closer to me. I can feel her heart racing against my chest. It's the most thrilling feeling. She's so awake. Alive. "I'm going to hold you to that."

CHAPTER THIRTY-FIVE
✦ ROMAN ✦

SENIOR YEAR OF HIGH SCHOOL, FOUR YEARS AGO

THE PENDULUM SWINGS BACK AND FORTH, BACK AND forth, becoming so hypnotic I keep forgetting what I'm doing and having to start over.

With a grunt of frustration, I shake my hand out and try again.

We're not allowed to use magic until we join the Order at twenty-one, but this is barely even magic. Kitchen-witchery. Or, it would be, if it was fucking working.

"You're doing that wrong."

I feel Etta's presence behind me, but I refuse to turn around. "Yeah? And I suppose you know better?"

She moves behind me, and a shiver travels up the back of my neck. I feel her leaning over my shoulder, as if to inspect what I'm doing. "What are you even looking for?"

"None of your business."

The truth is, I lost my wallet in the woods the other night, but I don't want to remind her of the party.

"Well, you can't just hang a pendulum over nothing and hope for the best," she says, her tone slightly bossy. "You need either a map, so you're scrying over it, or an anchor, like a part of whatever was lost. Preferably both. You're just waving a chain over a table, that's not going to do anything."

I make a non-committal noise in the back of my throat, but close my fist around my pendulum, giving up.

Finally, I look up at Etta as she plants herself beside me and lays her books out across the edge of the table. Did I miss something? Are we speaking to each other again?

"I thought you were pissed at me."

"Always," she says lightly as she takes her laptop out of her bag.

I furrow my brow. "Then what are you doing here?"

"Being the better person."

"Don't you mean 'the bigger person?'"

"No," she says sweetly.

I smile in spite of myself and stand to go look for a book of maps.

For some reason, I look back, and my stomach turns over.

I can't help but notice the way her skirt clings to her thighs, the way her blouse catches the light. The way her hair tumbles over her shoulders and how ridiculously, maddeningly beautiful she is.

Like she can feel my eyes on her, she looks up and smiles.

My chest pangs, and suddenly I can't breathe. Suddenly, everything becomes utterly clear, and a single, painful, rush.

I'm not falling for her, I'm already there—I've been here all along.

She's perfect—only she's not meant for me.

And I'm perfectly fucked.

CHAPTER THIRTY-SIX

·∗· ETTA ·∗·

PRESENT

IF I WAS TO BE PUT ON THE STAND IN COURT, AND asked to tell the truth, the whole truth, and nothing but the truth, I still wouldn't be able to explain exactly how I ended up at Roman Montague's house tonight. If I was threatened, tortured, or bewitched, I doubt it would make a shred of difference, because my memory simply slipped away into nothingness, becoming a blur of confusion and colors.

I remember the strongest urge to escape, then before I knew it, we were climbing down the balcony and ordering an Uber.

"I really need to talk to you," I mutter to Roman. "But..."

I glance at Cat, unsure if I should leave her by herself, and Roman follows my gaze. "She'll be fine with them."

"I know. I'm more worried about them, actually."

He raises an eyebrow. "You're not serious."

I only shrug. He'll see soon enough, I suppose.

Honestly, if I'd known Roman had friends over, I probably wouldn't have come, so in a way I'm glad he didn't pick up the phone. I'm not sure the same can be said of Cat, who seems wary at best of these guys who have never paid us the time of day before now. Teenage me would be eating this up, while simultaneously hating myself for giving into the desire to be accepted by this group of dangerous, forbidden, popular boys. They're men now, and no less forbidden or dangerous, and I'm still falling apart just a little at how easily Roman invited me into his world. Even if it isn't real. Even if Roman isn't really mine.

I lean over to Cat, speaking low, as if the rest of the room can't hear me. I jerk my head to the side, indicating that I'm going to leave the room. "Are you okay if I just—"

"Sure," she says, still eying Roman's friends like she's choosing a horse on Derby Day.

Roman takes my hand and tugs me behind him out of the kitchen and across a dark, eclectic living room full of dark oak wood and cozy leather furniture. On the right side of the room, a long hall with several closed doors on either side ends in a primary suite nearly the same size as the living room and kitchen combined.

I glance around at the bedroom, which just looks like the back half of a used bookshop, with a king-sized bed plunked in the center.

"How did you persuade Bennet to give you this room?"

He looks at me sideways. "*Give* me this room?"

"Yeah...don't you guys live together? I can't imagine there's another bedroom this big."

"There isn't, but I own the building," he says casually. "So, it wasn't really a discussion."

I blink at him, shocked. "You do?"

"Yeah, I guess you could say Bennet lives *with me.* Not that he's not also doing well. He likes to invest in the stock market, and he's good with star charts so he always knows when to buy shares and when to sell. He runs all our portfolios for us."

"So, he's a magical hedge fund manager."

"Yeah, I guess."

I suck on my teeth and lower myself to sit on the edge of his huge bed. "Interesting...but how do you own this building? I guess I thought..."

His dark eyes flash with amusement. "That my parents were moments away from disowning me for being an alcoholic, violent, fuck up and I was about to be destitute and homeless."

"I mean...maybe not in so many words."

I feel the back of my neck heat. I suppose, yes, that's sort of what I was picturing. I thought that part of why he had to get married at all was because his inheritance was being dangled over his head, like some sort of regency novel. If that's not the case, then...why is he doing this?

Roman furrows his brow, as if debating how much to explain to me. He relaxes his shoulders, in a gesture I've come to understand as "fuck it," and says: "That's half true. My father is constantly threatening to disown me because he's a prick, but even if he does, I don't need their money. Having it wouldn't be anything to scoff at, but it's not necessary."

"How?"

"I sell rare books. I'm good at scrying, especially for things I have a connection to." He grimaces as he says this, looking almost angry for some reason.

Scrying? The strangest memory pops out of nowhere—of Roman trying to scry over a blank table, with clearly no idea what he was doing. He can't be *that* good, right?

"I rarely see you use magic," I comment, voicing something that's been bothering me.

 A blind woman could see there's more bubbling beneath the surface than he's letting on. Not that Roman owes me anything, but the foolish part of me that knows I'm heading into dangerous waters with this man, wants him to trust me enough to tell me.

His eyes dart to the side and he licks over his lips. "I can find books thousands of miles away, sometimes even in other countries," he says.

I blink. I don't know what I was expecting, but that never would have crossed my mind. I guess he's come a long way since the day I had to teach him how to do it.

Scrying is a relatively simple practice, more akin to one of my spell jars, than casting complex runes. It involves holding a pendulum made of either crystal or conductive metal over a map, or the palm of your hand, and following the direction of the pendulum's swing. Generally, it isn't all that reliable and isn't used to find items further than a mile or two away. If Roman can find things thousands of miles away, he's not "good," at scrying, he's a savant.

"So, you do use magic?" I press, confused.

He shakes his head. "Not anymore."

"But your job? And your research...I'm assuming that's affected too?"

He barks a harsh laugh and sinks onto his bed next to me, pushing a hand through his dark hair. For a moment, all I can see is how we'd sit like this, in secret in cemeteries, surrounded by the scent of fall leaves and clove cigarettes.

With a jolt, I realize I can't smell the cloves. I bite my lip, wanting to ask about it, but not wanting to distract him if he's going to tell me something real.

"My sister disappeared two weeks after I graduated," he says, turning to stare at the wall. As if, looking at me at the same time as speaking is impossible. "I pledged the same night of graduation. You know how that works."

I tip my head—yes, of course I know. A tiny hint of bitterness climbs up my throat at the thought that perhaps I won't have the same experience, but I swallow it back down. This isn't about me. "Then what?"

He grins, almost embarrassed, looking down. "We threw lots of parties mainly." He jerks his head toward the door to indicate his friends in the kitchen. "They're all still in school with you, so it was like—"

"Having one friend who's twenty-one and can buy the beer?" I supply.

"Something like that. After that summer I was going to go traveling and find rare manuscripts for the Order, but then Marcia didn't come home."

I try to remember Marcia. She was younger than us by several years and never had much to do with me, but I was still sad when I heard she disappeared—more so when they found her body. Even my parents, who have nothing nice to say about the Montagues, were shaken by the death of a teenager.

"So you stayed because of your sister?" I hedge.

"And because I don't want to do the job anymore," he confirms.

He says it flatly, without any of his usual embellishment. I narrow my eyes. "I don't understand."

He runs a hand over the back of his head, seeming frustrated—though I can't tell if it's with me, or himself, or this conversation in general. Maybe a combination of all three, or perhaps simply with life overall. "Marcia was missing for three weeks before we found her body. Three weeks where I couldn't find her, but I could find a previously undiscovered original manuscript for *Dracula* two continents away. Do you know how fucking infuriating that is?" His voice rises, not quite yelling, but enough that I lean back. His black eyes track my movement, and he stops. "Sorry."

"No, don't apologize," I say quickly.

Shit.

I lean forward, reaching for him, but he pulls away. "Why did you come here, good girl?"

My stomach clenches. This time when he calls me "good girl," it doesn't feel like teasing or even fun. It feels like distance. Like a reminder of the ways in which he thinks we're different. I am the good girl, and Roman Montague will never see me as a whole person with flaws or himself as anything other than a villain.

I swallow thickly. "My parents want to move up my wedding."

Rage flashes in front of his eyes. "And you're just okay with that?"

Seated, we're still not eye-level, but I don't have to crane my neck to look up at him as I draw myself up. "You asked me why I was here. What part of my being here makes you think I would be okay with that"

The corner of his mouth tips up. "Is this your rebellion, good girl?"

I bite my lip. I don't know how to answer him. Maybe? Or maybe I'm just finally doing something I want, just because I want it. Maybe I'm struggling to say what I want out loud, to put my thoughts into words, so instead I have to show everyone who I am.

"Something like that," I say, knowing it's nowhere near enough. Nowhere near the right words for the magnitude of the emotions swirling just on the edge of my mind.

My heart beats in my ears as Roman's black eyes track over me. I hope he understands what I'm saying—or rather, what I'm not saying. What I can't quite admit even to myself.

"We'll figure it out tomorrow, good girl," he says finally, like the subject is closed.

"Yeah, if you don't mind us—"

"Don't even ask me if it's okay if you stay. I already told you I wasn't going to let you leave."

A thrill travels up my spine, and I glance down to hide how much those words affect me. They shouldn't, but *gods.* Why do I like it when he's demanding and aggressive? Why can I think of nothing else but how I'd like to see more of how dark I know he can be?

I ASK TO USE HIS SHOWER, AND ROMAN DIRECTS ME TO the ensuite off his bedroom.

The marble walls, floors, and countertops are all spotless and polished, the stone so smooth it's almost reflective. Fluffy, white towels hang from a rack next to the shower, and the fresh scent of shampoo and conditioner; a pine fragrance fills the air.

Gods—I could die here and be perfectly content.

I cross to the walk-in shower, shedding my clothes as I go. The tiled floor is cool under my bare feet but warms quickly as I turn on the water and steam fills the bathroom.

I step under the spray of the shower head and sigh as warm water pours over me, massaging the tension from my tight muscles. I didn't realize until this moment how right Roman was—I was stressed.

Reaching for the nearest bottle on the built-in shelf, I tip some body wash into my palm. The smell of pine and eucalyptus fills my nose and my heart pounds against my ribs. I run my hands over my body, covering myself in Roman's strong, masculine scent.

I wonder what he's doing in the next room. Is he thinking about me? Thinking about me naked and wet in every possible sense of the word. What would happen if I asked him to come in here with me? Excitement mixes with anxiety, and my hands are still on my stomach.

Although we've fooled around some, come close enough to sex that I know we'll get there eventually—possibly even tonight— everything we've done so far has been under the guise of "practice." It's a flimsy excuse, I know, but I'm self-aware enough to realize the deniability is making this all easier to process. I can't find a way to justify shower sex within the context of my own made up, paper-thin guidelines and I don't know if I'm willing to put myself out there without the barrier between us.

As I'm contemplating this, my eyes pop open at the sound of the door opening. My breath catches, and instinctively I cross my arms, trying to cover myself as a dark shadow appears outside the steamy shower wall. "What—"

The shower door opens, and I shiver slightly as the steam escapes in a woosh, and Roman steps inside.

I guess that answers the question of if he was thinking about me.

Roman closes the door behind him and turns to face me, his gaze raking over me. For a moment, I'm self-conscious, wondering what he thinks of my body. Wondering if I'm too curvy, or my tummy is too soft. But as his eyes graze over me, his eyes flashing with hunger, my anxiety dissipates.

Then, I take a moment to really process what I'm seeing...and h*oly shit.*

I've never seen his fully naked body, and while it's been clear, even under sweaters and jackets, that the man has muscles, I was not at all prepared to see the real thing. He looks like a statue. Or an Instagram model, at the very least. My mouth somehow goes dry and waters simultaneously, and I choke.

Roman laughs, his eyebrow ticking up in what can only be a challenge. "You okay, good girl?"

I shake my head, as surprised by his laughter as his presence. He's not really a laughing kind of guy—yet right now, he seems oddly... light. "Yeah," I stammer. "W-what are you doing?"

He takes a step forward, and I'm forced to back up into the wall. "Why do you do that?"

"What?"

The water pours over Roman's head as he leans forward, looming over me, but he barely seems to notice. "Ask questions you know the answer to."

My heartbeat pounds in my core, my clit pulsing with anticipation. I run my tongue over my lips. "Maybe I want to hear you say it."

His eyes flash with heat, "Yeah? You want to hear how hard I was waiting for you? Imagining you in here, just out of reach." Roman reaches down, spreading my legs apart with one hand and I quiver all over as he rubs soft, gentle circles over my clit. "Or maybe you want to hear all the ways I'm going to make you come? All the ways I can make sure you never forget who owns you."

I moan, pushing my hips up harder into his hand. "Owns me?"

"Of course, good girl." He buries his nose in my neck as he whispers in my ear. "Or I could just show you."

My mouth falls open in an O. I know it's a challenge as much as a promise, but something doesn't sit right. I know what I want instead...part of me is embarrassed to demand anything—to say any of these filthy things out loud, but another part of me wants to own it, and just say what I want—something that, for whatever reason, I only seem to be able to do with Roman.

I lean up on my tip toes, skimming my lips over his collarbone at the same time as I reach out, wrapping my fingers around his shaft. "As long as I get to own you too."

He jerks, his eyes going wide and serious as he looks down at me. "You already do."

I wrap my arms around his neck and Roman reaches down, gripping me by the backs of my thighs. He lifts me, pinning my back to the wall, and I twine my legs around his waist. For once, we're almost nose to nose, and the urge to kiss him is almost unbearable —but that's one line I can't cross. Not yet at least. Even though I know it's as pointless as flapping your arms when falling without a parachute, I need to cling to some shred of hope that I might come out of this alive.

Instead, I press my mouth to his neck, just below his ear. He growls in the back of his throat, reaching between us to line himself up with my entrance. I feel the head of his cock pushing against me as his thumb slides over my clit, and then I gasp.

My mouth falls open and my head falls back against the wall as he fills me, the sudden fullness and the size of him almost overwhelming. His head falls forward into my neck and for a moment, neither of us move. The only sound is our breathing, the water pouring down against the marble, and my heart pounding in my ears in time to his cock pulsing inside me. The steam rises around us, and I blink, droplets of water landing on my face. Our gazes meet, and for a moment my breath is stuck.

Then, the moment breaks.

Roman pulls out of me and slams back in, harder this time. I moan, my back arching as he hammers into me. I dig my nails into his shoulders, desperate for more friction, more speed, more everything.

Roman reaches between us again, rubbing two fingers over my clit as I writhe and grind against him. "Yeah, like that," he says. "Fuck yourself on my cock."

I whimper, bouncing harder, using the wall for leverage. Heat builds in my core, and my pussy clenches, a strangled cry threatening to escape from my mouth. I bite my lip, trying to keep myself from screaming.

"What have I told you about covering your mouth, Juliette?" Roman growls.

"I'm not!" I say indignantly.

"Close enough. I want to hear you come. I need to hear it. Don't deprive me of my favorite sound."

My eyes widen, and if possible, I grow even wetter. *Good gods.* "Well, you're going to have to work for it, then."

He leans over and turns off the shower. "Come on."

ROMAN DEPOSITS ME ONTO THE MIDDLE OF HIS BED, towel and all.

"We're wet," I complain.

"We're witches," he says reasonably.

Before I can make any further comment, he falls to his knees, grabbing my calves and dragging me toward the edge of the bed. I shriek, surprised, but my shriek turns into a moan of pleasure when he presses a kiss first to the inside of my thigh and then right to my core.

My knees fall open of their own accord, welcoming him in, and he sucks and laps at my already needy clit until I'm shaking and writhing beneath him.

"Fuck, you're so pretty like this," Roman says when he pulls back.

I raise an eyebrow. I don't know what I was expecting him to say, but that wasn't it. I don't know what to say in reply, and thankfully I don't have to, because he stands again, hovering over me.

He bends and laps his tongue over my right nipple, his fingers teasing around the left.

"Fuck me." I breathe. "I want you back inside me."

He doesn't make me beg. Roman slides back inside me, his hands on my thighs where my knees dangle off the edge of the bed on either side of his hips. He looks down at me, lying flat in front of him, and watches himself sliding slowly in and out.

"Touch yourself," he commands.

"What?" I say, half dazed.

"You heard me."

I did, but not only is that possibly too intimate—too embarrassing—to fathom, I'm not sure I can without shattering into a thousand pieces. He's got me so worked up, the slightest movement will have me melting into a puddle all over the bed.

But Roman isn't letting it go. "I want you to touch yourself while I fuck you. I want to hear what it sounds like when you make yourself come and say my name. Give it to me."

My mouth goes dry, his commanding tone and sexy words making my face heat. As if of its own accord, my hand snakes down my body, dancing over my breast and trailing down my stomach. A jolt of pleasure shoots through me when my fingers brush my clit, every nerve ending in my body sharp and too sensitive.

Roman smiles smugly, his eyes heavy with lust. "Good girl."

Tension builds in my belly and my breathing goes uneven as Roman fucks me, my breasts bouncing, my fingers rubbing faster.

"Fuck," I gasp. "I—"

"Yeah, good girl. Come for me."

"Roman, I need—"

Pleasure courses through me, and lights dance behind my eyes. My knees shake, my entire body clenching. Roman follows me over the edge, swearing as he pulls out of me at the last second, coming all over my stomach.

We lie there, panting for what feels like a long time, but really must be only a minute or two. Finally, Roman pushes himself off me. For a moment, I'm afraid he's going to leave—or ask me to leave, I guess, since it's his apartment.

Instead, he grabs one of the towels we brought in from the shower and cleans me off. Then, gathering me into his arms, he moves me to the opposite side of the bed before muttering something under his breath and drawing a rune in the air with his pointer finger. Immediately, everything rights itself. The water evaporates, our hair drying on the spot, and the towels zoom back to the hamper.

I frown. "I thought you didn't do magic anymore."

"I don't," he says flatly.

I glance at my now clean skin. "But you—"

"Don't make a big deal out of it, good girl." He yawns, leaning over to flick off the light. "Let's go to bed."

I stare at him in the darkness, a complicated barrage of feelings coursing through me.

I'm so completely done. So torn apart by this man, I don't know how I'm going to put myself back together when this inevitably comes crashing down around me. I should have realized from the moment he popped back up in my life at just the right time that I was screwed.

My heart pounds too fast at the realization that I'm falling. I'm on a runaway train—on a rocket sled toward a brick wall, and there's nothing I can do to stop it.

So I let myself go.

CHAPTER THIRTY-SEVEN
✦ ROMAN ✦

SENIOR YEAR OF HIGH SCHOOL, FOUR YEARS AGO

"HOW MANY TIMES HAVE YOU READ THAT?" ETTA ASKS. "Approximately."

I turn the page of my book, and don't look at her when I respond. Looking at her is when things start getting...difficult. "Six?"

She laughs. "This week?"

I frown. "It's a classic."

I can tell without looking that she's rolling her eyes. She always has a lot to say when I read a Palahniuk book.

So I keep reading them.

"It's giving...misunderstood emo boy who just took his first psych class."

"Did you hear that from Catalina Minola?" It sounds like something Etta's friend would say.

She pauses and I look up, finally meeting her eyes.

"No," she says, looking guilty. "Cat doesn't know I'm here."

Right.

The silence of the library's third floor is almost palpable, wrapping around us like a shroud. I'm ensconced in an overstuffed armchair, its leather arms worn to a sheen. Etta sits on the floor, her laptop and several books laid out around her, her fingers splayed across the pages of notes.

It might look like we're sitting together, but that would be incorrect. We didn't intend to meet here. We never do.

"Accidentally" meeting here, or in the cemetery, has become our delicate ritual, an unspoken truce in the silent war between our families. My uncle died last week, in another "mysterious" accident. I thought Etta might stop showing up to the library and was almost embarrassingly relieved to find her here.

I realize I'm staring at her and tare my gaze away. Fuck, I'm getting sloppy.

"What are you studying for?" I ask, my voice a strangled croak. "We're practically out the door."

Etta pauses, fingers poised above her keyboard. "I need to do well in finals."

I cock an eyebrow. Why? We're already accepted to Elsinore University...all the Order kids pretty much get in by default, and Etta is the Salutatorian.

That reminds me, I need to write my stupid fucking Valedictorian speech. Damn. Maybe I can get Bennet to write it for me.

It was a big surprise to a lot of people when Etta came in second to me in our class—apparently, everyone thought I was a fucking moron all this time, just because I don't like to study.

Admittedly, spending so much time in the library over the last year has helped. I used to only go to the library to make-out with Rosaline where Etta might notice. Who knew there were actually interesting books here?

I shake my head, realizing I've dropped the thread of our conversation and Etta has returned to her studying. "Why do finals matter?"

She wrinkles her nose. "I just...want to have options."

I frown. "What the fuck does that mean?"

"Oxford," she says simply, and the word hangs between us, heavy with implications.

"You got in?" I demand, unable to stop the sharp edge of... what, concern? From bleeding into my tone.

"Waitlisted," she admits, and I'm struck by the vulnerability she allows me to see.

My eyes widen. She's never mentioned this. Oxford is...well it's a long fucking way from Stratford.

A leaden weight settles in my chest. England. Oxford. Miles and time zones away. How am I going to "accidentally" run into her halfway across the world?

I lean back in my chair, folding my arms behind my head. "Good for you."

It sounds hollow, but I'm not sure she notices.

"Thanks," she says lightly. "I'm hopeful."

Our gazes lock, and there's an electric charge in the air, a silent acknowledgment of the crossroads we're approaching.

"Hopeful is good," I say finally. "It suits you."

CHAPTER THIRTY-EIGHT

ETTA

PRESENT

THE FOLLOWING MORNING, I WAKE WITH A SMILE ON MY face. The space in the bed next to me is empty, but the sheets are warm, and I can hear the shower running in the bathroom. I have half—okay more than half—a mind to hop in the shower too, but my growling stomach stops me in my tracks.

I barely ate dinner last night, given that I was so miserable the entire time, and I feel like my stomach is turning in on itself. I know Roman would not only not care if I eat what's in his kitchen, but he would also probably be offended if I didn't, so I get up and look around for my leggings before realizing they're still in the bathroom. Crap.

I pull the sheet from the bed, wrapping it around myself and pad across the floor to knock lightly on the bathroom door. When there's no answer, I knock lightly, and open it a crack. I might feel guilty if it were anyone else but given that Roman had no issue barging in on me in the shower, I'd call us even.

Steam billows out of the room in a huge woosh, and warm air greets me, moisture sticking to my face. The same scent of pine that clings to my hair fills the air. I turn, watching Roman's outline beneath the spray. Good gods—I may never get used to how insanely beautiful this man is.

"What are you doing, good girl?" he calls over the sound of the water.

"I just needed my clothes." I reply, bending to collect them from the floor.

I hear the glass door opening behind me and feel the woosh as even more steam billows out. "Don't think you can just come in here and then run. Get your ass in here."

"I'm hungry."

Roman's eyes darken. "Me too. Breakfast is the most important meal of the day.

I shriek as he steps out of the shower and stalks toward me, looking every bit the predator while I'm his prey. I step back a bit, instinctively, backing away even as I want him to catch me. Even as my nipples peak and my heart pounds in my core with the anticipation of what he'll do the moment he does.

I drop my bedsheet, and he strikes, moving, grabbing for me in a single swift motion.

I shouldn't let myself be so happy. Shouldn't let myself indulge in this, when he hasn't admitted any real feelings, and I've only just acknowledged mine in my head...but I can't help it.

I scream, half laughing, as he lifts me up onto the edge of the sink and pushes my knees apart, so I'm entirely exposed to him. It's not the first time, and I should be starting to get used to it, but I still feel a hint of nervousness at the full display.

He slaps my bare pussy with his open palm. "Who's is this?"

I yelp, surprised, by the sharp sting. Then, even more surprised when I realize I *like* it. "Yours?" I answer with a question in my voice.

"That's right, good girl." Roman smiles and sinks to his knees. "I love you like this."

"What? Naked?" I gasp.

He chuckles, running his nose up my inner thigh. "Completely at my mercy. It evens the playing field a bit."

I gasp as he reaches the apex of my thighs and laves his tongue over my throbbing clit. I try to force myself to think, as shivers travel up my spine. What did he mean, level the playing field? He's always saying things like that, without explanation.

"Roman, I—"

He licks a long delicate stroke up my center, and I shudder, losing track of what I was saying. I can't do anything but whimper and writhe as he continues licking me, interspersing his movements with hungry, open-mouthed kisses. Like he really is hungry, starving, for me.

I gasp, digging my fingers into his hair, moving closer and closer to what I need. "Fuck me."

I feel him smile against me. "You want to come on my cock, good girl?"

"Always."

He gets to his feet and pulls me down off the counter, flipping me around, and I come face-to-face with my own, wide eyes in the mirror, my own flushed cheeks. Oh *shit*.

Roman bends and whispers in my ear, making eye-contact with my reflection. "Watch me fuck you, good girl."

Oh my gods.

He places one palm on my back, pushing me down slightly as he lines himself up with my entrance. I'm so wet for him, so close to falling apart already, he slides all the way in in a single stroke.

This time I'm mostly expecting it when his hand comes down hard on the globe of my ass as he slides in and out of me in a punishing rhythm. "Fuck you feel so good. I knew you would be fucking perfect wrapped around my cock."

I arch my back, rocking my entire body, fucking myself on him as he mercilessly pounds into me. "You imagined this?"

"Every fucking day."

His hand comes up to band around my throat, forcing my face up to watch, his other arm holding me tight to his chest. I moan and sink my teeth into my bottom lip as the new angle grinds my clit against the edge of the sink. It hurts and simultaneously, confusingly, has me climbing higher and higher toward release.

"Roman," I pant. "Oh my gods."

"Come for me, Etta."

I don't want to look, but I also can't look away. My face is pink, my hair a mess, my eyes full of lust and so many other things. I whimper, then nearly cry, my eyes glued on to us as I shake around him, both of us forcing the other further over the edge into blissful oblivion.

"So. How'd you sleep?"

I finally leave Roman's room an hour later and find Cat sitting at the kitchen table, while Bennet Montague sits on the counter across from her eating a bowl of cereal.

Bennet. I tell myself. *Just Bennet.*

It's strange to realize who you consider a first name/last name person in real time, after spending all night fucking their cousin. Roman, at least, has moved into the just first name category—mostly. Thank the gods he doesn't have a nickname.

"I slept fine, thank you," I say primly, coming to stand behind the chair across from Cat. "You?"

She grins. "Not as well as you, judging from the sound of things."

My entire body clenches, the back of my neck heating. "Do you mind?"

Her grin turns into a laugh. "But seriously, I slept fine. The guest room is nice."

"Yes, it is. You're fucking welcome!" A male voice shouts from the other room.

I turn and realize that there is a third person in the room I hadn't noticed before. Pierce Avon—first name/last name—is lying on the couch in the living room area of the open concept apartment with a green throw-pillow covering his face. From the disarray of blankets at the foot of the couch, I take it that he slept there.

"He usually takes the guest room, apparently," Cat explains. "But I wasn't open to sharing."

"Miserable shrew!" Pierce calls through the pillow.

"That's '*Queen* Shrew,' to you," Cat replies without looking at him.

"Is that your stripper name or something?" Pierce snaps. "I thought you had to be attractive for that."

She shrugs. "I guess you'll never know, since you're broke as shit and wouldn't be able to afford the cover."

I raise an eyebrow, glancing back at the muscular torso of the moaning guy on the couch. "What is going on here?"

"She won the poker game," Bennet explains, swallowing his mouthful of cereal. "The house rule is you can only bet what you came in with. Otherwise, it's chaos. We end up with people running to the ATM and spending thousands, or betting boats and shit. But Pierce here, ran out of money and started betting favors. She's his queen now."

Ah. Well, I did warn Roman that Cat is more of a danger to his friends than they are to her. "Interesting. Is there anything to eat?"

"Help yourself to whatever." Bennet waves a hand toward the fridge. "Want some coffee?"

"Sure. I can make it though, you don't have to do anything."

"Get this," Cat says conspiratorially. "Rosaline Hathaway dropped by last night."

"What? Are you serious?" Anxiety shoots through me. "What did she want?"

"To talk to your boyfriend. We told her he was busy, and she didn't have to take our word for it because, well—" she grins "I mean, we could all hear yo—"

"I got it," I interrupt her, and turn toward the coffee maker, my cheeks flaming.

Cat doesn't press it, instead changing the subject with inelegant efficiency. "So what's the plan? For today I mean."

I bite my lip as I start the espresso machine and turn back to face her. "Well, I think it's pretty unlikely that my parents will notice we're gone until tonight at the earliest. The best-case scenario," I muse. "Is that my aunt says yes, and we can somehow persuade everyone to meet up to do the ceremony tonight. Otherwise, maybe tomorrow?"

It's Friday and we both have class today. Cat can and should go to hers, but I'm going to have to skip mine to go try and track down Aunt Angelica in Salem with Roman.

"Do you know who is going to stand in from every house?" Bennet asks.

"All except the Danes, I think is what Roman said, but I'm sure we'll figure something out."

Bennet leans forward toward me, swinging his legs. "Where is Roman, anyway?"

"Um...reading?"

"Seriously?" Cat looks incredulous.

I nod. "Seriously."

I have learned so much about Roman Montague in the last twenty-four hours that I've never picked up on before. Like, he's an introvert. A serious introvert. A part of me is tempted to say he's been managing to hide that for years, but now I think about it, that's not true.

He's not hiding it well.

He's not trying to hide it.

This is a man who genuinely wants to be left alone with his books. Who hates crowds and parties. Who clearly cares about his friends, but only wants to see them half as much as they want to see him. Except when he says that, he sounds like an asshole. Add on that he happens to be usually attractive, wealthy, and popular, he cannot escape people no matter what he does.

I remember when we used to sit in silence for hours. I always thought he just didn't want to talk to me. That he was only barely tolerating my presence. Maybe he just...likes being quiet.

That's fine. I've been quiet my whole life—I could do the talking for a change.

"Huh," Cat says. "Sounds perfect for you."

My stomach lurches. I'd been thinking the same thing, but I have no idea how to tell him that and risk the very real possibility that he'll completely shut me down.

CHAPTER THIRTY-NINE
✦ ETTA ✦

THERE ARE A DOZEN TAROT SHOPS IN SALEM, ALL boasting readings from "real witches," so it takes us nearly forty minutes to find the shop where my Aunt Angelica works. It doesn't help that she's using a fake name, and I haven't seen her since my grandfather's funeral ten years ago. Although there have been quite a few other deaths in the family since, that was the last funeral Angelica turned up to. I can't exactly blame her.

"I've always hated this street," Roman grumbles as we walk down the main tourist street in the city.

I turn to him in shock. "Seriously?"

"The whole thing looks like a godsdamn movie set."

"That's because it's in so many movies."

"Well, *stop,*" he whines. "Why cobblestones? If they were going to use honest to gods fucking cobblestones, they should have just made it pedestrian only, but instead it's just uncomfortable as shit to drive on with weird-ass tiny parking spaces. And if they're going to lean in on the history, at least be clear about the fact that the real historical site is under the Walgreens parking lot two towns over."

I raise an eyebrow. "I like it. It's cute, and there's really good coffee."

He grumbles. "Well, you didn't have to park."

I smile, in spite of myself. I have no idea why, but I'm glad to know he cares about *something,* even if it's an insanely niche problem like cobblestones.

Roman and I stand on the cobblestone street under the red and white awning of a shop called "Weird Wiles" and stare at a photo of my aunt plastered to the door under the heading: "READING TODAY!" The windows of the shop are dark, with herbs and glass witch balls hanging from the ceiling. It's all a little touristy for my taste, but I suppose that's where the money is.

Roman glances sideways at me. "Should we go in?"

"I guess there's no point in just standing here."

As we push open the door, the smell of incense and musty old books greets my nose and a tinkling bell rings in the depths of the shop, heralding our entrance.

The shop is dimly lit with candles and small lamps casting a warm glow over the entire room. A table in the center of the shop is covered in dried herbs, baskets of crystals, candles, and what looks to be voodoo dolls. Glass cases line the walls, some containing jewelry, others carrying silver knives or crystal skulls.

A pretty, petite woman leans against the counter, a huge, leather-bound book spread out in front of her. She's wearing thick black eyeliner and a cheap leather corset over a contrastingly expensive looking lace top. Her long, chestnut brown hair is tied back in two fishtail braids, woven together with wilted, yellow flowers. As we enter, she looks up from the book and smiles widely. "Hey," she says dreamily. "Welcome in! Are you the ones who called about the ghost tours?"

I clear my throat. "Uh, no."

"Oh, that's too bad." Her smile wavers. "They're wicked good this season. Lots of spirit activity."

Beside me, Roman clears his throat, obviously skeptical. I elbow him. He's a warlock for the god's sake, it's not like he doesn't know spirits are real. My guess is he doesn't believe that tourist attractions know where real spirits are and doesn't have any problem making that clear—no matter how rude it is.

The woman behind the counter wrinkles her small, freckled nose. As we approach, I realize she's younger than us—maybe only eighteen or nineteen at most. "Oh, a non-believer?"

I shake my head. "Ignore him."

She nods sagely at me. "Don't worry, I *completely* understand. If you need anything, my name is Ophelia."

I shake my head, a little thrown by her unblinking eyes. "We're actually looking for a tarot reader."

The girl looks me up and down before replying. "Right. She's just finishing up a reading." She gestures to a closed velvet curtain in the back of the room. "You can wait if you want, she doesn't have any readings scheduled this afternoon."

My back stiffens as I glance at the curtain, and my voice shakes as I reply. "Okay, thanks."

Roman and I step back from the counter and go to stand on the opposite side of the shop from Ophelia, while he unenthusiastically scans a shelf of books on tarot reading and pop-witchcraft.

"Do you think the ghosts are in the room with us now?" he mutters, sarcastically.

"Don't be an asshole."

He raises a brow at me. "I don't know what would ever give you the impression I'm capable of anything else."

I swallow, thickly. I know he's joking, but his statement has me thinking...why would I have that impression? Roman is an asshole, and unapologetic about it.

Except, sometimes, when he's different with me.

About fifteen minutes later, the velvet curtain pulls aside with a flourish and three people step out into the shop. Two, are clearly clients, while the third, I recognize immediately as my aunt.

Though it's been over a decade since I've seen her, Angelica looks, at least to my eye, exactly the same. She's wearing a red and black silk robe over a long, corseted dress, similar to Ophelia's, and has her dark hair pulled back in a tight bun. Aside from the dress, her minimal make-up and schoolteacher demeanor don't exactly scream "Psychic," Yet, there's something inexplicable about her aura that says she just knows things.

"Ophelia will get you scheduled for next week," she says to her clients as she walks toward us across the shop. "And you really should check out the ghost tours. They're wicked—" She looks up, and stops short, fumbling her words mid-sentence as she catches sight of me waiting by the counter. "—Uh, and happy Halloween! Bye, now."

Behind me Roman snorts, as Angelica ushers the confused couple outside. The moment the bell over the door jingles, signaling we're alone once more, my aunt turns back to me. "Well, it's about time you came to see me."

I blink in surprise, thrown off by not having to introduce myself. While Aunt Angelica might look the same, I most certainly don't, and I can't imagine how she knows who I am. Unless, perhaps, she's a better psychic than I was led to believe.

"Oh, don't look so shocked," my aunt says, before I can even comment. "I wasn't banished to a cave in the mountains, or a deserted island. I have social media."

A laugh bursts from my chest. "I'm sorry, I should have come sooner."

She waves me off. "I know why you didn't. Gods, I worried about you in that big house all alone with a mother like yours," she wrinkles her nose. "Not that I should comment. Not my business. Anyway, do I get a hug at least?"

I step forward tentatively. I'm not much of a hugger, but Aunt Angelica wraps her long, thin arms around me and refuses to let go until I return her embrace with equal pressure. My throat feels tight, and my eyes burn, and I have no idea why.

I take a step back and clear my throat, throwing my hand out like I'm waving on the next act. "This is Roman."

Aunt Angelica scoffs. "Montague. I know." She looks at him over my shoulder, scrutinizing his every feature. "You remind me of your father."

Roman's face turns stony, and I can practically feel the anger radiating from him. "I've never found that we have much in common."

Angelica shrugs, unbothered by his sharp tone. "Don't look so offended. You might be nothing like him in personality, but you could never go into hiding. Your face screams 'Montague.'"

Roman glances away, his lips pulled into a thin line. Angelica looks at me with a knowing smile before turning and striding toward the back of the shop. "I can't think out here. Too much incense, you'll have to come sit down."

Everything smells of sage and frankincense. I can't see how it would be better over there, but nevertheless I follow her behind the velvet curtain, Roman trailing behind me.

"Let me get another deck," Aunt Angelica says loudly as we duck under the fabric. "I use different cards for humans and witches, and then of course I'll use different ones for you two."

Glancing around, I'm slightly taken aback. I was expecting some sort of booth, like at a carnival, with perhaps a tiny table and some folding chairs, but the curtain hides a whole other room the same size as the magic shop. There is a table in the center, covered in several silks and surrounded by comfortable looking velvet armchairs. The lighting is tinged pink, and there are celestial paintings on the walls, giving the whole place an otherworldly feel.

"We didn't actually come for a reading," I tell Aunt Angelica quickly.

She cocks her head at me, her manicured eyebrows furrowing. "Are you sure?"

"Yes."

"Well, come, sit, sit." Aunt Angelica runs around to the far side of the table. "Let me just clean up then, and then we'll chat. That last couple had the worst vibe. Can you feel it? I need a *Dustbuster*, or something. Ugh!"

Her slightly manic demeanor as she buzzes around the room fills me simultaneously with warm nostalgia and slight anxiety.

Beside me, Roman is stiff, his entire body tight, as he breathes steadily through his mouth.

"What's wrong?" I ask.

"The smell is giving me a headache," he bites out.

I get the feeling that's not all that's giving him a headache. He hates my aunt's erratic energy, the ghost tours, the smell of cheap incense, and the cobblestones.

What would he do if I reached out and took his hand? I'd like to offer comfort, in what is clearly an uncomfortable environment for him...maybe thanks for tolerating it on my behalf. I bite my lip, unmoving, and stretch my pinky finger forward.

"Got it!" Aunt Angelica cries.

"Fucking hell," Roman mutters under his breath.

"Got what?" I ask, blinking a few times. I didn't even notice she'd walked away from the table.

"I don't have a *Dustbuster,* but I do have a rose quartz, which some might say is just as good." She glances around, before scrawling a quick rune over her crystal, causing it to glow slightly. She winks conspiratorially at us. "Don't tell. I tell people they're salt lamps."

Roman's scowl deepens, and he stares at the crystal like it personally offended him.

I sigh. "Do you want to wait outside?"

He debates it, then nods. He jerks his head toward the door. "I'll be over there if you need me."

I fight the almost uncontrollable urge to run after him, as I watch Roman exit the shop and stand directly outside the door with the posture of a sentry. As I watch, he tilts his face up to the sky, as if reveling in the fresh air then his shoulders slump—frustration, or exhaustion, it's hard to say.

"He doesn't like me."

I turn back to Aunt Angelica and find her watching me watch Roman. A hint of embarrassment colors my cheeks. Although, as I'm about to tell her we're getting married, I suppose it's alright if she sees me watching and draws whatever conclusion she likes. "I'm sure that's not true." I cast around for something she'll understand. "He doesn't mean I, he's just a Scorpio."

Angelica doesn't laugh as I expected, instead seeming to take my statement seriously. "Yes, I can see that. I've seen his whole chart before, back when I used to look at all the new babies, you know," she waves a hand. "But I can't remember all of it off the top of my head. I'd die to know all the placements. I'd bet there are some fire signs in his first house."

"Why?" I ask as I sit down. "Why does it matter, I mean."

She crosses her hands over her cards. "Professional curiosity...and I'm just nosey. Ah, well. I can dig it up later. I have all the charts I read filed away somewhere. So, if not a reading, what brought you two here today?"

I bite my lip. Roman and I didn't really plan out this meeting ahead of time like we did with councilman Lawrence, but I'm still a bad liar. Granted, Roman probably wouldn't be much better right now with how uncomfortable he clearly is. I wonder why he doesn't like it here.

"Actually," I begin, trying to stick to the truth as much as possible. "We were hoping you could come to our wedding."

The words hang in the air between us, charged with emotion. I'm shocked that Aunt Angelica doesn't immediately demand to know what's going on. To know how and why I'm marrying a Montague. Instead, she just stares at me for a moment before slowly letting out a long breath. "No," she says quietly. Her voice is soft, but firm. "I can't do that."

I'm taken aback. "Sorry, I should have started with *why*. See, we actually need a witness. It's really more for my pledging than for the wedding itself, see—"

She cuts me off firmly, none of her former manic energy left in her voice. "I'm sorry Etta. The answer is going to be no. I won't go into that temple again."

My chest tightens and I can feel my heart drumming in my ears. The tension rises in my stomach as tears well in my eyes.

It hurts more than it should, and I know immediately why that is —why it feels like my aunt has just shattered everything for me in a single word. I hadn't planned for a refusal, but there's really nothing else to say. Nothing to do, when all my wild plans are crashing around my ears.

"WE NEED TO LEAVE."

My words come out in a gasp as I sprint out of the shop. Roman looks up at me from where he's leaning against the window, legs crossed at the ankles, a bored smirk on his lips. "You okay, good girl?"

"Yeah," I say bitterly. "Great."

His smirk slips as he takes me in. My shaking hands, wide eyes, my manic, not even remotely normal smile. "What happened?"

I pause, licking my lips. Maybe I should wait and not tell him here? We could talk in the car.

His eyes flash with frustration, like he knows exactly what I'm thinking, and he adds: "Right fucking now, Etta."

"She said no. She hates the Order and she won't go."

"You're not serious." Roman looks from me to the shop, a mixture of emotions playing out on his face. "There has to be something else we can do."

I shake my head in frustration. "Like what? I don't know why I didn't realize this was a possibility. I mean, she was disowned and kicked out of the Order. It makes sense she would hate them."

Roman's face is torn with indecision as he glances back at the door. "I still think we can convince her. I'll just—"

"No! I don't want you to."

I shake my head in defeat. Part of me wants to keep trying but the other part is just too drained to even contemplate another attempt.

Roman's expression goes from concern to anger in record time. "So, you're giving up."

I take off in the direction of the car, leaving Roman no choice but to chase after me. "Yes," I snap. "Because I don't want to force her to do something that would hurt her, even if it helped us."

"Okay, fine," he says after a minute. "So she won't come. We'll find someone else."

My feet stomp against the cobblestones he hates so much. "There is no one else. That was the whole point of making an exception for Angelica."

"So, you're just done?" he demands angrily. "No more plan?"

"No. I'm not done with the plan. The plan is done with me."

He grabs my arm and yanks me towards him, the force of the spin taking me off-guard. His voice is low, his grip gentle on my arms. "Etta, stop."

I meet his gaze, the intensity of his eyes piercing into mine. "Why? Can I just have a moment?"

I get it, he wants me to figure something out right this second, but I don't work like that. I can't go from zero to one-hundred and not get whiplash, I need to think.

"Okay, so let's go somewhere then," he says, a hint of desperation leaking through his usually indifferent tone.

My anxiety spikes. "Go where?"

"Anywhere. Fuck the Order, we could just leave tonight."

No. No. We cannot. I bite my lip. "We can't just leave. It's not realistic."

"Only because you want to keep living here, have nothing really change, and force people to be different than how they are."

"That's not true." My face feels hot, my ears buzzing with pent-up energy. "That's a bad idea. It won't go well, you know that."

"Then if we can't leave and we can't do the ceremony in secret, the only thing left to do is go before the council," he says, his voice rising.

"What?" I squawk. "No! That's an even worse idea. It's way too dangerous."

"I don't *care*." He takes a step closer, practically growling in frustration. "Let them find out. I want everyone to know you're mine."

I freeze. Shit. We can't do this now. We can't. Not when I don't even know what I want. Not when he doesn't know why he even feels that way. What if he's not serious? What if it's not real?

I pull my arm out of the way. "I do. I care."

He scoffs, his face twisting back to its usual mask of indifference. "Of course you do."

I take a step back. "What's that supposed to mean?"

"You care what everyone thinks, Etta. You care more if strangers on the street like you than if you like you."

I reel back. "You don't have to be an asshole."

He narrows his eyes. "Yes, I do. I never pretended I wasn't."

Anger bubbles up in my stomach. "Yeah actually, you did. You haven't been an asshole to me. Not lately, anyway. You're choosing this right now."

"And you're choosing to be willfully obtuse."

"Excuse me if I don't want it to be my fault if my cousin kills you! I care, because I don't want it to be my fault if someone else gets hurt. I don't want anyone in my family to die or you to die because I was selfish. Why don't you get that?"

"Then what the hell are we doing here?" he sneers. "That was always a risk. You're the one who was more than happy to pretend this was about school or whatever the fuck else."

"Then what's it about for you?" I demand. "What do you want from me?"

"Are you even listening to me?" He takes a step closer, practically growling in frustration. "I'm telling you I don't care about anyone but you. I never have. I don't care if anyone finds out or what happens because I want everyone to know you're mine, no matter what the cost is. If you don't already know what that means, then you haven't been paying attention at all."

I hear him—hear what he thinks he's saying, and also all the things he isn't.

Maybe here at last is the answer to the question that's been lingering with me for days. What does Roman get out of this? He gets *me.*

Except that he's not saying, "I love you." No, he's saying he wants to own me.

And that's so very typical of Roman, isn't it? Didn't he warn me years ago? He likes to stamp his name on all the things he owns.

I suppose marrying me would accomplish that just fine.

My head spins. I don't have the energy to sort this out right now. I can't. "It doesn't matter," I say. "Because my aunt still said no, and I still just got a desperately needed wake-up call. I refuse to be the reason anyone else gets hurt."

He sneers. "Then what the hell are we doing here?"

I shake my head—right now, I have no idea.

For a moment, I thought the stars aligned, and I could have everything. The impossible fantasy. The things I only ever dared to ask for in the dark. But some things just aren't meant to be, and I need to stop ignoring what the universe was clearly trying to tell me all along.

Roman Montague and I will only ever be star-crossed.

CHAPTER FORTY
·ROMAN·

FRESHMAN YEAR OF COLLEGE, THREE YEARS AGO

I CHECK MY WATCH AGAIN AND RUN A HAND THROUGH my hair as I jog across the parking lot of Morgan and Son's funeral home.

I'm so fucking late.

My mid-term ran long, and there was traffic getting across town during rush hour. Since when is there traffic in Stratford? When I need to be somewhere, apparently, and never when I'm trying to waste time. This is going to be such a shit-show.

I jog past a guy playing bagpipes outside, and throw the door open with too much force, practically heaving for breath. A few elderly women dressed in black give me strange looks. Yeah, yeah. Calm your tits.

My gaze darts around the entry way, taking everything in at once —the fake flowers, the red carpeting, the unoffensive gold-framed paintings of landscapes on the walls. I spot a door that must lead to the coat room and duck inside to catch my breath.

I shouldn't be here—I'm tempting fate by just showing up—but there weren't a lot of good alternatives.

I'm leaning against the wall of the coat closet, surrounded by black wool and fleece, when the door creaks open. I freeze. This is all I need: to get shanked in a funeral home.

Or, probably not shanked, per se. I bet Tyberius Capulet carries around some gold-plated switch blade he doesn't even know how to use.

I rattle off a litany of creative swears in my head, cursing the gods for this whole stupid event. For putting me here in the first place. Then, the coats part, and I find myself staring into huge, gray eyes.

Never mind, gods. We're solid.

Etta blinks at me, her eyes red-rimmed and watery. She opens her mouth in shock and I can smell alcohol on her breath. She's clearly been crying.

"What are you doing here?" she asks finally.

My throat is dry, and the words feel rusty—out of practice. "Paying my respects."

The phrase feels almost rusty—out of practice. She looks down, shaking her head, and a strange pang of panic shoots through me. *Look at me.*

My first year of college has been a whirlwind, and it's already halfway through second semester. Even though Etta goes to the same school, I've hardly seen her except for glimpses across the quad or at Order events. This is the first we've spoken since last spring.

No more accidental meetings.

No more visits to the library.

There haven't even been any deaths all year, so I don't see her at the cemetery. It's been almost a year, and it's turning me into a fucking lunatic, almost hoping for someone to die. A distant relative—someone old—but *someone*.

I felt almost guilty when I heard that Etta's grandmother passed away. Like somehow, I caused it. I felt guiltier when I was thrilled that I'd get to go to the cemetery.

Well, the gods have a shitty sense of humor. They're cremating grandma, and the wake is today, the same day as my last mid-term. Not only is this entire place swarming with Capulets, so I'd be an idiot to leave this closet, but I'm positive I just failed my test because I couldn't stop thinking about seeing *her*.

I'm sick, I know. She's infected me, and there's no cure. I've spent half my life orbiting Etta, never able to reach out and grab her. She's the sun, and I will only ever be Icarus.

"Sorry about your grandmother," I say, just to fill the silence.

She opens her mouth, I think to say, "thank you," and instead sniffles, letting out a small sob.

Fuck. I need to say something—do something. Anything. I reach for her.

And then suddenly Etta launches herself toward me. Her lips meet mine, sudden and unpracticed, and I'm so shocked my arms come around her before I fully realize what I'm doing.

Her tears are wet against my face, but at least she's not crying anymore.

I slide my hands up her back, pressing her to me, and take charge. Covering her mouth with mine, licking over the seam of her lips and parting them with my tongue, and nearly groaning when she whimpers into my mouth.

This feels unreal. It's not how I would have wanted to do this, but I can't stop. My heart is pounding as I move my lips from her mouth to her throat, sucking on her pulse point. She gasps and digs her fingers into my shoulders.

I back her up against the wall, tangling one hand in her hair, and sliding her knee-length, black dress up to her thigh with the other.

She goes still in my arms as my fingers graze the inside of her thigh, and I pause, breathing heavily, and pull back to look at her. "Are you okay?"

She's biting her lip, looking unsure. Nervous, and upset in a way she didn't before—not like she's still sad about her grandmother and trying to escape it, but like her escape isn't what she wants after all.

She kissed me, right? Fuck, did I misread this?

I let her go and take a step back, as far as I can go in the small closet. This has never happened to me before. "Sorry…"

"No," she says quickly. "I've just never done this before. I'm fine now though."

She's…what? I give her a blank look, uncomprehending, and then it clicks. Oh. *Oh fuck.*

She tries to reach for me again, but I stay flat against the wall, avoiding her like the plague. My head spins with too many conflicting thoughts, and I grimace, warring with myself, over the right thing to do vs. what I want.

Etta scans my expression and her eyes narrow, clearly misreading my intent. "If you're going to make fun of me, I swear to gods I will punch you in the dick."

I shake my head. Normally, I would enjoy hearing her say "dick" but it's the furthest thing from my mind. "I wasn't going to."

"Then what's the problem? I know you're not a virgin."

No, I'm not—*at all*—and that's half the issue right there.

She doesn't understand what she's asking for. This is a terrible idea. She's grieving. We're in a closet at a fucking funeral home where anyone could walk in. There's not a chance in hell she won't realize tomorrow she's made a terrible mistake—not the worst mistake of her life or anything, it's just sex—but definitely something she will regret.

On the other hand, I'm suddenly, impossibly, harder than I was a minute ago. I don't think I have a virgin kink. But I definitely have a thing for Etta, and I didn't even know I could have her all to myself. Now that idea has taken root, I've never wanted anything more.

Wait. I shake my head. What the fuck am I thinking? I can't have her all to myself. I can't have her, period. Even if we did this, it would still only be once. She'd still end up married to that stock-photo she's betrothed to.

"Etta..." I start, unsure what I'm going to say. "This is a bad idea."

"Why? I said I'm fine, don't worry about it."

If only it were that simple, and I could just pretend she never told me, but now I can't get it out of my head. "Because you're upset and clearly going through something."

"Don't do that." She crosses her arms. "Don't try to be the nice guy now, we both know you're not."

"Is that what this is? The good girl is having a crisis and she doesn't want to be the good girl anymore, so she needs to be tainted by her personal villain?"

She scoffs. "How's that B in freshman psych treating you?"

My mouth becomes a thin line and I pinch the skin between my eyes. How the fuck did I end up here? Trying to talk a girl out of fucking me is going against every instinct I have. "Look, you can make your own decisions, good girl. Go get fucked by the next guy you see, I don't care, but I'm not going to be the guy who took advantage of the grieving virgin in the closet. That's too grim, even for me."

Her face scrunches up in anger. "Fine."

I turn toward the door to the closet, but she pushes past me to leave first. The result is we come tumbling out of the closet at almost exactly the same time.

I put out a hand instinctively to steady Etta, but she side steps me, shrugging off my help. Looking up, I see why. Sebastian Cesario is frozen in the hall, his eyes growing to the size of saucers as he takes us in. He must have been just arriving, as he's standing just inside the front door, only steps from the coat closet. The timing is shit, and further proves to me that either I have the worst luck in the world, or I'm being tested by some vengeful god. These coincidences are just too fucked.

I open my mouth to say something to smooth it over, but again, Etta beats me to it.

"Sebastian," she says calmly, as though she didn't just almost fall out of a closet. "It's good to see you. Thank you for coming.

"Er, yeah, of course," he says, recovering. Her flashes her a smile I know he's used on dozens of girls, many of whom were my exes. "I'm really sorry for your loss."

A shock of jealous rage shoots through me. I'll just fucking bet he's sorry for her loss. Sorry enough to comfort her? Sorry enough to take advantage of her?

I shake my head as if to clear it. What the fuck is wrong with me? This isn't high school. She isn't mine.

Etta sighs. "I'm not ready to go back inside just yet. Sebastian, do you want to get some fresh air with me?"

My stomach seizes, remembering what I said. *I don't care if you fuck the next guy you see.* I turn to look at her. I don't know what expression I'm wearing, but it feels like all blood has drained from my face.

She's determinedly not looking at me, a smile plastered on so wide she looks like a clown.

Sebastian looks at me for half a second. He's probably wondering if I'm going to kick his ass again, like Sophomore semi-formal, or if I've matured since then.

I don't move, giving him absolutely nothing. *I dare you to ask my permission, you fucking asshole.*

He doesn't ask, he just smiles at Etta. "Sure."

Etta doesn't look back at me once as she follows Sebastian outside, leaving me standing there alone.

Furious, I storm out the doors they just exited, planning to get right back in my car and head back to school. This was fucking stupid. I should never go to shit like this, I don't know what I was — "Oh, sorry!"

I jerk back and Councilman Lawrence and I stare at each other in surprise as he opens the door, just as I'm leaving.

"Roman!" the councilman says way too loudly. "What are you doing here?"

"Leaving," I reply. "Excuse me."

Chapter Forty-One

✦ ETTA ✦

Present

The scent of baking banana bread hits me like a bulldozer the moment I push open the door to my favorite local coffee shop, a burst of warm air whooshing out to greet me.

Sunlight shines through the huge, frosted glass windows onto worn leather armchairs grouped around steel bistro tables, and my mouth waters as Cat and I stand in line, waiting for the barista to finish with the man in front of us.

The atmosphere is cozy, but my mood couldn't be darker.

"Hey, Etta," the barista says brightly. "The usual?"

I blink, confused for a moment, and realize I'm standing a good two feet back from the counter, and the man who was in front of us is gone. "Uh, yes," I stammer. "Thank you. And also an iced quad americano, black, no room, please."

"You got it."

I glance around, wondering where Cat went, and spot her over at the bulletin board, reading some flyer. I can't read the fine print from here, but the bolded part says:

POETRY OPEN MIC NITE!

"What's up?" she asks, as I come to stand beside her. "You have that, 'I want to say something,' face."

I frown. "Is that a face I make?"

"Kind of like this." She hunches her shoulders, while making her eyes wide and sad. The effect is...unsettling.

"If I have ever looked like that, euthanize me."

Cat looks over my shoulder to where the barista is placing our drinks on the bar. She strides over to grab them, then returns and picks up the conversation as if there was no interruption. "Or, you could just say whatever it is you dragged me out here to tell me and defeat the face. Like exposure therapy."

I know she's joking, but I still frown. That's just it though, isn't it?

If I could say what I was feeling—what I wanted—I wouldn't have this problem. If I could voice my emotions immediately and talk about things when they happen instead of keeping them to myself for days and torturing not only me, but everyone around me with terror of what people will think, everything would be so much easier. But if I could do that, we wouldn't be here.

Damn. Why is this so hard?

I take a deep breath, and then, as if the floodgates have opened, I tell her everything.

Everything she already knows, but with more context, and a lot that she's never heard before going back years.

I tell her about the fight during my high school fundraiser, and the curse, and every fight afterwards. I tell her about when Roman beat-up Harrison Dane, even though he was only fifteen and Harrison was twenty, and about when Tyberius tried to poison Bennet Montague, so Roman cut the brakes on his car.

I tell her about when my mom nearly exposed the magical community on public television because Balthazar Montague called her a cunt and said he'd kill my grandmother; and about later when he *did* kill my grandmother.

I tell her about my father, and his affairs with girls in my college classes, about my mother and her impossible expectations, endless diets, and fixation on my weight. I tell her about how lonely I am in my empty, silent house, and how much I dread when anyone comes home; about how they ignore me and yet, I still want their approval.

And then, just when I think I'm running out of breath, I tell her everything I left out about the date with Harrison, and about Roman picking me up; about how we went to Councilman Lawrence's house and I didn't wear underwear and went to see my Aunt Angelica in Salem and had a fight.

And then I tell her about Roman.

Not about his teasing, because that's the one thing she doesn't need to hear again, but about the afternoons we used to spend in the library and the evenings in the cemeteries, and every stolen moment in the quiet of after a funeral; about the night at the gala; about how I'm afraid I love him, and maybe I always did.

"Fuck. What?" Cat interrupts. "Go back a minute."

I heave a breath, like I've been running a marathon, and try to backtrack to what I just said that's throwing her. My eyes widen, and I slap my hand over my mouth. "Holy shit."

She stares at me, and for a moment I'm terrified. Terrified that even though Cat and I have been friends for years, she'll tell me this is all too much for her. That I was right to keep it in all this time, or worse, that I have Champagne problems and they don't matter. That I'm spoiled and selfish for feeling this way.

"Well, I think your mother might have literally sold her soul, so I'd just disregard all that stuff about her."

I choke on a laugh, relief flooding me. "Yeah, maybe you're right. I didn't even tell you about the permanent Spanx."

Cat stands to get us more coffee, and I stare at the masts of the tall ships through the large, foggy windows. There's something about the air here. It's quiet, but not silent. I'm alone, but not lonely.

I take the mug from Cat as she sits down, nodding with thanks.

"Are you going to say it again?" she asks.

I purse my lips, wishing I could pretend I didn't know what she meant. "To you or to him?"

"Either."

"No!"

"Because it's irrelevant. My point still stands. I don't want to be the reason anyone gets hurt, especially Roman. I want to be the reason the feud is forced to end. I feel like the way things are going, we're more likely to end up causing more violence than ending it."

She shrugs as if to say: "So?"

"Not for nothing, but your family are all adults. They're doing this all on their own. Maybe they should worry if they're hurting you for once."

I try to let that sink in as she takes a sip of coffee. "It might be different if we were currently speaking. What if I said it and we still didn't work out? What if I love him, but he's planning to beat up my date to freshman formal, kill my grandmother, and cut the breaks on my car. It's not an entirely irrational fear."

I appreciate that she doesn't laugh.

"I mean," Cat says pursing her lips. "Judging from what I had to listen to all night in that apartment, you guys are hooking up *a lot*."

The back of my neck heats. "*Were*. And that's not the point."

"It kind of is, though. Aside from all the other stuff, you're fucking regularly and you're getting married."

"Were," I say over her. "*We were* doing those things. I have no idea what we're doing now."

"*Whatever*! I just mean that it would honestly be sociopathic if you didn't develop feelings for him."

"So, you don't think it's real?" I lean forward eagerly. "You're saying I'm getting caught up in the moment and it will go away."

She grimaces and I deflate before she even opens her mouth. "I don't know, maybe?" She picks at the split ends of her dark hair. "But honestly, no, I don't think that's what's happening. As much as I hate to admit it, this actually feels like the literal definition of 'if he wanted to, he would.'"

I furrow my brow. "What do you mean?"

"You know I despise all men, so the bar is lower than hell. It's in one of those deep-sea caves hanging out with a fucked-up, one-eyed, teenage, mutant, ninja-fish."

I sigh wearily. "I get it."

"Do you, though? I love you, but I wouldn't sit here and blow smoke up your ass. I'm saying that, objectively, no one said he had to agree to marry you. He didn't have to pick you up on the side of the road, or repeatedly risk his life to see you. That man is obsessed with you. It's honestly kind of shaking my world view. The bar might be, like, on the ground now."

I glance down, my face hot now. "Okay, but then why not even text me back?"

"What if he thinks you don't care anymore? Maybe you need to be the one to say something?"

"And what if I get rejected?" I ask, not really expecting an answer.

Predictably, she responds, anyway. "What if you don't?"

CHAPTER FORTY-TWO

·✦· ROMAN ·✦·

PRESENT

I CAN'T STOP THINKING ABOUT MY GRANDFATHER'S funeral.

It was only a few weeks after the initial incident that caused the feud with Etta's family to go from bad to nuclear overnight. I can't say I'd been pleasant to Etta before then, or that it got better afterwards, this being well into the years when I'd begun to build my obsession with her, but long before I would realize what it was.

I'd forgotten until now—lost in the intervening years of new memories—that until the day at the headmaster's office, Etta never spoke to me. She ignored me, always, with an almost dogmatic consistency.

So why come to the funeral?

I suspect I know the answer already. Know the answer to how we ended up here after all these years, and what spark ignited it. Etta has always cared too much. Cares more if those around her are comfortable than if she is. The same instinct that makes her want to save her family when they keep proving they'll throw her to the wolves without question has turned back on itself, twisting into an unhealthy fear of taking up too much space.

But that's neither here nor there, I suppose, when I hardly have the right to be judging anyone. Not when the only thing I can think of, aside from the overwhelming gloom pushing in on the edges of my brain, is wanting her. Needing her to come be like the sun driving out the darkness.

It's been twenty-four hours since our argument in the street. The argument that I still don't quite understand but infuriates me to think about. The one I wish I could go back and do differently in so many ways.

I'm lying flat on my bed in the dark, the only light coming from the hallway and from the phone lying face up next to me.

GOOD GIRL:

How are you?

I haven't replied, but not for lack of wanting to. It's such a simple statement with no simple answer. How can I say that with her, I'm fine but without her I can't breathe? That my obsession with her is unhealthy, and I don't fucking care. I'll never be normal when it comes to her, but none of this is normal. Maybe she'd accept that.

"Do you want something to eat?" Bennet asks from my doorway.

I have the strangest sense of déjà vu, glancing up at him, his outline only just visible. His image swims slightly. "No."

My cousin sets his jaw and he's quiet for a moment. "Are you just going to sit there?"

"Get out," I bark, in sort of a disconnected reply.

He wavers, going back and forth between his feet. Bennet hates conflict, with me especially. I've sometimes wondered if that's why he followed me around for our entire lives, despite the fact that I don't particularly like other people and never wanted to be in charge of our social group.

"No," he says finally. "Get your shit together, man. I don't know whether you broke up or—"

"We didn't break up. We weren't really together."

I keep trying to remind myself of that fact because it's easier to compartmentalize that way.

Bennet scoffs, ruining my plan. "I'm not hearing that. Just go talk to her."

I clench my hand into a fist. He's walking a fine fucking line right now. "I thought I told you to get out."

"Fine," Bennet says, backing out of the room. "Don't do anything. Sit in here forever, but you do know that you can't just pretend that no one else exists, right? There were other factors here."

I glance up, and again the room spins slightly and my head pounds. I mean to speak but can't find the words and only nod for him to continue.

"If you don't do anything, Etta will end up having to marry someone else."

"If Etta can figure out how to yell in the street she can yell at her mother. I think my work might be done."

In a way, I'm almost proud. Proud and fucking pissed.

Bennet crosses his arms, leaning against the doorframe. "You still have to think about your father and the Hathaways. What are you going to tell them?"

"I'll leave," I mutter.

It's an idea that's been circulating for the last twenty-four hours ever since I said it to Etta. I don't care about the Order anymore. I don't want to inherit my father's council seat. I don't even use magic. I have no reason to stay here except for her and Marcia's killer.

Bennet is right. Etta will marry someone else, and maybe I'll just have to move on and accept I'll never know what happened to my sister.

"Fine," Bennet says skeptically taking a few steps backward out of the room. "But this is some masochistic shit, Roman, even for you."

Despite my best efforts, I can't live with the image of Etta marrying Harrison Dane. I can't live with picturing her in another man's bed or kneeling in the Order's circle and performing the bonding ceremony, or not finishing school because someone told her she couldn't. I can't live with never hearing her argue with me again. I can't live without her.

The bell above the tarot shop door tinkles as I shove the door open with my shoulder. Probably rougher than I needed to, but I'm already bracing myself for the smell.

The other day, the shop was empty, but it must be peak hours because today it's crowded with tourists, the music playing overhead twice as loud, and the smell five-times as strong.

Perhaps it's my aversion to readers in general, given my one and only experience with one, but I hate it here. Willingly subjecting myself to this torment again feels like my worst instinct to self-sabotage, especially as Etta made it quite clear she didn't want to keep trying. But I have no idea where else to turn. I keep wishing I could go back and simply stay in the room, to hear if something was said other than the simple "No," Etta described. Something that would have panicked her to the point of wanting to give up on the entire plan.

I shove my way through the crowd toward the front of the shop. The same girl is working at the counter, today wearing an orange and white Halloween patterned dress even though it's November.

"Welcome in," she calls, keeping her eyes fixed on the cash register as I approach. "Gimme a second."

I say nothing, hovering in front of the counter while I wait for her to finish whatever she's doing. Finally, she slams the cash register closed, and turns to me. Her slightly far-away eyes narrow in recognition. "Oh, hello, non-Believer."

"Hey." I tense. I can't bring myself to find the energy to be charming, but I dig down deep and find something civil. "Is Angelica reading today?"

She sighs. "You aren't supposed to use the reader's real names. It's rude."

I didn't notice she had another name. I don't remember seeing it when we were here before. "Sorry?"

"To answer your question, yes, but she's booked all afternoon."

"I just need a few minutes."

She points down at the book on the counter—the same one I remember seeing last time. "They're fifteen-minute slots. She doesn't have a few minutes."

I run a hand through my hair. "Look. What would it take for you to just…" I glance down at the scheduling book. "Erase the next person. Fifteen minutes is fine."

My heart beats hard, sweat beading on the back of my neck as she considers. "You're from the Order, right?"

"Yes…"

I don't recognize her at all, but the only people who know about the Order are in it, or in extremely high positions of power in other ways—human politicians and the like.

"Fine," she says, scribbling out a name in her book. "You can just owe me a favor. That's worth more to me than anything you've got on you right now."

A *favor.* It's like a quest, and this woman, Ophelia, is the gatekeeper. The sphinx that must be defeated. The riddler on the road. The first obstacle to be bypassed in the hero's journey.

I frown—I've never been the hero.

"You still don't like me," Angelica says by way of greeting.

I sit down across from her in her little room beyond the red velvet curtain. "Not really," I reply, deciding it's better not to lie. And, anyway, I can't fucking deal with faking anything right now.

She grins, leaning forward, like that's the most interesting thing she's ever heard. It transforms her face, and she instantly looks twenty years younger. "Why? I'm dying to know."

"I'm dying to know why you told Etta you wouldn't help her."

She absently shuffles her cards in front of her, tossing a few on the table in no particular pattern with the same care of someone dealing poker. She reaches out, peeks at the one closest to her, and frowns. Shuffles the deck again, and tosses out more cards. "I hate busy days like this, I end up with such chaotic card energy." She holds out her deck to me. "Take one."

I humor her, hoping she'll get on with it and answer my question. "Why won't you help?"

She keeps shuffling. "The Order does a lot of great things. Here, I mean, 'great' in its original meaning. The Order does significant and powerful things in the world, but those are not always *good* things."

"They're not always bad things either," I say for the sake of the argument.

"True," she says simply, leaving my thoughts to spin off on what she might be thinking. "But I want no part in it anymore, and I don't want to help my niece join either."

I glare at her. "Etta isn't like that. She's a good person."

"And the Order corrupts good people. I've seen it happen before."

"Not her. This is a woman who wants to go to school and save her family. That's it. This whole insane thing is because she thinks she can single-handedly end a centuries long feud, and fix all the Order's problems just by wanting it enough. She's very...hopeful."

"You love her." It's just a statement.

I don't even bother denying it. "Yes."

"That's sweet, but it doesn't change my mind. You're both what, twenty-two? Today everything is wonderful and hopeful, but good people get disillusioned every day."

"No!" I insist. "See, you're not getting it. I'm not a good person. I've been a selfish, entitled prick my entire life and I haven't changed. I don't care about saving anyone or fixing anything, all I care about is her. All I want is to protect her, so if what you're afraid of is someone getting to Etta, that won't happen because I'd be standing in front of her and the Order can't touch me because there's nothing left to corrupt"

"It's a good speech kid, but I'm not the one to give it to."

I bristle, more at the word "kid" than anything else. "Never mind." I push my seat back. This was clearly a waste of time.

"Sit back down," she says, waving a hand. "I'm not done yet. Pick a card."

I look down my nose at her and slowly sit back down. "This isn't my thing."

"I don't understand that," she muses. "You cast runes."

"I don't," I argue, knowing it's somewhat hypocritical.

She clearly doesn't believe me and ignores it. "You had a star-chart done, but you don't believe in fate?"

I don't have the energy to explain to her that fate keeps trying to fuck me, that if I left things up to the universe or to the gods, I would spend every hour of my life wallowing in the abject fuckery of my existence. Of the prison of my own mind, in my objectively privileged life. Instead, I pick a card.

I'm not sure what I'm looking at, as I've never cared nor bothered to learn to read Tarot, but I hold it up to show her.

"Nine of swords. Well, at least my deck is energetically aligned again."

I scowl at her. "Can we just—"

"You pick, I'll talk."

"Fine."

She holds the deck out and I grab another card at random, handing it to her without looking. Satisfied, she says: "I take it you and Etta haven't compared star charts."

I stiffen. If she's about to tell me that this is pointless because we're incompatible, I'm going to flip this fucking table. "No," I say stiffly, taking another card. "How do you know?"

She grins and taps her temple with one finger. "I'm a psychic, remember? And I might have pulled some of my records—professional curiosity, you know—" she waves her hand "—and I noticed a strange pattern."

I lean forward. "What?"

"Pick a—"

"Fucking hell." I grab a card and shove it at the woman. "What was it?"

Her lip curves like a pleased cat. "Don't you think it's interesting that as heirs to two council seats, neither of you had betrothals at birth? Wouldn't highly ambitious, politically minded parents want to use their kids to further their roles in the Order?"

I frown, saying nothing. Yes, it is strange, but I know what happened to me. "There wasn't a good match when I was born."

She snorts a laugh. "The feud between our families goes back centuries."

I'm startled, and I suddenly remember that Angelica is a Capulet. It's strange—she doesn't seem like one, and it's so easy to forget. I tense, like she might suddenly attack, but she barely looks up as she continues.

"And?" I prompt, grabbing a card before she can ask.

"You may not know my brother well, but what do you think your father would have done if he found out his only son was fated for the daughter of his only enemy? Would anyone have told you?"

My mouth goes dry, and I can't form words. My mind goes entirely blank.

Angelica glances up, and I expect her to be smiling—like she's won something, beat me, with this revelation. But she just watches me with intense, gray eyes.

"So," I struggle to say. "Now what?"

It's not eloquent, and I despise asking anyone else for what I should do, but this whole week has been nothing but that. Nothing but laying down every shred of pride I had left as an offering of devotion to Etta. Now, maybe, I know why.

Angelica flips all my cards over and scans them, eyes darting back and forth as if reading words on a page. She nods slowly. "Now, you go get your girl. And do let me know when you finally have that wedding, I'm a hoot at weddings."

"You're coming?" I blurt out.

"Assuming you still need me, sure."

I'm reeling. "You just said I didn't convince you."

You didn't." She points at the cards. "These did."

I gape at her, even as I want to kick myself for questioning it and possibly fucking this up. I run a frustrated hand through my hair. I hate myself for not being able to just let things go. For having to understand everything. "I don't understand."

"Sometimes things need to happen in the right order at exactly the right time." She sweeps her cards into a pile. "Like, right now for instance, you need to go interrupt an engagement announcement."

My eyes narrow. "Did the cards tell you that too?"

She looks appalled. "No, it was on social media."

Chapter Forty-Three

ETTA

Present

A clap of thunder sounds outside my window and the rushing wind howls against the house, shaking my French doors for all they're worth. The rain hasn't started yet, but I can tell it's not going to be the peaceful kind of storm, but rather an angry one. One with teeth and claws and vengeance, wreaking havoc against the world.

I'm back in my room at my house as if nothing happened. As if I was never gone.

In a way, it's like I never left, since my parents never even noticed my absence. A folder with another of my mother's signature notes sits unread on the end of my bed, no doubt full of whatever decor she's chosen for the party after my bonding to Harrison. Just the thought makes me wish to go to sleep and never wake up.

I glance down at my phone, where my last text to Roman stares back at me unanswered.

. . .

ME:

How are you?

Hey, can we talk?

BOTH MESSAGES ARE BLUE, DELIVERED, AND LEFT ON read. My life is a joke.

After my conversation with Cat earlier, I thought I could just magically fix it, but no. He hasn't responded—either too busy or too stubborn to talk.

Apparently, my self-actualization came too late. That, or he was never going to be receptive to what I wanted. Either way, his silence is an answer all on its own, and now I'm stuck. I'm unwilling to go downstairs, get engaged and admit defeat, and too scared to face worse rejection by just going to Roman's apartment.

So, I'm just sitting here, quietly, letting things happen around me. I am the good girl.

A knock sounds on my door, and for a moment my heart leaps, only to come crashing down again. What the hell am I thinking? It's not going to be him at my bedroom door.

"Yeah?" I yell, unable to keep the bitterness from my tone.

"Etta?" My father's voice, tinged with a forced cheerfulness, cuts through the silence. "May I?"

"Sure."

Dad steps into the room, clad in his crisp suit, a look of expectancy on his face. "Your mom wants to know if you're almost ready."

I glance down at the latest party dress I've been stuffed into—white, of course. "Yup. Be right down."

He frowns, looking slightly concerned. It's probably because of my tone. I usually try harder to be pleasant—nice—but I'm struggling with that at the moment.

"How are you feeling?" Dad asks.

"Fine," I mutter, feeling the heavy weight of my arranged future pressing down on me.

My father shifts uncomfortably. His eyes search mine, a flicker of guilt passing over them like a shadow. "Is there anything I can do?" he asks finally. "Your happiness is important to us, Etta."

"No." I sound bitter. "Don't worry, I'm not going to pull an Aunt Angelica and run off with someone else."

The words are a little too close to an admission of guilt, but my dad doesn't know that. Still, he gives me a strange look. "Right. So, see you downstairs?"

"Ten minutes. I just need..." I cast wildly around for some excuse to stall, just a moment longer. "To touch up my makeup."

He leaves, the door closing with a loud snap. The sound reverberates through me, and I pause, listening to the silence of the room. The howling wind outside. The unevenness of my breathing.

I shouldn't have brought up Aunt Angelica, and how she left her betrothed at the altar, because now I'm thinking about it. Really thinking about it. Thinking about how she probably had all the same fears I do—about leaving her family, and not knowing how to function in the real world. About not knowing anyone outside of the Order, and not having any money of her own.

Except, a few days ago, when I had these fears I'd never thought of jobs I could do; like finding rare books, or running magical hedge funds, or reading tarot. I never thought I could be capable of something like that, but Angelica was, and she couldn't have possibly had as much of an incentive as I do to leave.

She couldn't have, because no one has ever loved anyone as much as I love Roman.

That thought is like a jolt to my system, bringing everything into sharper relief.

What the hell am I doing? I can't just not try.

I grab my phone and stand up from where I sit on the bed, dashing to the French doors. It's pitch-dark outside, the weather raging, but I hardly care. It could be snowing, and I still wouldn't stay here a moment longer.

ME:

Meet me at the cemetery

I type out the letters, hitting send before I can question it. Grabbing a sweater off the chair by the window, I slip my feet into the first shoes I see and throw the doors open. Cold air rushes up to greet me, but I hardly notice, adrenaline heating my skin. Hands shaking, I type out one more message.

ME:

I love you.

I know as the little "delivered" mark appears below the message that even if he ignores me, I still won't come back to this house. I want him—need him—but it's not only about that. If he doesn't want me, I'll leave. I'll go to England, or maybe move to Salem. I don't know, it doesn't matter. Anywhere, but here.

Taking a deep breath, I throw one leg over the balcony and look down, scanning for the first foothold of the trellis.

The wind kicks up, plucking at my hair and sending a chill through me, and I lean over, sliding my foot along the outside lip of the balcony.

"Etta?" My dad's exasperated voice sounds outside my bedroom door again, and I see the doorknob turn. "Your mother is very concerned about what's taking so long, could— "

My heart pounds out of control, panic rattling through me. "Wait! I'm not ready!"

Too late, the door opens again and my dad stares directly at me through the open French doors.

"Hi," I stammer. If I could pull myself back up, that would be better, but I'm not going anywhere at the moment—in either direction. "Dad, um, hi..." I say, trying to think of any believable excuse and coming up with zero. "See, this is..."

"Etta." My dad pinches the bridge of his nose. "As someone who has had their private relationships exposed a time or two, I recommend that you not try to explain this. It's never anything other than exactly what it looks like."

"What?" I sing-song, sounding more than a little guilty. "No, see—"

"Etta, stop." My dad shakes his head, looking somewhere between bemused and annoyed, and closes my bedroom door before striding across the room and stepping out onto the balcony. He leans against the house, looking entirely out of place out here in his suit. His graying hair is combed into a coiffe. He crosses his arms, and meets my eyes fully for the first time in my recent memory. "You're going to see the Montague boy."

I cough on air. "Excuse me?"

"Fine, don't tell me." He waves me off. "You don't have to, I already know."

I sit in shocked silence for what feels like at least thirty seconds, my mind spinning through possibilities. Did someone see us together? That's very possible, but we got seen together all the time back when I was in high school and I always explained it away. More importantly, my parents always confronted me about it. If we'd been spotted recently, they surely would have confronted me again. Councilman Lawrence could have told him, or maybe Aunt Angelica if she and my dad are somehow in contact. Maybe one of the witnesses?

The more I think about it, the more I realize how this was going to come out soon, anyway. We weren't going to be able to hide for much longer, even if it's over between us. People will still learn that it happened in the first place, and I probably always knew that somewhere in the back of my mind.

I swing my leg back over the balcony, rapidly coming up with a plan for damage control—of course, it might not matter now that the damage is done. I suppose the worst they can do is disown me, right?

I take a deep breath. "Are you mad?"

It sounds comical. "Are you mad" like I broke a dish. The words completely ignore hundreds of years of bad-blood, and all the very real violence that casts a shadow over myself and Roman.

My dad is silent, thinking, then finally says: "I'm...not sure I have any right to judge."

I blink in surprise. "That's...unlike you."

He frowns, but seems to decide to ignore the quip. "It's your life, Etta, and you've been practically an adult since you learned to walk. I think by now you have a good idea of what's right for you."

I gape at him. Where was this laissez faire attitude a few weeks ago? What about when I wanted to pick my own college, or hell, my own clothes? Who is this man and what has he done with my father?

"What about the wedding?" I blurt out. "You don't care if I get married?"

"I didn't say that," he says. "I'm not thrilled about this, I simply… empathize. I have started to wonder about the ethics of arranged marriages between strangers that can never be dissolved."

Huh. I can't decide how I feel about that, my dad being supportive because he cheats on my mom and thinks this is the same. It's not, but maybe I should take the wins where I can get them.

I glance into my bedroom and toward the door, half afraid that my mom will burst in next. "Does mom know?"

My dad looks down his nose. "Not yet."

I sigh. "Got it. So, not that it matters now, I guess, but who told you?"

"Dad looks painfully uncomfortable. "Well, a friend mentioned it."

I raise my eyebrows, uncomprehending. "A friend?"

"Yes," he runs his hand over the back of his neck. "A, uh, close friend was very upset that Mr. Montague wouldn't speak to her regarding the wedding. So, apparently, she got tired of being ignored and went over to his apartment."

I stare at my dad, blankly. "Dad, sorry, but I don't understand. Who do you know who would be at Roman's apartment?"

He clears his throat, and tries again. "My very close, very personal friend—" he widens his eyes at me, until they are taking up half his face "—could not get in contact with Mr. Montague regarding their mutual wedding."

My mouth falls open as realization floods me. "Oh my gods."

I can honestly say I have never seen my father look more embarrassed in his life. He wipes invisible sweat off his brow and looks away. "So, given her difficulty with contacting Mr. Montague, my friend arrived at his home late last night, where she was informed by several extremely inebriated twenty-somethings that Mr. Montague was otherwise occupied."

"Oh my gods," I say again, unable to think of anything else to say.

"My friend was very excited to learn of Mr. Montague's other affiliations, as she has recently gotten it into her head that she might want to "want" things." He rolls his eyes.

I furrow my eyebrows. I don't actually understand that part, but it doesn't matter. I'd rather fling myself off the balcony than ask for clarification.

"And you see," Dad says with an air of finality. "I heard this story at a time when your mother was not at home, thus she did not hear the story, and is not aware." He barely meets my gaze, seeming to look at my forehead instead. "Are we understanding each other?"

"Yes. Got it," I say quickly. "Thank you for, um, explaining that."

Dad looks physically pained. "You're welcome."

We sit in extremely awkward silence for a minute, before I force myself to break the tension. "So, are you going to make me go downstairs?"

He sighs loudly, sounding so exhausted I have to wonder if there's more on his mind than just me. "I'm not going to make you do anything. I'm going to suggest, however, that the garage door is out of sight of the great room and makes very little noise when opened."

CHAPTER FORTY-FOUR
✦ ETTA ✦

PRESENT

My heart pounds double-time as I speed out of my driveway and onto the road, heading toward the cemetery. The clock on the dashboard taunts me, reminding me that I'm already twenty minutes late.

Of course, he hasn't texted me back, so maybe I'm kidding myself.

I push the thought out of my mind, determined not to let panic set in. I can do this.

As I drive, the sky opens up, and massive raindrops begin to pelt my windshield, making it nearly impossible to see. The air becomes thick and foggy, blinding me. Thankfully, I know the way by heart.

My car screeches to a halt in front of the iron cemetery gates and my breath catches in my throat as I realize they're locked. How did I not know they locked the gates overnight?

I frantically search for any sign of Roman's presence. But there's nothing - no familiar car parked nearby, no figure moving within the gates. Could he be inside already? Or is he not coming?

All I can think of is Roman showing up to wait for me by our family's graves, only to find me not there.

Staring at the gates, I breathe heavily as if I ran all the way here. The rain pounds on my windshield, like it's mocking me, making everything all the harder. Daring me to go inside.

Screw this.

I fling open my car door and practically hurl myself out, feeling the impact of icy rain instantly soak through my clothes and chill me to the bone. But I refuse to let that stop me as I dart towards the pedestrian entrance of the cemetery, which miraculously remains unlocked despite the late hour.

My heels dig into the slippery grass as I frantically kick off my shoes and sprint barefoot through the freezing cold, my feet splashing through puddles and slipping on patches of slick grass. The chilling droplets sting my skin as I race past rows of solemn grave markers and finally, I spot the familiar cluster of headstones that mark the resting place of my family, and just beyond them, up a small hill, lies Roman's family—a silent reminder of our shared pain and loss.

Twenty yards back, my heart squeezes. There's no one there on that hill.

I scan the empty graveyard one more time and a sense of true hopelessness washes over me. I turn in a circle, the adrenaline wearing off just enough to realize how stupid this was.

Of course there isn't. Of course, he's not there. It's pouring, and I'm just...hopeful to the point of insanity, I suppose. I should have stayed in the car.

I wrap my arms around myself, the cold finally hitting me for real. The freezing wind is howling, dead leaves blowing everywhere, and another enormous clap of thunder says that the storm is only getting started.

"Etta!"

My heart leaps.

I turn, my numb feet barely able to move, and joy washes over me as a shadowed figure makes his way forward. My heart aches. I wish he wasn't always so hauntingly beautiful, dark eyes barely visible in this light, soaking wet, black hair falling in his face. He's wearing a wool overcoat over one of his seemingly endless supply of sweaters.

"What the fuck are you doing?" Roman demands when he reaches me.

"I—I texted you."

He scribbles a warming rune over me and it's like I'm somehow instantly wrapped in the warmest parka. He looks livid, and his expression only darkens as he looks down at my soaking wet party dress and sweater. "I saw your car, what are you doing out here?"

I tilt my head back to meet his gaze, raindrops sliding down my cheeks like tears. "I was worried we missed each other."

Practically growling with frustration, Roman reaches down, grabbing me under the knees and around the waist in a fireman's carry. "You're trying to kill me, good girl."

"No," I quiver. "This would have only killed *me*."

"Same thing."

Rather than walking all the way back to the cars, he walks twenty yards to our right and deposits me under the eaves of an old crypt.

My teeth chatter slightly, despite the warming rune, and Roman looks me over again.

He uses another rune to open the door to the crypt and practically shoves me inside. "Roman, no," I whine. "This is weird."

"Get over it," he says flatly. "You're the one who didn't stay in your nice, warm, car. We're going to wait for it to let up."

I take out my cellphone flashlight, already worried I'm about to see something out of a horror movie, but it's actually just a stone room with metal plates on the walls and a huge, stone, coffin in the center. If I don't think about it, the coffin kind of looks like a table, so...I guess I won't think about it.

I turn back to roman, and the entire reason we're here and everything at stake comes flooding back. My heart starts to pound too fast, leaping into my throat.

I'm burning to talk about my texts. To ask why he didn't respond, to ask him if coming here means he wants me too, to tell him I love him.

"My dad knows about us," I blurt out in a panic. "Assuming there's anything left to know, I guess."

"Yeah...that doesn't shock me." Roman takes a step toward me, his phone held out to the side, illuminating the floor. "I went to see your aunt again."

"What?" I hiss. I expressly told him I didn't want to keep pushing her. Even if I was angry. Even if it crushed me. "Why would you do that?"

His eyes glint with the first serious emotion tonight. "Because you were going to just walk away."

"Yes," I snap. "Because I didn't want to hurt her, and because it wouldn't have mattered, anyway."

"Well, you might care about that moral fucking high ground shit, but I don't and lucky for you, good girl, I'm selfish and all I need is to give you everything you want."

My chest constricts at the words and I don't think I'd be able to feel the cold even without the rune. He's always saying things like that—things that are almost impossible to misinterpret, yet aren't exactly what I want to hear. Meanwhile, I'm no better, never saying anything real at all.

"I wanted you to talk to me," I say quietly. "Why didn't you respond to my text?"

He frowns. "I did. I know it took a bit, I'm sorry, but...why are you looking at me like that?"

"I never got a single text." Even as I say it, though, we both know what happened.

It's Stratford, where technology bows to magic without warning and simply stops working. Part of me is dying to know what he said—especially to my last text—but as he watches me, dark intensity in his eyes, my brain refuses to focus on the question.

Instead, I step forward almost entirely closing the distance between us and his hands come up instinctively to rest on my back. His palms are warm despite the chill in the air, and I sink into his embrace. His arms encircle me tightly as if he never wants to let go; a reassurance that he won't leave no matter what I have to say.

I take a deep breath mustering up every bit of courage within me before whispering softly into the night air: "I love you."

Roman pulls away just enough so we can look each other in the eye, a small smile tugs at his lips as if these mere words are enough for him. He dips his head down until our foreheads meet, our noses grazing against each other. "Thank the fucking gods."

I choke, something like a laugh and an indignant huff coming out of me at once. "Seriously?"

His mouth hovers over mine, lips barely grazing, as if leaving the decision up to me. "In case it isn't obvious, good girl, I love you. I've always loved you, for years, even though it was slowly killing me. That isn't even a large enough word for how much I need you. You're the only fucking thing that matters to me, and I'm trying not to scare you with how, if I had my way, I'd lock you up and never let you leave because I need you to breathe."

My throat constricts as my eyes drift down to his lips and back up to his eyes. They're filled with desire and want and a hunger for me. I lean in, closing the last millimeters between us, then I press my mouth to his.

Chapter Forty-Five

PRESENT

I'M ON FIRE.

Even with the runes to protect us, it's cold and wet and so dark, I can only see the two feet around us illuminated by my phone. Yet, I'm being burned from the inside out, the flames turning me to ash in her arms.

For years I've been standing in the flames as she burned me alive, but now I'm on fire for a wholly different reason as her lips touch mine and her little hands wrap around my neck.

All I can think about is more, more, *more*.

I need her everywhere, all at once. I don't know if I want to be inside her or to have her come on my face or how best to worship her and make her scream.

What the fuck is wrong with me that the idea of fucking her here, surrounded by death and darkness has me hardening already? A therapist would have a fucking field-day with this one—I'm probably so messed up that I'm well beyond repair. Or, maybe, it's that there were only two places where I fell in love with Etta—the library and the cemetery. I've gotten to have her in one, and now I want both. I want everything with her.

I shake my head, trying to focus. Fuck, I came here for a reason. To tell her everything, yes, but also to ask her to come with me. To tell her what her aunt said and beg her to trust me.

I wrench my mouth from hers and it's almost painful. My voice is hoarse, like stone on stone. "Etta, wait."

Her voice is shaky, and almost nervous. "What?"

I briefly wonder if I should wait and do this differently. I've never pictured proposing, but I didn't think it would be in a goddamn crypt in the middle of the night, while I'm half distracted by my inconveniently hardening cock and Etta's wet, transparent, dress.

Then again, if I wait for the moment to be perfect it will never happen. Nothing about our relationship so far has been normal or easy or picture-perfect. If there's one thing we've never had on our side it was timing.

I pull my hand from Etta's hair, and reach into my pocket, unearthing the black-velvet box that my mother gave me. There had never been a moment when I thought about giving this ring to anyone else, so, maybe that cancels out the weird timing of the proposal.

I'm about to do the normal thing and get to one knee, when I'm distracted by her shaking. "You cold?"

"No," she lies.

I wrap my arms around her, pulling her in. "You're a bad liar."

"Just my feet," she admits, completely unaware of my pounding heart and the box clutched in my hand.

I glance down and realize her feet are bare. I raise an eyebrow. "What happened?"

"It's not important. I don't know why, but it didn't work on the bottoms."

She means the rune didn't work on the soles of her feet. Huh—that's a question for another time, I guess.

Transferring the box to my left hand, I grab her around the waist, lifting her off the ground and seating her on top of the stone coffin in the center of the room. Etta looks down, and frowns. "I feel like I'm borrowing someone else's bed, you know?"

"I don't think they mind, good girl."

She grins, and twines her arms around my neck, drawing me into her. "I guess you're right."

She wraps her legs around my hips, trapping me, and it not only makes it impossible to get on one knee, it does nothing to take my mind off bending her over this coffin.

It's got to be illegal to be this turned on while standing over someone's grave, yet, it's taking all my strength not to take her right here. Not to push her soaking wet dress up her thighs, to suck on her tits through the fabric of her cardigan, to thrust into her until she screams my name so loud that it would wake the dead.

Gods, this is the worst way to propose to someone. Or the best, I don't know.

I close my eyes, forcing myself to speak before I fully lose control. "Do you trust me?"

She looks up, her eyes shining. "Yes."

I hand her the box—more clumsily than I would have preferred in any other position—but it doesn't matter when her eyes go wide.

"Then I need you to come somewhere with me, now, so we can make this real."

She opens the box and looks down at the ring inside, a smile curving her lips. "Is that your proposal speech?"

"No, you already got the speech, but I was distracted by how fucking sexy you are," I tell her bluntly. "I can do it again. I'll tell you as many times as you want how much I've always loved you."

A pink flush blooms on her cheeks. Not embarrassment, I don't think, but happiness.

She snaps the box closed and grins. "You can put this on me as soon as we get out of here. I want to hear the speech again."

"Deal."

I start to step back, assuming she means we should get out of here right now, but she doesn't untangle her arms from around my neck. Instead, Etta adjusts against me, and I try to stifle a groan as she accidentally grinds against my cock. Or, maybe not so accidentally from the way her smirk turns wicked. "Do we have to go right now?"

I raise an eyebrow, glancing around at the crypt. "I thought you were cold."

Anyone would be cold—the weather is vicious, fall turning into winter, and she's soaking wet. I can't see any good reason why she'd want to be out here. Unless, she's thinking all the same depraved things I am. Unless she's even more perfect than I always knew she was.

"Warm me up," she says, a glint of mischief in her eyes.

Ah, damn her. "That's not very good of you, good girl. Maybe I've tainted you beyond repair."

"Maybe," she says, licking up the column of my neck. "Let's check."

I let out a strangled moan and capture her mouth with mine again, hungrily devouring her tiny sounds of pleasure. Reveling in the feel of her delicate fingers, and the way she writhes against me.

I move my mouth down the column of her neck, sucking and nipping at where I can still see the evidence of the bruise I left on her skin. Pushing her wet cardigan off her shoulders, I lave my tongue over that spot. Run my lips over her collarbones, and drag my fingers over her arms.

She lets her head fall back and she moans, the sound almost pained. "Roman. I need— "

"I know. Take off your dress, I want to see what's mine."

Her breath hitches, even as she pulls her soaking wet dress up. I reach out to help her, gathering the fabric of the skirt, and dragging it over her head. She raises her arms, and when it comes off in a cascade of wet silk she's sitting in front of me in nothing but her panties, all smooth skin and curves, entirely too beautiful to be real.

Her eyes widen slightly, I duck my head and wrap my lips around her perfect breast. I swirl my tongue, sucking, and nipping. She moans, her head tipping back, and reaches up to palm the other one herself. I notice her legs fall wider, like she can't stop herself from readying for me to slide into her. *Fuck.*

I move to her other breast, giving that one equal attention, and at the same time I reach down and squeeze my cock through my jeans, needing it to calm the fuck down.

Etta sees this, and misunderstands that I need to be less hard—not more. Her little hand snakes down to my belt buckle. I swat her hand back. "Don't, good girl."

"Why?" She pouts. "I want to feel how much you want me."

Holy shit. My mind is blank. She's finally grasping dirty talk, and I now realize I've played myself. I will never get another thing done for the rest of my life—there will be no blood available for my brain.

"Remind me, who does this belong to?" I ask, running my fingers over the front of her panties.

"You," she says without hesitation.

"Good girl," I praise her, all too aware of the double-meaning. "So give it to me. I want to play with my favorite toy."

She whimpers, seeming unsure if she should be annoyed or turned on. I don't give a fuck as long as she comes. I want her screaming, writhing and begging for it when I give her my cock.

I lean back over to kiss the scowl off her face, and a vague idea starts to take root in the back of my mind. I lick over the seam over her mouth, and she sighs, opening her lips for me and running her tongue over mine.

"Blessed be thy lips."

Etta immediately responds to the familiar phrase and tenses. "Roman..." she says warily against my mouth.

"Quiet, good girl, let me worship you."

I move back down to her breasts next, repeating all the torturous attention of my lips and tongue. Letting my teeth graze over her soft skin, and rolling her nipples between my thumb and forefinger. "Blessed be thy breasts."

Etta whimpers. "I'm supposed to get a turn, you know."

I know, but giving her free-reign to reciprocate won't have the effect I want. Reaching down, I dig my fingers into her hips and ass and pull her closer to the very edge of the stone coffin. "Blessed be thy cunt."

She laughs. "That's not the right words."

"It is when I'm going to lick every inch of your wet, needy cunt until you are begging for salvation and then I'm going to fuck you so hard you'll think you've already been saved."

Her laughter immediately dies as I grab her legs and pull her toward the end of the table, and bend to press a long, open mouth kiss to her clit.

"Oh my gods," she squeals, her knees clenching around my head.

I lick her over and over, tasting and sucking her down as my fingers probe at her soft folds. Her hips rise and fall as she writhes beneath me, fucking herself against my tongue.

I pull back for a breath, still pumping my fingers in and out of her, and marvel at how fucking beautiful she is, undone like this.

"On your knees," I tell her, straightening.

She whimpers in protest, thinking I'm done with her, but no. I just want more.

I climb up beside her, and pull her into my lap before lying down and dragging Etta up my body until she's hovering over my face. She moans at just the anticipation I think—it must be, because she won't sit the fuck down.

"Get your ass down here."

"No, I—"

I don't have the patience for this. I grab her ass and pull her down, thrusting my tongue deep, licking inside her, until her knees buckle and she falls forward, her hands bracing against the stone.

I suck her clit into my mouth and hold it there, like I'm savoring a piece of candy, rolling my tongue over and under, massaging small, delicate circles.

She whines, almost crying and I press my tongue flat, placing long slow laps against her entrance. She moans, bucking her hips against my face, desperate for friction.

"Please," she whines, grinding against my tongue. "Please, please."

"Please, what?" I ask, pulling back just enough to speak. To let her feel my breath and watch her tremble with want.

Her answer is to drag her pussy against my lips, demanding more. My eyes widen—I wasn't expecting that, and it's the hottest fucking thing I've ever seen.

I open wide, kissing her, devouring her, reaching up to pinch her nipples when her knees start to shake. Etta trembles, shattering, and screams loud and long as she melts against me; the sweetest goddamned thing I've ever tasted.

I don't let her rest. I can't. I need to be inside her right now, need to feel her tight around me, hear her screaming when she comes again around my cock.

I grip her hips, and move her back down my body to straddle just above my waist, trying to ignore the way my cock is aching so hard I think I might break the zipper on my jeans.

Etta looks up and meets my eyes as she reaches back and opens my belt without looking. This time, I wouldn't be able to stop her for anything. One of those damn midnight ghost tours could walk through here right now, and I wouldn't blink an eye.

Her hand snakes its way into my jeans, unencumbered by under-wear, and she wraps a hand around my shaft. She moves her fingers up and down, slow and teasing, and her lips curve into a smile. "So, does this belong to me, then?"

Fucking hell. "As long as you want me, I'm all yours, good girl."

According to Etta's aunt, that might be forever, and fuck I hope she's right. There will never be anyone else for me, no matter what happens.

Etta smiles, and slides backwards until she's hovering over my cock. She pushes my jeans down lower, then raises her hips, and drags the head of my cock over her center a few times before impaling herself on me.

Etta's lips fall open, and I moan, half with ecstasy and half with relief to finally be inside her. I swear nothing and no one else has ever felt this good. Like she really was made just for me.

"Fuck yourself on me," I tell her, even as she begins to move. "I want you to grind your clit just the way you like it, good girl, and tell me when you're ready to come again."

"Holy shit," she breathes, the lust clear in her eyes.

Etta presses her palms to my chest and begins to move faster. She rises and falls, riding me like the good girl she is in this very dark place. She whimpers, her eyes closing, and leans forward rocking her hips again and again.

I dig my fingers into her calves and watch, waiting for the little sounds and gasping breaths that mean she's close. I'm hypnotized, trying to think of anything other than how fucking good she feels, how sexy she looks above me, and how—

"Oh fuck," she breathes, eyes squeezing tight. "Roman."

Thank the gods.

"Are you gonna come for me, good girl?"

"Uh, huh," she rasps, unable to form words.

I sit up, intending to lift her off me. I'd planned to torture her just a little longer, prolonging her orgasm and sliding back to the floor. I'd thought I would bend her over the stone, her ass in the air, and hammer into her from behind.

But then, once I've sat up and changed the angle, she makes a little sound of pleasure in the back of her throat and I need to hear it again. Need to watch her fall apart.

She wraps her arms around my neck. Her eyes are still closed, her breath ragged as she tries to push herself over the edge.

I move my hips with her, going deeper, helping her bounce up and down. "Look at me."

She opens her eyes, and her mouth falls open again in a silent scream. I feel her tighten around me, her legs trembling, and finally I let myself explode inside her with a strangled: "I love you."

Chapter Forty-Six

✦ ETTA ✦

Present

You're not walking back in the rain," Roman says flatly. "I'll go and get the car."

I'm all too aware of the rain as I tug back on my cold, wet, dress, but I don't care anymore. "The gates are locked."

He gives me a sideways look, and dries my dress with a rune. "I think I can handle the lock."

"Sure, but I don't want to sit in here alone. I'd rather freeze."

He rolls his eyes. "Fine. I don't know any rune better than warming for this, but as soon as we get home I'm going to find one. I'll invent one if I have to."

I nod, but what I'm really focused on is that he said "home' as in: "when we get home" and I'm melting.

WE LEAVE MY CAR, DECIDING TO COME BACK FOR IT IN the morning, and Roman drives back toward the center of town.

My phone is working again, I think, but the only messages are from Cat several hours ago, and two calls from my dad.

It's almost suspicious.

Not a single call from my mother? No vicious texts from Harrison? Running out on yet another engagement party should warrant some reaction, right?

I'm almost offended.

"Are we going to your place?" I ask.

Roman pauses before answering. "I was thinking we should go to your house."

I look at him too quickly and crack my neck. "Why?"

"Because I'm done hiding this. You've walked out on two engagements, I assume that means you're ready to go public. That was the whole point of this, right?"

"Yes..." I say slowly "But the point was to already be married so no one can stop us."

"No one can stop us, anyway, good girl." He glances at me for a moment, for something like reassurance before turning back to the road. "There is nothing fake or convenient about this. I don't want to be with you for any political reason, or to protect anyone else. I just want you."

"I really do want to go to England, though." I attempt to make a joke and it falls flat, the seriousness of the conversation overshadowing all-else.

"Etta, I want to stop having to deal with your family setting up your wedding, or sneaking around."

"Okay." I take a deep breath. Who knows, maybe if it's all out in the open we could just...date for a while. I could finish college before we get married. We could have options. "Fine. My dad already knows, anyway, and judging from the radio silence on my phone, no one even cares that I left. So, I guess we should just go deal with it."

Roman turns to me and grins, that rare real smile that takes my breath away, and for a moment, it seems like everything will be fine.

But it's not fine.

As usual, things only get worse.

AS WE TURN ONTO MY STREET, FLASHING RED AND BLUE lights illuminate the familiar houses. Police cars block the driveway, and a bevy of officers crowd around the open front door. My stomach drops out and Roman and I look at each other. We both know what a scene like this means: either someone is dead, or they're going to be—very, *very* soon.

Roman reaches over and grabs my hand, and I realize I'm not breathing. I gasp, air filling my lungs too sharp and fast.

"What's going on?" I ask, as if he has any better idea than I do.

His tone is steady but somber. Like he's preparing for the worst. "We'll know in a minute, good girl."

I try to imagine the worst thing this could be. Like maybe, if I can imagine every possibility and practice living through it, it won't be so bad when I get out of the car. I won't be surprised.

Dad is dead.

Tyberius is dead.

Mom is dead.

Mom and dad killed each other, and now Tyberius is the head of the family and making me marry Councilman Lawrence.

I can't imagine anything else it could be—anything else just feels too absurd.

Roman parks along the side of the long driveway out of the way of the police. When he opens my car door, and I realize I didn't even hear him get out, or notice when he walked around to my side.

I blink in confusion and he reaches for me. "Come on, good girl."

Distantly, I realize that walking into my house with Roman beside me should be a big deal. Yet, fear of what I'll find inside has banished all the anxiety that came before it.

My every step is heavy as I approach the house, the gravel of the driveway deafening underfoot. I step up to the front door and stop.

"Hey," an officer in a sergeant's uniform puts an arm to block me. "You can't go in there."

"I live here," I reply dully.

"What's your name?"

Before I can reply, my mother's voice rings through the night, so loud it drowns out the sirens. "Juliette!"

Mom comes sprinting toward me down the driveway from the direction of the side yard, barefoot and disheveled. The cocktail dress that was no doubt perfect earlier, has wrinkled, and her hair is falling out of its bun. She looks younger, and frantic, despite her immobile forehead.

"Mom, what happened?"

I grunt as the wind is knocked out of me and my mother practically tackles me in a hug. "Are you alright?"

"I'm fine!" I say, pulling back from her. "What's going on?"

"Let's go inside," she says, her tone soothing.

Alarm shoots through me. My mother is never soothing, she doesn't hug, and she certainly never lets anyone see her with messy hair. "Tell me what happened!"

She looks a bit surprised by the tone of my voice, the volume of the command, but it seems to work. She looks at me kindly, almost sadly. "Honey, it's about Catalina."

There's a silence in my head. A buzzing. I think I say something, because Roman grabs my hand, but I don't remember what. All I can remember is my mom's next words: "She's missing."

Cat.

A lead weight falls into my stomach.

I didn't think to imagine anything happening to *Cat*, and now the surprise is just as painful as the news itself.

CHAPTER FORTY-SEVEN

⋅✦ROMAN✦⋅

Present

The scene in the Capulet's great room is eerily familiar to when Marcia disappeared.

The great room is little more than a formal living room, with towering ceilings, a stately stone fireplace, and warm, orange lighting. During the Founder's Day party, the wall of French doors along the far wall were open to the patio. Tonight, there is only darkness beyond the glass.

Etta is sitting on a long, leather sofa facing the fireplace, her mother beside her, whispering in her ear. Her father is still outside talking to the police. Harrison Dane is nowhere to be found—I can only guess he got tired of being humiliated and left.

I'm sitting on the stone base of the fireplace, feeling the eyes of Tyberius Capulet, who keeps glaring at me from where he leans against the wall on the opposite side of the room. It's only a matter of time before he erupts and says something to me, but he's keeping it together for now. Even Delphine Capulet is merely ignoring my presence, clearly more focused on her daughter.

It's clear that they think Catalina is dead, and I'm the least of their problems. I want to laugh at the bitter victory of avoiding a confrontation with Etta's family.

Nothing except a death could prevent a bloodbath.

I pull out my phone and scan the time again, as if it may have changed significantly from the last time I checked. It's been less than two minutes. Less than two minutes, which could mean life or death.

I'm not so sure Catalina is dead. At least, not yet.

All the other girls who disappeared showed signs of being held captive for some time before being dumped in the cemetery. I close my eyes, trying not to go to a dark place. I have to fucking think about this, because every detail could help.

"Is Bennet almost here?" Etta asks.

It takes me a moment to realize she's talking to me, and I look up and meet her wide, gray eyes. "Yeah, good girl. I'll call again."

Her mother looks at me sharply when I call Etta "good girl," but I can't bring myself to give a fuck. No one says a word when I stand up and walk into the kitchen to call my cousin again.

Etta was the last person to hear from Cat, about three hours ago, proving that she was at the party at some point. Three hours is hardly a missing person when it comes to an adult, as the human police have pointed out several times already. What they are failing to grasp is that with four—now five—girls from the Order missing or dead in under a year, every single witch with a shred of precognition in the whole damn state has been focusing all their energy on this. We know Cat is missing. What we don't know is where she is.

I lean against the Capulet's kitchen island, in almost exactly the same spot where I was standing when Catalina walked in on me and Etta. I press my phone to my ear.

It only rings twice before Bennet picks up. "Yeah?"

The background noise tells me he's driving, and picked up the call on Bluetooth. "Are you close?"

"Yeah," he says again. "We'll be there in five."

"We?" When I called Bennet earlier to bring my pendulums and maps over, he hadn't mentioned anyone else. "Who's with you?"

"Me," Pierce's voice replies flatly, none of the usual humor in his voice.

"Right." I glance up to where I can feel Tyberius's eyes tracking me again, having followed me out of the living room. "I'll meet you outside."

I hang up, and ignore Tyberius as I walk across the kitchen and toward the door that I know leads to the garage. All Etta needs right now is for her cousin to get into a fight with my friends in front of the cops.

Only, Tyberius refuses to let me ignore him. He stalks after me, giving the impression of a small dog trying to make itself seem bigger before a fight. *For fuck's sake.*

I pinch the skin between my eyes as I turn around. He's still wearing an emerald-green suit with a bronze tie, and his blonde hair is slicked back against his head. He looks like the fucking *Riddler.* "Let's get it out, now, Capulet."

"I can't decide if you're brave or stupid walking in here," he says, voice raised too loud for how close he's standing.

"I'm not doing this shit with you. Especially not today."

He looks completely lost, both because his worldview has been rocked, and because I won't fight with him. "What are you doing, Montague?"

He's really hard to be nice to, and I'm not nice. I need Etta for this sort of thing. I clench my jaw. "What does it look like I'm doing."

"It looks like you're fucking around with my cousin, but I know that can't be right because that would make her a fucking idiot."

Alright, that's it.

I keep my voice low. "I'm not going to fight you, Capulet, because it would upset Etta. She's not your concern, anyway, she's mine. Walk away."

He's indignant, unable to make sense of what I'm saying. "You think you can just mess around with my family, and I'll let it go?"

I grind my teeth. He's such a jackass, and always has been. I can't imagine spending a Christmas or a car-ride together without someone getting arrested, but this is what I signed up for.

I want everything with Etta, and unfortunately, 'everything' includes her lunatic family.

"I'm not messing around with her," I say flatly.

He rolls his eyes. "Yeah, right, like I'm going—"

I don't let him finish. "I'm going to marry her. I don't want to tell my wife I killed her cousin because he couldn't shut the fuck up, but I'll do it if I have to. This is the last time I'm telling you to walk away."

He gapes at me, lost for words, and I leave him like that—frozen —while I go wait for Bennet and Pierce.

THE NEXT TIME I WALK INTO THE LIVING ROOM, flanked by Bennet and Pierce, the number of people in the room has doubled.

Most of the council arrived while I wasn't looking. Representatives from the MacBeth, Hathaway and Cesario families are all standing along the wall at the back of the room. I freeze for a moment, when I see my father lurking in a corner, like a stalking shadow, dressed all in black.

He makes eye-contact with me across the room, and I know we're both thinking the same thing: what the fuck are you doing here?

"You're here!" Etta looks up, and her eyes widen with excitement. She jumps up and runs over to stand next to us. The sudden movement makes everyone else in the room flinch.

"Hey, Etta," Bennet mutters, his low whisper entirely audible in the quiet room. "I'm sorry about this."

"Thanks for bringing the maps," she says, glancing at Pierce as well. He isn't saying anything, just standing stiffly, staring into space. Strange.

I move back to where I was sitting on the base of the fireplace, and drag the enormous, stone coffee table a few inches closer with one hand.

"Can you find her?" Etta asks, as I begin laying out my maps.

I look up, and feel physically pained to meet her eyes. She's devastated, and I know exactly what this feels like.

"Maybe," I tell her. "I'm going to try."

I'm going to do more than try—I'm going to break the laws of physics if it means I can save Etta from losing her friend the same way I lost my sister.

"Scrying?" Tyberius says snidely, completely breaking the moment. "You're scrying for her? You may as well scream into the void for all the good that will do you."

"Shut the fuck up," Etta snaps, "At least he's doing something other than bitching and moaning over every tiny thing."

I smile, in spite of myself. I don't think she even realizes what she said, or why her family are looking at her like she's grown another head. I've corrupted my good girl, and her family has no idea what to do with this louder, cruder version of her. I love it.

Etta sits beside me on the lip of the fireplace, leaning over the map on the coffee table. She puts one hand on my leg in a way that can't be anything other than too-familiar. I can feel my father's eyes boring holes into my skull and Delphine Capulet's shrewd gaze on the other side, but miraculously they both keep quiet.

I take my pendulum out of the box. I have several—a clear crystal at the end of a silver chain, a standard copper one, and a pocket watch just for variety. The crystal seems right, and I go with my gut, wrapping the crystal around my middle finger and holding it over the map.

Etta's little fingers dig into my thigh, anchoring me as the crystal swings at the end of the pendulum, back and forth in a hypnotic rhythm. I focus as hard as I can on Cat's location.

Five minutes later, it keeps swinging and I grind my teeth.

"Fuck!" I hiss, resisting the urge to throw everything off the table. That won't help—I know from experience.

On the other side of the room, my dad turns away. He's seen this before, and I'm sure it brings back bad memories for him, as it does for me.

Etta squeezes my leg, encouraging. Out of the corner of my eye, I see Delphine Capulet make a jerky movement, as if she meant to move toward us and thought better of it. Etta doesn't notice.

"Are you looking for her?" Etta asks.

No shit. I close my eyes, willing myself not to snap at her. "I'm trying, good girl."

"No, not that," she says quickly. "I mean, you find stuff."

I stare at her blankly. I don't have time for this. "I don't understand."

"You find things, Roman, not people. People are complicated, things are ...just things. Try looking for something she was wearing."

My eyes widen and excitement rises inside me again. That's so simple, and yet I never thought of it before. Maybe it's fitting—assuming it works—Etta was the one who taught me to do this in the first place.

I look around to find all the eyes in the room on us, but this isn't the moment for anything other than finding Cat.

"Does anyone know what she was wearing?" I ask the room at large.

Again, it's Etta who answers. "Yeah." She pulls out her phone. "Here."

She shows me a picture in a text thread. The message above is from Catalina, asking Etta if the outfit makes her look, "fuckable in a way that Madeline Albright would approve of."

"This is perfect, thank you." I take her phone and zoom in, trying to find anything unique about Cat's clothing. Looking for a shirt could turn up any fucking shirt, but something unique, or at least rare...that will work.

I keep scanning the photo, speaking to Etta without looking at her. "You're not leaving my sight again without a ring on your finger."

"Roman," she mutters under her breath—not exactly scolding, but a warning. "Is this really the time?"

"I need to know I could always find you, good girl."

Then, I spot it. Cat is wearing a necklace, too small to see clearly. "What is this?"

Etta leans over. "Her mom died. It's her picture in a locket."

"Perfect."

Excitement roars to life inside me once more. If that doesn't work, then nothing will.

I don't explain it as I start swinging my pendulum again, picturing the locket in the photo this time, the same way I'd picture a rare book.

It's easier to find things that are connected to me, and I don't know Catalina well, so instead I think of how much I love Etta and how I want to do this for her. Beside me, Etta is holding her breath.

There's a crack as my crystal falls, and I look down, surprised. My chain broke. "Fucking hell."

"No," Etta hits my arm. "Look where it fell."

I peer down at my map of Stratford, unsure what I'm supposed to be looking at. It fell on the very edge of the map, hardly even in the town limits. There's nothing out there...

Then, all of a sudden, I understand.

"Has anyone spoken to Councilman Lawrence?" I look up, meeting my dad's eyes, then Delphine Capulet's.

"No," Etta's mother says. "I...well, it didn't cross my mind to reach him."

I grind my teeth. I take that to mean that she wanted to handle this alone, in hopes of getting Lawrence's job when he was forced out following Cat's death. Well, both she and Cat might be in luck.

"We need to go out to his house, now," Etta says, standing quickly. "We need to see if she's there."

"No," I say too loud. Etta looks at me with betrayal, and I quickly add. "You don't need to go. You can't cast runes yet."

She makes a noise of frustration, but doesn't argue, clearly seeing the logic. Instead, she looks up at her mother. "Mom—"

Her mother is already on her feet, barely hiding her excitement. "I'm on my way."

"No," my dad barks. "I insist on being the one to go. I wouldn't want you to *get hurt*." The way he says it makes it clear he's picturing her violent death.

Etta and I glance at each other. This could go on indefinitely and we don't have time for that. I'm reminded, strangely, of watching her from across the hall outside our principal's office—the longest godsdamn afternoon of my life. And one of the best, until that point.

"Why don't you both go?" Etta suggests hurriedly. "I'm guessing you might have some things to talk about on the way."

The room explodes in activity, the council preparing to move out, but Etta just turns to me. Her eyes are wet. "Thank you."

I'm almost uncomfortable—I don't know how to be thanked for doing the right thing, even by her.

I would launch armies for her, slaughter thousands to protect her. She has changed me yet again for the final time. I am no longer Paris, I am Agamemnon launching ships, I am Achilles marching into battle.

I've never been the hero of the story; but for her, I can be.

CHAPTER FORTY-EIGHT
✦ ETTA ✦

PRESENT

MASS GENERAL HOSPITAL HAS SOME OF THE BEST doctors in the world...and some of the shittiest parking I've ever seen in my life.

Bennet drives three times around the rotary, clearly confused by the never-ending road-work signs and one-way exits.

"We want the central garage," Pierce says emphatically from the passenger seat.

"No, that one's full. They're all fucking full," Roman complains.

I reach over and pat his hand. My engagement ring catches the light from the afternoon sun and sends dancing lights all around the backseat. "Deep breaths."

"I'll live, good girl."

He hates the crowd in the city even more than he hates cobble-stones, but Cat has to stay in the hospital for the next week and her family is struggling to get off their cruise ship in the Mediterranean, so Bennet, Pierce, Roman and I have practically lived here for the last several days. I'm getting really good at picking the best dinners from the hospital cafeteria.

After Roman found Cat, the seven other members of the council, including my mother and Roman's father, were able to burst in on Councilman Lawrence before anything too horrible could happen to her. "Too-horrible" being relative, after a kidnapping of course.

As it turned out, being the last living member of his family, and having no heir to take his seat had driven Councilman Lawrence to the point of true insanity. He'd kidnapped all those poor girls to replace the wife who had left him on the alter fifteen years ago —my Aunt Angelica.

Angelica really does seem to have a fine-tuned sixth sense, and it was she who called my father for the first time in over a decade, to tell him that Cat was missing.

Cat is recovering quickly, although her already low opinion of men is now lower than hell itself. Thankfully, I have a feeling that Roman's friends are working on changing that.

AFTER SPENDING THE AFTERNOON LISTENING TO CAT and Pierce bicker over the hospital TV remote, Roman and I finally find ourselves back at his apartment. It's *his* apartment, not ours, but I think we might get one of our own someday soon.

Roman opens the door and I follow him inside, tossing my keys and wallet on the table without looking around. I let out a long, exhausted, sigh. "I want to sleep for the next twenty years."

Roman doesn't reply, and I look up, confused by his silence.

"Dad?" he asks. "How the fuck did you get in here?"

"Mom?" I blurt out at nearly the same time.

I feel like I'm having a stroke. My mother is sitting on Roman's couch across from Balthazar Montague. No one is bleeding, and they seem to have been here for a while because there's a nearly empty bottle of wine and two glasses on the coffee table.

My mom looks up at me. She's wearing one of her power-business suits, but she's taken the jacket off and looks...almost approachable. She smiles tightly. "Juliette, come sit. Do you want some wine?"

Roman makes a disgruntled noise in the back of his throat, which I interpret as indignation at being offered some of his own wine. Our parents ignore him.

"Mom...what the fuck am I seeing right now?"

"Don't fucking swear," Mr. Montague says, unironically. "You're starting to sound like my son."

I know, and I don't care.

"I need someone to explain this to me right now," Roman growls.

"We're here to plan your next moves, of course," my mom says, as if this is obvious. "Now that we're down to seven council members, having two votes is even more critical. We've been discussing it, and we think we could easily take the voting majority for the next several generations. Tell me, Roman—may I call you, Roman?" She doesn't wait for him to answer, and keeps talking. "How opposed are you to...morally suspect means of persuasion?"

I tune her out, not really listening to the rest of her monologue. They're sitting here plotting blackmail, murder, and corporate espionage, but all I can think about is that they're here. Together.

"I told you they would have to get over it," I whisper to Roman.

He shakes his head. "I don't know about this, good girl. I think you've unleashed a curse here. It's going to be a plague on the world, getting these two in the same room."

"A plague of two houses?" I smile. "Eh, we've seen worse."

EPILOGUE
ETTA

THREE MONTHS LATER

WHEN I WAS A LITTLE GIRL, I NEVER PICTURED MY wedding day, the way I imagine that normal girls must. I didn't imagine parties or dresses or princes. Sure, as a teenager I remember picturing who I would marry. Picturing Roman, and hating myself for that—for that fantasy I could never have, which felt so silly and out of reach.

If only I could tell my younger self how it worked out.

As far as I am concerned, today isn't my actual wedding. I feel like Roman and I pledged ourselves to each other more than enough in that crypt, that we are married in every sense of the word. However, as far as the Order is concerned—and more specifically, as far as my mother is concerned—a real ceremony is the least I can do to make this "scandal" somewhat more acceptable.

My condition was that we honeymoon in England—on my break from school, of course.

The door behind me opens and I turn to find Roman striding in. "Nice robe."

I turn away from the window, where I was staring out over the tops of the Elsinore University buildings, and pick at the edge of my robe. "Right back at you."

The robe looks a bit like a bathrobe. If I'm being honest, it might *be* a bathrobe. I don't know what I was expecting—ancient, pagan, druid robes? Gandalf's cloak? The Order exists almost entirely in the modern age, with only a few small exceptions. There's no reason we wouldn't get our ceremonial robes from *Nordstrom* rather than spinning them from hair or something.

Roman grins at me. He's been doing that more often than not lately—actually smiling. "I like it," he says, coming to stand in front of me, his fingers spanning my hips. "Easy access."

My stomach swoops and I laugh as he picks me up easily, and my legs twine around his waist. "Roman, people will hear us. Put me down."

"*Fear* of sex is for other religions, good girl. We're at a temple and our gods want me to make you come. They get off on it. Worshiping you is my devotion to them."

Oh my gods.

He carries me across the room and seats us on the old-fashioned upholstered sofa on the far side of the room. I'm pretty sure it's only in here for the aesthetic, and it's really supposed to be used. I mutter a prayer that we're not about to turn it to toothpicks.

The sofa creaks slightly as I shift around, my knees ending up on either side of Roman's thighs, my hands on his shoulders. He reaches up and unties my robe, letting it fall open an exposing me to him. "Nervous?"

"Yes and no," I breathe.

He runs a hand up the inside of my thigh. "Not enough practice for you?"

I tilt my hips forward, pressing my bare center against him. "I guess not."

He groans and leans forward, his lips grazing my exposed breast. "Let me tell you a story."

My brow furrows. "Now?"

His fingers find my folds and trace over me in delicate, barely there touches. "You'll like it I promise."

"F-fine."

"Once upon a time," he starts, even as he slides the tip of one long finger along my entrance. "There was this girl in a white, princess dress."

Confusion fills me, and I dig my nails into his shoulders.

"And she went to a party, her engagement party actually, and even though she looked like a good girl, she snuck upstairs with—"

"If you say prince, I will leave," I tease as understanding floods me.

"No, I would never," he says with mock horror.

He grinds the heel of his hand against my clit, making my knees weak. Tiny involuntary noises erupt from me, and I roll my hips, desperate for more.

"She snuck upstairs with the villainous warlock," he says in between my moans.

"And then what?" I gasp.

"And then..." Roman grips his cock in his hand, dragging the head against my center. "...The good girl went back to her room and took off her pretty white dress, and she laid in the dark and rubbed her pretty little clit."

He pulls my hips down, impaling me on his thick cock. I gasp, my wide eyes meeting his. "What?"

Roman looks me straight in the eye as he sucks his fingers into his mouth then reaches between us to rub my clit. Despite myself, I'm hypnotized. It feels so fucking good, I need more, *more*.

I wiggle my hips, adjusting to the pressure of him inside me, and rise slightly, rocking back and forth a few times. Warm pleasure begins to build again in my core, as his talented fingers keep rubbing tiny circles.

"She rubbed her pussy and fucked herself until she came screaming the villainous warlocks name for anyone to hear," Roman says, every word punctuated by his movements. By the sparks shooting up my spine.

I'm so full of him, and my muscles feel so incredibly stretched. My mouth falls open. "Oh my gods."

I don't know if I say it as commentary on what he's telling me— what he's revealing he heard—or in response to his fingers driving me higher and higher, his cock throbbing inside me.

Roman reaches around with his other hand and grabs my ass urging me to rock forward. "Do you want to hear more?"

"No," I breathe.

I can't. I'm too embarrassed to know that he heard me. Too thrown by this tidbit of information that he's withheld until the perfect moment. The moment when he knows he already has me.

As usual, Roman seems to read my mind. "Don't be embarrassed, good girl. If you only knew how often I thought about you. How many times I imagined having you. How I hated myself for picturing you under me every time I fucked someone else. You have been in my head for so many years, I don't even remember what I was like before you."

Holy shit, I can't take this.

A whimper escapes my lips as I begin to move, rolling my hips to bring him deeper inside of me.

"Be a good girl and bounce on my cock, Etta."

I brace my hands on his shoulders and move faster. Both of our breathing picks up, and I can feel myself getting closer.

Roman leans forward to catch one of my nipples in his mouth. My eyes squeeze shut tighter, pleasure crashing over my entire body in waves. I clench around him, gasping, words failing me. He shakes, pressing his face into my neck, as he comes inside me.

DOWNSTAIRS, WE WAIT IN THE HALL OUTSIDE THE MAIN ceremony room before entering. I can hear the sounds of people moving around inside. The members of the council—now down to seven.

Personally, I think it sounds better. Eight was a strange number, anyway.

"Ready?" Roman asks.

I nod rather than answering, because if I have to talk right now I'm going to ask him to take me somewhere and do all sorts of filthy things to me—just the two of us.

He leans over. "Remember, good girl. This is a one off. I don't share."

I lean up, nipping at his lip. "Back at you."

The room is long and rectangular with white marble floors and high ceilings, similar to the event ballroom upstairs. I've been in here countless times for holiday gatherings but never when it was so empty.

Our bare feet echo as we walk, hand in hand, toward where the seven council members are standing together in a circle of black candles. They begin to chant, and their voices echo off the walls, reverberating all around the room.

As I turn to face Roman, I tune them out. It may as well be silent as I undo my robe and let it fall in a pool around my feet. Yet, for once, I don't resent the silence. For once, I'm not alone.

"Blessed be thy lips."

“I defy you, stars.”

William Shakespeare,

Romeo and Juliet, Act 1, Scene 5

About the Author

USA Today and International bestselling author Kate King loves sassy heroines, crazy magic, and alpha-hole heroes.

An avid reader and writer from a young age, she has been telling stories her whole life. Ever a fan of the dramatic, she lives in an 18th century church with her husband and two cats, and often writes in cemeteries.

STALK ME!

Visit my website at www.katekingauthor.com

Follow me on Tiktok and Instagram @katekingauthor